THE CONSTANT STAR

A Novel

BY

GEORGE BLAKE

COLLINS
14 ST. JAMES'S PLACE LONDON
1945

CONTENTS

5

CHAPTER ONE

FAMILY GATHERING

I

ALL THAT young Julius Oliphant had been told of Granduncle Ned's wealth and position, and all that a lively imagination and much reading had allowed him to envisage of these fabled splendours seemed pallid beside the realities of his first approach to the presence.

The very sight of the gig lying off the ferry quay at Ardhallow, ready to take him across the Firth, almost unnerved him. " Your Lordship's private yacht," old Peter the ferryman announced with familiar sarcasm, and Julius wanted to run back to the manse in Glen Cattan and upbraid his father for having failed to warn him of so much consequence in prospect.

The gig rode the water lightly, now and again lifting her curved forefoot out of the green waves as a spirited girl might show a pretty ankle under folds of lace. The eight tars who manned the oars were clad with something like naval uniformity in blue-and-white vests and white duck trousers. The young gentleman at the tiller sported a short blue reefer jacket, a brass-buttoned waistcoat, white shortclothes, white worsted stockings, and silver buckles on his black shoon ; on his head was a beaver hat, sloping inwards from brim to flat crown. Looking down from the quay upon this tiny floating, swaying world, Julius saw that in the sternsheets, where the young officer stood, was a place apart : a triangular yard or so of grating in teak, scrubbed nearly white. This was to be the place of honour ; and he, a simple country boy, had come from his father's small manse in Dugald Macfarlane's cart, which smelled of dung and was to take back to the glen a load of coal !

Julius thought modestly of the little oblong box, with brass straps, that contained his gear. It had been handy as a seat in Dugald's cart, and its polished bands had been admired by that simple Highland man, but Julius thought that it would look very mean in the sternsheets of the gig Granduncle Ned had sent to take him across the Firth to Garvel. With a pang of homesickness and pity mingled he saw his mother, only the evening before, in the candlelight, pack the box against this portentous journey.

" Your Lordship's private yacht," said Peter the ferryman again, the bitterness of the defeated Highlander in his tone, and waved to the boat to come in.

The boy in the sternsheets of the gig passed an order to his men. Eight oars made whirlpools in the green. The boat swung as on a pivot, its starboard gunwale laid neatly by the steps down the side of the ferry quay. The four seamen on that side shipped their oars and up-ended them as if they were saluting an Admiral of the Blue at least.

The young officer looked up and shouted :

" Mr. Oliphant's guest for Garvel ? All ready to take you across, sir. Fetch Mr. Oliphant's box, Macleod."

A man ran up the steps and lifted the brass-bound box from under Julius's feet. As they went down to the gig in procession the tar, holding the box under one arm as he might a toy, put out the big, hard hand at the end of the other to steady the boy's uneasy, landsman's progress down the greasy steps.

" Easy does it, sir," said the man comfortably : and Julius got the pleasing notion that seafarers have, at least, a proper understanding of the frailty of landlubbers.

The young officer saluted Julius, but with a grin as of understanding between youths. He was a dark boy, with a fine and distinguished profile and widely-spaced black eyes.

" Your hand, sir," he said, and his fingers were strong. " If you will seat yourself. . . . The box aft here, Macleod. . . . All set there ? Off ! "

The eight oars cut the water, making their inveterate whirlpools. The figure of Peter the ferryman dwindled on the Ardhallow quay. The boat surged ahead, lifting under Julius's buttocks, towards a smear of smoke below the line of hills on the other side of the water.

" Smart craft this," said Julius, making what he hoped was a proper opening with the young officer.

" Captain's gig of *Harmony*," the youth proudly agreed. " Old Ned. . . . O, I say ! Sorry, I forgot." He grinned. " Mr. Oliphant likes a bit of style. *Harmony's* the biggest of the fleet, you see, really the flagship."

The boy's tone implied a pride in belonging to a service as powerful and important as John Company or the King's Navy itself.

" But you know all about that," he added carefully.

" But I don't," Julius confessed. He waved a hand towards the mass of the Cowal hills astern. " I live back there in the glens. We have to climb Ben Bheag before we can see the sea. I've never been to Garvel before."

" Never been to Garvel before ! But you know Old . . . Mr. Oliphant ? Your granduncle, isn't he ? "

" Yes, that's right. But I've never met him."

The young officer was too polite to ask any more questions, but his look confessed that he itched to do so. Julius knew that this knowledge-able and much-travelled youth wondered at such inexperience and still more greatly wondered why the greenhorn from a Highland manse should have to be conducted across the Firth in this formal style.

"My name's Rait, by the way," the lad announced casually. "Bob Rait, midshipman in *Harmony*. Not that it matters." He laughed easily. "My ship just happened to be in just now."

"I'm Julius—Oliphant, of course," responded Julius eagerly, quite missing the point of Master Rait's speech. In all his fifteen years of life in the glens he had known hardly a half-dozen boys of his own age, and these the sons of shepherds and crofters, and his lonely spirit reached out for the comradeship Bob Rait might give it. Over these two lads at that very moment there flicked an edge of the mantle of destiny, but it was withdrawn as Bob called Julius's attention to the immediate scene.

The boat was in midstream by now, and though the salt, whipped off the tops of the short waves by an easterly breeze, was on Julius's lips, he could have believed himself on an inland sea. This upper, dog-legged stretch of the Firth was enclosed entirely by hills of all shapes and sizes, from the jagged mountains to north and west to the more solid but still portentous foot-hills on the southern shore, towards which the gig was heading. Even to the eastward, where the valley of the parent river opened out to a range of gleaming sandbanks, the gap that might have afforded a vista halfway across Scotland seemed to be blocked by a cone of solid rock, distant but massive ; like that Gibraltar, thought Julius, of which he had seen a print in one of the books in his father's library.

"There's *Harmony* lying over there by the Tartan Buoy," Bob Rait's voice broke in. He pointed east to where a great ship lay in towards a wooded promontory on the northern shore, and added defiantly : "You might not think it, but she can travel in the right wind."

"What's that one lying next her," Julius asked, "the boat with the two tall masts ? "

"Not ' boat,' " Bob corrected him with a friendly smile. " ' Ship ' for anything that's big. A boat is a small craft serving a ship. This is a boat we're in now. And it's always ' in ' not ' on.' But never mind. That's *Neptune*. Letters of marque—a privateer, you know, and quite a famous packet. Oliphants', of course," explained Bob Rait airily, " and I'll wager she's brought in a pretty penny in prizes. But there's not much in just now. Wait till we get closer inshore, and then you'll clap eyes on a ship worth seeing."

To Julius it seemed that his guide professionally underrated the

interest of the scene ; for him this upper estuary was a crowded
metropolis of shipping. Nearly a dozen vessels of size lay at anchor
in the deep water below the golden sandbanks, while inshore, off the
Garvel harbour-mouth and within the horns of the wide Bay of Tweek,
there fussed a whole armada, as it seemed to his country eyes, of small
craft—gabbarts and smacks and wherries and other floating things to
which he could not put a seamanlike name. He looked towards Garvel,
its buildings growing always larger and more detailed in the forenoon
light, and the spectacle of so much human activity so highly concentrated at once enchanted and appalled him.

In that summer of the year 1807 the town may in fact have contained some twenty thousand souls, of whom a large and incalculable
proportion were seafarers and other rootless men and vagrant women
brought thither by the chances and opportunities of Bonaparte's wars.
It was a town that, fronting the sea from under a nearly barren escarpment of volcanic hills, lived by the sea. As Julius Oliphant saw it
closely for the first time it seemed even to have something of the shape
of a ship, with the two granite arms of the harbour thrusting out from
the shore and arriving together at the mouth, for all the world like a
ship's bows. Through that opening between the pierheads he could
see that the main harbour was divided in two by a central quay, and
he guessed that he was at last beholding those fabled East India and
West India Harbours of which his father had so often told him.
Behind this harbour, and the fine range of tall mercantile buildings
that looked upon its waters, the town proper was crowded into a
shallow defile, but Julius got no more in those moments of approach
than a general impression of huddled roofs, some thatched and some
red-tiled, with smoke hanging over them and a kirk steeple rising high
behind. He noted an old church among tombstones on the westward
point of the bay, a congeries of warehouses and boatyards to the east
of the harbour and, on the steep slopes above the town, an occasional
villa or tentative terrace in the classical style.

"That's The Mount," Bob Rait broke in on his observations,
pointing towards a little hill that topped the kirk steeple itself and was
outstanding among other eminences of its sort in having a tuft of trees
on its top and, above the trees, a swirling guard of rooks. "You can't
see the house from here, but it's—it's a palace ! You've never seen
anything like it."

The little wave of apprehension turned again in Julius's breast. He
ceased for the moment to be the breezy companion of Midshipman
Bob Rait, a man among men, and became once again the awkward
and innocent Highland boy, suddenly called upon to go to the thriving
town of Garvel and submit himself to the judgment of this granduncle,

who was a legend for wealth and power ; whom even brisk Bob Rait
regarded as a sort of emperor ; who lived in a house above the town
so grand that it was hidden among trees, like the Duke's castle itself.
He remembered the admonitions of his father and his mother, both so
pathetically anxious that he should make a good appearance before
Granduncle Edward : both so proud and fussy and eager with their
warnings. They were so kind. They meant so well. They were so
simple. In the candlelight last night he had watched his father's face
and seen in the play of the muscles about that grave man's mouth the
signs of his concern.

"Now, look ! " Bob's voice cut in again. " Look at the lines of
that ship ! Ever seen anything like it ? "

They had come nearly under the bows of a brigantine which,
obviously new and in the process of fitting-out for sea, lay out of the
fairway within the western arm of the Bay of Tweek. Julius appreciated
the fact that Bob had shaped the boat's course so that he might see
something out of the ordinary, and at a glance he realised that this
new ship was indeed of quite another family than those he had seen
at anchor out in the fairway. These had seemed to him stout and
portentous ships, but monstrously pot-bellied and squat in the water ;
whereas this new vessel rode high and light, her bows soaring and
proud, her muscular lines towards the stern as tautly refined as those
of a greyhound. Above this slim hull the two high masts and wide-
spread spars seemed, for all their fragility in pattern, inordinately
wasteful in their proliferation. Could such a slender hull carry so much
sail ? Julius wondered. At the same time, he knew an inward surge
of excitement in the presence of this floating graciousness such as might
affect a man coming on a noble line of poetry or hearing a new, sweet
air on the violin.

"That's all Mr. Walter's work, of course," Bob was explaining
reverently. " He takes most to do with the building and the care of
the ships. All his own ideas. He's years ahead of everybody else in
the country. Those hollow water-lines . . . But here we are. That's
Mr. Ramage from the Counting House waiting by the steps. And
there's old Joshua."

The gig had passed between the outer jaws of the harbour and
was heading for a break in the eastern wall of the central quay. Bob
laid the craft neatly alongside a flight of stone steps, and down
these hobbled an elderly person, his hand extended in warm welcome.

"Master Julius, is it not ? " he cackled blithely. " Aye, you have
the look of your father, sir. Welcome to Garvel on behalf of the House.
Isaac Ramage is the name, sir ; fifty-six years in the Oliphants' service

and proud of it. Come, sir, your hand. Joshua—Mr. Julius's box here."

A large Negro with white teeth in a widely smiling mouth seized the case from a sailor and made up the steps with it. Bewildered by the bustle, Julius found himself following in the black man's wake to the level of the quay. He had the uncomfortable feeling of having somehow failed in a duty proper to the occasion.

" Bob ! " Mr. Ramage was calling down to the boat from the top of the steps. " While I remember, Mr. Edward's compliments and you're to report at The Mount at five of the clock this evening."

" Aye, aye, sir ! "

Bob saluted and followed this formal acknowledgment of orders with a special grin for Julius. Ah ! that was it, ran the warm flush through Julius's mind ; he had not wanted to leave Bob without a word of thanks and some hope of another meeting. He waved in return, and the boat wheeled towards the harbour mouth.

" Smart lad," said Mr. Ramage approvingly. " Bob Rait, midshipman in *Harmony*. Our biggest and finest ship, sir, as you will come to learn. A good boy. He will be in charge of you and your cousin while you look round."

" Oh, that's fine ! " said Julius happily.

" Yes, sir," Mr. Ramage agreed. " Now, Master Julius, cast your eyes on Garvel."

He spoke in the tone of one who at once exposes a triumph of civilisation and introduces a stripling to his heritage. This tone implied in the specific instance a flawless belief that the Oliphants were Garvel and Garvel the Oliphants' creation and fief. Young Julius felt anything but a princeling as they turned along the East Breast, but he recognised that the little procession of which he formed one shrinking unit had a consequence beyond the ordinary.

Striding before them with the box a mere trifle on his left shoulder, the giant Negro called Joshua was a commanding figure for stature and colour alone, but it was still more to the point that he was clad in a sort of uniform such as Julius had seen before only on the Duke's body servants—in this case a long coat of maroon cloth and knee breeches of the same material, with white worsted stockings and a loose waistcoat of yellow leather. His head, the hair crinkled like black parsley, was uncovered. In his capacity of grand vizier, Mr. Isaac Ramage likewise harked back to the eighteenth century in the consequence of his attire. His coat was of bottle green, his breeches of a fine black stuff. The waistcoat was of snuff-coloured silk prettily sprigged with little blue and pink flowers, and he wore a black three-cornered hat. The steel buckles on his black shoes were as bright as the silver bulb on the top of the stout malacca cane he carried.

Mr. Ramage was very respectfully saluted as they went along under the protruding beams above the doors of these East Breast warehouses with their pointed gables in the Flemish manner. One elderly gentleman, clearly of consequence, halted them to ask Mr. Ramage if this was not one of the Oliphant boys—would it not be Robert's son ? On being reassured as to that, he patted Julius's shoulder and said that he remembered his father well and hoped that he would find his granduncles very well. Many of the common folk of the place touched their forelocks quite obsequiously as the procession passed, and from the side walks loutish men and rough women, their heads covered with shawls, stood with a frank curiosity that confessed recognition.

This sense of being a marked man clouded the boy's observation of the town itself. From the East Breast they turned into a narrow thoroughfare which Mr. Ramage explained as the Cross Shore. It was but a rough track between rows of single-storey houses with thatched roofs, but they quickly passed through it into the considerable open space of Jibboom Square. Here Julius felt himself to be at the heart of a crowded and foreign metropolis, though a more experienced traveller would have thought little enough of a few groups of fishermen and sailors outside the taverns and alehouses at that hour of the early afternoon, of a coach standing empty before an inn bearing a gilt model of a Buck's Head, and of a handful of country folk roaring at each other in their coarse Lallan tongue beside a couple of carts while their horses drank at a rude well in the middle of the cobbled expanse. The whole southern side of the square, however, was taken up by a massive church that Julius, with some justice, thought very fine indeed, so hugely did it bulk above the meaner buildings of the old town, so high did the steeple reach up towards the fleecy clouds floating on the easterly wind against the summer sky.

Mr. Ramage paused so that Julius might appreciate the splendour of this edifice.

" The Mid Kirk," he announced, pointing the malacca cane at the corinthian portals. " Not our kirk, as you will come to learn, sir, but at the hub of our community. See now, Master Julius——" The cane pointed upwards to the model in gilt metal of a sailing boat that served as a weathercock on the very tip of the steeple. " ' The Gilded Gabbart ' the common folk call the boat up there, but it is the symbol of the town's prosperity on and by the sea. Mr. Edward would like you to appreciate that. Yes, sir."

" I'm sure he would," Julius agreed limply enough.

" But come, sir. He will be expecting us." And Julius almost felt that the personal pronoun should carry a capital " H." His own awareness of unimportance and innocence was not lessened thereby.

Their way now lay past the Mid' Kirk and straight uphill. The road was steep, but Julius noted that it had been surfaced and that the sidewalks were paved with Caithness flags. Above the eastern pavement, indeed, ran a high wall embanking a park, and into the nicely pointed surface of the sandstone a handrail had been set for the benefit of travellers up a brae so declivitous. This rail ended where an ornamental flight of steps, with a handsome stone balustrade and urns crowning the pillars, ran down from the park to the street.

" The Mansionhouse on our left. You can just see the roof from here," Mr. Ramage explained with a proud wave of the malacca cane. " Sir John's place, you know, though he prefers his country seat at Daff these latter days. Getting old, like the rest of us."

Julius noted that the steepness of the hill was certainly beginning to tell on his companion. The old man's breath had shortened to a whistle and a purplish hue had come into his cheeks in patches. They laboured together past the Mansionhouse gates, and at the first crest of the rise Mr. Ramage halted, turned to look seawards, and produced a large brown handkerchief to mop his brow.

" Hot," he panted an apology. " Steep. Old."

" We can take it easy," Julius suggested.

" Thank you, sir," the old man acknowledged. " Not what I was. But just a moment. . . ." His breathing eased slowly. " There, now. We stand above Garvel, on the level of the Gilded Gabbart itself, as you see. The anchorage, our harbour system, the warehouses—mostly Oliphants', I may say. Don't you smell something in the air, Master Julius ? A curious, heavy tang ? I always call it the Garvel Garland. G.G.G.G. . . . That is what the town's motto should be, I say. The Gilded Gabbart, the Garvel Garland. Good, eh ? "

" Very good," Julius agreed. " But what is that smell ? I noticed it whenever we landed—or didn't notice it, if you know what I mean."

" That smell ! " Mr. Ramage's tone protested with dignity against the use of a word so crude. " My Garvel Garland ! Master Julius, you have in your nostrils now the effluvia of Bailie Mair's tan works, of good Loch Fyne herring being kippered in John Baxter's shed, and —that sweet, heavy aroma—sugar boiling in the various sugarhouses. The cane grows on our own West Indian estates ; we import the raw stuff in large quantities. . . . But you will learn all that, sir, in due course. It is all very wonderful, is it not ? "

The malacca cane swept through an arc of some one hundred and fifty degrees, proudly embracing the thatched roofs and harbours of Garvel proper, the Mansionhouse with its ornamental stairways, the

Mid Kirk and its spire, the anchorage and its ships, and innumerable
square miles of Highland hills beyond.

"Yes, it's very wonderful," Julius agreed. "And all very new and
strange to me, of course."

"To be sure, sir," said Mr. Ramage, gratified. "But you will
learn. And now we'll be getting on, I think. A stout heart to a stey
brae—eh, Master Julius?"

Ruefully the boy reflected that the old saying suited his own case
very well indeed, and he doubted if he had sufficient stoutness of heart
to meet the situation now approaching. A queer little feeling of resentment against fate, with his own father and mother and the innocent
figure of Mr. Ramage as its symbols and agents, swept through his
mind. He felt it was somehow unfair that he, so rustic and simple,
should be bothered by so much novelty of experience and scene within
so short a space of time, and that on his way to the major, portentous
encounter with Granduncle Edward, in whose hands, he had been led
to understand, lay his future. He felt that they were overwhelming
him unfairly with this fusillade of novelty—the captain's gig; the
journey across the Firth; the bustle and colour of this, the largest
human settlement he had ever seen; old Ramage's Gilded Gabbart
and Garvel Garland; and the black man carrying his pathetic little
box. . . . It was all wonderful, but it was too much. Oh, for the turn
of the hill-road below Tighnafead and old Seonaid greeting him in the
Gaelic from among her scrabbling hens!

Then, there was the Other Boy.

Garvel had disappeared beneath the ridge, from the crest of which
they had looked down upon its wonders, and now they were following
a road, lined by great beeches, that ran across the farmlands of one of
the many escarpments of the hillside above the town. This track was
leading them to the dominant knoll called The Mount, and Mr.
Ramage had much to say of the scene and its associations, with
particular reference to the grandeur of the Oliphants' position within
it, but while Julius could politely acknowledge his guide's observations,
his inner mind was on the possible nature of his meeting with the
Other Boy.

Now he was to meet for the first time his cousin Mark, son to his
father's own brother; and the prospect strangely daunted him. Somehow, he was unable to realise that this Other Boy was as himself, a
country lad and a candidate for Uncle Edward's patronage. He hoped
that Mark would be friendly and likeable, like Bob Rait, but for some
subtle reason he took to fancying that it was all going to be very
difficult. It was absurd, of course, but under the eyes of Granduncle
Edward he was to meet a competitor.

"There, now!" Mr. Ramage announced with pride. "The Mount."

They were turning through a white gate with a little lodge to the side of it, and Julius saw at the end of a long avenue of limes, as through the wrong end of a telescope, the façade of a great two-storeyed house in the Colonial manner. A gardener was busy among the pots and boxes of the plants that adorned a white-pillared veranda ; another raked the gravel on a wide space before the main door. Every detail of the small stereoscopic picture spoke of wealth and comfort and assured position, and Julius's heart sank.

2

"So this is Julius ? "

Mr. Ramage bowed low from the waist, for all the world like some pompous vizier submitting a likely slave to his sultan.

"Good. And you told young Rait to report here at five ? "

"That I did, sir. Without fail," maintained Mr. Ramage, bowing again.

"Thank you, Ramage. That will do. You will see me at the Counting House in the morning."

The factotum bowed himself out, moving backwards through the doorway with the skill of long practice, and a hand fell kindly enough on Julius's shoulder, turning him towards the window.

"Let me see your face in the light, boy."

Julius looked frankly up into the face of his granduncle, Edward Oliphant, the head of his family. Look up he had to, for the old man, though a thought stooped about the shoulders, stood well over six feet in height. The face was clean-shaven and of a judicial cast, with a bold nose and a firm chin. The mouth was small and thin ; the eyes, their blue paling with age, were severe but not unkindly.

"Yes," said Granduncle Edward as if to himself. "An Oliphant and no mistake. That fair hair is your mother's, but you have the features. Not at all like Mark, who seems to take after his mother entirely. . . . Ah! But you two boys have not shaken hands yet. Mark ! "

Julius had been aware of the presence of his cousin in the room but only as a shape, a formless portent in the background of an almost theatrical scene. They were in what Julius took to be the library, a room so long and so darkened by the brown and red backs of row upon row of books—in numbers which made his own father's library seem a paltry affair—that the Other Boy had seemed to be lost like a wild animal against its protective colouring.

" Hallo, Mark ! "

" Hallo, Julius ! "

The cousins shook hands and considered each other, and Julius thought to see at once why the Other Boy had so naturally melted into the background of Granduncle Edward's long, dark library. This Mark was short and broadly built, and so dark that his black eyebrows met above his nose. The eyes beneath them were bright and observant. Though Mark's mouth smiled a greeting, those dark eyes did not smile. Julius got the clear impression of strength of character in his cousin, and he hoped that he would be able to like him. Already he knew that he could admire him.

" And you two boys have never met before ? " the old man was saying. " Strange ! I am very happy to see you together. After all these years. . . . Now, if my brother Walter would only come. Your Granduncle Walter, boys . . . We should be sitting down to dinner. . . . You had a good journey, Mark—I mean, Julius ? "

" Yes, sir."

Granduncle Edward did not pursue the topic. From a fob he drew a fat gold watch, glanced at its face, frowned and walked to the window. Julius saw in him a man aloof in his age and power. He glanced at Mark, and Mark was also looking at that enigmatic back, his heavy eyebrows drooping in a frown.

" Ah ! Here he comes," said the old man at last.

As if the boys did not exist he walked the length of the long room to a shining mahogany table at the back. From a silver salver he lifted a long-necked decanter and filled two long-stemmed glasses with a tawny wine and was replacing the stopper when the door opened to admit his brother.

" Ah, Walter ! "

" Edward, good day to you ! "

They shook hands with formality.

" A glass of Madeira wine, Walter ? "

" I thank you, Ned."

The little ceremony was played out as on a stage, and Julius, watching as it were from the auditorium, was deeply impressed by the grace of it. Granduncle Walter was the equal of his brother in height, but of a gentler cast of feature altogether. He had the same bold Oliphant nose, but there was something wistful about his eyes that took Julius's sympathy at once. In a dim way he discerned that these two made a perfect partnership : vigour and decision in one qualified by taste and refinement in the other. He was quite sure that they

made a perfect picture, standing together in the grave library of The
Mount : tall and slim in age, dressed alike in dark cutaway coats with
silver buttons, lavender trousers strapped under their boots, black
stocks and waistcoats of coloured silk.

" Your good health, Edward."

" I thank you, Walter."

The brothers bowed slightly towards each other and sipped their
wine. Only then, their glasses in their hands, did they turn towards
the waiting boys.

" So these are our young hopefuls ? " said Granduncle Walter
kindly. " And which is which ? Oh, you are Mark, are you ? How
do you do, Mark ? And this must be Julius. Welcome to Garvel,
Julius. Mark and Julius. And are you ' a plain blunt man,' young
Mark ? "

Mark stared at his aged relative, but Julius cut in quickly with a
little laugh :

" I hope, sir, he hasn't come to bury me," he said.

" You took the allusion, child ! " cried Granduncle Walter
delightedly, beaming on Julius. " You have read well indeed. Edward,
our grand-nephew Julius is a Shakespearean after my own heart. Do
you trifle with poetry, boy ? "

Before Julius could make answer, if he had any on the tip of his
tongue, the door was opened by the black man Joshua, announcing
with a grin and a bow that dinner was served.

" Come, Walter ! Come, boys ! " said Granduncle Edward
impatiently. " We must eat."

In contrast to the library the dining-room at The Mount was a
chamber of light. It was a long room, but its ceiling was high. Tall
windows looking on a smooth lawn filled it with the brightness of the
afternoon sun, while light walls, much white enamel and many glass-
fronted cupboards threw back the radiance in double strength. In the
middle of the vast room the small circular table in mahogany was an
island in a sea of thick mole-coloured carpet, and when they came to
sit down at it both of these boys from simple homes were bewildered
by such an array of napery, cutlery, silver and gleaming glass as they
had never seen in their lives before. Julius at least determined to follow
Granduncle Walter through the complicated steps of this ritual.

The food with which they were served was equally exotic. The
meal started with a soup which, though the look of it was uninteresting,
had a fatness and richness of flavour such as the mother of neither boy
had ever been able to extract even from the best home-fed mutton and
fresh garden vegetables.

" You wonder what it is, Julius ? " asked Granduncle Walter, chuckling, when he saw that grave boy's features pucker over the unfamiliar tang. " You are eating turtle soup, sir, like any Lord Mayor of London. This came from Captain Alexander, Ned ? "

" Aye, he brought in three beauties from Jamaica, one running to 170 lbs. I got my share."

" You see, boys," Granduncle Walter explained, " our trade—all the town's trade—is very largely with the West Indies. Try a drink of that stuff in the jug beside your plate, Mark. A trifle sharp, eh ? But you like it. That is lime juice from Granada. After dinner you will have a cup of coffee from our own estates in San Domingo. And remind me to-morrow, boys, to let you have a piece of sugar cane each. Eat and learn : that's the way of it here. Ha, ha ! "

It was Granduncle Walter who did all the talking ; his brother's remarks were only by way of punctuation. But Granduncle Edward was watchful. As the younger man plied the boys with friendly questions about their parents, their schooling and their tastes, Julius was well aware that the old man's eyes switched from face to face, marking how each took this or that question, as it were weighing up their different capacities. When at length the meal ended with dessert —an array of fruits utterly strange and extremely alluring to these country boys—Granduncle Edward resumed command of the proceedings.

" Now, boys," he announced, " you can run away into the garden and have a look round. I have affairs to discuss with my brother. Midshipman Rait will be here at five o'clock and will take you sight-seeing."

" You know, boys," Granduncle Walter amplified, " that Bob Rait is a connection of yours—far out, but still a connection. His father is second cousin to your own fathers—Captain Rait, a fine seaman, now in South America on a very important mission for our House, along with your cousin Alan Oliphant."

" Off you go, boys ! " Granduncle Edward repeated impatiently.

Though he regretted that cup of coffee from romantic San Domingo, Julius accompanied his cousin from the house in a mood of eagerness. He was a shy boy by nature and by virtue of his upbringing in a Highland glen, but he was a sanguine lad and he looked to find a friend in this cousin with whose fortunes his own seemed to be strangely bound up. Casting about how to open with his rather silent companion, he wondered that he should know so little of the Other Boy, save that his father, his own father's brother, was a parish schoolmaster in Ayrshire. Julius's father had never spoken much of his brother and had never described what manner of woman Mark's mother was, or said a word about her origin. It was as if there had been a rift somewhere in that branch of the copious Oliphant family, but Julius had generously concluded that between a parish in Argyll and another in Ayrshire nature had placed insurmountable barriers.

He was hesitating whether to start with the weather or the loveliness of the standard roses, each in its own circular plot on the shaven lawn before the house, when Mark startled him with an almost challenging question.

" Are they going to take us on, do you think ? "

" Well—I don't know—I hadn't thought of that." Julius's reply was weak but genuine. " It was all so beautiful and interesting inside the house. Didn't you like Granduncle Walter ? "

" Granduncle Edward is the one who matters. He'll do the deciding," declared Mark. " I hope I get into the Counting House. That's where the big chances are, right at the heart of things."

" I'd rather work with the ships," retorted Julius on an impulse that he realised a few seconds later to be a true expression of such ambition as he possessed.

" You mean, work in the boatyard ! "

" Yes." Julius stuck to his guns.

" That's daft," said Mark with rough finality.

" Perhaps," was all that Julius could find to say, " but it's what I'd like."

The downrightness of his cousin had him fairly nonplussed. He had to realise that here was a boy of another sort than his own, as it were of another race : a boy who in his middle 'teens had given hard thought to his prospects in business, or had been made to do so. He admired this quality in Mark and was ashamed of his own satisfaction with mere impressions, but he resented the shadow that his cousin's dark preoccupations had brought upon his enjoyment of novelty and of the beauty of the sunlit garden, and he was mightily relieved to see the stocky figure of Bob Rait approaching up the avenue of limes.

He moved to greet his friend, Mark following, and his face was bright with welcome.

" Hallo, Bob ! " he cried. " This is my cousin, Mark. Granduncle Walter told us that you are a sort of cousin too. What are we doing to-night, I wonder ? "

Bob and Mark shook hands, eyeing each other unsmilingly.

" I don't know," Bob answered Julius's question. " I'll go in and report to Mr. Edward."

He disappeared into the house, and Julius and Mark were left to kick the gravel idly.

" That's Bob Rait," Julius explained. " I like him, don't you ? He's a midshipman in *Harmony*, the biggest ship in the fleet."

" Is that all ? " asked Mark.

" You should just see the captain's gig I came across in to-day. Smart ! My word ! "

" I came up in the Irvine mail," retorted Mark. " Up on the box beside the coachman. Four horses, at the trot all the time."

" That must have been fine, Mark ! " said Julius generously.

" As good as an old ship's gig, anyhow," observed Mark.

If Julius had any reply to make to his cousin's truculence, so consistent as to be an almost amusing aspect of his personality, the occasion passed with the reappearance of Bob Rait.

" We're to go down to see my mother at Kempock," he announced. " That's about three miles away, but it's a nice walk along the shore if we cross the turnpike. Ready ? "

Down a minor avenue leading westward from the house and through a gate in the garden wall the three boys passed into the freedom of the evening. These slopes above and to the west of Garvel were laid out mainly in a regular pattern of hedged fields, with here an entrant of rough pasture rising unfenced to the heights of the hills behind, and there the walled garden and trees about a merchant's house newly built out of the increasing wealth of the town ; and the boys felt upon them the freedom of open country in the bright, soft light of a northern June evening. Julius, at least, would have gone dashing in his high spirits after the rabbits they started along the hedgerows or even the occasional hare they could see sitting up at comical attention in the fields, but Mark was more in the mood to talk to Bob about the countryside, and the social and economic interest of its features ; so that (it seemed to Julius's less orderly mind) his cousin had soon carefully discovered and tabulated the names of the new mansions they approached from time to time—Waulkenhill, Finnart, Kilblain and the rest—the style of their owners, and the origins of their fortunes. At the seriousness of such a mind Julius marvelled greatly, but Bob Rait also seemed ready enough to speak and boast of the new wealth and wonders produced by Garvel under the leadership of the Oliphants, and before long the three boys, rather conscious of being the heirs of all the ages, were marching abreast in grave, adolescent discussion of this difficult, serious but splendid prospect men called Life.

When they had crossed a stream, which Bob described and dismissed as the West Burn—telling his new friends how in its little estuary down by the Bay of Tweek the fisherfolk of Garvel moored their boats—the lads came upon a few terraces of new sandstone houses tending to stretch westward along the Kempock Turnpike, but these they skirted to cross the road and enter a region of rough land falling quite sharply to the sea. This had little of the charm of the farmlands

above. Here and there on the lower slopes another of those new houses
had been built, the new wealth confessing its first, inevitable instinct
to escape from the huddled township in which it was being made, but
the slopes were sour and rusty with damp even in high summer, small
defiles running down them were clotted with saughs and scrub oak,
and water dripped from small precipices overhanging small, dank
ravines into their muddy beds.

From the brow of this unpleasing slope, however, Julius had a
vision that was profoundly to affect all his way of living thereafter.
They looked down upon the Firth and its shipping, the panorama
stretched out in all its amplitude of detail below. Miles across that
great sheet of water, moulded into a fantastic pattern by lochs and
promontories, stood his own Highland hills, majestic against the
yellowing evening sky. But it was the sight of the shining sea that held
him fascinated as by a breathless tale ; for him it was history come to
life in a symbol. He thought not of the sea as a thing romantic in itself,
but his mind did fill with the thoughts of man's boldness in facing it, of
man's boldness in using it in skilfully-fashioned ships, and of man's
inveterate defiance of its enigmatic cruelty ; and his breast filled with
emotion and tears filled his eyes as he looked down upon it and sub-
consciously recognised that his own destiny was to be bound up with it.

" Oh, come on, Julius ! "

A shout from below shook him out of his absorption. Mark and
Bob had run ahead and were standing, looking up at him, on the strip
of flat ground by the water's edge under his feet. He waved and ran
down to join them.

His friends were on the foreshore proper when he reached them,
jumping from rock to rock, shouting as they slipped on the tangles of
weed, kicking limpets from their moorings, and otherwise behaving as
boys have always behaved in similar circumstances. With a much more
profound sense of novelty than they could ever know, Julius joined in
the scramble, but finding himself carried by one thoughtless leap to
the very edge of the tide itself, he was constrained by some odd impulse
to bend down, dip a finger in the water, and raise a few drops of the
stuff to his lips.

He raised his eyes to see that Bob was watching him with peculiar
intentness.

" Not nice to taste," said Bob quietly with a smile.

" No, but I have never tasted it before," replied Julius with a grin.

That intentness of Bob's look lingered in his mind, but soon they
were all at play again, their hands and pockets full of pebbles to throw
at the rabbits they started among the clumps of whins above high-
water mark. They paused for a while outside the palisade of a military

station Bob described simply as The Battery, watched the sentries pacing the earthworks, and gravely discussed the power of its guns to blast out of the water any one of Boney's ships that dared to show a nose round Kempock Point.

That promontory filled much of the view when they had passed The Battery, making a great bay with an expanse of muddy foreshore between. Fishing cobbles were drawn up on a strand of shingle at the head of the bay, and behind was a cluster of white cottages towards which the boys now walked direct by the turnpike that hereabouts dropped from the higher ground to sea level.

" Here we are," announced Bob at length.

He pushed open a gate giving on a path that led through an untidy garden to the white door of a two-flatted house, larger than the fisher-cottages near at hand, but on much the same modest scale, Julius reflected, as his father's manse in Glen Cattan. Shells from foreign shores, strangely-shaped and bleached, lined the path, and among shrubbery to one side of the house stood the figurehead of a ship long broken up : the effigy of some sea-god fearsomely bearded.

" Bob ! Is it Bob ! " trilled an excited female voice from inside the house, and a woman's figure appeared in the doorway, her pretty dress of sprigged muslin filling the width of it. " Ah, it is Bob ! *Mon cher . . .*"

The lady gave the midshipman a rousing kiss, much to the surprise and embarrassment of the two Scots boys raised in the Presbyterian tradition of suppression. They were both blushing when she turned her black eyes on them.

" And who are these boys, Bob ? " she asked. " Ah, the two new boys ! And how are they called ? Julius . . . How do you do, Julius ? Mark . . . How do you do, Mark ? No Luke and John, no ? " Her laughter trilled like birdsong. " And you are our cousins veritably. But no——" She shrugged her shoulders and shook her head in a most comical gesture of mock horror—" those Oliphants have no cousins. Those terrible old men are alone. Other men they only use . . . But come Mark, Julius, Bob ; I talk too much as always . . . *Entrez, s'il vous plait.*"

Hearing the tongue of the enemy in his country at war, Julius's surprise at the nature of this encounter was all the greater. And that this strange lady could dare to speak lightly of his Oliphant grand-uncles ! That was alarming—and puzzling ; and he recalled that, as they were crossing the Firth that morning, even Bob had thrown off a casual remark in the same sense. It was all very disconcerting. Bob's mother was a creature utterly new in his experience. Even her physical aspect was strange in his Scots eyes : a face still shapely and smooth in middle age but of an even complexion like ivory. She had narrow, long-fingered hands and narrow feet beautifully shod. Her ankles were slim, and to Julius's grave notions her dress was surprisingly girlish.

" Why look at me so strangely, Julius ? " she twitted him suddenly. " Am I a witch as Bonaparte is an ogre ? My French tongue, my silly English ? Yes, I am very funny, no ? Have no fear. I am only one of the great Oliphants' prisoners of war. You call me Aunt Sophie."

This alarming lady had led them into a sitting-room, which was prettily bright with chintz and muslin curtains but monstrously untidy with piles of garments heaped on the chairs and the tables and the floor. These she started to clear up with stormy energy until the lot lay piled in a corner of the room.

" *Alors !* " she remarked and then cried as if to the world at large : " Barbara ! Barbara ! "

A girl appeared in the doorway. She was Aunt Sophie's daughter and Bob's sister : no doubt of that. She was her mother in virginal form, slim and shapely, except that there was pink in her cheeks, and that she had hair of a deep chestnut hue. Her eyes were dark and calm, and the dark brows above them arched in a manner which gave her the air of one who asks a serious question and requires a sensible answer.

Her greeting of the new acquaintances was gracious and unaffected, but no more. Julius's sanguine temperament, indeed, was irked by her poised reserve. However, there could be no cold tension in any situation involving Aunt Sophie, and now she was sweeping the awkward little group of young people before her into action.

" *Eh bien, mes enfants,* and now you are friends. Barbara, Bob— take Mark and Julius for a walk . . . No, do not look so glum, Mark ! Smile for me. It is not all so serious . . . And while you are away I make supper. A French supper, young Julius ; it will seem strange to you, but you will like it. *Allez vous donc ! Psst !* Out you go ! "

She made as if to drive a flock of geese out of her path, and Julius at least felt very like one of those stupid birds, and he was not notably comforted when he realised that, as the procession took shape, he was to walk with Barbara, while Mark and Bob marched ahead with a little brown dog of the terrier sort—apparently another inmate of that unusual household—barking and dancing and bright-eyed to be one of such a notable and promising procession.

" You think it is all very strange ? " suggested Barbara, the question breaking with force into Julius's private world of preoccupation and shyness.

" Well, yes," he admitted awkwardly ; then suddenly confiding : " You see, I only arrived this morning. Our home—over there——"

he pointed towards the hills beyond the Firth—" is very quiet, and I
am not used to meeting strangers. Of course, I had been told about
my granduncles, but it was all sort of confusing—Garvel so big and
busy, the big house, Mark . . . And then——"

" My mother must seem very strange to you," she coolly helped
him. " She is a Creole, you see. If you do not understand, a Creole
is not, as some foolish people here think, a person of mixed blood.
The Creoles are the pure white population of all the Caribbean.
Maman was born in Martinique, but it was in New Orleans that she
met and married Papa. He was then on a voyage for Oliphants, of
course. Maman is wonderful ; you will learn to like her greatly."

She gave the French word its French pronunciation, and Julius
noted that her speech had something of both French precision and
intonation, as if English was not her natural tongue. But Barbara
differed greatly from her mother in the calm of her directness.

" You speak French ? " he asked politely.

" Mostly, with Papa so much and so long away. You yourself do
not speak English as they speak it round about Garvel here. Yours is
softer, clearer, purer."

" Oh, that is just because I come from the Highlands ! " Julius
explained modestly. " I am used to speaking Gaelic, and I suppose I
have to translate into English first."

" It is very charming," said Barbara.

Julius found this candour highly embarrassing, but it pleased him
warmly ; these accidents of birth and speech made a delicious private
bond between this strange girl and himself.

" I believe your father is in South America just now ? " he turned
the conversation away from a dangerous topic.

" Ah, yes ! " she sighed. " Very far away. To Potosi with another
of your family, Mr. Alan Oliphant. You know him ? No ? I do not
know myself what relation he is. It is a dangerous mission. They are
to bring home a treasure in silver dollars. Another of those Oliphant
enterprises, of course. Everything they touch turns to money."

Again that queer grudge of the Raits against the Oliphants, and
Julius winced in his mind. But what a picture the girl unconsciously
painted—of an expedition to Potosi, of a treasure in silver dollars, of
the Oliphant power reaching round the globe from the small Scottish
port of Garvel !

" But tell me about yourself, Julius," said Barbara. " Tell me
about your home in the Highlands. Are you coming to Garvel to work
for Mr. Edward and Mr. Walter ? I like Mr. Walter. I think that
you and he are—what shall I say !—en rapport."

Julius was not quite sure what this meant but knew that it was another of her embarrassing candours. However, it was much to be in Barbara's confidence, and they fell from then on into a pleasant exchange as to each other's circumstances, views, tastes and dreams.

By this time the party had climbed up a rough farm road to the crest of a hill-terrace from which Julius could see the Firth in still another splendid aspect. The point commanded a view not only of the anchorage up-river towards Garvel but also of the wider reaches below the point enclosing Kempock Bay, where the estuary took one of its many turns on the way to the open sea. Hereabouts the Firth was still a natural harbour safeguarded by a constellation of islands to the sou'-westward, but this upper reach of it, at least six miles across from shore to shore and its surface now whipping into turmoil under a wind rising sharply again from the east, declared its identity with the Atlantic. It was a region in which the salt tides of the ocean set the pace over and above the feeble flow of the mother-stream from the Lowland hills. It was just sea : brutal, enigmatic, gloriously challenging, and now with a tigerish splendour upon it from the setting sun and the fierce reds and golds and purples on the peaks of Argyll to the nor'-west away. Julius understood the meaning of this melodramatic scene. He saw why Garvel, looking westward to the New World from within one of the great ocean gates of the world, must prosper and make of its ruling dynasty, the Oliphants, the very princes of the new world of commerce ; and his heart swelled at the thought that he belonged to it.

His reverie was broken by a confusion of shouts and barking to the left where, among tufts of whin nibbled into the shape of neat cushions by hungry sheep, Bob and Mark and the little brown dog had evidently put up a rabbit. Instinctively Julius ran to join in the chase, and even Barbara picked up her full skirts and followed him. When they arrived on the scene it was to discover that the hunt had cornered a baby rabbit in the angle where two drystone dykes met. The little creature crouched by a clump of rushes in a paralysis of terror, its great ears flat along its back. The little dog danced with delight in its own prowess and barked an eager request to be allowed to go in for the kill. Bob was laughing as if the poor little animal was no more than the comic victim of the moment, about to be released from fear. Mark was grinning.

As Barbara came up to join them, Mark took action. Two quick steps forward, and one of his stocky legs shot out to kick the beast and send its small body crashing into the wall. It lay for a moment kicking feebly, and now Mark pounced, picked it up by the ears, and broke its neck by a blow with the edge of his open hand. Still grinning, he held the corpse out towards Barbara.

" That was cruel, Mark, and needless," she said coldly. Her eyes gathered Bob's attention. " Come. I want to go home."

" Yes," Bob backed her up uneasily. " Supper will be ready."

The return journey down the hill was not a very happy one, for Barbara was silent now, as if she must show her disdain of brutal masculinity, and Julius himself was altogether too embarrassed to be able to say anything either to her or to the two other boys. Mark, on the other hand, had turned garrulous and talked loudly of great shooting and ferreting expeditions along the sand dunes of his native Ayrshire, and Bob stoutly sustained the host's end of the conversation. Julius was sorry for Mark. He knew that his cousin had done a thoroughly boyish thing through a thoroughly boyish instinct to cut a figure before Barbara. He was merely puzzled that Mark had completely failed to see the sort of girl Barbara was : cool and clear-minded beyond any sort of woman he had ever encountered in his Lowland parish.

Aunt Sophie was out at the cottage gate to greet them.

" So you are back again, my little ones ! " she cried as they approached. " There is a lovely supper prepared for you—your own favourite salad, my Bob. Now I run to make the omelette . . . Did you have a nice walk, yes ? "

" Mark killed a baby rabbit. It was very silly and cruel."

Barbara's was a cold statement, passing judgment, and again Julius was mightily sorry for Mark. This new life was difficult enough, in all conscience, without this problem of how to encounter a distant cousin of a mysterious sex with foreign notions of behaviour and expression.

" Lot of fuss about a wee rabbit," mumbled Mark ungraciously.

" That's quite enough of that, Barbara," Bob warned his sister.

" Such silliness—all of you ! " trilled Aunt Sophie. " Come, Barbara, and assist me in the kitchen."

Mark was flushed and scowling now, the puckered lines on his forehead ominously complicating the junction of his black eyebrows, and again Julius was sorry for this cousin of his, whose strong natural instincts did not suffer him to fit easily into a subtler sort of society. It was a great pity that the evening had been spoiled between his roughness and Barbara's fastidiousness.

3

" And here, Julius," said Granduncle Walter, " is the holy of holies. I call it my study. This is the moulding loft. A big place, is it not ? "

He ushered the boy into the biggest chamber Julius had ever seen. While the roof of it was low and broken by numerous skylights, the loft, Julius reflected, must have had a floor area more than twice that of his father's kirk. That floor was of hardwood, as smooth and closely knitted and finely polished as he imagined that of a ballroom to be. Seeming a little lost on its expanse, three carpenters in white aprons were on their knees. Plying long-headed hammers in sharp, neat taps, they were nailing lengths of thin planking together into patterns so subtly curved that the boy recognised their exquisite shapeliness at once.

"Now you see, Julius, where we start the work you saw going on in the yard outside?" Granduncle Walter's air of antiquity seemed to disappear in the warmth of his enthusiasm. "How do the ship-wrights know exactly how to fashion a rib or frame, how to bend a plank, how to angle the sternpost of any vessel? For each ship differs from every other ship."

"I was wondering," Julius confessed.

"Well, look!" said Granduncle Walter triumphantly. "Those lines in chalk on the floor—the lines of a new ship still to be built—down to a fine fraction of an inch. Observe those curves coming closer and ever more sweetly to a point; these are the water lines curving in delicately to the very cutwater. Those lines that bulge outwards like the side of a fat bullock—the profile of the ship where she is bulkiest, where the cargo or the heavier pieces of cannon will go. Then fine again towards the stern. . . ."

The old man's hands made delicate passes in the air like those of a musician taking an orchestra through an exquisite passage. Julius began to realise that he was almost forgotten in Granduncle Walter's passion for his art.

"However," the latter resumed, as if laughing at his own foible, "that is the design, the creation, drawn out in rough chalk on an oaken floor. Now let us look at the material."

He led the way to the door, and as they passed out of the loft, with its atmosphere as of a monastery, the three workmen smiled to Julius in such a friendly way that he had the pleasant feeling of being admitted to the mysteries of their craft.

Behind the loft a space of ground was given over to stacks of timber in neat oblongs open to the weather on both sides but roofed over against rain. In these dim aisles, led by Granduncle Walter, the boy observed how the logs and planks were stacked in a careful criss-cross pattern, so that the air circulated freely within each pile. The old man was eager to explain the process.

"All this wood, Julius, is weathering, as we say, drying and hardening before it goes into the body of the ship. When they come in from overseas the rough logs are taken up-river in great rafts, and there they lie floating in tidal ponds till we need them. Then they are sawn and roughly shaped as required and brought here to be stacked and weathered as you see. All sorts of woods, beautiful woods, carried thousands of miles in ships, to make more ships, in turn to carry more goods ! You appreciate the progression, Julius ? "

" Yes, sir, I think so," the boy hazarded.

" Good ! Now, feel this wood. Smell it."

He had paused before a pile of timber which had, on its cut surfaces, a sheen in a colour somewhere between purple and light brown, and which gave off a faint nutty odour. The old man ran a loving hand along the planes of a hewn log and in the same moment raised his distinguished nose as if to savour the bouquet of a wine.

" This is teak," Granduncle Walter announced portentously. " A hardwood of the greatest distinction : so hard that it blunts the finest tools. It reaches us from India, and I may say that it is very hard to come by through the monopoly of the East India Company . . . But that is another matter . . Take, it, Julius, that we use this wood extensively in the building of ships of quality. As I trust you will learn in due course . . ."

With a wave of his hand he indicated another block of timber, fairer in colour on its sawn surfaces and clearly less obdurate than the teak.

" Oak," he said. " Our mainstay. All the planking of our ships is fashioned out of this fine wood. Here we depend on our friends in England. The Wooden Walls—you know about them, Julius ? The tree grows strongly in the southern and western counties. From the very earliest times the Sussex oak has been a part of English history. The Romans, the Normans—they discovered the virtues of oak and used it. The wood has the beauty of being at once tough and tractable. Whereas, over here . . ."

Impelled by enthusiasm for the niceties of his own subject, the old man stalked at high speed towards still another lot of logs. They were darker than the planks of oak, redder than the logs of teak, and they gave off a richer odour than either. Granduncle Walter rested a hand on one of the baulks of this strange wood, comporting himself as one who delivers an exalted address to a large audience.

" I think I may say," he began, " that we owe our ample supplies of this fine wood to the enterprise of the merchants of Garvel : in particular to that of my brother Edward. This is mahogany, most of it brought in our own ships from Honduras and other points in the Caribbean. It is less hard than teak, but quite as durable. It is rather more easily wrought. It has—you notice, Julius?—an even fruitier, more pungent aroma."

Again the imperial nose sniffed the air with satisfaction.

"But I would not say that we find it more useful than teak for the purposes of shipbuilding. Indeed, we import it largely for quite other purposes. This, Julius, is a wood most beautifully suited for the making of home furniture, so fine is the polish it can be made to take. The highest polish—like a mirror. Thus most of our importations go to cabinet-makers in the district. I dare to assert," the old man perorated grandly, "that there are now few houses of substance in the six counties round about us that do not contain at least one piece fashioned from the mahogany brought into Garvel in Oliphant ships. From the Caribbean . . ."

Julius was suitably impressed by this recital, if once more a trifle unhappy as to his own fitness to have a share, however humble, in this Oliphant grandeur, of which the evidence seemed to mount hourly. His imagination had been deeply stirred by Granduncle Walter's evocation of romance, however, and he could only too easily soar beyond his small personal worries to see the great trees of the sub-tropics tossing their feathery heads to a crisp breeze off a blue, white-capped sea, and to follow the ships, their sails puffed out by the breath of the Trades, surging nor'-westwards towards a remote Scottish estuary, the sun, the stars and a magnetized needle their sure guides across the waste of seas.

"Granduncle Walter," he started to ask. "Honduras is on the mainland . . . ?"

The speech was cut short by a concussion that gave him sensations of the most direct and unpleasant sort. It was a boom and crack together that made his ears tingle and weakened his knees under him. His throat tightened, and before he could speak a second shock made him start with the same unpleasant abruptness. His look of startled inquiry revealed Granduncle Walter with his right forefinger upraised, a smile round his lips.

"How very fortunate!" the old man was saying : "Why, Julius, it all seems to have been arranged for you! There go the guns again . . . a cannonade. That means a convoy in with prizes : possibly one of our own Letters of Marque. Nay, probably. Come boy! Quickly!" he urged excitedly. "Down to the harbour as fast as we can go and see what's afoot. You run ahead. Follow the crowd. I'll come as soon as my old legs will take me. Off you go!"

Another crash from the anchorage did not check the boy's flight towards such a gallant scene. As he ran through the shipyard he became only one of a crowd, for it seemed that all the artisans in the place, save a few elderly men, had downed tools and abandoned the unfinished vessel on the stocks and were possessed by the one feverish desire to see what sort of convoy had come in with such triumphant cannonading to the anchorage they called the Deeps. Its individuals cheering, shouting, jesting or merely panting, the mob streamed along Open Shore to meet on the East Breast other mobs pouring down Cross Shore and the Bell Entry until the approach to the Mid Quay seemed to Julius's country eyes to be nearly impossible and possibly dangerous.

The eagerness of his youth, however, and perhaps some awareness among the crowd of his local position, allowed him an easy enough passage to the end of the crowded jetty, and there he discovered Mark in the company of Mr. Ramage and Bob Rait. Mr. Ramage's authority, antique dress and, no doubt, malacca cane had cleared a small space at the tip of the quay within which the Oliphant party stood apart from the riff-raff of the place.

" What's afoot ? " Julius panted his question.

It was Mark who first replied just as eagerly.

" Prizes ! A Frog and a Spaniard ! Taken by our own ship ! Worth thousands of pounds ! "

" You are witnessing, Master Julius," announced Mr. Ramage more soberly, " a demonstration of our sea power. I mean the power of our own House's fleet as well as that of "—and here he obediently tipped his three-cornered hat with a forefinger—" His Gracious Majesty. The details again, Bob ? "

" Oh, it's very much the usual thing," said that experienced youth airily, " though it's a fine haul, I must declare. That's our Letter Marque *Favourite*—the smaller ship, Julius—and it looks as if she has taken a mighty rich prize. A Spanish galleon by the looks of her. See how her spars have been shot away ; see the holes in her upperworks. It must have been a rare fight. The Frog doesn't amount to much."

Panting after unwonted exertion, Granduncle Walter joined them then, and the story had to be told once more.

" Splendid ! " said the old man enthusiastically. " Captain Flett must be a proud man to-day. Has somebody informed Mr. Edward, Ramage ? "

" I have sent a boy with the intelligence to the Counting House," announced Mr. Ramage grandly. " And if I mistake not, sir, here comes Captain Flett to report in person."

All eyes followed a line indicated by the malacca cane ; it pointed to a white gig that had put off from *Favourite* and was surging shorewards. As it drew in towards the harbour mouth, Julius saw that it contained as its most important occupant a very tall and burly man of middle age with a very red face. This large figure leapt from the sternsheets of the gig before it even touched the steps, mounted these in three lusty strides, and briskly saluted Granduncle Walter even as it appeared over the edge of the quay. The crowd of rough men, gabbling children and shawled women behind raised a cheer, saluting this successful man and the Oliphant enterprise he represented for bringing new wealth to the town.

"Welcome, Captain!" Granduncle Walter greeted the sailor, warmly holding out both his hands. "This is a splendid return. And what have you brought in from the sea to-day?"

Captain Flett grinned. His voice was as deep in its own scale as the remarkable ruddiness of his complexion, and its Orcadian inflexions sounded very strange in Julius's ears at least.

"Spanish galleon *La Flecha* of Cadiz, sir," he explained. "We picked her up thirty leagues West of Cape St. Vincent and easily outsailed her, for she was heavily laden. They fought well enough, the Dons, but she struck after four hours of it, and I lost no more than seven men killed and twelve wounded. She carries the strangest cargo, sir, I ever clapped eyes on."

"And what is that, Captain?"

"So far as we can make out, sir, dyestuffs like Peruvian bark and cochineal. She had sailed from Mexico."

"Bark and cochineal!" cried Granduncle Walter. "Why, Captain, these goods are selling at exclusion prices! This is a fortune!"

"Then there's another big lot of queer stuff stowed aft, sir," Captain Flett boomed along. "Vicuna wool and chinchilla skins, our supercargo says it is. The stink of it's enough for me—if you don't misunderstand me, sir."

"Vicuna and chinchilla!" cried the old man again. "But these are at ransom figures! This is wealth, Captain Flett! This is prodigious! A mine of wealth! Eh, Ramage?"

"A mine of wealth, sir, as you say, sir," said Mr. Ramage, bowing agreeably. "This has been an enterprise that will certainly exalt our mercantile reputation."

Through these mellifluous exchanges there suddenly cut the voice of Mark, curiously harsh.

"How much will all this be worth?" he asked. "In thousands, I mean."

Mr. Ramage coughed and made a distracting pass with his malacca cane at the crowd which had closed in to pick up what it could of the news. Captain Flett, the colour of his large face deepening until it looked like an overripe fruit about to burst through his goggle eyes, stared at this strange and impertinent interrupter, but wisely restrained his seamanlike inclination to comment loudly and rudely. The old man bent on his grandnephew a puzzled and quizzical smile.

" That we shall not know for some time to come, Mark," he observed gently. " Mr. Ramage and his assistants will be busy for weeks. . . . But come, Captain ! My brother will wish to see you at once. Up to the Counting House, and we'll drink a glass to your success. Come, boys ! "

Mr. Ramage striding splendidly ahead, the Oliphant party passed up the quay, and the crowd of townsfolk and seafarers made way for them. Some of the sailors in the mob cracked jokes about Mr. Ramage's consequential carriage and were rewarded with laughter, but the majority bobbed or tipped their bonnets as the Oliphants went by, and some of the younger folk cheered again.

4

The fine weather was holding. In the late afternoon from the terrace before The Mount, Julius saw with emotion how, like the painted ship in Mr. Coleridge's poem, the Oliphant ship *Favourite* lay ahead of her prizes at the anchorage in a state of immobility that seemed quite unreal. Now her spars were bare of canvas ; she was utterly motionless on a glassy sea that did not even confess the pull of an ebbing tide. Beyond the Firth the mountains had somehow lost in the stillness their familiar air as of beasts about to spring and now rather suggested the forms of lazy kine that had eaten more than their fill. Vaguely but still intensely the boy thought of how the cannonade that had announced *Favourite's* triumphant return must have strangely reverberated and echoed along those golden slopes and up the deep, deserted glens.

Mark and Julius had again dined in state at The Mount, but with Granduncle Edward only this time, and they had heard from those grave lips a succinct, unsentimental account of *Favourite's* achievement and then a careful survey of how those operations of war benefited private enterprise and the interests of the Crown simultaneously.

" The arrangement is one of convenience between my Lords of the Admiralty and us merchants," the old man had said. " In effect, they invite the shippers of the United Kingdom to set aside units of their fleet as raiders on the enemy's commerce. Thus the enemy's communications are disrupted, and thus our national needs in the way of commodities are, in part at least, secured."

Granduncle Edward had sipped then at his glass of Madeira and stared out of the window as if contemplating the whole universe and its complexities.

"I would have you understand, boys, that the merchant pays through the nose for the privilege of assisting My Lords. Letters of Marque for a ship carrying more than 150 men cost three thousand pounds sterling. Three thousand pounds. The warrant for a lesser ships costs half that sum."

"Fifteen hundred pounds!" Mark had interjected eagerly.

"Precisely, Mark. Fifteen hundred pounds . . . Let me admit that since the great victory at Trafalgar—which, believe me, marked the beginnings of Boney's ultimate downfall, however victorious his armies in Germany may seem to be. . . . Let me admit that, since Trafalgar, the trade has been profitable. I might even say lucrative. And a point of morality may occur to you."

"But if Government asks you to do it——" Mark had broken in again.

"The point remains." Another sip at the glass of Madeira. "However, boys, you have seen to-day a singularly clear demonstration of the meaning of naval power and, if I may say so, the efficiency of the fleet belonging to our House. And now young Rait is coming up again to take charge of you for the evening. This will be a gay night in the town, and I have given him permission to let you see something of the fun—in celebration of Captain Flett's achievement." The glass rose again. "But I shall expect you to behave carefully. Your name is Oliphant, remember."

And here were the three boys in the garden again. While Julius contemplated the view across the Firth, Mark and Bob stood under one of the trees in the avenue of limes and argued with young vehemence. Startled out of his reverie by the hardness of their voices, Julius strolled over to join them.

"I don't care," Mark was shouting in his curiously rough way. "I'd take all I could off them—kill them—bash them! What are Frogs anyhow but a pack of greasy, unwashed cowards?"

"You won't find many sailors to agree with you," Bob replied mildly enough. "The Frenchie fights well. He's not a great seaman, but he isn't a coward."

"Who told you that?" was Mark's retort.

"Surely Bob ought to know," Julius intervened. "After all, he's met them and fought them."

"And not," Bob added with a laugh that had a little bitterness in it, "not for the fortune that the merchants get from the prizes."

Mark was also able to laugh, but his was the laughter of impatience.

"I believe you're on the side of Boney, both of you!" he said.

"Well," added Julius. "Granduncle Edward himself said that there's a point of morality about the privateering business."

" I don't know what that means, and I don't care," Mark observed, adding impatiently. " Come on and do something ! "

" We'll go and see the alligator," announced Bob.

As the trio went down the hill towards the town Bob explained the strange nature of this animal. It was, he said gravely, of the same amphibian species as the crocodile, which infests the banks of the Nile. The alligator, however, belonged to the Americas, and this specimen had been brought to Scotland in the ship *Triton*, Captain Nimmo. The town was flocking to see it where it lay, not expected to survive very long, in a room in Morrison's Land at the foot of Highland Close. Mark and Julius listened carefully to Bob's account of the affair and felt again that this Garvel life was full of wonders indeed.

At a fast pace Bob led his charges through the crowds that were already filling Jibboom Square with colour and noise, and the excitement of a special day in the life of this seaport town infected Julius at least with a sense of gay unreality, as a glass of wine might touch an older man to a new feeling for the confused glory of living. In the arcades under one solid but ornate building a crowd was milling to gain a passage through a doorway, beside which Julius saw playbills announcing the appearance that night of Mr. and Mrs. Henry Siddons, at very heavy expense, in Shakespeare's comedy of *The Merchant of Venice*, followed by Davis's celebrated scena, *The Castle Spectre*. And this was the theatre—the New Theatre, said the playbills ! The urgent scene outside the building rather frightened Julius, who had been taught in his father's manse to think of playgoing as rank sin and playactors as sinners and harlots.

Still, he began to see the scene about him precisely as the playgoer accepts the illusion of the lighted stage. He was in that medley the young man abroad for the first time, a little drunk on too many impressions of a life and a rough vivacity more fantastically intense than his darkest Presbyterian forebodings had ever helped him to envisage. Sailors from the ships newly in, their coarse faces either flushed or haggard with drink, shouted outside every tavern or, arm in arm with their shawled, rough-tongued doxies, took the crown of the causeway, elbowing the quiet foot-passenger into the drainage by the roadside. Loudly they all swore, shouted, spat, sang bawdy songs, fought with their fists, kissed, or passed water with a carelessness complete. Witnessing this display of coarse candour, Julius felt that he was plumbing the depths of this world's iniquity. He realised that there were to be passages of his first experiences in Garvel that could never be told to those parents who had been hitherto his absolute confidants.

He was frightened, horrified. He had never known that life in crowded places could be thus. He was too young to know that war, with its abandonment of whole peoples to death, so that they fall in love with death, must see the collapse of all the sanctions.

He was afraid. And still he was enchanted. Colour surged and flashed about him. The mariners, home from the sea, seemed very gallant in coats red or blue, striped guernseys, red or yellow or bright blue shirts, white ducks or blue serge trousers, white or red stockings, or any other combination of garments and colours that had taken the individual fancy. Some wore earrings ; all had skins darkly coloured by wind and spray and sun. Julius saw one man with a frightened monkey in the crook of his arm. And then there were the wild women of the town, so many of them with the flaming hair of the Celtic people ; all of them in brightly striped short-gowns and bold shawls of tartan, green and red ; all ready to link arms and shout with the tars. Among these wild people the artisans of the town walked dourly and disapprovingly, but still with the alertness of Julius himself.

All this came to Julius in flashes, for Bob hurried his charges through the crowd in Jibboom Square and up an alleyway off the main street of the place. At the end of this cul-de-sac Morrison's Land was entered through an archway under a high tenement building, and so they passed into a courtyard, muddy and fouled by a sow and her litter. A handful of citizens at the door of an outhouse beyond indicated where the great natural curiosity was to be seen.

A penny each, paid to a hag who sucked at a short-stemmed pipe, admitted the boys to what had probably been a washhouse in the palmier days of Morrison's Land, and the alligator lay in what had perhaps been a wash-trough of wood. It was in size a disappointment to Julius at least, no more than five feet in length. It lay utterly motionless, its eyes closed, in about a foot of water that steamed faintly in the near darkness of the chamber ; it was no doubt one of the hag's duties to maintain the temperature from a kettle that steamed on a fire behind her stool. Still, the ugliness and strangeness of the alligator, heightened by the mystery of its torpor, were to be marvelled at, and the boys did so, arguing eagerly about its habits, diet and temper.

They were still debating Mark's proposition that the alligator is a ferocious man-eater when, out in opener and fresher air again, Bob suggested that they might now turn westward and see the Loyal Corps of Sharpshooters drilling on Salmond's Field. Eagerly the cousins agreed that they would dearly like to add this martial spectacle to the evening's wonders, and the party climbed up and out of the town again by a country road. Salmond's Field proved to be a gorse-tufted expanse of common land to the westward of The Mount, and of the Loyal Corps of Sharpshooters not more than two score had turned out

on parade that evening. But there they were in their doublets of
bottle-green and trousers of hodden grey, the officers trailing enormous
scabbards, and the country boys thought it very fine to see the Sharpshooters kneeling to receive cavalry, forming squares and at the deadly
rate of three rounds a minute go through the motions of loading and
firing their long muskets.

"They're smart, I must say!" Mark exclaimed proudly.

"O, not bad for soldiers, and volunteers at that!" Bob coolly
agreed. "These were almost the first company of volunteers in the
Kingdom. Give me the cutlass and a good boarding party of
tarrybreeks any time, all the same."

As by second nature he turned then to look out to sea, and his cry
of surprised interest trained the gaze of his companions in the same
direction. Another great ship had come into the anchorage. Her black
sides were chequered by yellow squares about the ports, and the blue
ensign hung limp in the still evening air from the gaff.

"My goodness! A ship of the line!" Bob's professional calm had
quite deserted him. "120 guns at least. Come on, lads, and we'll
get down to the harbour. If her men are ashore there will be wild
goings-on in Garvel to-night."

The three boys ran all the way downhill, and even in the mean and
narrow thoroughfare called the Vennel, leading them from the upper
parts to the waterfront, it was clear that the men of His Majesty's
ship had come ashore in numbers. From every tavern door came a
greater uproar than ever. Among the bright and varied garments of
the merchant seamen the soberer uniform of the tars maintained its
own distinction, and for Julius their greasy pigtails almost alarmingly
suggested the exotic. The trulls of the place were even shriller in excitement than an hour before, and fist fights for possession of them were
being cheered by rings of delighted spectators in alleyways and pends
here and there. Even a country boy knew with a thrill of delighted
alarm that folly and wantonness were at large in Garvel that night.

The three boys moved slowly among the throng, awed and unnoticed spectators of carnival. Bob had quite forgotten both his
responsibilities and his sailorly wisdom. He was as the two Oliphant
cousins, a child at once bewildered and fascinated by madness in his
elders. Only when they had stood for the best part of an hour near
the well in Jibboom Square, watching a show livelier and more varied
than any theatre could ever purvey, did he realise the passing of time
and recollect the weight of his duties.

"We ought to be going," he said. "This racket will get worse
and worse. They can get dangerous, these people. I don't think Mr.
Edward . . ."

"Oh! Just one turn round before we go home again!" Mark pleaded, and Julius backed him up.

"Well," Bob hesitated. "Oh, all right! We'll walk down to the West Breast and back. But you must be home at The Mount by nine, or I'll be in for a keelhauling."

The rabble seemed thicker and noisier than ever down the Cross Shore, and when they turned the corner on to the West Breast the boys saw that some particularly fierce commotion was agitating a crowd along by the gates of the graving-dock. It was a crowd that seemed, from its noises, to be made up of two elements equally amused and angry, and in the heart of it could be discerned the flat, black hats of naval men and the flash of the evening light on metal.

Bob Rait stopped short in his tracks and spread out his arms as if to hold his companions back.

"My God!" he gasped. "The Press! Come along! Out of here as fast as we can go!"

"Oh, Bob!" Mark and Julius started to protest.

"It's just the likes of you they would pounce on," Bob explained urgently. "There would be hell to pay. Come on."

He turned and sought to push the cousins back along the way they had come, and Julius saw that he was now in a real agony of concern. Mark, however, resisted the pressure.

"I don't care," he cried. "I'm going to wait and see the fun."

"Come along, you fool! They can take you unless you're bound apprentice. Julius——"

"Yes, Mark. Come along," Julius added his plea to Bob's and started tugging at his cousin's arm.

The contest of wills lasted a shade too long. Mark's determination to resist endured until the crowd by the dock-gates had broken up and was trailing towards them, some shouting angrily, some laughing. Between the disorderly lines of excited townsfolk marched the Press Gang in a tight knot surrounding a handcuffed prisoner with, stumbling behind them in bare feet, an aged woman.

Every lightest detail of that sorry picture lived in two minds at least for many years to come. The trophy of the Press was a gangling long-haired youth with the open, wet mouth and the flopping limbs of the half-wit. The ancient who hobbled in bare feet behind, shrieking her plea that he be spared, was a harridan with bedraggled grey hair, a tattered shawl and the ingrained dirt of poverty in the skin of her lined face. Some of the crowd jeered at her in her unbeautiful torment, and one of the tars in the rear rank of the escort suddenly turned and, jocularly enough, grabbed her by the hair, twisted her round on her bare heels, and left her lying on the cobbles.

It was then that his companions missed Julius. They could not know, any more than he did, that the cruelty of the scene was to him so intolerable that all his discretion and gentleness of spirit were swept away on a hurricane of passion. They only saw him run forward, straight towards the manacled idiot in the heart of the Press and, like a pygmy seeking to smash with his bare fists through prison walls, batter at the outer rank of sailors. They heard him shouting.

For his own part Julius knew nothing between that moment in which the pity and cruelty of the scene had blinded him with anger and that in which his mind cleared sufficiently of blackness to let him realise that he had acted in extreme folly ; also that he was being hurt and humiliated for his pains. Two burly sailors had seized his arms in their iron fingers and were twisting them, while a third kicked his shins to hurt. A fourth member of the Gang, no doubt some sort of petty officer, had thrust an empurpled face into his and was snarling at him through discoloured teeth.

" Attempt at rescue, eh ? Fine bloody cocksparrow you are ! You just better come along wi' the idiot, see. Spreadeagled and a rope's end for your backside, Master Spitfire. The darbies for this young fire-eater, Dusty. Take that, you——"

The man's half-clenched fist swept across Julius's mouth. The boy had to screw up his muscles and blink against the pain. The tears came hot, there was a numbness in his lips, and he felt the salt taste of blood in his mouth.

The crowd had closed round the knot of commotion. His eyes appealed to it for sympathy, but it seemed to have gone sullen. Then he saw Bob thrusting against the outer file of sailors, and in a strange detachment he observed that Mark was with Bob, square shouldered, his fists clenched, his dark face set for battle. Mark was his friend. . . . Then Bob, shouting at the petty officer with all the authority he could put into his young voice.

" Belay there ! Let that lad free ! You can't touch him ! "

" Oh, I can't, can't I ? " The sailor chose to be sardonic.

" No, you can't ! " Bob insisted, squaring his trim figure against the larger man. " If you do, by God ! your commanding officer will hear of it within the hour. That's Mr. Edward Oliphant's nephew. He's bound apprentice to Mr. Oliphant. Let him go at once, or I'll see you in irons in double-quick time."

" Attempted rescue, just the same," the man insisted. " Breakin' into the ranks. . . ."

But his tone confessed a set-back, a weakening of his rough assurance. He looked a little uneasily at his companions, and when he did so the crowd, always feeble, started to threaten him with heavy murmurs. Bob thrust his advantage home with a gallant lie.

"So you're going to take a bound apprentice, you fool?"

At that moment there stepped forward from among the mob an elderly man in the drab clothes of an artisan.

"The sailor laddie's richt," he addressed the petty officer in his hard Scots tongue, "and you're wrang, man. Ye've ta'en a bound apprentice to Mr. Walter Oliphant himsel'. I saw him in the yaird this vera day wi' his granduncle, decent man that he is. And to that I'll tak' oath when ye like."

The sailor took refuge in crispness.

"Let the cocksparrow go, Dusty. We'll stick to the loonie. And you"—he rounded on Bob—"you tell this whippersnapper, 'prentice or no 'prentice, to keep 'is bloody nose out o' where it isn't wanted. See?"

"Ach, you go to hell!" said Mark stoutly, looking indeed as if he were quite willing to engage the whole Press in fisticuffs.

A ragged section of the crowd sought to follow the boys along the West Breast, but some decent working men, headed by the elderly artisan who had intervened, prevailed upon them to leave the unhappy trio alone, using the great name of Oliphants as a warning to the riff-raff.

Julius was almost carried along. He sagged on the strong arms of his friends. Over his drooping head and his bruised face Bob confided to Mark.

"We'll take him to Mr. Walter's place first. The old man will just raise hell. . . . Come on, Julius. Get your left arm round his waist, Mark. . . . God, what a keelhauling I'm in for!"

"Hoist him on my shoulders," suggested Mark.

"No, no! I'll manage. Thanks, Mark!" gasped Julius.

He was grateful to his cousin, recognising in him for the first time a special sort of integrity. But he was in no shape to think or care much what they did with him or where they took him. He was sick through and through with the sense of folly and failure.

5

"I am very much displeased," said Mr. Edward Oliphant. "I grant you, Walter, that the boy showed spirit. But does that not simply confess a complete lack of judgment? He is an Oliphant. He had been expressly warned, only this afternoon. And now—brawling on the West Breast, daring the Press, having to be rescued almost by force—with one of your carpenters intervening. . . . A carpenter to get an Oliphant out of a brawl!"

"Our Saviour intervened in many a brawl, Ned," interjected Mr. Walter, chuckling quietly, "and he was a carpenter, they say."

"Nonsense ! Clever words ! You won't get round me. The boy's a fool. He had better go back to that manse in Cowal and—and grow cabbages."

"You are very much less than your reasonable self to-night, Ned," his brother insinuated. "Are you feeling quite up to the mark ? "

"This confounded sciatica again. In my left thigh. In the month of June, if you please ! The height of summer ! "

"Perhaps we might go indoors ? "

"No, no ! I enjoy the evening in the garden. June—hardly any darkness—the perfume of the roses."

"Exquisite, Ned ! " Walter was quick to agree, glad to be over the nastiest part of the interview that young Julius's folly had forced upon him.

The two old gentlemen were pacing the lawn before The Mount. Walter had deliberately persuaded his brother into the garden, feeling instinctively that the sweetness of the late June evening would play agreeably on that austere and dignified spirit. It had been an awkward job, breaking the news to Ned. The air in the library had been electric. Ned felt strongly about the dignity of the Oliphants. But that, Walter knew well, was only one aspect of an exquisite sense of form : the very sense to which the loveliness of the garden in the long northern twilight was now ministering so subtly. He let the magic go on working for a space of minutes before he spoke again.

"In the meantime, Ned," he broke the silence almost confidentially, "the boy had better spend the night at my house. He was quite sorely knocked about and was suffering distinctly from shock. And remorse, I need hardly say, bitter remorse. I had to send for Blackhall to give him a sleeping draught."

The head of all the Oliphants received this intelligence with a grunt.

"To-morrow morning," Walter persisted, "he should be fit to go home as arranged. He will call here for his box, and he will wait on you to make his apologies. These will be handsome, Ned, and from the heart, I assure you."

"They had better be," said the old man severely. "And I'll have a word or two to say to Master Robert Rait."

"No doubt, no doubt ! " Walter hurried on. "As to the future of these two lads. I think you have formed a good opinion of Mark's capacities. He is sharp and vigorous : no doubt about that. You will want him in the Counting House. Probably you will think of sending him abroad to gain experience in one of our enterprises. I am sure he will do well. But as for Julius. I take him to be of a gentler sort altogether, more sensitive, more imaginative——"

" A fool ! " declared Edward forthrightly.

" No, Ned ! " retorted his brother with spirit. " Not a fool. Nor a coward. His folly was one of generosity, and it took courage. I don't think," he added grandly, " that generosity and courage are qualities of which any Oliphant need be ashamed.

" Well, let him be indentured at once, and no more of this brawling with the Press ! " snapped the old man.

And there was Walter's whole point gained at a stroke. Still, an artist in situations, he proceeded to develop that which he had staged in his mind beforehand.

" I found that Julius took very keenly to my side of the business. His interest in design and in the materials—the woods—was most eager and intelligent. His natural bent lies that way, I am quite sure. Now I take it that we may look to the need for maintaining our fleet for a long time to come. I take it that we may go on expanding indefinitely. Why, Ned, only this very day Captain Flett brought in that Spanish prize and a fortune beyond the wildest dreams ! There seems no end to the prospect of expansion . . ."

Walter's eloquence began to falter at that point.

" Go on ! " came the sardonic voice of his brother through the gloaming.

" I merely suggest that it would be well to apprentice Julius to me personally, so that—if I may say so—the not unimportant shipbuilding side of our enterprise be maintained in—I think I can use the phrase— a sort of direct succession."

" That's what I said," the colder voice cut in. " Indenture him and be done with it."

It sounded as though Edward had quite lost interest in the subject of Julius, his faults and his future. He stopped short in his walk and paused as if to rest, his right hand outstretched against the trunk of a chestnut tree. Again Walter thought with alarm that his brother had overtired himself, and then he turned rather indignant to realise that Edward was chuckling richly as if over some private joke.

" Man, Watty ! " the older man dropped into the familiar dialect of their boyhood. " That's a grand sermon you delivered about this pet laddie o' yours. Ye're sae honest, man. Ye tak' ither fowk to be as honest's yersel'. I could see ye comin' at me ten mile aff."

" But, Ned ! " poor Walter protested. " I was only concerned to put things right as between you and the boy. What is really in your mind ? You speak very strangely."

" Never mind, Watty ; you did well."

Walter felt the unaccustomed pressure of his brother's fingers affectionately squeezing his arm. The brothers then resumed their pacing of the lawn.

" Something on my mind ? Yes." Edward returned to his normal mode of speech. " Nothing tragic, nothing even alarming. I suppose it's just that I am getting old. We are both getting old, Walter. But the thought came to me when these two boys were dining with me only this afternoon. They were excited after seeing the Spanish prize brought in ; they were eager to understand the Marque system. Eager—that's the word—especially for Mark. And I realised that the boy has no sense of time or history. He sees it all as a simple business of sending out privateers and bringing in rich prizes, for ever and ever, amen. As if war were a natural state of affairs ! Why, Walter "—he chuckled again—" I had to borrow an old argument of yours and suggest to the lad that our use of the system raises a moral question."

" Yes," Walter agreed quietly. " But this is an unusual line of thought for you, Ned."

" Aye. Growing old. It must be that." Then he spoke with vehemence. " But I do not like—I say, Walter, *I do not like* to hear such an infant as Mark assume that commercial success is nothing but the result of aggressive action. That confesses lack of understanding, lack of vision, and a purely acquisitive spirit. I do not like it."

" These children were born and reared in time of war," murmured Walter gently.

" Aye, there's that ! " his brother agreed readily enough. " But they must understand that wars end. Are they taught nothing in their schools nowadays ? This war will end. Bonaparte will fall. Perhaps not to-morrow ; perhaps not in my lifetime ; but fall he will. His last chance of domination went when Lord Nelson smashed his fleet at Trafalgar two years past. He will fall. And what then, Walter ? "

" I foresee," maintained Walter stoutly, " a long period of profitable colonial expansion before this country."

" There will be that," the old man allowed. " It will last our time. These two young boys need never lack fortunes. But Garvel itself, man, this little town we take to be one of the hubs of the universe ? "

" I do not understand, Ned," said Walter with concern.

" Look——"

Edward led his brother to the brow of the slope, and from there they looked down on the collection of streets and houses that was the huddled capital of their empire. Lamps were still burning in the houses down there and flares above booths in the streets although it was near midnight now. The sounds of shouts and singing rose faintly to their ears.

" There is Garvel," announced old Edward Oliphant, and to his brother his tone sounded ominously prophetic, like that of one conscious of death in the offing. " You remember it when you were a young boatbuilder, Walter, and I was the captain of a coasting brig—a handful of fishers' huts at the mouth of the West Burn ? And now it is one of the busiest small ports in the country. Extraordinary ! "

" You did much to make it what it is, Edward," said Walter.

" Do you remember the university, Walter ? " the old man persisted in his own line of thought. " That was your idea. We believed ten years ago that Garvel was to be a commercial capital and ought to be a seat of learning. Tom Crauford of Kilblain was with us, and Hugh Oughterson, and the two Leitch's. . . . We were bitterly grieved when the Bill was thrown out of Parliament."

" Yes, I regret it still. Here we have leadership in our commercial sphere, infinite prospects of expansion. Our bare duty . . ."

" No, no ! " the old man interrupted sharply. " That is my point. Not those infinite prospects of expansion. Perhaps it was right that we did not get our university. Look again, Walter. This has been in my mind for a long time past. Sometimes I think we would do as well for ourselves—for ourselves alone, I say—to transfer our headquarters to London."

" Ned ! You surely can't mean——"

" Look again, Walter. The River, man ! You don't follow me. The River. There's your key . . ."

The tide was out. Over the anchorage and the sandbanks above it had fallen the deep colour of the sunset's long afterglow. To the eastward the sinuous line of the river proper gleamed in the smoky half-darkness settling over the land.

" There it is as clear as you could wish to see it, Walter," the old man said quietly. " Now that it's low tide, observe how Garvel stands at the bridgehead of the estuary—a fine deep-water anchorage before it and only a shallow, silting river above. The big ships can go no further ; here they must anchor and unload. But that river will be deepened some day—ten years, twenty years, fifty years from now— but it is coming. You know how those city merchants "—he pointed towards the east—" have spent and are spending a fortune on surveys and works. And they will succeed. Even now they have fourteen feet of water on the height of the springs at Dumbuck. They will go on digging and dredging and banking. They will make docks. They will have the ocean trade up to the doors of their warehouses. And it will pass our doors, all but a fraction."

Old Edward Oliphant sighed.

" Change, Walter. Steam. Remember Symington's boat on the

Canal. Then this restless fellow Bell over there. Yes, change . . . But
I am looking far ahead. We have had our day ; the young folk will
have theirs, though a different sort of day from ours. It all changes,
and yet it never changes. Come, Walter, into the house and we'll
drink a glass of spirits before you go."

6

Even as *Favourite* lay at anchor before Garvel, the green hills of
home about her and her Spanish prize swinging to the tides astern,
a man who knew and loved that northern scene as well as any lay
dying on a slab of brown rock, baked by the equatorial sun.

The rock was in Peru, on the foreshore of the glassy Pacific and
beneath a craggy range of mountains that got its colour of death from
the ordure of innumerable seabirds falling pallidly on the tawny native
stone. There was no green thing about this man as he died of
hæmorrhage from the stump of a leg that had been cut off by a Spanish
cannon-ball. It had been fired that afternoon by a *guarda costa* with
the fine name of *Almirante di Lima*. Another man, who bent over him
solicitously, was uninjured, but on his pinched, scorched face was the
look of failure. With a kerchief he had soaked in a pool of sea water
he dabbed hopelessly at the cracked and swollen lips of the dying
man.

" No good," croaked the latter, as if criticising this kindly effort.
" Go home, Alan Oliphant ! Go home—if you can."

" Now, now, Bob ! " the other protested, but emptily.

" Not long now," the wounded man's croak dwindled to a whisper.
" Dear Christ, this heat ! Keep that bloody sun out of my eyes, Alan.
Better now . . . Then go home. To hell with the silver ! "

" Those peons. The mules."

" They can live in this hell. You can't. Go home. More than I
ever will. See Sophie, my sweetheart. Young Bob—tell him to look
after his mother and the youngsters. My love to Barbara, dear girl.
Tell her her daddy thought of her. . . . Oh, that bloody sun in my
eyes again ! "

" There now, Bob. That's better. I'm staying with you."

" Go home, Alan Oliphant. See Old Ned, and tell him how I died.
Tell him I died for his filthy silver, curse him ! Tell him that all the
silver of Potosi is not worth the life of a man, not worth Sophie's
broken heart. Nor worth the life of a mule. . . . Curse him ! "

The swollen tongue seemed to stick in its thickened juices. The last
breath rattled in the throat of Captain Robert Rait of the ship *Garthland*

of Garvel. Alan Oliphant draped the kerchief over the dead face with its ludicrously swollen lips and stood up.

He looked towards the blue and distant peaks of the Andes and considered how barren and unfriendly were even their golden foothills. A figure on a knoll some five furlongs above high-water mark, a figure statuesque and symbolic in a striped blanket, reminded him that in the hollow beyond were some seven score pack-mules and their attendant peons—the army that bore its useless load of Oliphant silver and looked to him for leadership.

Alan Oliphant was in his twenty-third year, and he knew fear and bitterness in that dreadful moment. It had been a grim enough business to haggle for months with the Spanish merchants in the thin, baking air of Potosi, trading *Garthland's* cargo of Scottish textiles for bar after bar of silver. It had been hard enough to gather the train of mules and attendants and to secure reliable guides. Then to lead the expedition to the coast had been to pass through Purgatory : day after day, week upon week, over the mountain passes under a remorseless sun that hid itself only behind choking mists off the sea. And the crowning bitterness of reaching the coast, a king's ransom in silver intact, only to watch the waiting ship silenced and dismasted barely a league offshore by the heavier guns of the *guarda costa*, and then to wait on the rocks until a drifting spar brought in his kinsman, his last possible link with his own people, in the very article of death.

Alan Oliphant stood for a long time beside the body that was now the unbeautiful symbol of his defeat. His now experienced eye picked out, high up against the brassy sky, two black specks : a couple of condors waiting to pounce on the corpse of Captain Robert Rait and, tearing at flesh and muscle with their greedy beaks, leave it a cage of white bones. He thought of the long line of those blanched rat-traps that marked his trail from the uplands of Bolivia to this hopeless point below Titicaca, the skeletons of men and mules fallen by the wayside so that the Oliphants might have their treasure. To think of retracing those innumerable, weary steps was itself an agony. There were loaded pistols at his belt and one motion, one effort of decision, would end it all.

Alan Oliphant was young, however. Conscious of the name he bore he might not be, but some inherited sense of responsibility worked within him. Somewhere in the hinterland of his mind stood the figure of old Edward Oliphant, severe, exacting, just. Perhaps he heard that austere voice speak of duty and of the obligations of enterprise.

He braced his shoulders and, turning away from the body, started across the rocks towards the sentinel figure on the skyline.

CHAPTER TWO

I

MR. WALTER OLIPHANT lowered the flute from his lips. Holding it out before him, he appeared to admire its slim black body. His fine fingers played a soundless tune on its bright stops. He smiled.

" My music does not disturb you, Julius, I trust ? " he asked.

" Not in the least, Uncle Walter," his companion replied cheerfully.

The young man sat at a round table in the middle of the room. An open book, loose sheets of paper, compasses and a protractor lay before him within a circle of light down-cast from a shaded lamp. A pencil in his right hand traced a series of algebraic notations on one of the sheets of foolscap.

" How goes the work ? " the old man asked.

" It's coming nicely," Julius replied. " This book Dr. Spence recommended has given me some real good ideas. Did you have a look at it ? "

He passed the volume across to the aged relation whose lean frame filled an easy chair by the blazing coal fire. Mr. Oliphant placed the flute across his long knees, adjusted a pair of steel-rimmed spectacles on his distinguished nose, and held the title-page up at the level of his eyes.

" Fluids," he read, " if my French does not betray me. By Bousset. Never heard of him. And why fluids, Julius ? "

" Well, sir," Julius laughed. " there would be little point in designing a ship if we hadn't a fluid to float it in."

" Granted, my boy. But the sea is an element and, except for tides and storms, static. It is not a river, a stream, a——"

" But that's just the point, uncle ! " the young man urged, laying down his pencil. " When the ship is in motion under sail the sea *does* become a current—in relation to the ship's position. Therefore—I argued to myself—if this man Bousset can tell us something new about the behaviour of water in motion, then we may discover something new about the behaviour of ships in motion. And he has told me a lot, I assure you."

" God bless my soul ! You have a good head on you, indeed ! " Granduncle Walter used forceful words, but he spoke with the mildness of old age. " But I must not interrupt you. Don't make those bows of yours too fine, boy. I have been afraid lately that you were going too . . . However. It will not disturb you if I play myself another air ? "

47

"Not at all. I like it."

The young man picked up his pencil and bent again over his papers. The old man raised the flute to his lips and blew into it the tune of his fancy, quaintly filling the little room with inoffensive sound. It was one of General Reid's admired pieces, gallantly entitled *Miss Constance Gilchrist of Abertocher*, and it was a bleak and harmless little melody, decorated with funny small runs and graces, and as neat in its form as a lady's fan. It had no power of passion to intrude between Julius and his symbols and visions.

The tune ended in a neat recital in reverse of its beginning. The flute was laid again across the old man's knees. His white head drooped, nodded over and then was still in sleep. A coal fell from the grate.

"Got it ! " cried Julius.

"God bless my soul ! " the old man protested, starting out of slumber. "Got what, boy ? "

"Sorry, Uncle Walter ! I hadn't realised . . . I was thinking of something else."

He rose from his chair by the table and stepped to the fireside, resting a hand on the mantelpiece. Had Mr. Walter Oliphant been a younger man he would have discerned tension in his grandnephew's fine, pale face—so like his own in youth—and in the mere strength of the lad's clutch on the edge of marble.

"No, that's it now, Uncle Walter, or I'm just a fool," said Julius, pursuing his own line of intense thought. "It's what you yourself guessed at years ago. Now I think that it can be confirmed by scientific proof. All my figures and drawings seem to be as safe as the Bank of England. To-morrow——"

"I'm afraid I have missed the point, Julius . . . Dropped off . . ."

Julius's frown into the fire was transformed into a smile of kindness. He turned and laid three fingers on the old hand lying along the arm of the chair.

"We'll leave it till to-morrow, sir," he said kindly. "You are tired, and I am tired. Look—it's after ten. Bed, Uncle Walter."

"But Julius, I am most interested. This work of yours."

"To-morrow, sir. Look, Uncle Walter, do you think you could manage up to Nellie's Pool by eleven o'clock in the forenoon ? I'll have something to show you, I promise."

"Nellie's Pool ! On the Dellingburn ! Eleven of the clock ! " cried the old man indignantly. "Why, Ginger and I set out just after ten every morning at the latest ! Nellie's Pool indeed ! "

His indignation petered out suddenly.

"Did you say Nellie's Pool, Julius ? I don't quite grasp . . . ? "

"An experiment, sir. Using the flow of the stream on models. I've thought out a bit of apparatus, and Nellie's Pool is just the place for it, with that strong run of water under the bank above it. Tom Aitkenhead and Sandy Crum will run the thing up in no time. But come, sir. It's past your proper bedtime."

"You have me all excited," the old man chuckled as he rose obediently from his chair. He swayed a little on his feet and Julius put out a quick hand to steady the tall, ageing form. "Experiments in Nellie's Pool, upon my soul ! What next ? You have worked hard these four years, Julius. I told Ned that your talents lay that way. I am very proud of my pupil."

He was moving slowly on Julius's arm towards the door, and he turned his gaze to beam affectionately into the young man's face.

"Thank you, Uncle Walter," Julius laughed easily. "And I am rather proud of my master."

"A great joy to me," old Walter Oliphant pursued his own sentimental line of thought even as they passed through the hall, lifted the candle from the table there, and went upstairs together. "Like a son in the house. It has made a very great difference to my old age . . . Did you tell me, Julius, that Mark is coming home ? "

"Yes, sir. Mr. Ramage tells me that he will be coming back in the *Sovereign*, due any time before the end of the month."

"Dear me ! It seems an age since he went away. An extraordinary experience for a lad ! More than a year on the island of Heligoland, and virtually in charge of all Europe's supplies of coffee ! That was a remarkable enterprise of Ned's. But Mark has a talent that way. Eh, Julius ? I think he understands the value of money better than you and I do."

Cackling over his little joke, Granduncle Walter suffered himself to be shown into his chamber and warned to be careful with his candles and falling coals from the fire that burned in the grate. Julius in his turn was warned to see with care to the locking up of the house and against burning the midnight oil over his papers.

This was their ritual. Downstairs again, Julius made to turn the heavy key in the front door but then on an impulse opened it and went out into the night. The October air was frosty, and a full moon above a ground mist suffused everything with a chill but gentle radiance. The silence was complete, as if the town below and the anchorage beyond had disappeared completely under cover of the seasonal haar. Julius turned and stared at the white, harled walls and irregular roofs of his granduncle's house of Goldenhaddock.

It was a mansion much less grand, more natural to its northern setting, than Granduncle Edward's place at The Mount. It had been indeed the small mansionhouse of a family of bonnet lairds, little more than a large farmhouse, with only a few crowstepped gables and one pointed turret in the Baronial manner over a turnpike stairway to suggest its feudal status. Julius regarded its moonlit walls with affection. The gleam of candlelight from Uncle Walter's room upstairs and the stream of whiter light through the window of the lamplit parlour below warmed his heart. This was home ; herein existed between the old man and himself such a wealth of sweet cordiality, far beyond even that of the manse in Cowal, as he could never have dreamed of knowing in his lonely boyhood.

The night air worked through his garments, and he shivered and hurried indoors. The big key turned in the hall, he sought the warmth of the parlour, sat down at the table, picked up his pencil and bent once more over the sheets of foolscap.

2

At dawn next morning young Mr. Julius Oliphant led a small expedition up and out of Garvel. It had a quaint look, as of a party bent on scaling the hills behind the town with the aid of sundry mechanical devices.

Julius himself, now a tall and lean young man, led the way over the frosted grass, an assortment of books, papers, cords and small tools under his arms, in his hands, or stuffed into the pockets of his ankle-length surtout. A yard or two behind him marched two solid artisans with blue bonnets and white aprons tucked up round their waists, each of them laden with a straw tool-bag, small pieces of fashioned wood and, over their shoulders, a selection of blocks and pulley-wheels. Considerably in the rear, panting for breath and at the same time wasting it in comment on these strange proceedings, two apprentice boys staggered over the rough ground carrying between them an array of battens and planks of timber.

The cavalcade's way beyond the town lay up a small defile through which the Dellingburn tumbled cheerfully to reach the sea hard by the Oliphant Shipyard. The stream was of no great volume, but it came over the escarpment blithely enough in a small series of falls and through bushy grottoes of its own making. On the first plateau, however, it ran sedately through a series of meadows with only an occasional stunted hawthorn to mark its course, and hereabouts, in a basin below a second of the foothills' interminable terraces, it formed the considerable stretch of Nellie's Pool. Above that, as Julius had reminded Mr. Walter Oliphant, there was a fine run of fast-moving water between high banks.

"The very thing!" said Julius to himself, surveying the scene again. "Now, Tom, Sandy——" he addressed the journeymen. "Drop all that gear and come and see what I want done."

For an hour and more thereafter that upland hollow echoed to the sound of wood being sawed, hammered and nailed. As the autumn sun came through to warm the day, urchins from the town, arriving to play with model boats in Nellie's Pool, paused to watch that sheet of water being prepared for a finer regatta than it had ever accommodated before. When Uncle Walter's red spaniel Ginger came loping along to fawn on Julius, intimating to him that he and his men had put in fully three hours of work, that stretch of the Dellingburn had been strangely transformed indeed.

"God bless my soul!" cried the old man, pausing on the edge of the pool to stare.

On each bank of the stream they had set up a stout post, the tops joined by a crossbar that bridged the race of water emptying itself into the pool. From this crossbar hung three pulleys, and through each of these a length of fine strong cord had been rove. The three cords each supported a metal weight, their free ends being tethered meanwhile to a peg driven into the ground where Julius stood among his men, smiling at his granduncle's surprise. On the grass at his feet lay three ship-models in solid wood, painted red, white and blue respectively.

"A gibbet!" cried Uncle Walter, gaily recovering from astonishment. "Have you invited me to see a triple hanging, boy?"

"No, sir," Julius laughed. "A single birth, I hope—of a new idea. Let me explain . . . You won't be tired standing, sir : not too cold?"

"Tired—cold—rubbish!" returned the old man testily. "Proceed, Julius, if you please."

"Well, sir——" The young man's manner seemed to become professional of a sudden. "You see the three models here—we'll call them Red, White and Blue. They are all of the same wood, all of the same weight, and all of the same general dimensions. But take Red here——"

Julius stooped and picked up that model with his left hand ; the fingers of his right felt the little ship's bows as a potter's might fondle the curves of a vase.

"You see that these bows are of the usual design—bluff and blunt. with the bulge outwards. In fact, she's an exact model of that *Pandora* we built for Mr. Crauford."

" Yes, yes. I see. Proceed."

" But here's Blue, sir," Julius continued, stooping again. " You see how I have fined the bows away as far as I dare go—at present that is."

" Too fine by far," interjected Uncle Walter sharply.

" That may be. We shall see," Julius agreed. " But there it is for the purposes of the experiment. The stern is also rather fine, the water lines forward are hollow. Otherwise, of course, Blue is exactly the same ship as Red."

" Yes, yes ! " Uncle Walter was getting excited. " And White ? "

" Just a compromise, sir, half and between the two extreme outlines. She is not the shape of anything I should care to build. But White is our control—in the sense of this experiment, I mean."

The old man considered the three models on the grass. He touched each one with the point of his stick. But when Ginger thrust his nose against the fresh paint, the stick poked the dog aside impatiently.

" You are an extraordinary boy, Julius," he said, smiling on his grandnephew. " Now, let me hear how you will order the demonstration."

" The gibbet, as you call it, sir," Julius pointed to the frame over the stream. " Three pulleys or drums, each with exactly the same resistance. Three counterbalancing weights, true to a fraction of a grain. Three lengths of cord of the same material and exactly the same length. All that has been checked and checked again."

" I accept that," said the old man, testy again. " And then ? "

" Well, sir, we float the models in the current here and watch how they behave." Julius laughed a little uneasily. " I may be proved a fool, but my reasoning certainly is that the finest of the three designs will oppose the least resistance to the flow of the water, will therefore put less strain on the counterbalancing weight, and will *therefore* lie further upstream than the others. And of the three models, sir," Julius concluded rather defiantly, " I expect Blue to win."

Mr. Walter Oliphant considered the models again. He looked at the tackle so strangely arranged over the Dellingburn. A clearing of the throat hinted at reservations in his mind.

" We can only put it to the proof," he announced at length.

" Yes," agreed Julius crisply. " Sandy—tie up these models to the lines. Red on the right, White in the middle, and Blue on the left. And see that you use exactly the same length of cord on each knot. Rab "—he addressed one of the apprentice boys—" off with your boots and stockings and get ready to wade in with the boats."

The small boys up from the town had by now gathered closely about the Oliphant group. They listened open-mouthed to all that passed and now stared, goggle-eyed, at Sandy and Rab preparing to launch the little ships. One, who had elbowed his way almost under Julius's elbow, suddenly darted out of the circle and made an announcement to his playmates.

" Hey, lads ! " he shrieked. " There's gaun' to be a race ! "

" The child is not far wrong," murmured Julius to his granduncle. Mr. Walter Oliphant did not smile.

" This may be an historic occasion," he intimated with severe dignity. Then, he suddenly swiped at the legs of the children with his stick, missing by yards. " Run away, you boys ! This is no time for foolery."

" Watch now ! " cried Julius, grasping at the old man's arms.

The three models were afloat in the Dellingburn, bobbing to the small waves and eddies of the race above Nellie's Pool. A brush of rising wind across the stream disconcerted them.

" Confound that breeze ! " snapped the old man.

" No," Julius demurred. " An average weather condition. Just what we want."

The coloured models survived the small tempest and settled to breast the current. Each put upon its tethering cord just such a strain as a trained terrier might upon its leash. The spaniel dog called Ginger barked at those strange animals that could ride the running waters so much more lightly than he.

Julius's fingers closed round the old man's wrist.

" There it is ! " he whispered tensely. " The fact stands out— proven ! Blue lies ahead. Red is far behind. White is in between. And—mark this, Uncle Walter !—White is closer up on Blue than Red is behind the rest. That proves it. All I thought and calculated . . . The suspicion of fineness towards the stern. The hollow water lines forward. We've got it ! "

The small boys on the bank of the burn were shouting at the pitch of their voices. This was for them better than a fair, and their adolescent pipes cracked as they shrieked the odds.

" On wi' the white yin ! . . . Blue's winnin' . . . Rid, Rid, Rid ! . . . Blue's winnin' . . . White—come on the White ! "

The riot of young voices died away on a long " Aw—aw—aw . . ." The models had steadied in the stream. The fine-lined Blue lay ahead, riding the force of the stream serenely. Then, as one man, the urchins of the town cheered the winner of this notable race. Julius breathed the tautness of excitement out of his chest and turned to his granduncle.

" Is that my proof, Uncle Walter ? " he asked as easily as he could.

" No ! "

The objection was decisive, and Julius felt himself stiffening to resist the refusal of all his hopes.

"Have I got something wrong?" he disciplined himself to ask mildly.

Mr. Walter Oliphant pointed his stick at Blue.

"That ship's in the beat of the current," he said. "Obviously she has the advantage over the others. Your test, Julius, is not soundly contrived."

The young man held back the anger of disappointment.

"Yes," he agreed thoughtfully. "I should have foreseen that. All the better! We can ring the changes. We'll have them all ways. His voice sharpened with eagerness. "Red, Blue, White . . . Blue, Red, White . . . Blue, White, Red . . . Anything you please."

"If you will just exchange Blue and Red meanwhile," Uncle Walter cut in calmly, "that should be quite enough to go on with."

Julius merely motioned his men to do what the old man suggested. Sandy the journeyman exchanged the lines attached to Red and Blue, and Rab the apprentice, wildly cheered by the children on the bank, waded once more into the stream to set the little ships for this second test.

"Anither race! Anither race!" cried the boys from the town. "The blue ane'll win again . . . Naw, it'll be the rid this time . . . Watch you the white ane!"

"Silence, you brats!" commanded Mr. Walter Oliphant, waving his stick at the mob of infants.

"Let them go, Rab," said Julius.

Once again the model ships danced in the stream as they took the stresses of current and cord and weight. The cross-wind blew still more freshly, and Blue had the strongest eddies of the stream under the inner curve of the bank to contend with, but it was as before. Her fine bows gave her the obviously superior power to forge through the water, and when the models assumed their final positions she still lay ahead, with White behind and bluff-bowed Red lagging and snubbing at her cord behind both.

Mr. Olipant's stick was raised on high.

"Prodigious!" he announced. "Julius, I congratulate you. This is a demonstration of historic importance, far-reaching, revolutionary . . ."

"And see, sir!" cried Julius happily. "See how dry her decks are! Blue's, I mean. Red's are wet. Those bluff bows splash the stuff about."

"The thing is clear," boomed Uncle Walter. "Capital! Prodigious!"

"And now I'll absolutely prove it," said Julius, suddenly grim.

"But, my dear boy——"

" No. This is quite necessary, sir. The proof absolute. Just watch this. Rab—into the burn with you and fetch in Red. Sandy—that sharp plane of yours."

The model in his hands, Julius held its bows against the bole of a hawthorn and with a few strokes of the tool shaved away the bulges forward until the block of wood had roughly the shape of White. He carefully picked up the shavings and handed them with the model to his carpenter.

" Try them just once again, Sandy. But lay these shavings on Red's deck. We must keep the weights exactly the same."

Once again the miniature flotilla rode the stream. When the models had curtsied to their positions in the dance Blue was still serenely in the lead. Then——

" God bless my soul ! " exclaimed Uncle Walter.

This time Red so eased the strain on her counterbalancing weight that she lay even with her new bows slightly overlapping those of White.

" Careless dynamics ! " laughed Julius. " I must have fined her down more than I intended. Still. I think it proves my point quite decisively. Do you agree, Uncle Walter ? "

" Agree ! I am a convert of the most abject kind," Mr. Oliphant laughed in return. More seriously he added : " This is important, Julius. This may take the science and art of shipbuilding along quite new paths. This requires thought, calculation, application. Nay, Julius ! This requires demonstration on a full scale. . . . Let me see. Now, if I could persuade your Uncle Ned to sanction a new and most interesting addition to the Fleet. If we could build at our own risk— and why not ? This is a splendid moment . . . Ginger ! Ginger ! Home for dinner, sir. Will you be with us, Julius ? "

" When I have got this gear back to the yard, sir. Within the hour."

" And we'll crack a bottle of wine, boy ! " the old man exulted, poking his grandnephew in the ribs with the point of his stick. " And a florin to you, Sandy. Treat the lads and drink the health of your young master. You have seen history made to-day. Yes, sir. Ginger ! Ginger, you rascal ! Home, sir."

The red spaniel rooting among the rushy tufts and small bushes before him, a very happy old gentleman made his way down the glen. He left behind him a young man whose cup of content was full and overflowing.

3

The Reverend Colin Lambie was preaching against the sin of fornication and gave the impression of enjoying himself hugely. Basing himself on a full-blooded text from Deuteronomy, he seemed to belabour his audience with words much as he smote the pulpit desk with his clenched fist or slapped the Holy Bible before him with his large palm. His accusation was all-embracing. They were guilty every one of them, it seemed—old men and decent housewives and even the terrified infants in his congregation. What he described as the long and bloody wars brought upon the world by the insensate folly and satanic ambitions of that fiend in human shape, Bonaparte—with this curse there had come among them in Garvel, his own beloved corner of the Lord's vineyard, a raging infection of moral laxity. Hordes of loose-living, God-defying mariners, troops of painted Jezebels, had descended upon the town like a plague of locusts, seeking what they might devour. They were in a fair way, roared the preacher in a quaint phrase, to make of the place a Sodom and Gomorrah ; and the towns-folk, he implied, were equally guilty in the sin of homologation. They would go down the pit, they would burn in hell fire. Mr. Lambie did not even find it possible to take a hopeful view of the outcome of repentance at such a late hour.

The awed children apart, very few members of that congregation took the commination to heart. They were students of style in preach-ing rather than of doctrine. This was common form in their Kirk, its theology based on close and literal reading of the Old Testament, its corporate mind fixed on the doctrine of Original Sin. It could fairly be said that they enjoyed the sensations of guilt and of being the victims or cockshies of their minister's verbal brickbats. After more than an hour of Mr. Lambie's threats and recriminations they would gather in the open kirkyard among the gravestones, and nod to each other gravely, and even grin uneasily, and say, " Man ! The meenister was in rare fettle the day ! " or " Powerful ! Powerful ! He was in rare form the day."

One at least of that congregation heard the Reverend Mr. Lambie declare against fornication sometimes with amusement, more often in disgust with the preacher's orgiastic revels in near-indecency, with the licensed sadism of his whirling words. Sometimes he winced for, sitting alone in the Oliphant gallery, Julius had only to lean his elbows on the ledge and rest his face between his hands to see below him, where she sat among her brothers and sisters in the body of the kirk, the aloof, chaste, chiselled face of Barbara Rait under a bonnet more adventurous in *chic* than any other woman in that congregation, even Sir John's lady herself, dared to wear. Barbara, of·all the poised women in the world, to have this filth out of a fool's mouth thrown at her ! This Lambie might even throw a gibe at her for the neat, discreet gaiety of her clothes.

Julius leaned a lot upon his hands. Like many a young man before him and since, the eternal youth of the ballads, he heard the Word of God as an intrusion upon his privacy of thought and feeling. All the way from Kempock Barbara had come to church for once in a while, a delicious response to the impulse that had taken him there when he might very decently have stayed at home. Barbara was beautiful and intelligent and calm. All the wildness of Mr. Lambie's preaching could never touch her, except with a faint disgust which her fastidiousness would pick up and drop in the gutter as often he had seen her pick a thread from her sleeve with fine fingers and drop it in the fire. Barbara.

He wrenched his eyes and attention from her figure. She would never look up in any event. That was not Barbara's way. He must not draw attention to her by his doting. He was an Oliphant, alone in the Oliphant loft, elevated above the mob and watched by them.

This enclosed pew in the gallery of the Old West Kirk had come to the family with Uncle Walter's purchase of the mansionhouse, lands and appurtenances of Goldenhaddock, and it was a distinction that Mr. Edward Oliphant greatly appreciated. He had really loved, Julius knew, to sit there in state beside his brother and among such relatives as chanced to be in Garvel, calmly and rather splendidly taking over from poor Walter the headship of the clan. He had liked to look across the body of the kirk to that other, more ornate gallery in which, under his armorial bearings carved in bog oak, sat Sir John and his lady : fat and red-faced and quite undistinguished-looking as both those scions of the local nobility might be. All that had ministered pleasantly to his acute and dignified sense of position.

Julius himself was not insensible to the traditional interest of his situation. Alone now, he was aware of responsibility to the Oliphant legend. He would be very strangely placed, he reflected, if Uncle Edward and Uncle Walter, both growing so old and frail, were never to sit in this pew again, leaving him to hold the family citadel ! Mark was coming home, to be sure. That would be interesting. Had Mark changed greatly during his years abroad ? How would their reunion go, and how would they get on in partnership ?

Uneasy questions ; and Julius turned his eyes to the Sailors' Loft that filled the whole rearward portion of the gallery. He always took pleasure in this arrangement, so true to the tradition of a seaport town, even to the apparently irrelevant but artistically just model of a 20-gun frigate suspended in mid-air above the heads of the mariners. He liked to know that the ships' captains sat in front on a bench upholstered in blue cloth with brass-headed nails, while mates and junior officers in the row behind sat on blue cloth indeed but were denied the splendours of brass studs. Right, too, that the ordinary seamen should occupy plain deal benches behind their betters—honest fellows, their rugged faces quite unmoved as the Reverend Mr. Lambie enlarged on their sins of carnality. And on a cutty stool beside the captains' bench old Bauldy Pin the beadle of the Loft, a hero of Trafalgar, less a leg shot off by the Froggies' guns in that engagement, and a martinet among the seafaring worshippers.

The sermon seemed to stop suddenly. Even that vehement preacher's flow of invective must somehow exhaust itself. In an access of tolerance Mr. Lambie gave out the 23rd Psalm, and that they sang in the metrical version to the tune *Covenanters*. Shortly Julius found himself among the tombs in the kirkyard, exchanging courtesies with Sir John, his lady, and Miss Lavinia, their only child. Yes, he was sorry to say that Uncle Edward was now no longer fit to make the journey downhill from The Mount and up again. Yes, Uncle Walter had a slight chill and at his age . . . Sir John said he knew what it was.

" It's a peety of the auld gentlemen," he said in good braid Scots.

Sir John looked the prosperous lowland farmer to the life, and he was indeed little more than that. The Laird of Garvel had been small fry until such as the Oliphants came to make a huddle of fishermen's huts an international seaport. But Sir John had been at least eager to see his property developing, sensible enough in concession, and shrewdly fair in the feuing of his lands, and Julius respected him for having no baronial airs. He was only fascinated by the rough brosy face and plain manners of the little man who could call his blood blue and by the forthright vulgarity of his Leddy—a Sangster of the Dreeps, as she incessantly reminded you, and a wondrous figure of fun in her nodding plumes and innumerable rings and bugles and brooches, adorning a body as stocky and rotund as a bollard. But Julius was always most interested in the personality of Miss Lavinia, the sullen, shy, pathetic, pasty-faced girl, who seemed to hide behind her father and mother and regard their interlocutor with a long look in which the deepest suspicion and the most feverish hopes were pathetically represented. It had been suggested that a match between Miss Lavinia and one of the Oliphant boys would be in the right historical order of things.

Barbara waited for Julius by the gate. The children had run on ahead, eager for the delights of the long walk home by the shore path to Kempock, sure that their favourite cousin would follow with their sister.

"I shouldn't go down to Kempock to-day, Barbara," he explained to her as they shook hands formally. "Uncle Walter is not well at all."

"But Maman will be so disappointed, Julius!" she exclaimed with that air of sincere concern which always defeated him. "And I was to tell you that she is cooking a very special dinner for you. She says you are the only guest she ever cooks for specially. She says you have a natural *goût*—and you know what that means to Maman! Is your granduncle really ill?"

"Well," Julius was weak, "he certainly has a chill. I kept him out too long over an experiment the other day. And at his age——"

"He has good servants in the house. You can return early in the evening. Oh come, Julius! You have news for Maman, she loves to hear the news. It is so long since you visited us. You must tell me about your experiment."

If Julius had seriously thought of breaking an old custom even for one day, he was unnerved now. The sweet seduction of her voice, her little foreign tricks of speech, the directness of the dark eyes under the arched brows—these were quite beyond his power to resist. Apart, too, from the emotional hold that Barbara's calm personality had upon his, her physical person enchanted him artistically. In terms of his natural symbolism she was for him like a fine ship. She had matured into a woman of medium height, but so slimly proportioned that she seemed tall. Since the news of her father's bleak death on the Peruvian shore came home she had worn black on formal occasions, and in the fashion of the hour her sheath-like dress confessed the perilous beauty of a perfect figure.

So on they went together towards the cottage in the bay, the young people content to leave them alone. Only Barbara, subtly understanding the delicacy of his mind, subtly but justly flattering him, could make Julius talk so gaily and candidly. Soon he was off on the loveliness of hollow water-lines and his plans for the dream-ship he and Uncle Walter were to build. He spoke of the virtues of oak and mahogany and teak as a poet might of gilded mountain tops or a mistress's tresses. He sought to enchant his companion with his own almost delirious delight in line, and he, one of the grave and important Oliphants, sketched large curves and exquisite whorls in the air with abandoned hands.

"You are so charming sometimes, Julius!" Barbara murmured through a little laugh.

"I beg your pardon?" Julius inquired gravely. Then he blushed.

"Oh, I see! I am truly sorry, Barbara. Making an exhibition of myself. Wearying you. I seem to get so excited about ships."

"Dear Cousin Julius!" she smiled at him. "But please go on. I do like to hear of your work."

Julius did not in the least relish her careful mode of address, but he did not often encounter such an understanding listener, and he was still maintaining and elaborating the case for the fine bow and hollow water-lines when they passed at length up the untidy path to encounter Aunt Sophie beaming, on the doorstep of her cottage.

"*Ah, Jules! Mon cher*," she greeted him ebulliently. "I am happy to see you. And so handsome you are growing! That is why I cook a fine lunch for you—a lobster in our American way, then *canard rôti*, then *crêpes Suzettes*. And all because you have a fine figure, and I am an old fool of a woman!"

During this recital Aunt Sophie put forward her ivory cheek for him to kiss, and this Julius had at length learned to do without a blush. He had come to love this strange woman if only because of her complete, cool and kindly understanding of himself, and greatly to admire her for her spirit. She had aged since her husband's death. The lines about her mouth and nose were sometimes hard. Invariably she wore black, but always with the style of a Frenchwoman in these things.

"It is kind of you, Aunt Sophie, but I really should not have come," Julius started to explain. "Uncle Walter is not at all well."

"But Barbara smiled at you, and your foolish heart went rat-a-plan, rat-a-plan. I know."

"Maman!" Barbara protested, though more in defence of Julius than of herself.

"Maman! Maman! Maman!" mocked her mother. "Have I not eyes in my head and an understanding of these things? It would become you, *ma fille*, to blush like dear Julius. Had I your age and your looks—ah, I should not pretend! But you are half *Écossaise, fière et froide . . . Cepedant, le dejeuner*. I shall hear your news at table, Julius. Barbara, see that these infants sit down with clean hands at least."

Laughing merrily, Aunt Sophie trotted away to her kitchen. Barbara glanced at Julius even as he averted his eyes and said:

"I am sorry you should be so embarrassed, Cousin Julius. Maman has not been the same since my father died."

"Oh, I understand Aunt Sophie's little jokes by now," said Julius, airily dismissing as nothing that situation of which his real self so passionately wished to take advantage.

But soon they were all seated at table, and now Aunt Sophie was

categorically demanding news from Julius in between her spasms of
filling empty plates or chiding, even cuffing if he or she was within
reach, one or another of the children.

"And why should you not have come to see me to-day, Julius?"
she would ask. "And to miss such a dinner as this?"

"I would have missed a feast," Julius replied gallantly, "but
Uncle Walter is ill. He caught a chill, and all my fault. I kept him
too long in the cold the other morning, watching a foolish experiment
of mine."

"Foolish?" asked Barbara candidly.

"Well, no. But I shall have to leave rather early to-day, Aunt
Sophie."

"That Walter," observed Aunt Sophie judicially, "has a certain
fineness of—what is it?—*esprit*. Not unlike your own delicacy of
feeling, Julius. But he is old. *C'est la vie.* Yet that Edward goes on.
There is a type of Oliphant I cannot love."

"I know, I know," Julius hastened to cut short Aunt Sophie's
chronic tirade against the Oliphants. "But Uncle Edward has many
great qualities. I wish I had some of them. And he, too, is growing
very old and frail."

"*Je m'en fiche!*" said Aunt Sophie contemptuously.

Barbara, watchful over the raw patches in the integument that
bound her kin together, intervened coolly.

"That we understand, Maman," she said. "But Julius has also
some news of Bob."

"And I am not informed! At once. The one woman in this world
most passionately concerned!"

"*Chère Maman!* You would hardly listen," remarked Barbara
gently.

"It's not real news yet, Aunt Sophie," Julius abetted the girl
swiftly. "But I do understand from Ramage that Bob is almost certainly
on his way home by now. One of our ships made a very fast passage
from the Plate, and the skipper reported Bob's *Venture* standing in to
Montevideo. There was also word that my cousin Alan had reached
that port with the treasure of silver from Potosi after all."

"Not one of these Oliphants could be parted from treasure in any
form," interjected Aunt Sophie bitterly, adding: "Even if my
husband must die."

"Papa was a sailor. It was cruel for you and for us all, Maman,
but it was the risk of his profession." That was Barbara bringing her
cool mind to Julius's aid.

"It was sad indeed," he agreed, "but still I think you will not
deny Cousin Alan's pluck, Aunt Sophie. It is nearly four years now

since the expedition set out, and yet he has done what he was asked
to do. I believe the journey was terrible, fantastic—back to Potosi
from the Peruvian coast ; down through the jungles and plains to the
valley of the Parana. One Scotsman fighting through at the head of
a gang of cut-throat half-breeds. Four years ! "

Julius was warming to his theme. His face was flushed under his
fair hair.

" One may think what one pleases about the morality of modern
commerce. One may condemn the privateering system. I think I do
myself. One may even have private griefs and bitter regrets. War is
like that, always. But "—declared Julius grandly—" when I think
of Alan Oliphant's journey, the dangers he ran, the terrible sufferings
he must have known—and all to do his bare duty—well, I think it's
splendid ! Splendid ! He did his duty. And that was good enough
for Lord Nelson himself."

This exordium had a more immediate effect than Julius could have
bargained for. Aunt Sophie seemed to leap from her chair. Her arms
folded tight round his neck. From behind her eager, babbling lips
kissed his hair and then, formally, both of his cheeks.

" *Mais, comme tu es charmant, Jules ! *" she cried. " *Si jeune, si probe !
Voilà* . . . It is over now. I am happy. My Bob comes home again.
And I have in my little cellar a bottle of Chateauneuf-du-Pâpe.
Alors . . ."

The rich, dark wine of the Rhone was carefully uncorked and poured
into fine glasses. Even the children were allowed a modicum well
diluted with water. Julius gave the toast.

" To Bob and a speedy return ! "

" My Bob ! *Cher enfant* . . ."

" Bob ! "

It was solemnly drunk, and then all the Raits, Barbara excepted,
started to chatter at once of Bob's goodness, Bob's ship and what he
might bring home to the children. Infected by the gaiety of this
cheerful family, Julius proposed another toast.

" We ought to drink to my Cousin Mark now. He is returning
from Heligoland, you know, Aunt Sophie."

" That is a lout," said Aunt Sophie firmly.

" You have not seen him for nearly four years, Maman," Barbara
corrected her coolly.

" That is so," her mother admitted. " My temper to-day is good.
We shall drink to Mark and a speedy return. *Bon santé !* "

This second toast was duly honoured, if with less enthusiasm than
the first commanded, and now Aunt Sophie was in the mood for
celebrations all round.

"And to whom shall we drink now?" she asked, her dark eyes shining maliciously.

"We should drink to the new ship Julius is building," said Barbara, perhaps only to steer her mother away from the embarrassingly personal.

"A new ship! What ship is this? Why am I not informed of these matters?"

The whole story of the experiments and of the decision to build a vessel to Julius's new design had to be gone over again for Aunt Sophie's benefit, her many and shrewd questions carefully answered.

"That is good," she pronounced finally. "I knew you to be a young man of genius, Jules. Your glass, *mon ami*, and yours, Barbara. *Alors* . . . But how do you name this ship of yours, Julius?"

Julius was happy and confident. His spirit was strengthened by friendly company and good wine. He smiled round the family circle, his bright eyes coming to rest at length on Barbara's face. He saw that she was watching him intently.

"With the lady's permission," he announced boldly, "I am going to call her the *Barbara Rait*."

A great clapping of young Rait hands greeted this intimation, Aunt Sophie leading the salvo. Suddenly shocked by his own boldness, however, Julius turned his gaze from the happy, laughing faces of the children to Barbara. She was blushing, and her head was bent in embarrassment. He was bitterly sorry that he had so brashly exposed her to this notoriety even within the family circle. Her eyes were levelled from under their long, black lashes on his, and he realised with sudden joy that her look was not resentful. It was appealing, rather; it was the look of a young, lovely, trustful girl.

"You do me a great compliment, Cousin Julius," she murmured.

"Cousin Julius!" mocked Aunt Sophie, almost with a snort. "What manner of speech is this? Is this a convent school? Never," declared Aunt Sophie with decision, "never have I known a proposal of marriage more gracefully made."

"Maman!" Barbara was horrified now.

"Maman! Maman! Maman! I have an understanding of these matters. I also have eyes. So let us not waste words. That is as it should be. *Alors*—Pierre, little Sophie, Edouard, let me see this table cleared before I return with the coffee. You enjoyed my cooking, Julius?"

"Superb, Aunt Sophie! It always is."

"*C'est bien fait*," concluded that surprising lady.

Julius could have wished to be left alone with Barbara then, even if his shy spirit hesitated before the delicacy of the situation her mother had created, but it was not in Aunt Sophie to foster sentimental attitudes. Though the children were dismissed with much scolding and hand-clapping, she kept bustling about the little sitting-room while the coffee was drunk, and then she must have Barbara and Julius into the kitchen to help her with the dishes and sustain her delight in conversation.

When that task was done, the autumn evening was beginning to fall and Julius, remembering the lonely old man in his sickroom, prepared to go.

Barbara came down the path with him to the gate. They seemed to have nothing to say to each other, but when Julius turned to her with a smile and an outstretched hand, she spoke in a rapid whisper, strange in one at other times so exquisitely poised.

" I apologise for Maman, Julius. Will you ever forgive her ? She is so reckless in what she says. I am ashamed."

" But there is nothing to forgive," he said softly. " Perhaps . . . Well, perhaps I would rather have said it myself. Barbara ! "

She could not take his eye. Again she hung her head, blushing.

" You will let me name my ship after you ? " he persisted.

She looked up at that and smiled at once radiantly and tenderly.

" It is a beautiful compliment, Julius. I——"

She stretched out her hand as if she would lay it on his, and his heart pounded with hope, but suddenly, with a little cry of " Oh ! " she turned and ran from him towards the house, leaving poor Julius, whose knowledge of women was small, sorely puzzled to know what ailed her.

4

The wind of early winter hurled the rain in drenching gusts across Jibboom Square. Sheltering in the archway of the Buck's Head, Julius watched how, in the beams of a lantern swinging from a bracket over the carriageway, the rounded surfaces of the very cobbles and the puddles in the roadway beyond came to liquid life under its lash. Outside that small world of yellow light the night was dark and noisy with storm. Julius could hear the slates of the houses about him rattle softly as their edges were lifted and dropped by the gusts. He wondered idly how it went with the Gilded Gabbart up there on the tip of the spire which he felt rather than saw looming above him in the darkness.

A fit of coughing from a squat, muffled figure by his side brought him back to earth on a wave of compassion.

" You shouldn't have come out on a night like this, Mr. Ramage," he said. " Why not go home now ? The Mail looks like being late. Or go inside and wait."

" No, no, Master Julius ! " the old man wheezed an indignant protest. " The very night of Master Mark's homecoming, and his two dear granduncles so poorly ! My bare duty."

" We don't want a third invalid," said Julius curtly enough.

" I am perfectly content here, sir, by your leave. I should feel unhappy otherwise."

They had not long to wait, in fact. Within five minutes, even through and against the drive of the wind, Julius caught the rumble of the coach's approach along the tunnel made by the warehouses lining the turnpike. Soon its twin lamps swung into the square round the corner by the Wheat Sheaf. Gleaming on the wet backs and harness of the four horses, they made a circle within the open space and anon shone through steam as the beasts were drawn up before the archway.

The square came suddenly to life, the storm seemed to recede. Ostlers and other servants poured out of the inn and through the carriageway from the stables. Julius, with Mr. Ramage behind him, had to shoulder his way to where the passengers were clambering from the coach.

" Mark ! " He had immediately recognised a figure, bulkily clad in a wide-skirted riding-coat of thick, buff-coloured material.

" Julius ! "

The cousins shook hands firmly. The onlookers drew back, and the two young men, parted for nearly four years, eyed each other. It was the same old Mark, thought Julius, and still a new Mark. He had grown greatly about the shoulders so that, though he was not tall, he gave the impression of possessing stature. The face had filled out to something just this side of fatness, but it was handsome in its dark way. The air of the man, as distinct from the familiar physical linea-ments of the boy Julius had known so well, spoke of experience, assurance and decision.

" My best welcome to Garvel, Mark," said Julius heartily. " It's a poor homecoming, I fear, but I'm glad you are here."

" It's bad, I suppose ? " Mark returned. " I had your letter when we berthed at Leith. Thanks for that, Julius. And there's not much hope ? "

" Very little for either of them. But shall we get your gear up to The Mount first ? "

" Yes. Hoi, there——"

Mark's call for service was loud and imperative. It was immediately answered by a rheumy, deferential voice.

T.C.S. E

"Welcome home to Garvel, Master Mark! I could wish the circumstances were happier."

"Oh, it's you, Ramage! You got the snuffles, too? You should be in your bed, at your age. But have you got Joshua here? We can't stand kicking our heels in this storm. See he takes this case and has a lantern to light us up the hill. And go you home at once, Ramage. Much better in bed, and I've some private business to discuss with my cousin."

"By your leave, sir, I will," said Mr. Ramage not without dignity. "It has been a privilege to welcome you back to Garvel, and I merely repeat, sir, that I wish the circumstances were more propitious. Master Julius, a very good-night to you."

So saying, the old century bowed itself out of the presence of the new and was lost in the darkness, traceable therein only by a cough that sounded feeble against the howling of the wind; and Julius felt bitterly sorry. It was not that Mark's tone had been rough or peremptory. It was just off-hand and—yes, masterful was the word. No doubt it had come on him with his great responsibilities in Heligoland and through his dealings with foreigners. But to drop the small honorific before the old man's surname, to send him home unrewarded even by a handshake for an act of fidelity! It was a pity, thought Julius, that Mark had forgotten the old homely, patriarchal ways of their House. But now Mark had a new phase of the proceedings in hand.

"Ha, Joshua, you old black rascal! This case. Off you go, and hold that lantern high. This is a most damnably dirty, dark hole on a night like this. Come along, Julius!"

They passed out of the small globe of warm light before the inn and plunged into the blackness round the gable of the Mid Kirk. The wind contested their attack on the road uphill. It buffeted them, so that they rocked and gasped and were at pains to hold their hats on their heads and control the swishing skirts of their coats. Only when they reached the first crest and turned along the lateral road leading to the gates of The Mount was it possible to speak coherently.

"Hell's candles!" cursed Mark, shouting above the new noise of branches thrashing overhead. "A bloody place this to come home to!"

"A wild night," Julius agreed. He was feeling tired.

"Wild? And those two poor old gents dying! . . . Ah, that's better."

The road had dipped and turned again out of the worst of the wind. The sudden relief from noise and pressure was blessed.

"But you and I will have a mighty lot to talk about, Julius," said Mark, as if his mind had been engaged on nothing else all the way uphill. "The wealth of the house—I mean, our huge interests, spread over half the globe—no cousins of ours in the direct line. Then you and I, the two grandnephews, with our own rows to hoe, eh ? ''

" I hadn't given it a thought," said Julius candidly. " Dr. Cameron had not given up hope when I saw him last."

" Of course, of course ! " agreed Mark. " But these two years on Heligoland have taught me that the wise man is the man who looks a bit farther ahead than the next. The Trust Dispositions will be there, of course, and the Deeds of Co-partnery. But I'm telling you, Julius, the undertakings are so vast, so lucrative——"

" Do you mind, Mark ? I am too tired to think of all that, even if I wanted to. Up all night since last Sunday. Just about three hours sleep. I'm very tired, I am afraid."

" Of course you are," said Mark heartily. " It can wait till to-morrow surely."

Their passage up the avenue of limes to Granduncle Edward's mansion was a renewed experience of assault and battery. It was a blessing to enter into the peace even of a house of death.

Julius dropped, yawning, into a chair in the library. He laid his tingling arms along its mahogany arms. He stretched out his legs. He felt weak and indecisive in the face of Mark's virility.

" Just the same old place," the latter observed gently enough. " One misses the old boy—and the decanter and glasses on the table back there. Remember our first day, Julius ? "

" Yes, indeed ! "

But he was thinking rather of a verse from one of Mr. Moore's *Irish Melodies* that had disturbed him from time to time ever since he had first read it : the lines about him " who treads alone some banquet-hall deserted " and knew the desolation of a visitant to scenes of past glory. He was so tired, so sorry for two old men : the last of the Elizabethans dying.

The cousins were waiting for Joshua to serve them with wine and such solid food as could be found in a distracted household when Dr. Cameron, pulling on his coat, looked into the room. He was a small old man with a wizened face and eccentric manner, and he shook his head, as if with mere annoyance, as he entered.

" It's bad, bad," he announced. " You can hardly feel the pulse on the poor old creature. Age—arteries. And this is you back from your foreign travels, Mr. Mark ? You have timed it nicely."

" And there is not much hope ? " asked Mark with due solemnity.

" Hope ! " snapped the doctor. " This is not a question of hope. It's a question of time."

Joshua appearing then with a silver tray, the odd little man stopped him and poured himself a glass of wine.

" I needed that ! " he said with a gasp of pleasure, returning the empty glass to the tray. " And now, Mr. Julius, I have still the other old gentleman on my hands. It's just a weak heart and no will to live with him, but there it's a most terrible congestion of the lungs and a weak heart forbye. Are you coming with me ? "

" I think I will," said Julius, rising wearily. " It would be as well if Mark waits here while I wait . . . at the other end."

Mark nodded, and Dr. Cameron motioned Julius to the door.

" And there will be a nice how-d'ye-do if Garvel loses its two great Oliphants within the day," he remarked brightly.

5

So it happened. Old Edward Oliphant passed to his fathers before it was light next morning, and in the gloaming of the following day his brother Walter drifted into the crisis of his illness and did not come out again.

At neither death-bed were there acts of drama, last words or distresses of any sort. In coma the brothers slipped out of life like old ships—thought Julius as he waited for the end at Goldenhaddock —fine old ships that have had their day, been laid up for a space in a romantic backwater, and have then, without warning and in the twilight of a late summer's day, sunk noiselessly under the unruffled waters. The double passing was a matter for wonder and sadness, but not for bitter tears. The simile of the banquet hall deserted returned to Julius's mind, but it gave place to the memory of a mood that had come on him when, on a trip to the boatbuilding yards of the Moray coast, he had turned aside to look on the battlefield of Culloden. It had been very quiet up there where so much history had been violently made and unmade ; the moor lay empty to a windy sky, saying nothing of what it knew. Larks sang heedlessly above the barrow-graves of the clansmen. Nothing—just an emptiness, shadowily peopled by wistful ghosts and folk-memories.

The marks of awe were on Mark too when Julius went down in the evening to see him at The Mount. Mr. Aeneas Caldwell the writer was there in his high capacity of man of affairs to all the Oliphants, but the cousins shook hands and looked intimately into each other's eyes as if they had the library to themselves.

" A black day this, Julius," said Mark. " Uncle Edward, then Uncle Walter ! It's . . . Oh, I don't know ! . . . like something in a storybook."

" That is what it is, Mark," agreed Julius, eager in friendship. " But a true storybook—a book of history. I feel like somebody just playing a part, not belonging. I hardly know my own grief yet. You and I have so much to talk about."

"That's so," agreed Mark cautiously. He seemed to be breaking away from his cousin's warmth of confidence. "But here's Mr. Caldwell. There's a lot of detail to discuss first. The funeral——"

"I was saying before you came in, Master Julius," the lawyer appeared to resume a formal discourse, "that this is beyond the family now. I had Sir John himself and the Baron-Bailie in this afternoon about Mr. Edward's funeral alone. Now Mr. Walter's on the top of that ! It will be the biggest thing that has ever been seen in this town."

Mr. Caldwell had that air of remoteness from the ordinary human feelings and failings which comes of traffic in niceties on paper. The colour of paper was in his once-handsome face, of which, however, the long jaws, ridged by a line of grey hair, seemed as it were to have been extended by the solemnity of his profession from the measure of foolscap to that of demy. Now he was in a sort of lugubrious enjoyment of the climactic moment of a career as adviser.

"You two young gentlemen," he said, and he was little more than twenty years the cousins' senior," are the only beneficiaries who can act. All your cousins in London and Honduras and the rest of those places—they're away, and that's that. There's no means of informing them ; they have no means of getting here. I tell you, gentlemen, the responsibility is yours."

To Julius this oration seemed ludicrous, a pompous fuss about nothing. Of course, the Oliphant uncles would be buried with public honours. That followed. They belonged to Garvel as much as Garvel had belonged to them. It did not matter. They were dead. The disposal of two aged, decaying bodies . . . There was so much more of their heritage that mattered so much more profoundly.

Even with this in his mind, Julius was startled to hear Mark cut in with :

"It must be a public funeral, of course. I'll take the responsibility for that."

Julius was still in the condition of acting a part against a background of enormity, but the assumption hurt him. Mark would take the responsibility, would he ? Mark was welcome to the responsibility, but that he should assume it was—well, wrong. A look from Aeneas Caldwell encouraged Julius.

"I shall also take the responsibility," he said.

A sharp sweep of the lawyer's eyes took in the elements of the situation and weighed them nicely within a matter of seconds. Julius discerned the cynicism of experience behind that rapid glance.

"That is very satisfactory," said Mr. Caldwell equably. "You both agree. Well, we'll just let Sir John go ahead. And I hardly see how it could be otherwise. I'll see about having the vault opened. Now, gentlemen——"

A knock at the door checked his hand as it was reaching out for a valise of papers he had brought with him, and Dr. Cameron was ushered in. The little man had utterly lost his professional alertness. He had the droop of more than age upon him ; his eyes had withdrawn into blue-shadowed recesses.

"That's number three now," he announced bitterly. "Old Ramage died on me half an hour ago."

"Ramage!"

Three voices echoed the name in three utterly different tones, and Mr. Caldwell added :

"God save us all ! Three at one burial now ! "

"You are not suggesting," Mark's heavy voice broke into the chamber of awe that enclosed the others. "You are not suggesting that we've got to bury old Ramage too ? Along with my uncles ! "

"Why not ? "

Julius knew that his voice must sound sharp, and he saw the anger darken on Mark's heavy face, but the situation had suddenly become real and vital to him.

"It's almost a lovely thing, poor Ramage's death at this hour," he vehemently urged. "His last act of fidelity, after all those years ! It's lovely, it's poetry ! If we didn't let him go to the grave with our uncles, I'd be ashamed for the Oliphants, and this town would despise us forever. But that is the least of it. It's what you said yourself, Mark ; this is history. We are living in it. For God's sake, let us live up to it ! "

Mark, his arm along the mantelpiece, drummed on its surface with his fingers and glowered down at the fire. The silence that followed Julius's outburst was broken by the grave voice of the lawyer.

"If I may advise you, Master Mark, what Master Julius says is sound. Poetry and history are neither here nor there, but the general effect—on this public occasion—there's a question of credit in it."

The brittleness of fatigue in the little old doctor's voice exploded within the circle of solemnity.

"It would be a damned shame if you left old Ramage to be buried like a pauper ! The man hasn't a relative in the world. You couldn't survive it, Mark Oliphant, not with all your cleverness and power. And is there anything to eat and drink in this house ? I'm fair famished."

Mark turned to smile at Dr. Cameron. It was a superior smile, as

Julius saw it, based on his great reserves of just that power the little man had spoken of. As he had something of the air of a successful young villain of the stage, so could he now make a gesture and throw off a telling line.

" We don't want for corpses at the funeral, to be sure."

He strode to the thick silken cord by the mantelpiece and pulled it so that the bell in the distant kitchen clanged with vulgarly cheerful abandon throughout the house of death. When Joshua appeared :

" Bring us wine—food—all you've got. And quickly ! " he commanded.

And so it came about that Edward and Walter Oliphant were buried with such ceremony that the funeral is a legend in the town to this day ; and that not least because the common folk were delighted that the great Oliphants in their wisdom and generosity took their old servant, Ludovic Ramage, to the grave with them, and on a gun-carriage at that, with the Berwickshire Militia's band of music playing that solemn piece from Mr. Handel's *Saul* immediately behind his indifferent corpse.

Sir John and his colleagues had managed the occasion with a just sense of its importance. Not only had they persuaded Colonel Howe of the regiment of militia then stationed in Glasgow to lend his music and a guard of honour ; they had so impressed the greatness of the occasion on Captain Fetherstonhaugh of His Majesty's Frigate *Neptune*, then lying in the Deeps, that a detachment of tars, their trousers white, their greased pigtails swinging in unison, marched behind the foremost band ; and mighty handy they proved to be when it came to the lifting of the coffins. The gun-carriages were provided by the Loyal Paisley Regiment of Artillery, and the teams of draught horses to pull them were drawn from farms over an area of a hundred square miles of Sir John's own estate. The Loyal Garvel Fencibles were out in full strength, and they provided a second band of music to brace the marching of the rear of a column that was ultimately reckoned to be a full mile in length : the last detachment of it—a regrettably jocose band of apprentices from the shipyard—only starting down the gravelled avenue of The Mount when its head was nosing, serpent-like, round the wall of the minister's glebe towards the gates of the kirkyard by the sea.

The cortege was multi-coloured and most variously composed. The military apart, the Crafts of the town—the Wrights and the Coopers and the Masons and the rest—marched behind and under their banners and shields. The journeymen from the shipyard had paraded in their uniform Sunday best—white duck trousers and long blue coats with brass buttons. The town's drunken piper, Jock Tosh, defying the military music, played his instrument bravely all the way, alone in a gap between the Masons and the Oliphant counting-house staff, and was the only individual to raise a cheer from among the townsfolk lining the streets. Tam Rennie, the town's drummer, marched and pounded his instrument in a little enclave of his own. Joshua the Negro sobbed bitterly and continuously in his special place behind the family party. The day was bright and still after a sharp morning frost.

Walking beside Mark at the head of the column, Julius wished that he could see it as a spectator. It would have been fine, he thought, to stand on the escarpment before The Mount and from there, pensive and aloof, watch history pass in a moving picture under his eyes. To be one of the procession, with Sir John puffing behind, and the indifferent soldiers marching dutifully by the biers, and the bands of music competing in the vanity of it all—that was to be imprisoned in a coil of pomp and hypocrisy and convention. This was no way of expressing how he felt about his beloved Uncle Walter. About Uncle Edward, yes ; the old man had always been just history monumentally embodied. But Uncle Walter had been such a tender, subtle old gentleman, who took delight in playing empty little airs on the flute and was happiest when contemplating the sweet lines of a goodly ship. He should have been laid quietly to rest, in the presence only of those who had loved and understood him.

When the coffins were lifted from the carriage in the churchyard Julius could have cried out at the bleakness of those rigid boxes, to be boxed in turn in a box of bricks under the cold earth. How much finer, cleaner, and free in death the Viking conception of the drifting ship, burning to the water's edge !

Uncle Walter would be so lonely and cold down there ; and Julius began to realise most poignantly his own loneliness now. Lonelier than ever, now that Mark was home again ! A comic thought that, if bitterly so. Even as the minister's voice announced the great phrases of committal, he began to feel afraid, thinking of the wealth and influence and power he and his cousin must now proceed to share as best they and their adviser might contrive.

He set out that evening to walk to Kempock, his only justification a hunger to find the company of loving friends : to have about him the brittle good sense of Aunt Sophie and the cool tenderness of Barbara. He took the turnpike for it, walking fast under the stars, and as he was coming over the brow of the slope behind Fort Jervis, he paused on that small eminence to consider the multiplicity of the stars, their brightness and their insistent, mocking warning of human impermanence and Time's endless patience.

As he stood there at the end of the Drum Farm loan, there

approached him a squat, muffled figure, and he braced himself for unpleasantness. The stranger, however, declared himself friendly with a subdued hail.

"Is that you, Master Julius?"

The hoarse voice alone told Julius that his interlocutor was Bauldy Luke, one of his own most reliable journeyman shipwrights. As he peered through the starlight to identify the man's familiar face with certainty, he saw that the other grasped in his hand a small telescope.

"But I didn't know you were an astronomer, Bauldy!" cried Julius warmly.

"Yes, I watch the stars," said the small man. "God's wonders in the heavens. Have you seen the Comet? This night it's as clear as clear."

"Where?"

"Up there to the nor' east. Take my glass, Master Julius. Fix the Pole Star first." The man's horny fingers closed gently round Julius's wrist and guided his aim. "There to the east a little and down where four might be on a clock-face. . . ."

"Got it!" cried Julius at length. "Magnificent!"

He stared at the phenomenon till his eye ached and his arm trembled. He lowered the glass with a sigh.

"What a spectacle, Bauldy! The naked eye gives one no idea of its size and brilliance. That trailing tail!"

"The astronomers have calculated that it is upwards of a hundred million miles in length, that tail," replied the man with almost proprietorial gravity. "They can even tell us that the comet will disappear and race through space and return again after three thousand years."

"Space. Time," Julius repeated in a whisper of awe.

"God has so ordered it in his wisdom," announced Bauldy Luke as one having authority. "We are as chaff in the winds of time. We are as specks of dust in space. All flesh is grass. The nations are as a drop in a bucket."

"Yes," Julius agreed. "That is a thought for us all to-day. And now I must get on my way, Bauldy. Thank you indeed for the use of your glass. Are you walking on?"

"No, Master Julius," said the man. "I have a good hour of quiet study before me. I bid you good-night."

"Good-night, Bauldy, and thank you again."

From this strange encounter with one whose personality and revelations were surprising Julius turned away, conscious of a calm in his spirit he had not known twenty minutes before. By a small miracle of knowledge and optics he had been vouchsafed proportion and philosophy. He saw that his urge to be with Barbara was fretful

and selfish ; he had found his own place in the immensities of space
and time. Through the magical starlight he walked homewards,
promising himself a peaceful, useful evening among Uncle Walter's
private papers.

6

"And there you have it, gentlemen," concluded Mr. Aeneas
Caldwell, folding the document in heavy demy parchment, stitched
with blue silken cord, from which he had been reading. "I will only
add that I urged your Uncle Edward to be more explicit about his
wishes as to the direction of the general business, but he would go no
further than this simple enough division of his monies. Maybe he had
his reasons, but I must say it puts both you gentlemen in a delicate
position *ex adverso* one another. On the face of it, you are rivals for
the headship of the House, with any one of your cousins in London
or abroad free to say his say. But it is not coming to that, I trust. I
simply state the position as a lawyer must see it."

They were in solemn conference in the library of The Mount, the
lawyer and Mark and Julius. Julius was miserable that this reading
of wills must by immemorial custom so quickly follow the misery of
burial and parting. But Mark was eager and interested, his dark face
bent keenly across the table at which they sat.

"But as I understand it," he said, "Julius and I come out about
equal in the simple division of the monies."

"Yes—and no." Mr. Caldwell frowned over the awkwardness of
the question. "As regards Mr. Edward's property, yes—a clear
division of the estate as at the time of death *pari passu* among the
surviving descendants. And as for that," added the lawyer with a
flash of bitterness, "I doubt it may have to come to a Multiple-
poinding."

Now we are getting lost, said Julius to himself, the unhappiness
writhing within him. This is where bitterness and cupidity and the
dark asperities of the law come worming into the warm body of
decency. . . . The lawyer braced himself for another effort in ex-
position.

"Mr. Walter's will," he said, "is another kettle of fish altogether.
As you have heard, gentlemen, a large part of his fortune goes to this
notion of his—the foundation of a Technical College in the town. We
may think what we like about that, but there it is in black and white,
signed in his own hand and properly attested. I engrossed the deed
myself."

Mr. Caldwell's knuckles, reinforced by a thick golden ring on the little finger of his right hand, rapped on one of the folded documents before him.

" I am very glad that Uncle Walter thought of that ! " cried Julius, innocent and eager. " It's what we need in Garvel—and it's so like him ! I wish he had left all his fortune for that."

Julius saw Mark turn his head rather deliberately to look at him, but there was a tolerant pitying smile on the dark face. The smile about the lawyer's lips was wintry.

" That's as may be," Mr. Caldwell commented dryly. " I venture no opinion. But to return to the point. The balance of Mr. Walter's estate goes to Master Julius. And the testator goes so far as to express the hope that Master Julius will assume the direction of the shipyard."

" And I hope he will," said Mark promptly. " But——"

Julius wanted to cry out for escape. He most horribly saw the talons of jealousy and self-interest close upon him. If they would only let him say what ought to be said, disclaim the lightest dream of hunger for wealth and power, plead to be left alone to build lovely ships !

" But that begs a large question right away," Mark insisted.

" It had occurred to me," agreed Mr. Caldwell dryly.

" We don't know how the affairs of the shipyard are involved with those of the main Oliphant business. Did Uncle Walter own the shipyard separately and individually ? I think not. Then, do we know exactly—or can we ever know exactly—how much of Uncle Walter's ostensible estate is really a part of Uncle Edward's estate ? "

Mark, thought Julius kindly, is really enjoying himself now. Not really being selfish or grasping in a conscious way ; just making his relentless way towards the actuarial truths of such a situation as engaged his deepest interests. Mr. Aeneas Caldwell was nodding his approval of these remarks.

" It seems to me," continued Mark with a harsh little laugh, " that the uncles have left us all at sixes and sevens. And just to take first things first—if you don't mind me putting it so for us both, Julius—the uncles had worked together all these years without a really watertight co-partnery arrangement between them ? "

" That is so," agreed the lawyer patiently.

" Then that is the very first thing we must fix for the future," announced Mark with decision.

" Agreed, agreed ! " Mr. Caldwell began to display some signs of impatience. " But these estates have still to be detailed and computed. Your cousins have still to be consulted. We still have to determine the relationship between the two businesses."

" Surely there can be an adjustment without any wrangling or ill-feeling. There is more money than any of us could possibly need."

This came explosively from Julius; forced from him by distaste and impatience. Mark had risen from the table and was pacing the long, lamplit room.

" Yes, yes ! " he said. " But——"

" I am glad to hear you speak like that, Master Julius," interjected the lawyer eagerly. " We ought to be able to discern from poor old Ramage's books how profits were customarily divided between The Mount and Goldenhaddock, if I may put it that way. As for capital values, a little friendly arbitration. . . . Tolerance on all sides. . . . Ample means to go round, to satisfy everybody. I foresee no great difficulty."

" No, no ! It's not that."

Mark's pacing from the bay of the window to the semi-circular alcove at the back of the room seemed to become more decisive. He had the air of one who communes raptly with himself. The fingers of the hands clasped behind his back worked tensely.

" The property can be fairly enough divided, no doubt," he threw at the other two over his shoulder. " The details can go to arbitration. You won't find me standing out for a guinea here or there. But I know this, gentlemen——"

He swung round to point an almost accusing finger at his cousin and the lawyer.

" —— The leadership of the House has to be settled once and for all. Here you have one of the greatest mercantile properties in the United Kingdom to-day, and I tell you, even if you suspect me of personal ambition, that this huge enterprise will go to pigs and whistles unless there is a recognised superior, a senior partner. This is cold sense I'm giving you. I am frightened when I think of divided authority among the second generation in any business. When I think of the pickle we are in simply because the uncles never took the trouble to define their relative positions, I am more convinced than ever. You may not like it, but I'm giving you good sense."

" Uncle Edward was the head of the firm, surely," suggested Julius mildly.

" Seniority in age," snapped Mark.

" No, Mark. A matter of temperament entirely, I assure you."

" Temperament ! Fiddlesticks ! "

Julius had laughed lightly as he interjected his small note on the importance of character, but he knew only too well and too bitterly the nature of the struggle into which Mark's attitude threatened to draw him. He looked appealingly towards the lawyer, but that large bleak head was shaken unhelpfully.

He understood Mark. He saw that his cousin was right and just and shrewd according to his lights. He knew that the leadership of the House of Oliphant was something for which he himself had only a small capacity and less than no desire. This was the moment to declare his own abdication of those queer things called " rights," his desire to be left alone with the shipyard and freedom to buy good woods for shipbuilding on favourable terms.

Something in him, however, held out against Mark and his ideas —if they were not positive pretensions. He perfectly understood his dark cousin to mean what he said : that a guinea here or there was of little account. But he did most clearly understand that Mark was in love with power, hungered to possess power, and would fight to gain power as the greatest need of his soul ; and something tough in Julius had to hold out against the aggression in the other's personality.

The moment of renunciation passed. It was Mr. Caldwell who smoothly closed the discussion.

" That, I think, is an issue which must wait awhile."

" It may wait a bit too long," retorted Mark roughly. " I don't mean to." He paused to tap his cousin's shoulder. " D'ye hear that, Julius, my boy ? "

" Yes, I hear," said Julius, miserable again.

7

Julius completed a calculation in a few short scribbles of his pencil and pushed the pile of papers away from him.

" There you are, Gavin," he said. " That's the new ship on paper as near as we can get it till the lads start work. You can start the laying of the keel in the western berth to-morrow. Then you had better get ahead with your quantities. Give me a rough estimate in cubic feet of all your needs in the various woods—to-morrow afternoon will do. I thought our stock of oak was running short."

" Yes, sir."

The lad who stood by Julius's desk was tall and gawky in the extreme, and thin sandy hair and a cast in his left eye created a first impression of fecklessness. This was offset, however, by strong hands and a general shrewdness of visage. His tone of voice, even as revealed in a couple of monosyllables, declared him to be what in fact he was— a pupil-assistant to Julius, trusted and intelligent.

" Yes, Gavin," Julius laughed lightly. " If this idea of mine is sound, you should be one of the most highly qualified ship-designers in Britain. All I know will be in this vessel, and there's no more I can teach you."

"The idea is sound, sir ; no doubt about that," said the youth stoutly. "Now, if you please, I'll take the papers and get those quantities worked out. I could put in a couple of hours on them to-night."

"Don't overdo it, then."

Gavin Semple gathered his papers, bowed slightly, and retired. Julius leaned back in his chair and yawned. It was hardly dark outside, but an oil-lamp burned softly above his desk, and there was a merry fire in the grate. Looking round on the ship-models under their glass cases, Julius reflected on his own affection for this private office of his that had been his Uncle Walter's. He had had an early portrait of the old man brought down from Goldenhaddock and hung above the mantelpiece ; through the dusk of the room outside the circle of lamp-light it contemplated him with what he believed to be an encouraging affection. A dear, cosy room, full of memories of kindness and of work shared : remote from the bustle of the yard, in an old white-washed building, once a farmhouse, that they had bought to serve as offices for the expanding business. This room had been the kitchen, the scene of rough rural domesticities, full of the smell of the fields and of wet clothes and of coarse cooking, loud with the noises of children and overworked women's tongues. How strange that it should have become a department of science, the birthplace of the *Barbara Rait*. Ah, Barbara—dear, dark, mysterious girl ! It seemed an age since he had seen her, death and obsequies grimly intervening. He must go down to talk with her, tell her about the ship, get strength and encouragement from her steadiness of mind and spirit.

A knock at the door shattered his reverie. Gavin Semple thrust his sandy head round the door's edge.

"Captain Bob Rait to see you, sir."

Behind Gavin there loomed and then advanced the burly square-cut figure of Barbara's brother, heavy in his thick blue seaman's coat, carrying the freshness of the evening air with him.

"Bob ! "

"Julius, lad ! "

"But I didn't hear your ship was due in ! "

"We weren't spoken once all the way across, either by friend or foe. An odd tops'l'e on the skyline once or twice : nothing more. I touched at Portpatrick yesterday morning and sent a signal to the counting house. But I don't suppose your cousin Mark troubled to let you know."

" So you know Mark is home again ? And about the uncles ? "

" Aye, the agent at Portpatrick—what's his name ? Douglas—told me the whole story. That's why I have come straight to you, Julius. Master Mark and the counting house can wait," Bob added bitterly.

Julius had already seen that the man carried a burden of special anxiety. He was not the old, cheery, brisk, efficient Bob, loudly happy to be home. This was a shipmaster with a frown and a worry, as if he had been forced by stress of weather to pledge his ship in a bond of bottomry.

" I've got Alan Oliphant on board," Bob hurried on to explain grimly, " and it's not a very nice parcel of cargo, believe me. The poor soul's half-crazed, Julius—more than half. Now it's just drink for him, to help him to forget. I was keeping him short at a bottle of rum a day. He cursed me up hill and down dale all the way across. Damn that Potosi silver ! "

" Poor Alan ! " cried Julius, who had never seen the man.

" Aye, you can't help liking the poor devil," Bob went on. " A good lad broken, wasted, humiliated. And that's why I have come straight to you, Julius. By God ! I said to myself "—he burst into vehemence—" I'm not going to land this poor devil right into the tender hands of Mark Oliphant—to be treated like that rabbit, years ago ! One kick in the guts . . . I have a fair idea how it is with the succession to the business. A bit of a muddle. Even Douglas knew that. So I thought I'd best get a decent man on to the job with me before poor Alan is thrown to the lions. And you are the man, Julius."

" But what can I do ? " cried Julius, unhappy.

" I don't know. I have no idea. I just want you to come out with me to the ship now and see that passenger of mine. Two heads are better than one. We can perhaps work it out shipshape. But I want you to see him before Mark does. Come on, Julius. The boat's waiting for us at the quay."

A small rabbit, near the known point of death, tried to make itself small and unseen among tufts of whin, its muscles retracted tight. Then came an overwhelming power to put it out of life with a kick. And that small matter had been remembered all these years by one witness of the scene ! Very, very strange—thought Julius as the boat sped under the rising moon towards the ghostly shape that was the ship *Venture*—how the smallest event may shape lives !

Bob opened the door of a deck-house, and a shaft of soft light fell across the planks. This came from an oil lamp that hung from brass gimbals above a figure crouching before a stove within. Julius saw the small interior as if it had been a scene on the stage of a theatre.

That first sight of his cousin was so lucid and comprehensive, he could have described thirty years later, and with particularity, the man's long face, sallow and strained, with a straggling yellow goatee on the chin, the hunch of the shoulders as of one perished with cold, the hands folded and locked between scraggy knees. He marked how the shoulders winced in a sideways movement away from the door as it opened. The tell-tale bottle and a glass half-full were on a table beside this figure of a man prematurely aged or reduced by suffering to a near-animal condition.

"Alan, this is your cousin Julius," said Bob Rait gently. "He is a good friend of mine and yours."

"I am glad that you are safely home, Alan," said Julius.

He made to offer his cousin a hand to shake but, seeing the other keep both of his locked between his knees, laid it gently on the man's shoulder. It communicated the tremor of nerves that passed through Alan Oliphant's body.

"I want to help you if I can," Julius went on. It was like talking to a frightened child. "Bob and I will see to it that nobody worries you, Alan. Be assured, please, that there is no business to talk about— nothing to discuss until you are rested and well again."

"Thank you, Julius."

The voice was at once hoarse and subdued, as if from a throat long parched by thirst or relaxed by shouting, but the tone in which even these formal words were uttered let Julius understand that he was in a fair way to engage this broken man's confidence. Over Alan's shoulder Bob nodded vigorous encouragement.

"You'll have heard that we are all at sixes and sevens here. Uncle Edward and Uncle Walter died a fortnight past, on the same day."

Alan nodded his head, but without any apparent emphasis.

"So," Julius went on boldly, "you need not think of them any more. That is all finished now. You are like myself now, Alan, just one of all us cousins who succeed equally to the estates. Indeed, I can tell you from what I know already, none of us needs to work any more. There are ample means for us all, and if you would wish to rest, in a quiet place in the country, until you are better—why, Alan, we'll find a place for you to-morrow and you can go away with an easy mind. If it is not an impertinence, I would willingly watch your interests until you are in shape again. Or recommend a good man?"

"What the devil do I care?"

It was as if Alan Oliphant had suddenly returned to the full, pugnacious vigour of his original manhood. Suddenly he released his hands from between his knees and stretched one out to grasp the glass on the table. He gulped down all it held.

Only then did he turn to Julius with a smile. It was a feeble, almost pathetically silly, grimace.

"All right, Julius," he said huskily. "You are kind. Different from most of our breed!"

"I only know, Alan," returned Julius earnestly, "that you have had a terrible time."

"A terrible time," his cousin repeated emptily. Then his voice rose to near a scream. "I've been through hell, man! I am still in hell! I'll never get out of hell!"

"Tell Julius something about it, Alan."

This quiet suggestion, strange in its simplicity, came out of Bob's mouth. From a dark corner of the cabin he brought two stools, placed one for Julius and settled himself on the other. A forefinger motioned Alan to help himself to the bottle. Julius was puzzled by these preliminaries but discerned that Bob in his rough seaman's wisdom had staged this uncanny scene.

Alan Oliphant began to speak, indeed, to pour out his story, a tempestuous, incoherent and at moments intolerably vivid narrative of his adventures and sufferings on the way from Potosi to the coast of Peru and back again, then down through the jungles from the thin Andean air to the estuary of the Plate. Bits of it came pouring out in Spanish; fragments were spat out in a rough tongue Julius, horrified but fascinated throughout, took to be the speech of the Indian muleteers.

The narrator gesticulated. He made faces, and wild passes with his thin hands. Ever and again he reached for the bottle, refilled his glass, and gulped raw spirit; and Bob Rait made no move to check him. When the narration languished and Alan Oliphant seemed to grow tired of his own excesses; when the voice faded away and the noise of the tide, slapping against the ship's side, rose to fill the deck-house with primitive sound; then Bob would put in a question to bring Alan back to the point of cleansing and exhausting confession.

The man spoke of heat and corruption and death and thirst and stench. He was a thing degraded by physical ordeals and possessed by his own degradation. The narrative had a shape of sorts—it traced the fantastic journeys from Potosi to the coast and from the coast back again to Potosi and, after a bitter sojourn there, the fantastic trek south-eastwards over mountain tracks, through jungles and swamps, and across the pampas—but the lines were blurred by a profusion of physical detail. Not the least iota of the saving consciousness of duty heroically done remained to sustain Alan Oliphant.

Julius listened to the story with horror and compassion. Some of his cousin's phrases, brilliant in their violence and as furious as the dazzle of the sun in the thin air over the Andes, he was to remember his life through, as even an old man will remember the monstrous injustices endured in infancy.

" The brute's belly came oozing out between his ribs and swelled up like a bubble of soap. The stink in your nose was as if a leper's fist had smashed it. . . . Seven men died that evening, spewing their guts out. Green vomit with a stench that must have sickened the condors . . . Thin, thin air up there—like your lungs being sucked empty. Your heart hammering till every beat was a blow on the head. Your throat like sandpaper on fire. Stones, sharp as razors and hot as fire-bricks, cutting through the rotten soles of your boots to the raw skin. . . . Blinding light. It shut your eyes in behind scorching eyelids till you could only see the mad things inside yourself. . . . Chimborazo is an ugly pimple, the colour of raw leather. It never moves. I tell you, Julius "—this on a scream—" *it never moves* ! It just stays there, useless, sneering. Christ, how I hate that mountain ! "

Such phrases, thought Julius, were like the jewel in the fable—strangely embedded in a dungheap of personal humiliation. Only now and again did the agonised man admit a flash of decency in his experience.

" Those merchants of Potosi ; they did keep their word and give me shelter. Old Conchita was as ugly as a witch, but she brought me food regularly. I believe she was sorry for me, Julius . . . God ! It was a foul hole of a cellar, stinking and wet, like the bilges of an old ship, but it was better than that Mountain of Silver, a bloody, scorched, brown pyramid of useless muck against a sky like a sheet of blue enamel, and the glare of the sun on those white adobe walls.

" Down in the jungle the leeches stuck to your ankles. White, like chunks of dog's dung, but flushed with the red of your blood. You didn't care after a bit. You were too tired and sore to knock them off. The bruise just suppurated when you kicked yourself."

Alan Oliphant's head nodded over the edge of the small table.

" Suppurated," he repeated drowsily. " Like yeast working. Yellow. Stinking."

His torso slumped forward, and it was clear to see that he was at length beaten by the alcohol he had taken to escape from his self-disgust. His face on his hands, he sobbed with a bitterness and abandon that were at once terrifying and absurd. Julius regarded the spectacle of surrender helplessly until a touch on his arm and a nod of Bob's head took him out of the deckhouse, with its reek of rum and human un-cleanliness into the fresh air on deck.

" Come aft to my cabin for a moment," Bob suggested.

The masculine tidiness of that apartment was refreshing after the sour fug of Alan Oliphant's quarters. Bob filled two glasses from a decanter of wine and handed one to Julius.

"I have had to stand that for weeks on end," he said.

"But it's—it's intolerable!" Julius exploded. "The price of silver! My God!"

"But what is to be done?"

"Done! I don't know," said Julius bleakly. "My only instinct, somehow, is to keep him out of the sight of my cousin Mark." •

"Well said," Bob agreed with a grim smile.

"I know, Bob!" Julius was suddenly inspired. "We'll take him to my people in Glen Cattan. They'll understand. They'll be good to him. Alan will be—safe in Glen Cattan. Till we see how things shape."

Bob tossed off his wine with decision.

"That's sound talk," he said. "The sooner I get him off my ship, the happier I'll be, I confess. To-morrow?"

"Yes, I could arrange that."

"I'll have a boat at the Mid Quay steps early—say, eight. Just the two of us and a picked crew. You'll have to help me to blarney the poor devil into going ashore at all. He is mortal afraid. He would stay in *Venture* until he had drunk himself to death. But come, Julius, I can put you ashore now. And thanks for coming. . . . Don't worry about him," he added, answering a look in Julius's eyes. "My steward can manage him better than anybody."

8

Venture's boat, the lug-sail drawing sweetly to a breeze from the east, sped towards her parent ship at sunset the following day. The evening was magnificently fine ; the sky a rare powder blue, the hills nobly clear against the golden glow in the nor'-west. Ahead, the smoke from Garvel's winter fires, sheltered from the prevailing airt, curled cosily above the roofs of the town in its bay.

Yet, with this loveliness about him, Julius felt again like one who returns from a funeral. Morose, he was almost unaware of Bob Rait beside him, his arm over the tiller, his eye cocked on the peak of the sail. Julius had on him the sweetly melancholy feeling that, just as he had lately buried Uncle Edward and Uncle Walter, so had he that day assisted at the interment of Alan Oliphant : a second burial at that. There was still Mark to face over the consequences of his impulse.

It had been one of those days on which lunacy seems to get entwined with the order of ordinary life or, thought Julius ruefully, is exposed as the terror always underlying life. He and Bob had lived through a fantastic scene in the ship that morning when, in the deck-house, they had for an hour on end reasoned with Alan, sought to deceive him, then to cajole him into a movement he could not com-prehend, and Alan had run about the cabin like a rabbit, or cursed them roundly, or begged tearfully to be left alone, or begged for drink. They had finally got him over the ship's side and into the boat on some daft, dishonest pretext that they were, all three of them, going on a day's outing with much drink and hilarity in prospect. (Bob had to pocket a bottle for the journey.) Then the fantastic arrival at the manse in Glen Cattan by cabriolet, hired with difficulty and at fantastic expense, and the swift, sketchy explanation to his own ageing father and mother, both of them torn between scandal and pity, between respectability and loyalty. Old Dr. MacCallum had come up from Ardhallow on his garron, and Alan had fallen at the sight of his white beard into an extreme state of alarm, and the doctor and Bob had gravely discussed the daily allowance of liquor that would be necessary to keep the crazed man from Potosi in life. Finally, his own mother : melting to the pathos of Alan and his story, getting his confidence, making friends with him, showing him the chickens and the Ayrshire calf on the glebe ; taking him into the byre on the gay pretence that he could most usefully and gallantly help her to milk the ageing and docile cow, Betsy. Alan's tears when they left him in Glen Cattan ; the questioning look in his mother's eyes.

Julius thought miserably of his own part in these transactions. He saw himself as having fobbed off a personal problem and responsibility on two good and simple people to whom he owed a better duty.

" Bob ! " he suddenly addressed his companion. " I have made up my mind."

The seaman took his eyes from the boat and turned them on his companion.

" Aye, and what's that ? " he asked gravely.

" To have nothing to do with the Oliphant fortune or the Oliphant business. To stick to the shipyard and what Uncle Walter left me of his private fortune. That, at least, is clean."

Bob Rait seemed to give the set of his sail long and special con-sideration.

" It's your affair, Julius," he said, " but it's a bit too much like leaving everything to Master Mark for my taste. That is what he's waiting for, if I know my man."

" He can have it—the power and the money and all the silver that's lying in that ship of yours. It's just so much ordure."

" And poor Alan's interest ? "

" Why, Bob, his share will be all the greater ! And we'll get a curator, or whatever it is, appointed to protect his interest better than I ever could. I'll see Caldwell to-morrow."

" It won't stop Mark from sending another lot of men to Potosi if he feels there's a profit to be made," observed Bob sourly. " However . . ."

He started to whistle softly. The boat was approaching *Venture*. The sun was quite gone and the easterly air nipped.

" I think I'll go straight ashore with you," Bob announced suddenly. " I must see my mother and the children. Do you feel like coming with me, Julius ? "

" Yes, I'd like to see your mother again."

Bob Rait smiled, mentally adding " and Barbara " to his friend's eager acceptance of the invitation.

CHAPTER THREE

A CLOUD OF STEAM

I

THE COMET OF 1811, of which the spectacle had so kindly worked to soothe the spirit of Julius on the night of the great funeral, worked with an equal effect of miracle on the minds of many men besides.

For generations thereafter both Portuguese peasants and rubicund English merchants, marvelling at the splendour of the vintage of that year, gravely attributed it to a sidereal influence acting subtly on the vines of the Douro valley. Under the comet's mysterious sway, others held, Napoleon conceived his fatal plan to march on Moscow. It is beyond any doubt that the phenomenon was noted with characteristic interest by a restless man who, working and calculating and planning on the shores of the Firth of Clyde (if with more enthusiasm than accuracy and more impatience than probity) launched upon the world a portent even more explosive and permanent than the Grand Army.

Mr. Henry Bell and his project of a steamboat were the matter of a jest long before the latter took the water. In Garvel the sailormen and longshoremen of that thriving town called upon each other with rough jocularity to witness an impending miracle of smoke, steam and flame. The sailing ship had brought them prosperity and they could not see beyond it. The man was daft. The merchants and solid men of the town, Julius among them, wondered that a builder so experienced and respected as Charles Wood in the Port should so far lend himself to the harebrained scheme as to undertake the creation of a hull for the man's infernal machinery. In pulpits and inn parlours alike men waxed angry, fulminating as against witchcraft, prophesying something like the end of the world and, if not that, a holocaust of lives in a noisy catastrophe of nature.

Fear was at work in all the critics, in the jocose as well as the messianic, the old fear of change. They were as children, hating the unknown, and behind the hate there worked powerfully in the majority an unconscious desire to cling to the security of the known, proven ways of doing. These men of 1811 were as the men of 1911 who heard of Bleriot's flight across the English Channel : witnesses, either eager or unwilling, of the human juggernaut in the act of changing gear. Most of the men of Garvel, contemplating from their windows the graceful masts and spars of sailing ships, looked back on the eighteenth century and found it good enough. Only a few among them, and not all these had identical motives, could peer through the cloud of smoke and see, as magic palaces floating in a cerulean sky, the glazed rotundities of the Great Exhibition.

Mark and Julius Oliphant quarrelled openly over the meaning of Mr. Bell's project. It was no more than a brush, an exchange of rough words, but it was an exposure, if only in a second's flash, of a profound and dark abyss between two philosophies of living. Men about them noted the significance of this cleavage, and for Julius himself it lingered, all his life afterwards, as the bitter memory of a portentous and unhappy moment.

They were with others of their own generation in a room in the Buck's Head that served the young merchants of the town as a sort of club. It was the hour after the day's work, and wine was circulating among the group of talkers. Julius stood with young Mr. Hugh Crauford of Kilblain at the window overlooking the Square, while Mark was with his own cronies by the sideboard near the door. By the absurd chance of life it was a rivalry of laughter which brought the cousins face to face in anger along the length of the room. One of Mark's boisterous tales of social adventure in London had raised a roar of masculine mirth in his circle when a cackle from young Crauford, high and shrill like a girl's, seemed subtly to compete with it and to satirize it.

A silence, sudden and irrelevant but ominous, made Julius turn his head to look down the room. There he saw Mark's face, dark and flushed, offer a challenge.

" And what's the grand joke up at your end ? "

" It's Julius ! " young Crauford went on cackling. " What he said about Bell and his steamboat. He said—ha, ha !—that its tale will be a good deal shorter than the real comet's. TALE—TAIL : you see it ? Thundering good, eh ? "

"It was a damned silly thing to say, if you ask me," said Mark.

"It was a mild joke among friends," retorted Julius, stung to severity. "But if you are going to take it seriously, the future of the steamboat is surely a matter of opinion."

The coldness of Julius's voice as against the wine-flushed heat of Mark's vehemence made an arena of that inn parlour. The cousins were nakedly against each other in the ring, their friends, shocked or hopeful or merely amused, the spectators of a duel.

"A matter of opinion it is," said Mark truculently. "And yours is mighty far behind the times, my friend. You are living in the last century, with your sails and your wooden tubs—sticking knives into the mast and praying like a heathen for wind. I tell you : Bell has the right idea. No crawling on his belly to the Almighty for him ! This man is going to take ships where they are wanted and when they are wanted ; and that's what I call Progress. You'll see—and perhaps to your cost—I warrant you."

Julius, though perceiving acutely the indignity of the quarrel and hating the very fact of quarrel, had to make his chill retort.

"The steamboat has still to be proved. I think the sailing ship will last my time—and yours. That is an opinion I am entitled to hold. And I think, Mark, we had better leave it there."

He turned his back on Mark, returning to young Mr. Crauford and the outlook on to the Square ; and though it seemed that his cousin would very willingly carry the argument further, their friends, recovering from the shock of melodrama, formed a screen between the disputants and, in the old human way, were belatedly wise in advising Mark to drop it, to take a joke as it came, and to see that the open quarrel had, in a manner of speaking, never happened.

But it had happened ; and as he walked up the hill to Golden-haddock that evening Julius was unhappy, thinking of the difficulty of human relationships and doubting, on reflection, the validity of his own faith in the old ways of doing.

2

This discomfort of mind returned to Julius when, a good many months later—indeed, on a warm afternoon of August, 1812—he stood on one of the weedy slipways of his own shipyard among much the same set of friends as had witnessed the quarrel in the Buck's Head.

It had come to pass. The *Comet* was coming down the river for the first time, carrying passengers. On the desk in Julius's office lay an advertisement cut from the *Chronicle*. "A handsome vessel to sail by

the power of air, wind and steam. . . . The elegance, safety, comfort
and speed of this vessel requires only to be seen to meet the approbation
of the public." He remembered laughing at the phrases with his
friends, drawing attention to what seemed to them all the highly comic
juxtaposition of the words "steam" and "safety." But since the
vessel had remarkably survived her trials and since the day was
admittedly a great one (and with some instinct to salve his own
conscience) Julius had invited the party to the yard from which they
would see the ship pass within a stone's throw.

Mark was there. Young Mr. Crauford of Kilblain was there.
Barbara was there, one of a bevy of the young wives, the positively
betrothed and the merely coveted young ladies of Garvel's merchant
princelings. With the spirited assistance of Aunt Sophie a cold repast
had been set out in Julius's office rooms and uproariously enjoyed by
all.

Aunt Sophie was there in person, but she declined to join the formal
party.

"*C'est le jour de la jeunesse*," she prophetically countered Julius's
protests when he went into the improvised kitchen to tackle her. "My
position on such a day is here. *C'est mon metiér.* These are matters I
understand. How else, *mon cher Jules*, could your stupid Scottish
servants serve *le dejeuner* to your guests? *Alors, j'y suis, j'y reste.* And
now you will kindly forget old Aunt Sophie and return to the elbow
of my Barbara. That is a good girl, but a fool where you are concerned. Every woman is a fool where one man is concerned, however
stupid that one man may be. . . ."

She broke off this rapid discourse to chide one of the apprentice
carpenters who was acting as a servant of the high table on this
great day.

"*Cochon!* Fool! Dolt!" she cried at the boy's fair, innocent
face. "Does one lay a fish fork for *la soupe*, a spoon for *saumon froide*?"

She turned to Julius, her black hair falling in untidy but romantic
wisps over her bold features.

"This requires my attention. *Va donc!* Here I am *affairée*, therefore
happy."

The repast, served in the yard's airy moulding loft, was excellent;
the whole occasion was one of those on which, according to the whim
of circumstance, every participant is in exactly the right temper to
enjoy and share enjoyment. Even Mark, when they were all trooping
out into the sunshine, took Julius by the elbow and whispered:

"Well done, Julius! As pleasant a party as ever I have attended,
and beautifully managed. I congratulate you."

That made Julius happy, doubly happy when, having seen his

guests disposed in various positions of vantage about the staging, he took his own place beside Barbara under the stern of the new ship that was to bear her name. The mood of holiday was abroad. Over the waters of the ship channel, smooth under the August sky and apparently still, save for the small eddies of the ebb near its end, their voices echoed in jest and laughter. One young man had made up a ladder to the deck of the new vessel and was scanning the sandbanks to the eastward.

" I think I see her ! " he suddenly called. " Coming round the bend below Finlaystone there. See the smoke and steam above the trees."

" That's a cloud you are looking at, Henry," somebody else shouted and was rewarded with a laugh.

" A cloud ! " cried a third. " That's Bell and his infernal machine gone up in smoke."

That day, on both banks of the River along a length of twenty miles, men waited in parties like this and, here and there, in crowds to see the *Comet* pass. Small boys ran with her along the banks for miles at a stretch ; old men openly and loudly cursed her as a symbol and, in messianic phrases and tones, denounced this bold and ungodly man, Henry Bell, for launching his monstrous craft in defiance of the clear laws of God. Most of the spectators that day, however, had assembled in the mood of Julius's party—to make a holiday of a fantastic occasion, which (most of them believed and hoped) must end in fire and explosion and, so, a melodramatic exposure of Bell's presumptuous folly.

" The man is quite crazy," young Mr. Crauford of Kilblain was heard explaining to a dimpled daughter of John Howie of the Tan-works. " I've often been across at those Baths of his and heard the man talk. Talk ! He'd talk the hind leg off a donkey. Full of the maddest schemes, but not a single idea of detail or finance or anything reasonable. We'll never see his *Comet* to-day. I'll wager she is lying in bits on the foreshore about Bowling."

Young Mr. Crauford got the lie to his gallant prophecy almost immediately. The watcher with the telescope on the deck of the new ship cried out again, this time to announce in high excitement the approach of something much more tangible than a cloud, something portentous moving round the bend of the ship channel before the Port, moving slowly enough with a great churning of paddles and belching of smoke, but moving inexorably.

The party on the staging bunched and crowded and craned to watch her approach along the Davie shore. The hope that she would blow up or stick on one of the sandbanks was forgotten. She was coming, the *Comet*, the new steamboat, with only a mile to go before history should be decisively made. She approached, and they saw and heard a piper blow defiantly in her bows. Smoke belched from the vessel's tall stack. The noise of the machinery, a medley of grinding, clanking and hissing, conveyed a disturbing sense of irresistible urgency, and if the twin paddlewheels on each side of the ship turned gawkily and slowly enough, they were forcing a goodly plume of water off the ship's stem and themselves left a turbulent wake to churn in silvern whorls behind her.

As the vessel bore down upon the young people of Julius's party they laughed and cried facetious warnings to one another. Then, as she still came on, the laughter and the jests died on the summer air. As she passed they were silent, held perhaps by some profound apprehension of the shape of things to come ; and as she went away again, moving in towards her berth at the new Customhouse Quay, they rose and cheered her heartily, led by Julius himself.

" What do you make of it, Julius ? " asked Mark in his ear, but not aggressively.

" Bell has certainly done it," Julius replied, adding lightly, " though I think I could show him ways of doing it better."

" As how ? "

" Length and shape. He has put machinery into the hull of a herring buss. . . . But if you will forgive me, Mark—my guests. Would you help me to collect them for cake and wine in my room ? "

He went himself to conduct Barbara indoors and deliberately lingered behind the others so that she might see, and perchance admire, the ship he was building to her honour. He led her along the staging to the vessel's bows whence, he knew very well, anybody with an eye for form must perceive the special quality of his design. He waved a casual hand upwards and was rewarded by seeing Barbara's grey eyes run slowly down the lines of the ship, her head tilting to appreciate the concourse of elegant curve that was his doing.

" How do you think she shapes ? " he asked, off-hand in a boyish way.

" But she is very fine, Julius—I mean *fine* in the French sense. The curves flow as good poetry flows."

" Do you really mean that, Barbara ? " he cried, flushing with gratitude.

" Don't I usually mean what I say, Julius ? Your ship is very lovely."

" *Your* ship," he protested warmly. " And she would need to be lovely—with a name like that ! "

" Julius ! "

Her protest was a whisper, and she blushed. With a great gladness he realised that it was miraculously in his power to turn Barbara at will from a woman with a cool and detached mind into a girl warm with sentiment and defenceless. He would have said more there and then, but she forestalled him, touching his wrist in an intimate gesture.

" Come ! Your guests will be waiting."

They joined the others at cake and wine and found that rational conversation was impossible amid the babel of chatter and laughter. They were moving to one of the windows, unconsciously seeking for themselves a place apart, when Mark, his face wearing a strange look of preoccupation, bore down on them among the gossiping groups.

" I say, Julius ! " he hailed them. " You will excuse me, Barbara ? But that point you made about Bell's ship. It interests me greatly. The point about length and speed."

" Do you really wish a lecture on marine architecture ? " laughed Julius.

" I would very much value your views," returned Mark gravely.

" Ah, well . . . If it will not weary you, Barbara . . . You see, Mark, this man Bell has demonstrated that machinery can be applied to drive a vessel with safety—and there I eat my own words. On the other hand, he has failed to demonstrate that his method is any improvement on the old. Why, his boat took upwards of five hours to come down the River to-day, and you know that one of our old flyboats, using only wind and tide, can do it in less."

" Yes, yes. A good point ! "

" Now, I know nothing of machinery, but I do know that Bell must get more power into his vessel if her speed is to be improved. That may come through an advance in engineering methods, to be sure, but since that is immediately improbable, he can only get extra speed by putting in more machinery—two engines instead of one, say ; and to accommodate his machinery he will have to build a lengthier ship. I think, I repeat, I *think*—it will be found that in steam vessels speed will be very closely related to length. If you must have speed, you must have length. Or so it seems to me."

" That is interesting, very interesting," said Mark, his dark eyebrows together in a frown of cogitation.

" More than that," Julius went on triumphantly, " he must change his design. This is the bee in my bonnet, no doubt, but those bluff bows, all very well in a herring buss or a coal gabbart, won't do. They must be fined away, made hollow. If I were ever to design a steamboat——"

" Why not ? " asked Mark sharply. " There's a future in it."

" No, no, Mark ! The problems of sail are difficult enough for me.

But if ever you want a design, and don't ask me to have anything to do with engines, why——"

He laughed at his own flight of fancy, but Mark took it gravely.

" You never know," he said. " Anyhow, Julius, what you have told me is interesting. I am grateful."

" And my fee," added Julius, still in the mood of jest, " is that you lend me Bob Rait to skipper my new ship on her trials. Is it possible?"

" By all means ! " agreed Mark cordially. " Bob should be home from Honduras within two months, and I mean to offer him a spell ashore. We need a good man here as a sort of marine superintendent. You can have Bob's services, with pleasure."

" Thank you, Mark ! That's a promise."

" Surely. By your leave, Barbara . . ."

He left them then and turned away into the assembly, the dark look of preoccupation still on his face. Julius turned to Barbara.

" Sorry, Barbara ! Was it all too dry for you ? Mark seems to be taking the *Comet* very seriously."

He saw that her eyes were warily following Mark's progress through the crush.

" Be careful, Julius," she muttered. " I suspect our cousin Mark when he is serious like that. He is a very clever man."

3

A day of April, 1813. Only a remnant of the Grand Army that had assaulted Moscow was back across the Beresina, licking its wounds and re-forming as best it might. Leipzig and Waterloo were still to be fought. Thousands of men were still to be maimed, to die in agony, or simply to die suddenly without any warning of the approach of death, in Napoleon's wars. Henry Bell's *Comet*, embodying in its small bulk the ultimate strength of the grandest army ever assembled, lay beached on a West Scottish shore : à failure so far ; too short, too slow for its destined purpose. Mr. Bell was having his vessel lengthened, putting in a new section amidships. Those who had cheered his ship's first passage down the River were again prepared at any moment to say that they had never believed in the steamboat ; and that the *Comet* was but the matter of a jest. An Englishman called Jeremy Bentham was enunciating social doctrines which most of the young merchants of Garvel regarded as pernicious. " The fellow should have his neck drawn," Mark Oliphant had declared stoutly.

Time and history were, in fact, flowing on with their wonted vivacity, but the seeming importance of the crowding events of the great world, mused Julius Oliphant, was mocked by the inscrutability of the sea. It was all about him as he stood by the helmsman on the poop of his new ship, and it was in violent movement. The clouds were low over Rathlin, and under them, off the Atlantic, the sou'-westerly wind came strong and chill. It was kicking up great seas which, white-topped, raced in feverish procession towards the mouth of the Firth, and was itself so urgent to get on that it ruffled each breaker with a secondary set of wavelets. The waves hissed as they charged with the *Barbara Rait*, lifting her from shoulder to shoulder in a gentle pitch. The wind filled her canvas with dispassionate fury, driving her on towards the islands where a single shaft of wet sunlight had pierced the lowering ceiling of clouds to make a bronze splash on the lower slopes of Goatfell.

It was just another day of boisterous West Coast weather, that day of April, 1813. There had been millions of days like it before, and there would be millions after. Yet no other day had been or would be precisely like it. Never did wind and tide and sun and cloud repeat themselves. The sea was always the same yet always novel and exciting. Contemplating the steamship and the humiliation of the Grand Army and the new ferment in the minds of men, Julius smiled to think that, for variety with implacability, the sea had human history beat. The fancy pleased and comforted him, the creator of a thing which used wind and wave so sweetly.

He crossed to the windward side out of the shadow of the great mainsail (for he had chosen to have his ship rigged as a brigantine) and studied the dial of a patent log of his own devising he had had set up on the taffrail.

" She's logging over twelve, nearer thirteen," he turned to observe to the steersman.

" She iss a beauty," the Highlander returned, " and she iss as light on the helm as a pony. If my trick was to last all day I would not be noticing it."

Julius nodded with pleasure and walked forward. Another sailor stood there, a gigantic figure of a man wearing a red cowl, his body braced against the mainmast.

" Taking much over ? " Julius asked the man casually.

" Not what would make a shower of rain," the sailor replied. " She's as dry as a bone, this packet. I watched her when we was butting into the dirt on the trip out, and she just threw it off her forefoot."

" That's the hollow lines," Julius explained, gratified again. " That was one of the ideas in my mind—that as well as speed."

" You were dam' right, then," said the sailor, the steady gaze of his blue eyes raised to appreciate the set of a foresail.

Aft again, and there was Bob Rait on deck, sturdy evidence of the fact that Mark had kept his promise. His hands deep in the pockets of his reefer jacket, he stood close behind the helmsman, studying both compass and the set of canvas over the man's shoulder.

" 'Morning, Bob ! " Julius greeted him. " Did you have a sleep ? "

" An hour or two. Enough." Bob returned. " I don't like these narrow waters, and I wanted to watch this ship of yours in a bit of a sea. She'll do."

" Do you really think so, Bob ? "

" I know. She'll do. How your ideas would work out on a big ship in heavy water, I don't know, but I'll undertake to sail her for you when you build one."

" That I certainly will ! " declared Julius. " This is only the model, the trial piece. Now we have seen her in action in approximate service conditions. I—Hallo ! Our friends enjoying themselves already ? "

" Aye, the sun was over the yardarm for them as soon as my steward had cleared the breakfast," Bob explained with a grin.

Julius's discourse had been interrupted by bellows of masculine laughter coming through the slightly opened window of the coachroof lighting a saloon below decks. Now he stepped forward and, smiling, peered down on a convivial gathering.

There they were, his guests—Mark and young Mr. Crauford of Kilblain, John Howie, Jr., of the Tanworks, and Erskine Tannahill of the Sugarhouse—bottles and glasses on the table at which they sat. It had been Julius's own idea to make an outing of the *Barbara Rait's* trial trip. Perhaps if he had examined himself he would have had to confess to a need of witnesses to his success, even to a secret need of his nature to challenge Mark. He did not now in the least grudge them their hilarity and their indifference to the performance of his ship. He turned back to Bob with a smile.

" And no sign of the ladies yet ? " he asked.

Bob pointed forward, and Julius's happy eyes saw Barbara standing there amidships, staring ahead. She had bound a red kerchief tight round her dark head, and the folds of a voluminous cloak in navy blue streamed behind her in the wind which, at the same time, emphasised the height and slimness of her figure. Julius started towards her, and as he did so she, without having seen him, likewise moved forward to the ship's bows. It was useless to shout against the clamour of the wind, and he was abreast of the deckhouse from which she had emerged before she turned to look astern, a hand at her head to control the wisps of flying hair. Just then a gust of wind, lusty and whimsical, filled her coat as it might have filled a spinnaker and took Barbara down the slope of the tossing deck at a speed utterly beyond her control. She had the quaint, pretty, helpless air of a girl running an unwilling race downhill, half dignified, half abandoned.

Julius's immediate thought was of the danger she was in. He knew only too well the wounding force with which a body out of control on shipboard can fetch up against an obstruction. He ran, his arms outspread, to check her flight. Her body bumped into his with such vigour that his head knocked against the varnished teak of the fore end of the deckhouse. His arms were round her in a protective embrace.

" Not hurt, Barbara ? " he asked anxiously.

She shook her head, laughing breathlessly.

" No . . . Only foolish." Her eyes steadied on his. " Your head ? "

" Nothing."

She was in his arms. Their faces were close together. He marvelled at the large intensity of the pupils in her grey eyes searching his. Near and dear, the warmth of her body against his had him suddenly trembling with passion.

" Stay there, Barbara," he whispered. " Stay there—for ever."

" Is it my true place ? " she whispered back.

" Yes, yes, yes ! You know it is ! "

" Yes, Julius, my dear, I know. *Chèri* . . ."

It was their strange fortune thus to plight their troth on the open deck of a ship at sea. Barbara was the first to shake herself out of the trance of kisses. She withdrew from his urgency, her hands against his shoulders, and laughed again in her happiness.

" Is there not enough scandal in this ship, my dear ? " she asked him blithely, both her hands now busy with her hair and headgear in the oldest of feminine gestures.

" Not a soul in sight, darling ! " he protested, his mood answering hers ; and indeed they had the foredeck to themselves. " Come and kiss me again."

" No ! " she declared with mock ferocity, and then, as if relenting, she took his hand. " Come, dear, and we'll talk to my solemn big brother. But not a word of—of us—till we get ashore. Promise ! I have my reasons."

" But your mother ! "

" Maman ! " Barbara's laughter tinkled in the wind. " She thinks only of death. Come, Julius."

Aunt Sophie was, in fact, the now unhappy subject of that scandal about which Barbara had jested. It had seemed to Julius's simplicity only fitting that Barbara should sail on the trial trip of the ship that bore her name, and he had been vastly puzzled by the almost public question of propriety the notion had evoked. Mark in particular had been strong on the duties of an Oliphant in such matters. A girl in a ship alone, even with her own brother as skipper ! Out of the question. The thing would be the talk of five counties. . . . Aunt Sophie had resolved the affair in a lightning decision.

" Then I shall accompany my daughter on this voyage," she had declared in her grandest manner. " The sea I do not like. It is brutish and uncomfortable. But this ship of *mon cher Jules* is, in a manner of speaking, Barbara's ship also, and it is fitting she should be of the party. *Alors !* I go with my Barbara as chaperon. *C'est comme il faut.* Let the small pussycats and the large tomcats talk as they will."

Now Aunt Sophie, a martyr to duty, lay green and groaning while that matter in which she would have been most vividly interested had been concluded, and the parties thereto (their eyes so shining that even Bob twinklingly suspected something afoot) paced the decks of the new ship together, close and confidential and thrilling to the wonder of intimacy confessed, while the vessel sped past the sheeted islands towards the clearer weather in the upper Firth and Mark and his cronies stood by their bottles and their jests in the saloon below.

The noises on deck of men preparing to bring the ship to anchor brought them up to survey the familiar scene at the Deeps. The hills and townlets on both sides of the water had the near, new-washed look that follows heavy rain, colour and shadow heightened in this case by the play of scudding clouds before the sun's face, so that shafts of its early afternoon brilliance moved like searchlights over the landscape, here gleaming on an array of slated roofs, there bringing up a cottage gable in pearly white or giving vivacity and significance to a planting of firs across the shoulder of a hill.

It was clear enough to their companions of the voyage that the four cronies of the saloon were in no mood to dwell on the beauties of nature. They all wore the look of men enclosed within that small, complacent and yet vulnerable world which alcohol builds about the persons of the convivial.

Julius smiled tolerantly to see Mark, his face red, control his balance with elaborate care and assume his role of hailfellow : cnowledgeable and tolerant. It was a pity, he thought, that Mark kould never shed the taint of patronage, the besetting defect of his virtues of leadership. It was almost laughable to see Mark brace himself for an effort of lucid, off-hand speech.

" So you are pleased with your new ship, Bob," he addressed the captain jocularly.

" Yes," said Bob curtly. He was intent on certain operations proceeding on the fo'c'sle. " The finest ship I have ever sailed."

" You and Julius should go into partnership," Mark retorted.

And why, Julius asked himself, could he never keep that sneer out of his tone ?

" You never know," said Bob, laughing automatically.

He turned away to bellow orders forward, and Mark took Julius's arm and led him aside. The whiff of drink on his breath surprised Julius as a revolting triviality.

" You are a great man, Julius," he started with surprising direct- ness, " and I mean that. No : you may think that we were only boozing down below, but I was watching. I know a good ship when I see one ; I know it better when I sail in her, and I take Bob Rait's word for these things. You've got something here—this new design. Sail or steam . . ."

" My dear Mark," Julius protested, " you know perfectly well that I am only interested in sail."

" Good and well ! " Mark agreed, slurring the words and gesturing largely with one arm. " But I mean what I say. Look at old Bell's *Comet* on the beach over there." He pointed to where the hull of that vessel could be discerned, drawn high up the northern shore. " Just what you said—too short, too bluff in the bows. You were right, Julius. You're a great man. But what about an engine in one of your ships, eh ? What about an engine in one of your ships ? The hollow water lines *plus* the power, eh ? "

The question was put with a sort of triumphant truculence, but Julius could only take it that the drink was working in his cousin.

" Mr. Bell and I are working along different lines," he said coldly.

The conversation was interrupted by the appearance of Aunt Sophie from the deckhouse. She was fully, even excessively, dressed for going ashore and carried on one arm a hatbox of enormous size.

" And now," she addressed the world at large, " will somebody direct me how to get off this ship, and just as quickly as may be ? Never, never, will my stomach recover from a voyage so disgusting ! "

4

Mark Oliphant smiled faintly as he scanned the missive, in which Sir John's fine embossed coat-of-arms and Sir John's boyish hand- writing and erratic spelling formed a neat composite picture of the then state of feudal culture.

" Is Sir John's man waiting for a reply ? " he asked without looking up at the clerk, who stood by the great desk that had once been Uncle Edward's.

" Yes, Mr. Mark."

" My compliments to Sir John, then, and I shall be pleased to wait on him at the Mansionhouse this afternoon."

" Yes, Mr. Mark."

When the door closed behind his man, Mark rose from his chair and walked to the new three-light window he had had cut in the corner of the room overlooking the Square. To secure that commanding view of the main focus of the town's activities had been the unconscious expression of a temperamental necessity. Now he had the place and the people always almost under his eye ; he knew, or could accurately deduce, what was happening or likely to happen in this capital of his mercantile kingdom. No spy or Peeping Tom was Mark Oliphant. All who cared could look up and see him standing there, and good luck to them ! His attitude was that of command ; what he saw from his new window provided the raw material of a policy.

This sunny morning, in the hour before noon, the Square was quiet. An occasional fish-hawker trundled a barrow out of the Bell Entry and across the Square towards the Rue End ; and the sight told Mark that the herring busses had come into the mouth of the West Burn with a good catch that morning. The caddies were away up the road to sell the fish in Cartsburn and the Port, and Mark's mind trifled with the notion of buying in bulk from the fishers and organising the hawkers to work for himself as middleman on a percentage basis. This did not strike him at all as an act of exploitation. To him it seemed an obvious and proper ordering of trade : his superior resources, indeed, providing the vagrants of the sea lochs and the urban streets alike with a reasonable guarantee of steady employment. This chaffering among ruffians at the West Burn-mouth, this unregulated hawking of good food for the poor over a wide range of prices, if not by sheer barter—all that was waste, and Mark abhorred economic waste.

But this was small beer for the head of the House of Oliphant, just one of those notions a shrewd fellow tucked away at the back of his mind. The long wars were assuredly drawing to their close, and no man could foresee the trend of trade. Meanwhile, since the fishermen were clearly enjoying a good season, there was that accumulation of ships' junk down in the yard on the East Breast. Bob Rait had condemned the lot for the use of the Oliphant fleet, but those coils of rope, bits of spars, kedge anchors and so on could be disposed of to the small coastal fisherman—a small profit out of a book loss. He crossed to the desk and made a note of the fact.

Back at the window, Mark saw with a renewal of lively interest that old Reuben Baine of the Orchard Sugarhouse had emerged from the Linen Bank and was walking slowly towards the Mid Kirk, his eyes on the ground. This was interesting. In seeing John Tasker the agent

about his balance, if any, poor old devil ! It was that hell-raking son
of his ; drink and women. Mark had no moral scruples about the use
of drink and women. He had had his share of both pleasures and would
go on having them as he saw fit. But he had long ago made it his rule
to have no truck with the women of Garvel, save on the most honourable terms. The joys of the boudoir were for his regular trips to London,
to be conducted as discreetly and economically as any other bit of
business. Mark utterly despised Ben Baine for having been caught by
a trull and married into an Irish cattle-dealer's rapacious family.
Meanwhile, it was a case for a few discreet inquiries about the Orchard.
Oliphants' brought the stuff in in their ships ; might as well go in for
boiling as well. There was a future in sugar now that more and more
folk were taking to tea-drinking.

From Ben Baine's failure as an amorist Mark's thoughts turned
naturally to one of the items of the day's business with Sir John. There
was an unconscious smile of superiority on his face as he turned from
the window, with its view of a small town's market place and human
failures, to a sort of cupboard arrangement in another corner of the
room. Sliding panels and the forward drop of a hinged shelf revealed
a washbasin of burnished copper, a copper jug of water in the recess
below, soap, a comb and brushes, a towel, and macassar oil in a
crystal bottle. It was a bold bit of business he intended to arrange
with Sir John. The wide scope of the project pleased him. The price ?
That was the least of it ; that merely amused a gentleman of means
who had frequent occasion to travel to London on affairs, rented rooms
of his own in Norfolk Street, Strand, and carried a list of agreeable
ladies in his pocket-book.

Mark smiled confidentially and deliberately this time to the
reflection of his own dark face in the mirror above the copper basin,
and the word " Byronic " floated across the surface of his mind. It was
that confounded, gushing old fool, Sir John's lady, who had used it
of his appearance, in his own presence, if in a sort of aside to Miss
Lavinia. A damned poet ! Mark had a poor view of scribbling as a
job for a man, but he allowed that this fellow Byron had launched
himself and his belated patent of nobility into the writing business with
a great deal of success. The fellow, club-foot and all, had picked the
public pocket of a very nice parcel of cash, by all accounts, and Mark
respected the feat. He was not ill-pleased to share the dark glamour
of Newstead. But now to the Buck's Head for a chop and a pint of
claret. It was a large programme that which, over several weeks, he
had planned for Sir John to invite him to discuss.

The Mid Kirk clock under the Gilded Gabbart was striking two
as the paunchy little baronet and his friend, Mr. Mark Oliphant,

came over the eastern shoulder of the Broomiknowe and paused on a knoll to look down on Garvel. The town was so deeply embedded in the foothills, the slope so steep, that the undulating note of the kirk bells rolled upward from below the level of their feet. Indeed, Garvel lay in a pocket with such curious acoustical properties that the cries of children at play in the streets of the town, a mile away and some four hundred feet below, rose to their ears with a very strange effect of remoteness, as of orphan voices calling on the living from the world of the dead.

No fanciful notions of the kind, it must be said, disturbed the thoughts of Sir John and Mr. Oliphant. These were running along practical lines. Their eyes did not even take in the outspread splendour of the anchorage in the afternoon sun, the wilful intricacy of pattern made by green peninsula and grey point and golden sandbank on the glass of the sea, or the magic of jagged peaks, cerulean in the distance against the brassy horizon of a hot day. Their eyes were on the soil about them, its features and its uses.

" So you think we can count on a period of expansion, Mr. Oliphant, peace or no peace ? " Sir John asked, burying in the turf the point of the tall shepherd's crook he affected and leaning on the shaft. " I needna' tell ye how the question affects ma management of the estate. I think ye understand ? "

Mark understood this completely and said so. He understood that the man beside him, for all his country ways and paunchy habit, was Sir John Wedderspoon, seventh baronet of Garvel and Gallowbrae, rightful owner of all the lands on this side of the Firth within a radius of eight miles from the Mid Kirk steeple. He knew that the estate, the ancient title notwithstanding, had been but a bonnet lairdship for centuries on end, and he appreciated Sir John's acumen in associating himself as a man of business with the later development of Garvel as a port. That Sir John should now, like himself, be looking to the future as a sensible man moved him to considerable respect for his homespun companion.

" There will be no stopping the expansion of Garvel," said Mark, measuring his words, " if we set about providing for it. Mind you, Sir John, the end of the war is going to close some of our channels of revenue. There's going to be no more easy money from prizes and the like, and I wouldn't say but what there's going to be trouble with the workpeople." He added violently : " There are too many damned Blacknebs about the place already ! "

" Ye mean them that are crying for Reform ? A pack of bluidy rascals ! "

" Aye, but we'll deal with them," promised Mark grimly, " and the best way to deal with them is to give them work to do. Keep them at it ! Now, we are a seaport first and foremost, and that will remain. There may be no fine prizes coming in, but there's a huge trade going to develop with our new possessions. What some folk don't under-stand——" and here his voice took on its sneering tone—" is that the war was won for British shipping nine years ago at Trafalgar. The command of the seas is ours, Sir John ! Trade is going to flow like a river to ports like Garvel—aye, even if we have to smash the monopoly of John Company."

" That's gey big talk, Mr. Oliphant," Sir John demurred cannily.

" And for big possibilities ! " cried Mark, carried away by the splendour of his own dreams and happy to have the opportunity at last of expressing them to the man best placed to make them realities. " If you were to ask my advice, Sir John, I'd say : Dig more harbours, dig them wide and deep, and you'll fill them for two generations to come ! What if the city magistrates have deepened the River ? Of course it'll take some of the trade past our doors, but there will be plenty left, believe me."

The two men considered in silence for a space the estuary laid out like a map below them—the blue water below the squat sandbanks, the muddy grey of the winding ship channel, the yellow of the shallows over the hirsts. They saw it coming to new life ; they saw the anchor-age crowded with laden ships, the harbours extended along five miles of waterfront, bustling with the movement of swinging cranes and of ant-like hordes of stevedores and of streams of horse-drawn lorries bearing the rich goods into a metropolis of tall, new transit sheds. Mark at least saw the dwellings of the workers creep up the steep hillside to where they stood and hungrily envisaged billows of industrial smoke, true earnest of the new prosperity, rolling across the hirsts towards the Lennox hills.

" Man, I'm wondering," said Sir John in the vernacular. " I'm whiles mindet to gang cannily. The estate's doin' no sae bad as it is."

" And that'll no' tak' us far, Sir John," returned Mark in the same tongue and with a laugh. " Will we step westwards a bit ? There's another notion of mine I'd like to have your views on."

The two men, figures in British history, symbols of forces that were to change the face of the country and the fortunes of its people, moved from their point of vantage and, cutting across the brow of the hill, now dipping into a rushy hollow, anon splashing through the mire stirred up by the horny feet of milk-laden cows, made towards another of those nobby outliers of the foothills encircling the town. As they went, Mark developed his theories.

" We'll keep our shipping and our shipbuilding. Shipbuilding can even expand if somebody has the sense to see that Bell was right, and that the steamship's the vessel of the future."

"There's your ain cousin," suggested Sir John pawkily.

"Julius!" Mark laughed. "Julius would as soon build a boat with wings as one with honest engines. He'll build Noah his next Ark if he lives long enough."

"A nice fellow, all the same," Sir John seemed to deprecate the hint of blasphemy.

"One of the best!" agreed Mark heartily. "But he's like too many of them—he doesn't see, or won't see, that we are passing into the age of machinery. Machinery, Sir John! The use of power! Factories, engineering shops, woollen mills—that's what Garvel needs to back its overseas trade."

Sir John's short form came to rest with a grunt against one of a group of birches on a knoll behind The Mount. He leaned there for a while, wheezing heavily, his face red with effort, but Mark studied that face out of the corner of his eye and saw with satisfaction that the shrewd, acquisitive mind behind it was working busily.

"Factories!" Sir John contrived to ejaculate at length. "That's a michty tall order, man. What's to attract them here?"

"Cheap power."

Mark dropped those two words with the greatest deliberation of casualness and noted that, as he had planned, the laird was baffled by superior knowledge.

"Cheap power?"

"Cheap power, Sir John," Mark repeated the magic phrase gently. "You know what it costs to bring a load of coals to Garvel from the nearest pits. Fair ruinous! But we can dispense with that. We can use the white coal."

"White coal!" Sir John's intelligence seemed to be reeling under a series of shocks.

"Water."

"Water!"

Mark smiled slightly to see how his pupil in economics had something of the air of one who receives the knock-out blow. He had rehearsed his approach to these high matters with some care, but now he allowed a peremptory note to creep into his tone.

"Look, Sir John!" He pointed up the slopes behind where they stood. "Think of your own moors up there, and nothing on them but perhaps a couple of hundred blackface sheep. But the moors are fair dripping with water—water running to waste down fifty glens. Waste! And it could all be dammed and led to the town to drive as many mills as we could pack along the length of the stream."

" And where did you get that idea ? "

Sir John spoke slowly, giving each word a sort of reverential emphasis. His eyes were as near goggled as their small size permitted. Mark evaded the question.

" It can be done ; that's the point, Sir John. And at no great expense. Man——" He was carried away into the familiarity by his genuine enthusiasm for an economic idea. " Water power costs nothing. Sell it as cheap as you like, it will attract all the more enterprise and still return a fine dividend on your capital."

" Capital . . ." Sir John began.

" That can be provided," said Mark easily. " It only needs your word as ground landlord."

" Aye ! " said Sir John. " Aye ! Juist so."

Mark had a perfect understanding of his companion's state of mind in that moment. He knew that he had aroused in the little man the most eager interest and the hungriest sort of cupidity. The phase of digestion and demurrers had been reached. The ideas must have time to pass through the filters of a mind as shrewd and cautious as that of any peasant. Boldly but adroitly Mark proceeded to complete his picture.

" But that was not exactly the notion I had in mind. That was just in the bye-going. What I thought would interest you most, Sir John—though it must have occurred to you already, to be sure—was the direction in which the town itself is bound to expand, as I see it."

" Aye ? " Sir John ventured cannily.

" Assume the natural growth of the place, with or without water power. Call it the inevitable growth. No doubt about it, Sir John, the town must expand in this direction. It will grow uphill, up the glens running down to the Bay of Tweek. I have little doubt but that, in fifty years' time, the factories and the workers' homes will have spread uphill to where we are standing now, and beyond—aye, up to Ewerton itself."

" And d'ye mean to tell me," asked the little man roughly, " that the Mansionhouse, no' to mention The Mount and Goldenhaddock, are going to be swamped under a rickle o' smokestacks and tenement buildings ? "

" Inevitably, sir," Mark persisted suavely, " if your property is to develop profitably, as I think you will wish. And this little notion of mine arises out of the fact. Now just think, Sir John, of the number of men of real substance in Garvel ; their names will occur to you ; at least two score men who have acquired considerable fortunes these last thirty years or so. They are still content to live in the town proper, some of them in auld-farrant houses cheek-by-jowl with slums and stews and taverns, and we'll have to persuade them out of that. They owe it to their own dignity as leading citizens ; the time's coming when rich and poor will not find it comfortable to live close together—like bugs in a rug. Look then, Sir John——"

Mark pointed westwards to where the Kempock turnpike ran among trees and enclosed fields and then out of sight behind the bluff above Drums.

" Was there ever a stretch of land better suited for laying out in elegant feus ? A fine flat terrace above the Firth—though I don't see why you couldn't build along the Laigh Road as well—and a view you'd search the world to find the equal of. Handy to the town and yet cut off from it by the West Glen. Free from smoke, with our prevailing wind from the south-west. Big feus, mind you, Sir John, at least an acre apiece. You could ask feu duty at a high rate, and I'll wager you'd get it. Onerous conditions in the feu charters, such as that each house be of at least twelve rooms and built in an elegant style ; it might be a villa in the Italian manner or anything you fancy. Man, it's a gold mine lying to your hand ! It only wants one man of substance to make the first move. And upon my soul, Sir John, I wouldn't be loth to set the example if you were to give me a bit of encouragement."

With eyes apparently dull Sir John pondered that part of his domain indicated by Mark. The bucolic face betrayed not the slightest sign of either interest or disapproval. Mark was simply content to know that an idea had been planted as fairly as it could be, and that, like any competent and patient gardener, he must await the fact of germination and prepare to tend the crop to the point of ripeness.

" Aye ! " said the Laird at length, turning his back suddenly on the field of possible expansion. " Weel, we'd best be stepping towards the Mansionhouse. I was to tell you that Her Leddyship and Miss Lavinia would be glad to offer ye a dish of tea if ye're in the mind to look in."

" Nothing could be more delightful."

The two men walked eastwards in a silence broken only by an occasional explosive " Aye ! " or " Mphm ! " from Sir John. As for Mark, he went along in a state of easy satisfaction. He had set out in the most favourable conditions a plan long and carefully considered, and it was clearly working in the quarter to which it had been deliberately addressed. Things were going very well. A judge, a connoisseur of acquisitiveness, Mark Oliphant was satisfied that he had put in a good afternoon's work.

Lady Wedderspoon's reception of him was flattering in the extreme. With perfectly good-humoured cynicism he enjoyed the oddity of the fact that a woman of the Scottish landed gentry brought to their encounter much less poise, and much more fussiness, than he himself, a merchant, had learned to regard as proper to a lady of position. Failing in his judgment of permanent values, as he was destined to fail all his life long, he confused grace with worth and, in his fascination with profitable novelty, had no eye for the value of a tradition rooted in the soil.

It equally gratified him to see that his presence had a profound effect on Miss Lavinia. She was so eager ; she so easily blushed when he advanced to take her cup ; she would so excitedly gabble such stupid things. At all events, she was honest and simple and, probably, sensible and domesticated. He took pains to bow over her person, to half-whisper a near-confidence.

Things were going very well indeed.

5

Young Mrs. Julius Oliphant sat in the drawing-room of her fine house of Goldenhaddock. Her armchair was set in the bay of the window, and Barbara was very consciously enjoying the warmth of the evening sunlight, the glow it shed over the anchorage, the hum of the bees in the snapdragons outside, and the light drifts of perfume the fitful breezes of a hot July carried from the tea roses growing against the harled walls of her house. She was with child, and she smiled now and again at the liveliness of its quickening within her. Inside that moment of time Barbara Oliphant placidly reckoned that no other woman had ever been happier than she.

The grace of the high-ceilinged room alone gave her profound pleasure. This had been the most wonderful of Julius's wedding gifts. They had agreed that the marriage ceremony must be a quiet affair—to Maman's loud and voluble disappointment—but in the making of Goldenhaddock fit for its first bride in fifty years Julius had been gloriously extravagant. This was to be her room ; she had only to indicate her dreams and desires and they were gratified. He had gone to Edinburgh and even to London for those precious, rich hangings and that delicate furniture. He had corresponded direct with Mr. Girtin and Mr. Constable in the matter of the English water-colours that gleamed from the walls. (The panelling and the enamelling in white had been entrusted to a firm of specialists in Beith with a Royal Warrant and a regal way of doing business.) He had seen Mr. Broadwood himself regarding the construction of the pianoforte and the decoration of its case. Even Mark, who had been most complaisant

in providing transport by sea for the goods from the South, had been
moved to a jest, remarking that he was reminded of the brave days of
the Spanish prizes.

With all her French instinct towards economy Barbara had never
grudged a penny of the money they had spent on the beautifying of
their home. It gave them both exquisite pleasure, and no value in
sterling could weigh with her as against their joint happiness. It was
like the child in her womb, a symbol of their incredible delight in
each other.

She was wearing black that evening, the waist of her dress caught
high under her filling breasts. Its only decoration was a frill of white
chiffon about the neck, just as on her thin fingers there was nothing
but the single band of gold. She had, however, been wearing a scarlet
cloak while walking in the garden on Julius's arm, and this now
flowed in glowing curves over the arms of her chair and on to the
floor by her feet, most effectively framing her grave beauty in its
severity of dress and giving her person in repose the very breath of
expectant motherhood.

She thought of the child and of childbirth, but rather lazily and
without alarm. That there must be pain, and that there would be
risk, she knew, but all the apprehensions were sublimated within her
by the great strength of her happiness and the great force of her
unconscious will to perpetuate the love that she and Julius bore to
one another. Indeed—as she smiled again to think—most of the
practical burden had already been shouldered by Maman. At great
length and often in embarrassing detail Maman was at any moment
ready to descant on the feats of accouchement and the triumphs of
nursing she was ready at the right moment—and not only ready but
supremely competent—to perform and achieve. *Chère Maman!* She
would talk and talk of her own unique mastery of any given situation,
but it always had to be allowed that gallant spirit that her competence in the practical was of a high order, that she never promised
what she could not brilliantly perform. Already a wardrobe of small
garments, exquisitely stitched, was accumulating in the cottage at
Kempock.

"You will have the goodness to leave these matters to me."
Barbara could hear her mother's voice—" *C'est mon métier. C'est moi
qui parle*—I, who have brought five children into the world. The
labour? The pain? Pff! These things are forgotten overnight by a
woman who is a woman. What imports is the feeding of the infant
thereafter and the warming of the body. *Alors!* I shall be present
to see that these matters are attended to *comme il faut.* You will therefore rest, *ma chère fille.* I permit you to be thoroughly lazy until the

child is ready to appear—about the day of Guy Fawkes as I calculate. I have a regard for the health of my first grandson."

Barbara stirred to the sound of footsteps along the terrace outside. Her eyes brightened when she heard Julius humming the little Highland air he was so fond of, *Crodh Chailien*. He had had a conservatory built to the west of the old house and, like any good young husband, settling down, made a great business of the culture of grapes and nectarines. Then the sounds of another pair of feet coming up the drive from the main gate had her stiffening a little with disappointment, for she saw that they were about to have a visit from her cousin by marriage, Mr. Mark Oliphant.

The two men entered the room together, and with a quick " Please do not rise, Barbara," Mark hurried to greet her. He bent low and solicitiously over her hand.

" You are keeping well ? " he asked. " Looking after yourself ? That's right ! We must be careful about my first—what will he be ?— second cousin. My godson, I hope."

In terms of the conventions Mark's avuncular reference to her condition seemed to Barbara significant. Rightly or wrongly, she could never take this masterful cousin of hers for granted. Their respective minds and temperaments were inevitably hostile, and she could only see him objectively, examining every one of his attitudes to discover the motive that prompted it.

" You will stay for supper, I hope ? No ? Then at least a glass of wine. Julius dear, would you kindly ring ? "

" There is certainly an excuse for a glass," said Mark, settling himself comfortably on a divan. He was clearly in great good humour. " Indeed, Barbara, I am really here to take you and Julius, the nearest to me in the family, into my confidence in a highly personal matter. Can you guess what it is ? "

" You are betrothed, Mark ! To——"

" Yes, Barbara. To Miss Wedderspoon. Are you surprised ? "

" No," said Barbara heartily, " but I am delighted. I congratulate you indeed, and wish you and Miss Lavinia every happiness."

On Julius the effect of the announcement was much more stimulating. His eyes glowed with pleasure, he shook his cousin's proferred hand with both of his.

" Mark, old friend ! " he cried. " This is capital news ! I am delighted. You must be happy. I hope you will both be very happy always. When will that wine come ? This calls for a bumper ! "

They were all very jovial over the toast which Julius proposed with boyish gusto, and Mark played the part of successful suitor as heartily as his temperament allowed. Shortly, however, he turned grave as befitted a man of position and substance about to take an onerous step, and his next remark was sententious.

" I think it could be called a suitable match, don't you think, Barbara ? "

" I think it eminently suitable, Mark," returned Barbara, her calm unruffled.

" It's perfect ! " Julius insisted generously. " All sentiment apart —if you will allow me to put it that way, Mark—this is a proper union between two of the most influential families in the district. Why, it's quite a bit of local history ! "

" That is precisely how I look at it, Julius," agreed Mark almost demurely. " Clearly, the marriage may lead to—well, shall we say ? not unimportant developments. And that reminds me of one thing I'd like to say to you right away, Julius. You will understand, considering Lavinia's position, it may be desirable, if it is not actually forced on me, to move out of Garvel and into a mansion in the country. After all, the Wedderspoons belong to the landed gentry, and—but you will appreciate the point. And so, Julius, my friend, how about The Mount as the home of your technical college in terms of Uncle Walter's will ? "

" The Mount ! But this——"

" I know that you are having difficulty in finding a site in the town proper," Mark went on in his grandest manner, " and there is The Mount lying to your hand ; quiet and still convenient to the town, and a big, rambling place that could easily be converted to your purposes. What a saving in building costs to begin with ; all the more for your capital funds ! "

" It is like poor Uncle Walter's dream of a university come true," whispered Julius as if to himself.

" It will be yours if you agree," Mark announced firmly. " And in honour of my betrothal, my friend, I am prepared to make a solid contribution to the cost of the building and the site."

" Really, Mark ! This is wonderful. But the idea is so new, and so attractive. I hardly——"

A wave of Mark's hand dismissed his cousin's hesitation.

" It can be very simply contrived," he said decisively. " Let us get Caldwell, or any other independent man you care to name, to put a value on the property. Whatever the figure may be, you shall have The Mount for half of it. The other half is my gift to the college— and, damme, if I don't throw in the legal expenses as well ! It's not every day a man finds himself betrothed."

Barbara was aware of Mark's dark face turning towards her. She knew very well that he did not look to her for approval. She knew that Mark was as keenly aware as herself of the sheer impossibility of his ever gaining her sympathy. It was much like dealing with another woman, and Barbara respected Mark's astuteness in playing on Julius's weakest spot and so triumphing over herself. She acknowledged his look with a brief smile, but her eyes moved swiftly to Julius for whom she was suddenly afraid.

" But this is overwhelming, Mark ! " he was saying excitedly. " This is generosity on a princely scale. And such a good and simple solution of a problem that was beginning to beat me ! Isn't this very wonderful, Barbara ? "

" Mark has done a handsome thing," said Barbara.

" Not another word ! " commanded Mark, rising from the divan. " I'll put the business in hand to-morrow . . . By your leave, Barbara, I must go now. Will you see me to the door, Julius ? No : just one other matter before I go. Now, I pick your brains, Julius, I warn you, but it arose in conversation with Sir John the other day. You remember throwing off a wild notion of impounding the moorland waters and using them for the supply of power to the town ? "

" One of my harebrained schemes ! " laughed Julius, adding swiftly. " But perfectly feasible, I assure you."

" It was only a point of detail," Mark insisted. " That the water was up there, lying idle, I have always known. But I am no engineer, and what beats me is how you could get it down to the town through the fringe of hills. Was it a tunnel you contemplated, Julius ? "

" No, no, no ! " cried Julius, interested. " Look, Mark ! You know how the land lies up there, over the brow of the hill. It's all a great, sodden moorland, square miles of it, but draining off to the West— that is, *away* from Garvel. Where's my pencil ? "

He delved into a variety of untidy pockets and dredged from them at length a stub of joiner's oval-barrelled pencil and a dog-eared pad of paper.

" Look now, Mark. There's the Moss, I don't know how many square miles of it, fed by innumerable springs and streams off the hills round about. It's the bottom of a bowl ; in fact, a natural reservoir. But the bowl won't hold water because—look at the sketch—there's a big bite out of it at the western end, near Outerwards—*here*." He stubbed his pencil into the paper to indicate the position of that mountainy farm. " So the water runs away down the Langhill Burn "—another swift score on the paper—" and if you think of the huge amount of water the Langhill carries on a run of only four miles to the sea, then you can realise how much power is being wasted."

" Yes, yes ! I see that," said Mark, his dark eyes intent on those few square inches of paper. " But——"

"No 'but' about it, Mark," retorted Julius out of the superiority of technical assurance. "You simply dam the Moss at the western end, from Outerwards across to Rullian Top, and within a week of closing the sluices you have millions of gallons of water on hand. A tremendous weight of water, Mark, with a fall of at least three hundred feet before it gets down here to the town ; enough power to drive a hundred mills ! The dam would be nothing—less than a mile of strong embankment and a few sluices. Child's play from the engineering point of view."

Barbara sat watching her husband's face. In this distributive mood he was, she reflected, at his most charming. He could never be secretive. For him an idea was a delightful thing to be spread about and shared. The mere conception of the idea, and the richness of it, were enough for him. Like a woman bearing and giving birth to a child, except that Julius's mind conceived and threw off its fruits so freely.

"And still the problem of getting that water to the town," Mark was saying. "A tunnel——"

"A tunnel ! At least two miles in length, under six hundred feet of hill, through the hardest igneous rock in the geological system of Great Britain ! Why, man, it would cost a million and take a lifetime ! No, Mark, look——" Julius's pencil slashed again across his sketch-map. "There's how the water comes to Garvel. *Round* the hill, not *through* it. An aqueduct cut into the slopes of Rullian Top from Outerwards round to Ewerton—high up on the hillside—a simple, inexpensive job for a hundred navvies and a competent engineer. It could be done within the year, and the outlay no burden on the undertaking worth mentioning."

"I see, I see," said Mark softly. "A bold notion, Julius."

"Obvious," retorted Julius gaily and not without vanity. "The inevitable solution of a given problem in dynamics."

Mark laid the small pad of paper on the occasional table in the bow of the window, and Barbara watched how his eyes seemed to brood on it. She knew that his mind had borrowed from Julius something of value, and she knew also that purpose was shaping in that mind of his which he would never display candidly to any other human being. Then he looked up suddenly and gave her one of his rare but not unattractive smiles.

"Your pardon, Barbara. Julius made this so interesting. Now I must hurry off and leave you two to your own devices." He bent once more over Barbara's hand. "Good-bye, cousin ! You will promise me to take great care of yourself ? "

Julius was chuckling when he returned from seeing their guest to the door.

"Good old Mark and his waterworks !" he laughed. "He is like a terrier when he gets an idea into his head. He bites deep and won't let go."

"As usual," observed Barbara drily, "Mark has a plan, probably for making money, and you as usual, my dearest love, allowed him to pick your brains."

"Oh, Barbara !" Julius protested mildly. "There is nothing in that water scheme. If a man is interested, he has only to glance at a map. And you know perfectly well, my dear, that I would never have the energy to take up such a project."

He stooped and pressed his cheek gently against hers, whispering :

"Why should I care ? I have my ships, and I have always you. Is that not more than enough ? "

" I am very content, my dear heart," she whispered and kissed him lightly on the ear.

<h1 style="text-align:center">6</h1>

A bonfire blazed on the Craigs Top, for the battle of Waterloo had been fought and won and the terrible legend of Bonaparte was now but a bad dream, still portentous and unforgettable, but the edge of its terror turned in the fires of a new morning.

Barbara watched the leaping play of the flames from the window of the upper chamber in which Walter Rait Oliphant lay asleep, a morsel of warm, dear flesh in his crib. She had thought to hear his infant cry for her breasts and had hurried upstairs, the nursemaid being out with the rest of the town, celebrating the distant victory. It would have been little wonder if the child had stirred in its sleep ; the clamour from the town below rose to her ears in a high and almost strident buzz. All the ships at the anchorage, that had saluted the victory with salvoes at noon, had now sent their men ashore, and the streets and taverns down there were loud with shouting and song, bawdry and disputation. Not a few couples or small groups of revellers, seeking the dark places for the fulfilment of their desires, had wandered uphill and now and again broke the special silence of the Golden-haddock grounds with their bawling.

Still, the infant did not stir, and Barbara watched the sombre play of the bonfire from the window. She could see many another fire on the hilltops above and about the Firth, a ring of fires from the uttermost of the Cowal hills right round the northern arc of the sky to the summit of the great rock upstream. These, however, were but pinpoints of light, small and individually unimportant flowers in a festoon ; whereas the beacon on the Craigs, although a full mile away, loomed portentous and personal, as she felt it. In the late evening of a northern June it should have been a tame confusion of pallid flame and black smoke, but the day had been wet, the sky was still heavily overcast with low cloud, and against that louring ceiling, and reflected from it, the bonfire glowed truly red and the smoke rising from it in oily whorls against the glow made the stuff of a child's vision of hell. Barbara imagined that she could see over that distance the small, black figures of people darting across the base of the fire, adoring the fire and feeding it, hierophants of a primitive cult.

She turned from the window at length, picked up the child and put it to the breast. As it muzzled and sucked with the vulgar vigour of perfect health, she smiled the delight that only mothers know in the lusty and remorseless greed of their babies ; but as the child settled down to his feed and then took to drowsing at intervals, so she drowsed with him, letting the stream of thought flow unchecked through her mind.

The bonfire still flamed in her mind's eye, with the small, black figures darting about in its glow, and she wondered vaguely enough what victory meant to such people and, more sharply, what they thought it meant to them. Aloof from the popular excitement, Barbara had no feeling that a great and portentous change in men's lives had suddenly been wrought by the destruction of the Grand Army on a distant Belgian plain. War had been the condition of living throughout the twenty years of her life. It had been the means, however indirect, of her father's death. It had given her dear brother his meed of adventure and his share of wealth out of prizes. Her own comfort in this big house of Goldenhaddock rested to a great extent on wealth gained by conquest in the war at sea. A woman nursing her own man-child at the breast, she was happy that the victory portended an end to the slaughter of mothers' sons. But this fact of victory, over which most men and women were deliriously rejoicing—did it portend Change ? A still warmer solidarity between a woman and her man ? Less poverty and drunkenness and disease ? A clear future, into which Walter Rait Oliphant (now gorged and asleep, his pouting mouth dropped away from the nipple, as if in disgust) could advance to fulfil without arbitrary interference such talents as lay within him ? A spacious and quiet age in which the genius of her own Julius might flower in lovely completeness ?

She was a woman ; and she smiled to realise how her thoughts ran along the groove of possessiveness. But as she laid the infant back in his cot, the smile faded in the light of the single candle she had lit and was replaced by a look, strange in a face so well-modelled and calm, in which strain and apprehension were subtly blended. It was not peace . . . That hard knowledge was at the back of her mind. Distracted by the business of putting the baby down to sleep, she could not define the causes of her uneasiness. It was simply there : a premonition, an intuition. She went down the broadly sweeping stairs with the feeling that something ominous had happened or was about to happen. She wished that Julius would come home. If he was happy with his friends on this night of celebration let him stay out, and all her love and trust with him. But she could not be happy until he came home, alive, happy, confident.

Downstairs again in her lamplit drawing-room, she made first to the windows to draw the curtains, but there she paused again to watch the bonfires, a girdle of diamonds round the waist of the deepening night, on the hills across the Firth. She deliberately decided to leave both shutters and curtains open. The glow from her windows would be her modest salute to victory and a sign to Julius that she lovingly awaited his return. She was turning to her chair under the lamp and to her book—the romance of *Waverley* by the new author of exciting anonymity—when she was brought up abruptly, startled, her hand on the chair's back, to hear the voice of her brother Bob raised in anger, then the quiet tones of Julius seeming to protest against his companion's vehemence. They were coming up through the garden to the door.

Barbara's thoughts tumbled into a vortex of womanly alarm. Julius and Bob had quarrelled. Or Julius and Bob had been drinking and had picked a foolish quarrel. But it was never the way of Julius, the fastidious, to take wine to excess, and this must really be a quarrel between the two men she most dearly loved and faithfully trusted in all the world. Terror and shame and horror ! Then the fighting spirit and the clarity of mind in crisis she had inherited from her Creole mother disciplined her alarms. She sailed to the door and into the hall, her head high and imperious, to face and deal with masculine folly at its crudest.

"Such a great noise, Bob," she greeted her brother icily as he came through the door, Julius in his wake. "I have a child asleep upstairs."

"Noise !" cried Bob passionately, ignoring her reproof. "If I had a pistol in my hand and Mark Oliphant in front of me you'd hear a noise, I promise you ! That would be me blowing the brains out of a damned, treacherous, swindling dog ! "

"Easy now, Bob ! Easy ! " Julius murmured behind him.

T.C.S   H

" What is all this ? " Barbara asked.

" A damned rascal ripe for hanging ! " Bob continued to insist recklessly. " Give me that swab on the main deck of my own ship and the knotted end of a rope in my hand——"

" Meanwhile," Barbara interrupted him tartly, " you are in my house, and not on the fo'c'sle of a ship at sea. Let us go into the drawing-room."

In the brighter light of the great room she looked from her brother's face to that of her husband. The one was darkly red with honest anger, the other pale and set as if by pain. She saw that Julius had in fact suffered a profound and recent shock, and she had to control herself to await the story.

" And now ? "

" Just that Mark Oliphant, is a swindling, black-gutted . . ."

" Allow me, Bob," Julius interrupted quietly, turning to his wife with a wan smile. " The fact is, Barbara, Mark has sprung a very unpleasant surprise. Only this evening, and only by accident, I learned that he has taken over Bennie's boatyard on the Cartsburn Shore and really means to set up business in—well, I suppose I must be frank—in opposition to me. Bob and I have spent the evening making inquiries, and I'm afraid we can't see it as anything but an unfriendly act."

" Unfriendly ! " Bob exploded.

" He has taken over Bennie's place ? " Barbara repeated deliberately as one who, in detachment, seeks to marshal facts. " Now he is going to add boatbuilding to his interests ? As if he had not enough power, enough wealth . . . I suppose," she added bitterly, " he believes in the steamboat ? "

" I suppose so," agreed Julius, nodding miserably.

Bob, who had been pacing the long length of the room, up and down, stopped in his tracks, pointed a rigid forefinger at his brother-in-law and appealed vehemently to his sister.

" But he has only told you the half of it ! " he cried. " Mark Oliphant building ships is one thing. That we can face. It's his way of contriving it, the damned greasy, pot-bellied, twisted, oily, upstart son of a——"

" Bob ! Your story, please."

" The fact is, Barbara," Julius intervened again, " I got the first hint of it from my assistant, Gavin Semple. You know the lad."

" Squint-eyed rascal ! " Bob explained gratuitously.

" I was sitting there this evening," Julius went on, " working on the drawings of a new vessel for the Maclays. I called Gavin in to ask him to get ahead with some preliminary work, and then he told me that he could not do so. He was leaving me, he said Mark had engaged him as manager of the new yard. And that was the first I heard of it ! "

" And you see how it is, Barbara ! " added Bob, flinging his arms wide apart in indignant appeal. " It's not just that our Mark—damn his eyes !—sets up against Julius without a how-d'ye-do ? or a friendly hint. The damned rascal has to steal Julius's pupil—the very man who has learned from Julius all he knows ; the very man—and the only man—who has Julius's secrets of design at his finger's ends ! "

" Hardly secret," murmured Julius. " A development—inevitable . . ."

" So inevitable," Bob rounded on his brother-in-law with surprising bitterness, " that even Mr. Mark Oliphant could discover them for himself ! Don't be a bigger, soft-hearted fool than you can help, Julius."

" That will do."

Three monosyllables from Barbara silenced her brother. She moved to the window, and now she made a show of drawing the curtains. Only when this task was completed in a series of vicious tugs did she realise that she had quite overlooked the closing of the shutters in the first place. But she turned to her menfolk with calm.

" Very well," she said. " Mark is a treacherous man. That one has always known. I am not surprised. But is this an end ? "

" By God, I should hope not ! " Bob responded.

" Very well. I only ask questions. Perhaps I speak of things I do not fully understand. But if Mark intends to take up building for steam, am I to take it that you both now despair of sail ? You, Julius ? You, Bob ? "

" Good God, no ! " This from Bob.

" Hardly that, Barbara." This from Julius.

" Very well. Let Mark have his steamboats. Let him have his Gavin What-is-his-name ? He may even have some of your secrets, Julius. But does the Oliphant yard thereupon close down ? Or am I speaking foolishly ? "

" Lord ! It's like Maman all over again," commented Bob in a hoarse whisper.

Barbara saw her husband and brother exchange glances that were almost sheepish.

" You are quite right, Barbara, of course——" Julius began in his reasonable way.

" You dislike the unpleasantness of it all, my dear," Barbara said. " So do I. But if one must quarrel with Mark, or fight Mark in business, then I am not in the least afraid."

" But the man is my employer ! " Bob broke in loudly. " Do you think I can go back and take his dirty money and his orders now ? Do you think I'm going to spend the rest of my life managing a line of stinking steamboats for Mister Swindling Mark Oliphant ? "

They were just a pair of boys, thought Barbara, bewildered and indignant and foolish boys because their romantic code of honour had been outraged. Like a boy, Bob must now throw his rhetorical questions at her head, transferring all the responsibility to her ! She braced herself for another effort of patience and reason.

" Is it impossible that you and Bob should now work together, Julius ? " she asked blandly. " I know nothing of these matters, but if Mark is likely to turn his fleet over to steam, and you believe that there is still a future for sail, is it not something to consider—that you should build your own ships, Julius, and that Bob should manage them for you ? You would do well in partnership, I am sure."

The two men stared at each other, with the stupid air of those who hear wisdom from unexpected sources. It took their dazed minds an appreciable time to realise the bold simplicity of Barbara's suggestion, to examine it for flaws, and then to accept the creature of a woman's mind.

" By Gad ! " shouted Bob at length, smacking his knee.

" Barbara ! " Julius's tone was quieter, but his face glowed with pleasure, gratitude and admiration. " You have got more sense than Bob and I put together ! "

He turned eagerly to his brother-in-law.

" You see it, Bob ? With your great experience of the trade and my building resources. Capital ? Why, I've got ample ! We could——"

" No trouble about capital ! " Bob insisted recklessly. " I had my share of prize money in the good days. No, Julius ; the thing is to open up the Indian trade. John Company's monopoly won't last, you mark my words. Give me two—four—good ships . . . I could write you down a specification now. . . . Where's that bit of keelavine I had . . . ? "

Barbara rose from her chair and knew that her rising would pass almost unnoticed. They were off on their romantic voyagings again, these two men of hers. Her own idea was now theirs, and she was as happy as they were. But she felt tired. Men never knew what it cost a woman in energy to maintain their peace of mind.

" I must go upstairs now," she said. " You will stay the night, of course, Bob ? You know your room. . . . Do not stay up too late, Julius, my dear."

They rose formally as she passed from the room, but the eager argument broke out again as soon as she had closed the door behind her. Barbara did not expect her husband to come to his place beside her as she had bidden him. They would be at it for hours.

Holding the candle away from the cot, she drew aside the muslin curtains and looked down on the sleeping, innocent face of Walter Rait Oliphant.

All children . . . but, no ! Not Mark Oliphant. Mark had guile, the guile of the woman and the serpent. She trembled a little with hatred as she thought of that ruthless man but, still holding the curtain of the baby's cot, she disciplined herself not to waste her strength in hating Mark. She was not afraid of him, and she knew that he was at least a little afraid of her. She would need all her strength for a duel that might be long and painful. Her only fear was for Julius and his gentleness ; for herself she had no fear. She knew that, in the long issue of things really significant, Mark was vulnerable because he did not understand and never would.

And still she felt she could not sleep. She tried to read by candle-light, but the rumble of men's voices in the room below was an obsession. Now they rose in altercation, then they eased, but only occasionally, in laughter. At length she went downstairs again.

The men looked up, startled, from their wine as she slipped into the room.

" Not a ghost," she said with a soft laugh, " only a poor woman who cannot sleep for your chatter. Come, you have talked enough for one night. Is everything not arranged by now ? "

" All cleared up, Babs, shipshape and Bristol fashion," Bob told her enthusiastically. " A new shipping line for Garvel—Oliphant and Rait. O. and R. How's that ? "

" Surely you can imagine something more romantic on a day like this," she chaffed them. " The Waterloo Line—the Wellington Line . . . No—look ! "

Barbara was leading the way from the room, and she paused in the hall to see a bright star perfectly framed in the oblong of the still open door. The night remained overcast, but the clouds had broken towards the north, and there was this one bright star, its neighbours either pallid or occluded, to be the mystic, sentimental symbol of their enterprise.

" The North Star ! " cried Barbara.

" The Pole Star ? " Bob amended. " And our house flag designed for us free of charge—a silver star on a blue ground ! "

" Better still," Julius suggested.

He had taken Barbara's hand in the darkness.

" Shakespeare was always right. The Constant Star ! Our purpose, our ideals . . ."

" Got it ! " cried Bob joyously and gave his brother-in-law a seaman's buffet on the back. " The Constant Star ! That's the name for the line and the first new ship we build. And that house flag—a sort of middle blue, not too dark, not too light, with the silver star, five-pointed, well in towards the spar. Capital ! "

" And if you promise to go to bed now, *tout' suite*," said Barbara laughing again, " I'll promise to sew the first flag for your first ship. No, Bob . . . No more wine, no more toasts . . . *Allons !* "

7

Alan Oliphant saw the Waterloo bonfires and was stirred by the glow of them. Even from the depths of the Highland glen two of these beacons could be seen flaring against the sullen sky, one on the summit of Beinn Fidhleir and one, farther away but higher in the firmament and more exciting, on the peak of the Stack itself. On the bemused mind of this broken man the fires worked strangely, filling it with memories of a life that had been rich and convivial, of the days when he, one of the Oliphants of Garvel, had been a kenspeckle man among men. They strengthened the recurrent instinct of his confused inbeing to escape from the prison into which terrible circumstance and considerable weakness had thrust him.

Alan Oliphant's malady had stopped short of lunacy and its divine release from reality. Years after his ordeal on the Andes and in the forests he could still waken out of sleep, screaming with terror, all the horror of those desperate hours on the Pacific Coast and the interminable days and weeks and months in the forests as fresh and raw as spilt blood. Even so, the memories were fading, losing their edge. The slow tempo of life in the glen was creating in Alan the counter-irritants of boredom and impatience. The wreck of a man had enough of its egoism left to give it purpose. Cunning gradually took the place of fear within him. With one of the tricks of near-imbecility, in his endless conversations with himself as he took his daily walks, he told himself that he was a fly man. From one of the crofters of the glen he had picked up the Gaelic phrase for it, *an gille corach*. This he used in to himself as if it were a codeword. He had always the feeling that his lovely and secret intentions were being spied on.

" Come and see the bonfires, Alan ! " old Mrs. Oliphant, Julius's mother, had called from the door.

She had been out, as was her custom, enjoying the perfume of the

roses and stocks she had contrived to cultivate in the thin, sour soil
of the fastnesses. Alan answered the summons with a boy's leap from
his chair at the parlour window, and the old minister shuffled after
him. They stood together, all three, regarding with awe the fires on
the high peaks.

"Victory!" murmured Julius's father. "But Thine the power
and the glory. They shall beat their swords into ploughshares, and
their spears into pruning hooks; nation shall not lift up sword against
nation, neither shall they learn war any more. Amen."

He was failing, and his wife laid a hand on his arm.

"Come indoors, Roderick. And you, Alan," she turned to her
charge with a smile. "It is time for bed."

"Yes, aunt," he replied dutifully. "Good-night! Good-night,
Uncle Roderick!"

"You will not be needing a candle this evening," said Julius's
mother. "Sleep well, Alan."

She was good to him, and he cherished for her all the devotion of
which he was capable, even if it was the devotion of a dog, lacking
both true respect and self-respect. He knew that she managed him
with wisdom as well as kindness. She dispensed his regular tots of rum
and never sought to preach at him. (He did not know that Cousin
Julius had contrived this regimen and provided the liquor as he might
have a pension to a needy relative.) Even when, twice or thrice in
the year, the hunger overwhelmed him and he escaped to drink
himself into stupor and filth at the Inns down at Claddich, she did
not upbraid him but took him into her house again, and cleansed him,
and put him to bed.

Still, she was one of those others who stood always on watch
outside the walls of his prison. Even she could not exact respect from
the ghost of Alan Oliphant's soul. When he was safe in his upstairs
room, unembarrassed by a tell-tale candle, he stayed for a long time
by the window watching the blaze on Beinn Fidhleir, hugging to
himself a wild intention, waiting. The hunger was on him again.
The fires were calling him back into the stews where alone, now, he
could realise himself. He dreamed passionately of the lights and the
noise and the liquors of the Inns down at Claddich.

It was in his mind a dark and subtle plan, with himself as a brilliant
and ruthless plotter, but it was all as easy as it had been many a time
before. The old minister and his wife, innocently asleep in their room
at the back, did not hear him pad down the stairs in his stocking soles
nor stir to the turning of the handle of a door that was never locked.
They did not hear the familiar slam of the gate in the drystone dyke
that kept the sheep out of Mrs. Oliphant's bare bit of garden, for Alan,

the fly man, *an gille corach*, knew where he could step over a nick in the wall where Para Lamont's garron, taking fright at a seagull swooping under her nose, had backed a cart with a load of peats in it against that nicely balanced structure.

The Inns at Claddich was not more than a rickle of hovels. Three single-storeyed buildings of two rooms each, roofed with clay and heather, hung together in such an irregular line that the miry space before them formed a sort of courtyard and provided for Alan Oliphant at least the illusion of community. As he neared the place he saw heartening streams of lamplight pouring through the doorways and heard the gallant noises of friendship and celebration, mainly in the Gaelic tongue. A platoon of dogs of the collie sort wuffed and growled and barked or fawned as he crossed to one of the lighted doors, their eyes gleaming green in the quarter-light.

That was a great night at the Inns of Claddich. Not only was it the night of victory ; the drovers had come down from the high Highlands with a great herd of cattle for the tryst at Falkirk and were making of this low-browed tavern their caravanserai. It was their dogs that had challenged Alan's approach to the Inns. You could see their fires burning and hear their beasts lowing on the bit of pasture-land beyond the brawl of the Claddich Burn. They had come hundreds of miles from the North, over mountain passes and moorland tracks, and now, at this uncouth halt, those of them who were free from the care of the bestial were making merry according to their custom, with the downfall of Boney giving them a fair excuse for a carouse beyond the ordinary.

The shouting of them, the higher shrieks of the women who marched with them, and the reeks of sweat and raw spirit assaulted Alan as he crossed the threshold of one of the three low buildings. There visited him a small, fleeting wisp of a desire to race back to the peace of the manse and the secure kindliness of Julius's parents. This decent, vestigial instinct was wiped out by a roar of greeting from the landlord of the Inns of Claddich.

" So it's yourself, Mr. Alan Oliphant ! And it will be a gill of the best to begin with ? "

Damn this sly and brosy man for proclaiming his name and identity so loudly ! But blessings on him for the gill—good raw stuff, neat, filling the tumbler. He drank, holding his elbows close to his sides so that the uncouth drovers might not perchance spill the lovely liquor from his hand. He paid for it out of a leathern purse, and, such was the feebleness of his physical movements, anybody who cared could see that over and above copper and silver, the purse contained eight golden guineas.

A woman was watching him. She was out of Garvel. She had gone foraging in the north after the soldiers, and had taken up with the drovers coming south again. The glint of the guineas inspired her, and the naming of an Oliphant set a shrewd mind to work. With plenty of drink taken on her own part, with the proprietary arm of a drover tight about her, Joanna Baxter marked her quarry down. She was a woman of bold and striking looks—tall, high cheek-boned, light skinned, with red hair on her head and a shawl of red tartan about her shoulders.

She watched with the patience of a cat, marking how her man swallowed gill after gill, his throat and stomach revolting against the crudeness of the stuff but his appetite insatiable. She saw the daze of helplessness come over his face and into his eyes and, judging her moment to a nicety, she slipped from the drover's embrace and had Alan in her arms as, reeling with nausea, he sought to make through the crowd towards the door. Nobody, not even the drover, now benevolently drunk, had eyes or attention for such a trivial incident.

Joanna elbowed her man into the courtyard, feigning a drunkenness as abandoned as his.

" Come on, ma bonnie lad ! " she crooned to him, " come on an' we'll lay oorsels doon thegither in the byre, canty an' couthy an' warm. I'll be ye'r bit wifie for the nicht, an' ye'll no' find me blate. Come on, hinny, an' we'll bed thegither."

She might as well have been addressing an ox for all Alan Oliphant knew what was happening to him. Even within his private prison all the lights were out. He was only so much living matter, so that when Joanna slumped on a heap of dried bracken in a stall of the rude byre, he fell with her and was promptly unconscious : his handsome head comically (and tragically) pillowed on the great bosom of his snoring doxy.

In the morning he was wakened by his head, the two ears in the strong grasp of Joanna Baxter's hands, being shaken into the friable, sweet-smelling moss of the bracken. His tortured eyes sought to focus on a boldly handsome face seen for the first time. That he was in disgrace and humiliation again was his very first emotion ; and he might have had the heart to rid himself of this strange woman, her warm person so close against his, except that she thrust a bottle to his lips, cajoling him with " Drink, hinny, drink ! Here's the stuff that'll mak' ye a man again."

He drank, and the strong stuff immediately set the ethers of the night before working again, and Alan Oliphant was once more helpless, careless, reckless.

" Come on, lamb ! " the woman coaxed him, but dragging him

to his feet. " You and me are on the randan now, and there's plenty more in the bottle."

With that she picked up her petticoats to the knee and, on shapely legs, pranced through a reel of her own invention, singing as she danced :

> *A Highland lad my love was born,*
> *The Lawlan' laws he held in scorn . . .*

Alan nodded a dazed approval of her gaiety, but when she led him out into the yard and down the track towards the sea, he tried to shake himself free. Somewhere in his muddled mind was the knowledge that he ought to be heading uphill, towards the manse.

" Come on, hinny ! " the woman urged him cheerfully. " It's no' every day ye get a strappin' lass like me for your bed ! Here—anither wee sup at the bottle and we'll ha'e anither for luck down the road, and then anither and anither. You and me's on the randan, and de'il tak' the hindmost."

He was helpless against her gay vitality. Joanna took his arm and, a very strangely assorted pair, they set off down the glen as the cocks were only beginning to crow, taking the width of the road in their unsteadiness, and Joanna loud in snatches of bawdy song.

At length they came down to the sea at Ardhallow, and there at the quay lay one of the new steamboats. She was in the ownership of Mr. Mark Oliphant, and Angus Macphail, the skipper, eyed his two new passengers with concern, wondering how he might have to justify himself to a hard and proud employer. He cannily concluded that it was no affair of his, and shortly the *Prince of Orange*, touching here and there at the coastal hamlets, was on her way across the Firth to Garvel. Alan Oliphant slept all the way, his head in the crook of Joanna's arm, his shoulders wrapped in an ample corner of her red tartan shawl.

From the top of one of his paddle-boxes Angus Macphail watched the couple stagger ashore at Garvel and gyrate across the new Custom-house Quay towards the door of Lucky O'Halloran's tavern. He knew quite clearly whither Alan Oliphant was bound now, and that was to oblivion in the stinking slums of the Low Vennel, hard by the great Mark Oliphant's counting house. He wondered again, and anxiously, where his duty to his employer lay ; but when his engineer, Jock Archibald, came on deck with a hank of waste between his greasy hands, Angus pointed a finger towards Joanna Baxter and her capture and bitterly remarked :

" There's ane o' the Oliphant chickens come hame to roost."

CHAPTER FOUR

I

Sir John Wedderspoon, seventh baronet of Garvel and Gallowbrae, could read only with difficulty, but he was at pains to decipher every syllable of a report in the *Advertiser* of April 18th, 1821. His steel-rimmed spectacles down on his snub nose, his thick forefinger trembling along each line of small print, his lips dumbly shaping each word, Sir John worked down the column for the third time that afternoon :

" The 12th of April, 1821, will long remain a memorable day in the annals of Garvel. Rapid as was its advance from the obscurity of a fishing village to the consideration which belongs to one of the first sea-ports of Scotland, we trust it is destined from this day to exhibit a still more rapid progress as a manufacturing town, for which it has acquired facilities it did not before possess—and, we may add, which no place in the United Kingdom now possesses in the same eminent degree.

" To form an immense artificial lake in the bosom of the neighbouring alpine regions, and lead its liquid treasure along the mountain summits, at an elevation of more than 500 feet above the sea, till, in the immediate vicinity of the town, it should be made to pour down, a resistless torrent, in successive falls, for the impelling of machinery to a vast extent—such, in a few words, was the magnificent conception of our enlightened fellow-citizen, Mark Oliphant, Esquire, under the progressive and open-handed patronage of the Superior, Sir John Wedderspoon, Bart. ; and never, probably, did the first trial of so novel and extensive an undertaking demonstrate its capacity and entire adaptation to its purpose, or excite such unalloyed and universal gratification . . ."

The article proceeded to describe how he, Sir John, accompanied by his coadjutor in this distinguished enterprise, Mr. Mark Oliphant, embarked at the first sluices below Loch Wedderspoon (as the reservoir had been appropriately named) in a rowing boat decorated with flags, and floated along on the first tide of the stream out of the lake they had caused to be fashioned among the hills. The *Advertiser* did the occasion justice :

" The spectacle of a vessel skirting the mountain's brow, and tracking the sinuosities of the alpine chain at so great an elevation, seemed the realisation of a dream of the wildest fancy ; and the course of the boat was followed by crowds of delighted spectators. It arrived at Ewerton, in the vicinity of the town, at exactly quarter to three, where it was received with cheers and a salute of cannon."

This writing chap had made a proper job of it, Sir John reflected, making a mental note to send the fellow a bottle of wine and a boiling fowl with his compliments. It was wise to keep in with these " chiels takin' notes " as Rabbie had called them. He rose from the table and went to the window, which, overlooking the row of French guns on the terrace that were the town's trophies of the victory at Waterloo, commanded the wide prospect beyond them of the anchorage and mile upon mile of Highland peak in jagged and lovely confusion to a distance of twenty leagues away.

Sir John Wedderspoon was not interested at that moment in the beauty of pure landscape. The sprawl of Garvel at his very feet, as it were, gave him much more satisfaction. Losh ! The place had grown and was still growing. New mills over to the east there, down the line of the new waterfall. Big lands, or tenements, for the work-folk rearing their four-storey heights and their slate roofs farther and farther up the slopes, so that the Mansionhouse itself was now nearly surrounded by dwellings and, to keep the Policy decently private, he had had to plant fast-growing poplars along its inland boundary. He could not see it from his window, but Sir John thought with satisfaction of the town's extension westwards along the Kempock turnpike, one merchant after another following Mark Oliphant's example, taking a good bit of ground for the erection of a villa and not caring, so it seemed, what feu-duty or annual ground burden he must pay to the Estate. Its income had trebled in seven years. This was a better return than a landowner could ever get out of a wheen sheepfarms. This was progress.

A shrewd fellow his son-in-law, reflected Sir John Wedderspoon ; a right canny chiel. It was a great day for Garvel when the two of them had come together. Energy and property working hand in glove —there was nothing like it ! Mind you : there were moments when he, Sir John, found his son-in-law a thought trying, not to say a bit too big for his boots ; the fellow had whiles a domineering, do-what-I-tell-you kind of a way with him, and gey hot in the temper if he was crossed or had a dram inside him. Still and on, Mark Oliphant was an able man and a rare catch for the Garvel estates at this stage of affairs, just sent by Providence to be Baron-Bailie and keep those

Blacknebs and trash in order. And now, if what the women folk said was right, Mark Oliphant was going to make him a grandfather. Lavinia, now he came to think of it, must be gey near her time, though, the Lord knew, she had been long enough getting herself that way. It would be a boy. Sir John would not permit himself to think otherwise.

. . . The mother-to-be was at that moment confiding the secrets of her condition and the fears of her mind to her cousin-by-marriage, Barbara Oliphant. They sat over the tea-cups in the great florid drawing-room of the new house Mark Oliphant had built himself to the westward of the town and called Dunclutha. Herself the mother of two children now, for Walter Rait Oliphant had acquired a brother Ivie in 1820, Barbara was in the position of adviser to her kinswoman in distress.

Indeed, she was there that afternoon in response to a note from Lavinia, almost furtively delivered by the hands of a semptress who went to and from Dunclutha daily to sew garments for the new baby. Five years of marriage had neither strengthened nor matured Lavinia Wedderspoon. She was still in company the diffident, foolish, confused girl whom Mark Oliphant had chosen for his bride, much as he might have chosen a clerk for his counting house.

Considering the girl with her loose, large mouth and pale eyes and, now, grotesque figure, Barbara was sad to realise how pitiable was her position. From her mother—her person a-jangle with foolish ornaments, her mind as empty as her prattle—Lavinia could never have either understanding or support. For her father she was an object of the landscape, a bit of property, and a disappointment in not having been born male. For her husband she was—but who could tell Mark Oliphant's precise attitude to any other living creature?

She had nothing in her to help herself; she was utterly without understanding or sense or knowledge. Sentimental, she knew not the splendid agony of love and passion. Feckless, she had not even the housekeeping virtues. Lavinia Oliphant was negative, a female body now with child, and no more. Her case was pitiable to the point of tragedy.

This afternoon, her time almost upon her, she discovered herself to be for once unique. That countless millions of women before had conceived and been in labour and given birth was a fact outside her imaginative range and could therefore give her no philosophical comfort. Her timid soul was filled with physical fears.

"Ah! But that is not so very dreadful, Lavinia," Barbara assured her with a kindly laugh; adding on a little wave of French impatience:

" It is true that a first child may give a little trouble. But it is only a matter of hours, surely. One day at the most, and then you will have the child at your breast and be happier than you ever were in your life before."

" I wish it was all over," said Lavinia, but listlessly.

She sipped at her tea-cup, put it down awry in the saucer and, blushing, appealed directly to her companion.

" Will you come and be with me, Barbara, when—when it starts ? I would feel better with you near me. There's nobody . . ."

Barbara furtively but shrewdly studied the uninteresting face of her cousin-by-marriage. Its helpless vacuity touched her.

" If you wish it, Lavinia," she replied, " certainly. But have you consulted Mark—the doctor ? There are certain——"

" No ! " said Lavinia quite briskly for her. " But I don't care. It is going to be my baby, isn't it ? "

" That is so," Barbara agreed. " And if I can help you, Lavinia, I certainly will."

" There's nobody else," said Lavinia, the brief flame of independence dying within her. She concluded colourlessly : " I hope it is a boy."

" Boy or girl," Barbara was a little impatient, " it will still be your own child, will it not ? A girl baby is a great joy."

" Yes, but I was thinking of Mark. He talks about it as a boy already, arranging everything. He will be disappointed if it is a girl." She added almost casually : " You mightn't think it, Barbara, but Mark is difficult to please sometimes. But if you were there . . ."

Barbara had known exactly why her unhappy cousin must appeal to her. Without strength of her own, she must borrow from the nearest and likeliest giver. But this confession of fear and unhappiness was tragic in its listlessness. Once again she, Barbara Rait—and what could she do about it ?—was to stand between Mark Oliphant and a gentler soul. Barbara thought poignantly of Julius, then of her own mother. *Eh bien !* . . .

Meanwhile Sir John had been joined at the Mansionhouse by his son-in-law. They had dropped into the habit of an almost daily conference on their joint and engrossing affairs.

" You would see the piece in the *Advertiser* about the opening of the Water Works ? " Mark began when he and his father-in-law were settled, each with a tumbler of whisky-and-water beside him.

" I did that," said Sir John warmly. " Laurie made a guid job o't."

" Laurie knows which side his bread's buttered on," retorted Mark

dismissing as unimportant the issue of editorial independence. He drew
from the tails of his coat another sheet and, passing it across the table,
pointed to an item prominently displayed below the title. " But have
you seen this lot ? "

Sir John adjusted the steel-rimmed spectacles and peered at the
sheet, which bore the strange title of *The Cleg*. In the Scots tongue
the cleg is the horse-fly, and the journal that trembled in Sir John's
hands lived up to its name. It existed to sting and to inflame. It
was a product of its historical period, one of the scores of sheets
which, in that Age of Reform, briefly but numerously existed to express
with reckless impertinence and no great regard for accuracy the revolt
of the new industrial masses against the autocratic power of the
employers.

" But this is fair damnable ! " snorted Sir John.

" Read it," Mark commanded.

With a touch that would have passed for modern in a later age the
article was headed, " O, Oliphant ! O ! " and it started thus :

> " Lest these pearls of wisdom have escaped the lofty gaze of
> Mr. Mark Oliphant and his high-born father-in-law, The Cleg
> thoughtfully puts on record certain cogent observations dropped
> last Tuesday afternoon by Mr. Julius Oliphant at the Presentation
> of Prizes for the winter session of the Technical College endowed
> from funds acquired (we will nor inquire too closely how) by his
> family during the wars with Buonaparte. On this occasion Mr.
> J. O., not hitherto notable for any zeal for Reform, delivered
> himself to the budding Newtons and half-baked Watts of divers
> sentiments which must have uncomfortably stirred the ghost of his
> progenitor, Uncle Edward O., last tenant of The Mount, into a
> state of considerable agitation."

" Damnation ! " cried Sir John, having struggled so far. " Laurie
never prentit this in the *Advertiser*."

" Laurie knows better," said Mark curtly. " Go on."

The article proceeded to furnish a version of a speech which,
within its period and setting, would have been sensational on any pair
of lips. Julius was represented as having drawn a horrific picture of
the state of Garvel in the throes of its new industrial development. He
was quoted as referring in the face of his youthful audience to " stews
and brothels and slums "—and here *The Cleg* had cunningly inserted
an oblique and unmistakable reference to the now notorious fate of
Alan Oliphant—and to have said that the future of the town was
likely to be grimmer still unless men of rectitude and enlightenment

were prepared to come forward and guide their fellow-citizens out of the morass into which the workpeople of the place were being thrust by the rapacity of the masters. Employing a trick of journalism in advance of his time, *The Cleg* made adroit use of quotation marks :

" We do not hesitate," he proceeded, " to say that an audible shiver of astonishment passed through his audience when Mr. J. O. was heard to declare in tones of vibrant emotion : ' Not a steam-boat touches at the Customhouse Quay but brings its unhappy load of Highland or Irish peasants to labour under conditions of slavery in the mills and deepen the squalor of the warrens of the Vennel, the Rue-end and the Crossshore.' " Whereupon *The Cleg*, with the defence of printer's error always behind him, ran cheerfully on, " and it is notorious that the vast majority of the steamboats now engaged in this profitable emigrant traffic are the property of Cousin Mark, that most highly-respected citizen.' "

Sir John lowered the sheet and peered over the rims of his spectacles at his companion.

" But this is fair damnable ! " he repeated. " Dy'e believe Julius would ever talk such a feck of confounded nonsense ? "

It was a just question, and Mark knew it. He knew, perhaps more shrewdly than any other living soul, that the eponymous proprietor-printer-editor of *The Cleg* was without scruple in his bitterness of frustration. He knew that his Cousin Julius was by his very nature incapable of angry attack on anybody or anything, by his complex intelligence incapable of seeing any question from one side only and of making a pronouncement, public or private, without almost stultifying qualifications. Mark did not answer the question.

" There's too much of this damned Reform nonsense getting about ! " he exploded passionately. " We beat Boney fair and square, and now we are plagued with the very nonsense that started him off ! Do you wonder that he made himself an Emperor ? . . . That fellow Owen up at New Lanark ! Shorter hours, higher wages—and much he made of it ! A pack of weavers in Lancashire ! I'd take the lash to their backsides. . . . And now we have it here in Garvel ! It's spreading, Sir John, and it's got to be stopped. It's not just the common folk. It's not just a shopkeeper here and there. Men of the merchant class that should know better—the Crauford boys, young Tannahill, Dan Gregor's son, and now this precious cousin of mine. They have a Club—Philosophical they call it ; they say it's for ' political study.' Political my Auntie Kate ! Sheer, damned dangerous, dilettante nonsense, Sir John ! "

Mark had worked himself into such a fury that his face was flushed a deep red and the veins swelled on his neck and forehead. He banged the table so hard that his father-in-law thrust out a hasty hand to steady his glass.

" Damned rascals ! " agreed Sir John, but not passionately. " Still," he mused, " I wonder if Julius said all that *The Cleg* makes him say. Thon's a dangerous fella ! "

Mark rose from his seat. His anger had abated, but now its place was taken by the sardonic mood that, in him, was the sign of a positive decision made.

" Where there's smoke, there's fire," he observed, much as if he were throwing superior wisdom into the dull face of his father-in-law. " My distinguished cousin has said quite enough for me. The Oliphants have a name in this town, Sir John, and not a little property, and I'm not the man to stand by and let one of the name throw mud at it or lower the value of the property. My steamboats are bringing vagrants to the town, are they ? " His anger was rising again. " Bringing the Irish and the Highlanders into conditions of slavery, by God ! We'll soon put a stopper on that sort of nonsense."

Leaving his father-in-law with little ceremony, Mark stalked down the hill to his counting house. There, waiting for him in his room, was Julius, pale and clearly on edge. The sight of his cousin took Mark considerably aback, but it was his way to meet a contretemps of the kind by passing immediately to the offensive.

" You here ? " was his first rough thrust. He was angry that, late in the evening, there had been nobody in the front office to warn him of a visitor. " I suppose you've come to try to explain this ? "

He threw his copy of *The Cleg* on the desk before Julius, and Julius nodded miserably.

" Yes, Mark," he said, " if you think it needs explanation. As it stands, the thing is damnable—offensive to you to a degree— monstrously upsetting on all counts. I am bitterly sorry, Mark, that anything I may have said in public should be open to this abominable construction. I only ask you to believe that the thing is a hideous parody of what I did say on a special occasion, that more than half of it is wicked invention—political prejudice put into my mouth by a wicked man—and that the reference to you and your business is one that I would never make. I have more respect for the family name and, if you will let me say so, for you personally."

The unhappy dignity of Julius's speech was not altogether lost on Mark. That was indeed, in Mark's view, the confounded thing about this cousin of his. The damned fellow was so gentle and reasonable, and no coward at that ; and that made a practical man angrier than ever. He lashed out again at the spectre which so greatly irked his inner conscience.

"That's a fine speech ! It's a pity, Julius, you couldn't take the same care when you are spouting for the Blacknebs—bawling at Tom, Dick and Harry to go out and burn the town about our ears, or as near that as makes no odds."

"That is unreasonable, Mark, and unfair," said Julius sharply. "I have my convictions. I must honestly believe that this town is developing too rapidly. I think that wise government would try to control the flow of immigrants or plan, at least, to give them decent accommodation before they are brought in. I think that we are heaping up trouble for ourselves—precisely the sort of trouble which you, Mark, when you jeer at Blacknebs, fear most of all. All that I believe profoundly ; all that I feel bound to say, whether in public or private. But I do not associate, and never have associated, and never will associate, your name or interests with my personal convictions. If a blackguardedly scribbler does so, with most obvious malice, I am sorry ; and I apologise for any sentences of mine that may have been less carefully shaped than I intended."

"Words !" snarled Mark. "Too many damned words !"

"I offer you my apology," Julius insisted. "Mark—you know very well that I, of all people, would never seek to injure you."

"This isn't the finish of the business. What you say is all very well. But . . . Oh, to hell ! There's the door. I've had enough for one day."

In the very act of making this angry gesture, one which he knew to be abrupt and unreasonable, Mark was conscious of the appeal in Julius's gaze. It was an appeal to reason—and be damned to that sort of reason ! Deliberately he drove the appeal from his consciousness. He reached out for a pencil and drew some papers under his eyes. He did not even look up to see the back of an unhappy man pass out through the door. But when he heard the outer door of the counting house close behind his cousin, and his footsteps, loud in the silence of the growing night, pass round the corner and up the hill towards Goldenhaddock, he was aware of frustration and, though this he could never phrase, of what less vehement men might call defeat.

He reacted in terms of anger, the black anger like a form of drunkenness that was always the devil on his back. When he heard the front door of the counting house open again he bawled on the new arrival to come in and face his wrath.

A fair boy of some fourteen years with a sensitive face appeared, apprehensive, before him.

"And where the devil have you been?" Mark growled at the child.

"To the Buck's Head, sir," piped the boy, "with the London mail, sir—to put it on the coach, sir."

"And leave the counting house empty for every Tom, Dick and Harry . . ."

"Mr. Julius was here, sir," the innocent treble explained. "He said he would wait, sir, and watch the counting house for me. I thought . . ."

"You're not employed here to think. I'll do all the thinking that's wanted."

Mark was now in the mood to play with weakness, that quality he could not abide.

"I suppose you want to go home for your supper?"

"Yes, sir."

"Aye! Well, you can take the long way round for it. Away down to the West Breast and tell Hannah the printer I want him here at once."

"*The Cleg*, sir?" The boy was suddenly eager.

"Mind your own business and do what you are told. Hannah— and quick about it!"

When the boy was gone, Mark drew a blank sheet of foolscap before him, seized a quill from the sheaf in the pewter holder on his table, dipped it thoughtfully in his pewter inkwell, and started to write. He wrote slowly, frowning as he worked, but soon the pen was moving fluently enough through the bold capitals and the decisive down-strokes that characterised his hand of write. It was not a long piece; and when it was finished Mark held it up to read; and, reading it, he smiled. His quill fell on the paper again to make a few deletions and alterations, and even as he was dredging the sand over the wet ink, the boy knocked to announce that Hannah the printer awaited his pleasure in the passage without.

In the flesh The Cleg was an elderly, skinny, shuffling man with a tilted shoulder and a pale, weasel-like face. He was garbed in the old-fashioned way in a long coat and knee-breeches of rough brown cloth with sagging worsted stockings. There were dark stains of snuff about his nose and mouth and on his greasy waistcoat. So far from suggesting the buzzing vitality of the horse-fly, the creature's person spoke of poverty and meanness, cowardice and slyness all at once.

"Aye, aye, Hannah!" Mark greeted the man with dangerous joviality and in the doric speech. "I see ye've ta'en into your head to have a go at the Oliphants. I suppose The Cleg maun aye be stinging."

"Just in the way of business, sir, just in the way of business," the printer grinned uneasily, revealing toothless gums.

"Just so, just so ! " Mark agreed cordially. " A body maun live. But, man ! Ye're awfu' backward wi' your information. If it's a right slap at the Oliphants ye're after ye shouldna' thriep on a wheen Hielanders and Irish using the steamboats. Cast your eye on this."

He tossed the sheet of foolscap across the table to the printer, who had to hold even that bold writing close to his red-rimmed eyes. The pantaloon's shoulders began to shake with delight, and he even cackled.

"Hot, sir, hot ! And a very bonny retort to his lordship, if ye'll allow me, sir. A wee bit of dressing up the The Cleg's ain way, and this'll make a column of the best."

"These are your facts," said Mark curtly ; then, relaxing again : " Things will be a bit slow in the printing line these days ? *The Cleg*'ll no' be making your fortune, man ? "

"Juist so, juist so ! " the old man piped. " Strugglin' awa', sir, juist struggling awa'."

"That's bad," Mark observed. " Well, there's a bit subscription to your news-sheet. Between you and me, you understand ? Good ! And that'll do for to-day."

Mark drew from his fob and tossed across the table a couple of golden guineas. A dirty claw clutched at them then touched an obsequious head, and the printer bowed himself out backwards.

The next issue of *The Cleg* appeared with remarkable prompitude. It was a joke in Garvel that, like the insect from which it took its name, the sheet came out only on fine days. The wits looked for it to be available about noon each Friday, but none was surprised if it made a sluggish appearance on the Saturday morning. Now, for the first time, it anticipated its due date of publication, and by four o'clock on the Thursday afternoon a copy lay on Mark Oliphant's table, another on the raised desk at which Julius had been working on a set of drawings.

Why Hannah the printer was so eager to publish was not hard to guess. It was a choice morsel of spice he had ready for his readers. Excelling his effort of the week before, advancing far ahead of any of his contemporaries, he had a headline in black type spread across the width of his front page :

O, O, O ! OUR OLIPHANTS AGAIN ! O, O, O !

Under this The Cleg opened with a characteristic flourish :

" *Quis custodiet.*—The Cleg begs to ask with the ancient scribe —*quis custodiet ipsos custodes* ? Or, in the homelier vernacular, can the pot afford to call the kettle black ?

" The Cleg's faithful readers will readily call to mind that, on his last hebdomadal appearance, he drew the attention of his fellow-citizens to certain remarks dropped by Mr. Julius Oliphant at the recent Presentation of Prizes at the Technical College, of which the youthful *alumni* are the dearest of his spiritual children. Lest it has escaped the attention of any who have the cause of Reform at heart, The Cleg has pleasure in rehearsing the gist of that remarkable oration."

What followed was more than the gist of the previous report. It was a cunning elaboration thereof. Mark's name had disappeared from the story : The Cleg had cleverly slewed the finger of ridicule to point directly at Julius. Then he proceeded triumphantly :

" In the eyes of any fair-minded reader it must be obvious that the eloquent boatbuilder (now self-styled ' shipbuilder,' so large have we grown within a decade !) was, with a degree of loyalty The Cleg does not take it upon himself to assess, directing the finger of scorn towards an enterprising member of his own family, who, not without success, has been notoriously responsible for setting up a useful and inexpensive traffic of steamboats on the Firth. As to that, The Cleg refrains from taking sides. He does, however, ask if Mr. J. O. has ever troubled to look for the mote in his own eye ; and that for the reasons herewith appended.

" The eyes of The Cleg are everywhere, and it has not escaped his notice that the ship *Pladda* (Capt. Crombie), the property of the aforesaid Mr. Julius Oliphant and his brother-in-law, Captain Robert Rait, is now at sea, bound for Halifax, Nova Scotia, with, on board, some 120 souls, men, women and children, evicted in circumstances of the most cynical cruelty from Ross-shire and certain of the Outer Isles.

" The facts, susceptible of copious and unimpeachable proof, are that the vessel anchored off Stornoway on March 18th this year, and embarked 77 souls, many of them aged and enfeebled persons, of the Tolsta district, driven off their ancestral holdings by the rapacity of the landlord and his hireling agents. On March 27th— the hapless victims being meanwhile confined in the ship's hold in the most miserable conditions—the *Pladda* weighed anchor and, two days later, put into Loch Broom, there taking on board some 50 creatures (the term is not too extreme) uprooted in conditions of the most grievous hardship from their hearths and homes on the Dundonnell Estates. On the 31st day of March the vessel set sail for North America.

"The conditions prevailing on board these emigrant ships need no description here. Like the sheep that are to take their places on the Highland hills, the hapless victims of brutal landlordism are literally herded below decks in conditions of which the merest sketch would be offensive to any polite understanding. Whither they go, to what drear fate on foreign shore, they know not. How much less fortunate those exiles than the handful of Irish and Highlanders who, assured of a reasonable livelihood in an expanding community, seek of their own free will a place by our hospitable hearth?

"To sum up. The Cleg, arch-and-sworn enemy of hypocrisy in high places, puts his question to Mr. Julius Oliphant direct. If the aforesaid Mr. J. O. can on one day rend our hearts with the plight of a few immigrants into our civilised town, and the next banishes scores of his hapless fellow creatures to a mysterious fate— *Quis custodiet ipsos custodes?*"

A feeling of physical sickness came over Julius as he read. When he was done, he stood for a long time staring blankly at the pink paper. Miserably he reflected that this charge might, after all, be well-founded; he was guilty of having left the shipping side of the business entirely to Bob Rait. Not that Bob could be thought of as having allowed an Oliphant ship to be used for such a traffic. But could he not? Cargoes were scarce in these days of post-war disturbance.

His eyes downcast and bareheaded in spite of the spring rain that was now falling heavily, Julius passed out of his drawing-office and across the yard to the old office building. He found his brother-in-law busy checking a list of stores with the supercargo of the *Pladda's* sister-ship *Ulva*.

"Bob," he interrupted them. "Where is the *Pladda* just now?"

"The *Pladda*? I couldn't tell you," answered Bob, looking up from his papers. "She has been on charter to Fullarton of Irvine these six months past. He had her bound for the St. Lawrence the last I heard. She's maybe not out of the ice yet."

"We have no control over her movements?"

"None whatever!" cried Bob, laughing at his cousin's vagueness. "Why do you ask?"

"Nothing," said Julius listlessly. "We'll have a word later."

He returned to his drawings, but he could not work. His mind and

eyes kept losing focus and peering beyond the lines and emblems so
fairly drawn on the thick paper into a world of misery. He was unhappy, and unhappy he had to remain, for it was not in his gentle
spirit to shift the blame for this humiliation on to other shoulders.
It did not even comfort him that he was technically innocent of a sin
he abhorred.

The satisfaction with which Mark perused The Cleg's effusion was
not so profound as Julius's distress. He chuckled as he read the piece,
admiring at once the printer's extravagance of phrase and his own
power to command such a forceful pen. For the rest, however, it was
no more than a bit of business neatly executed ; a stopper on a lot of
confounded nonsense and a shifting of public attention from certain
commercial matters that were none of the public's concern. Mark
tossed the sheet aside, promising himself a thorough reading of it later
on. Meanwhile, there was work to be done over a batch of reports
from his agents in the West Indies, and—he remembered again—the
onset of Lavinia's pains had taken place at noon. The rest of the day
would be full.

It was after six before his work was done. He stood for a while
at his window and saw that the rain had ceased ; no need to call out
the carriage he had set up to go with the consequence of Dunclutha,
though it was one of his most profound pleasures to pass in it like a
lord through the streets of the town. This was an evening for a
reflective walk home : a sort of showing of the flag by a man of
position about to be a father.

Mark felt positively benevolent towards the world as he stepped from
the counting-house door, but he had hardly gone five paces when a
young man suddenly appeared to block his path.

" Sir," said this youth in a loud voice. " You are a blackguard
and a cowardly knave ! "

Mark stared at his surprising interlocutor. He looked into a face
handsome beyond the ordinary in an almost girlish way : a fine and
sensitive face prettily flushed with excitement and emotion and, if
Mark had had the eyes to see it, strangely pathetic in its tilt of gallant
and hopeless loyalty. The boy, for he was little more than that, was
the youngest of the Craufords of Kilblain, and Mark knew him to be
one of those new, foppish, dilettante young fools who followed Julius
in this dangerous business of so-called Reform.

" Say that again," growled Mark dangerously.

" With pleasure ! You are, sir, a blackguard and a cowardly knave,
and you will be branded throughout the town as such," the youth
maintained. He went on hurriedly, stammering slightly over the
phrases of a charge that had clearly been rehearsed. " You inspired

that dastardly attack on Julius's honour in *The Cleg*. I saw that rascal Hannah slinking from your office this night a week past. He has been seen by some of us this afternoon, and he doesn't deny it, for he can't. Neither can you, sir. For a guinea or two you persuaded this hypocrite to perjure himself and you—yes, you, sir !—for you know very well that the *Pladda* is on charter. You malign your cousin, one of the finest men . . ."

The young man's dignified periods began to falter, and Mark observed that the high, clear, indignant voice was causing passers-by to stop and stare.

"And what do you propose to do about it, you booby ? " he asked, forcing a sardonic laugh.

" If Julius does not call you out, I shall ! "

At this gallant challenge Mark acted swiftly. A thrust of his heavy shoulders sent the youth staggering backwards among the miry dubs that had gathered, rain upon sewage, in the gutters of the square.

" Get out of my sight before I take my cane across your back," he snarled and passed on his way.

He walked westwards with deliberation and dignity, outwardly the very exemplar of a solid merchant whose decency has been most outrageously offended. Within, however, he seethed with the old, black anger. Damned rascals ! Misguided idiots ! A generation of interfering fools ! All the way up the road by Kilblain and along the Kempock turnpike Mark thought of retorts that should have been made to young Crauford, physical lessons he should have taught him there and then in the publicity of the square ; and he took a bitter pleasure in thinking out new moves in the battle. But he knew, however uneasily, that the walls of his private fortress had been breached, and that a dark and ominous cloud was upon him.

So deeply was he involved in these sombre and private thoughts, it was not until he had set foot on the lowest of the fine flight of steps leading up to the main door of the new house that he raised his eyes to see, standing there, the slight but intense figure of Aunt Sophie. Her arms, akimbo, were bare to above the elbows ; she wore an apron ; over her left shoulder was a towel.

" What the devil are you doing here ? " he asked, genuinely baffled by this apparition on his doorstep.

" I attend your wife in her confinement," said Aunt Sophie, holding him at length. " If you will employ for such an occasion that Dr. Cameron who is in his dotage ; if you entrust such a case to a midwife who is a drunken fool. . . . *Alors*, it becomes a matter for persons of experience. My daughter Barbara was with Lavinia, *bien entendu*, but she also is without sufficient experience ; and therefore, the case being of some difficulty, she sends for me, who understand these affairs. *C'est bien fait.*"

All this Aunt Sophie rattled off at high speed but with supreme composure. Then she stretched out a hand, adding :

" Now I congratulate you, Mark, on the birth of a fine son."

As he had dealt with young Crauford, so Mark ignored the hand and shouldered his way past this vain and aggravating woman into his own house. It seemed to him that Julius's damned friends were everywhere, even biting deep into the most cherished acres of his private property.

2

The heat of the summer afternoon was tempered by a breeze from the south and west. The rippled surface of the Firth was of a passionate blue, blending with the green and gold of hill and island and with the lighter, serene blue of the nearly cloudless sky to make a colour pattern more dazzling than any peacock's tail. In this enchanted light of the North the sails of yachts were points of white fire against the water's blue, and the tall, brightly-painted funnels of the steamboats, even the feathers of smoke they trailed, added their happy notes to the chorus of colour.

Barbara Oliphant found her eyes more often on the splendid scene than on the fine bit of needlework in her hands. She was conscious of being happy, her mind filled and soothed by beauty, and conscious too of the rare human happiness of being carefree to enjoy it. But such a day of glory could not wait and must be enjoyed through every minute of each hour until sunset ; for if there might be others like it in summers to come, there could never be another with the same completeness of perfection ; and Barbara was now mature enough to know, with that little, not unpleasurable sinking of the heart which is fate's intimation of a middle period reached, that never again might she be in a mood so completely receptive of beauty, so willing to surrender utterly to it.

And still she was supremely aware that even her own inherited mental trick of analysis could not break down the solid fabric of her present happiness. There was so much to be happy about, to be thankful for. Her very physical position, at her ease in a garden of a villa overlooking the Firth, was in itself a milestone on the slow and difficult road to happiness. Herself and Julius and her children the guests of Mark and Lavinia and their children in Mark's new villa at

the Coast ! It was all very different from the early years of separation
and conflict. Time was the healer indeed. They were all older, more
mature, perhaps wiser—Mark and Julius, Lavinia and herself alike—
but were they happier ? Barbara, her eyes but dreamily focused on
the white patch made by the washed walls of a farm-steading against
the golden flank of a hill six miles away across the water, reflected that
life for a woman is at its happiest when her children are developing
out of infancy, and she herself has learned patience and discarded
vanity, and has still the grace of body and the youthfulness of mind to
hold a husband's passionate devotion. Not youth ; that was the hour,
though bright, of folly and regret and wildness and pain. Far better
this placid noon of satisfaction and so-willing service.

 She glanced up the slope of the rough lawn out of which a small
terrace had been cut to take the garden seat whereon she lounged ;
and there he was still—her first-born, Walter. He sat on a rough bench
that his Uncle Mark had had built round the bole of a venerable beech.
He was still deep in his book, a work on botany. So like his father
in his capacity to be absorbed in technical study. He was going to be
a doctor : his own firm decision. Already he was acting apprentice
to Mr. Broadfoot, the new young surgeon who had come to Garvel
when old Dr. Cameron had died. In the autumn he would be going
to college in Edinburgh. That raised a host of small problems in
Barbara's mind—his body clothes, his lodgings, his allowances in
money—but she thrust them out of it. Dear Walter ! So like his
father, too, in his quietness and sweetness, but with always the hard
core of detachment in those who study to understand perfectly and do
not find it easy. Yet like her own people, the Raits, in his darkness
and slimness. Even finer than his father . . . Dear Walter ! Seventeen
past now. So long ago since her own body had been racked in agony
to let him come into the world.

She could hear the voices of Lavinia and the three younger children
at their games among the whins on the lower slopes of the estate. Lavinia
was still a dull woman by adult standards, and a dull woman she must
always be. But Lavinia was kind, and good with children, and Lavinia
was a happier woman now, strengthened by motherhood. Listen to
the laughter of the infants as she led them at their play, herself an
infant ! There was no pleasanter sound in all the world.

Time was the healer. It was strange that only two children had
been born to each of the cousins—her own Walter, and then Ivie,
still a fair-haired boy ; and Lavinia's John and Edward. It might
be that the bitterness had gone out of the relationship between the
parents just because they had come to see that the future was with the
young. Even Mark had mellowed beyond belief in at least his im-

mediate dealings with other human beings. Barbara smiled to think
that he was now quite reconciled to Reform and almost approved the
new Act for confining the voting right to persons of property ; and
she guessed that Mark could see himself as a future Member for Garvel.
He did not seem to care that his office of Baron-Bailie was gone, for
Sir John was dead. No doubt he was recompensed by seeing himself a
future Provost of the town.

The click of a latch brought her head round to see the two men
enter the garden by a side-gate off the old farm-track up the hillside.
They seemed to be deep in grave and confidential talk. It would be
about boats, for they had gone down to the Yacht Clubhouse to meet
the famous English gentleman, Mr. Assheton Smith, reputed to be
thinking of placing an order for a new yacht, though he must already
possess a fleet as large as his renowned stable of hunters. She could
see the eager eloquence of Julius's hands sketching his beloved curves
in the air, dear creature !

Mark was the first to look up at her with a smile and salute her
with a sweep of his fawn beaver hat.

" Enjoying the sunshine, Barbara ? " he asked cordially.

" And the view, so perfect on such a day ! Yes, Mark, you chose
the site of your new villa very cleverly."

" I think I did not too badly," he replied with satisfaction.

Mark looked up the slope to the new house crowning the eminence.
It was, though perfectly in the taste of the period, a squat, square
building as ugly as any fortalice its architect may have copied. At
each corner was an irrelevant tower, and the flat, harled wall between
these protuberances was broken only by a few tall windows in the
pointed gothic manner. The roof was flat, with a crenellated parapet
right round. Mark had given this house the fine name of Mount
Oliphant.

" Why don't you persuade Julius to build you a house at the
Coast ? " asked Mark seriously. " Look ! Only an hour by steamboat
from Garvel yet we might be a hundred miles away, and safe on an
island the riff-raff can never reach. You have the sea-bathing at the
door, clean air, glorious prospects . . ."

" Barbara and I have to leave those luxuries to you men of wealth,
Mark ! " Julius interrupted his cousin with a friendly laugh.

" I don't know about that," returned Mark slowly. " I don't know
about that. This Coast is going to develop, and begging your leave,
Julius, thanks to the steamboat. I said something just now about the
common people, but the day will come when they will have their
fling. Big developments, Julius. You'll see these little coastwise
hamlets growing into towns, built on pleasure. You'll see villas spring

up on every decent bit of shore and hillside for fifty miles down the Firth. You'll see steamboat competition up and down the River such as we daren't dream of yet. Yes, and I tell you that a man of foresight, with even only a little cash to spare, could lay here and now the foundations of a tidy fortune ! "

" And I haven't even a little cash to spare ! " Julius laughed again. " And it's no use talking to me, Mark, along these lines, sound as I know your judgment to be. I can never think that way. All I care is that you villa-folk may want a pretty yacht built now and again—a sailing-yacht, Mark !—and then I'll give them what they want. Lovely yachts . . ."

Mark stared out across the Firth. He was interested.

" Yes. I'll grant you that, Julius," he said. " There will always be a market for the sailing yacht on these waters—if you have, first, the wealth to have them built and to sail them. You've got hold of something there, Julius."

" Listen to that, Babs ! " cried Julius happily. " I've had one commercial idea that Mark thinks well of ! Come, Mark—it is only fair—give me my first order for a fine yacht, even if you are a steamboat man. It will be a very lovely thing, I assure you."

" Well," grinned Mark amiably, " I'll think of it."

" I'll start designing it now ! "

A pleasant jest between these two, thought Barbara, busy again over her tambours. Mark left them to cross the grass to where Walter was still deep in his book ; Mark had always had a queer, sneaking affection and admiration for his dark nephew. And now Julius, as absorbed as Walter in his botany, had produced a pencil and the sketch-book he always carried and, with those light strokes in which the natural draughtsman works, was sketching the lines of the dream-yacht he would build for such a man of substance as his cousin, Mark Oliphant.

Barbara watched him carefully. This was the happiest Julius she knew, the artist lost in the delight of free creation, selfless. The spectacle gave her both pleasure and satisfaction but brought her also a little shiver of apprehension, for it always reminded her that if to watch over him was a privilege, it was a responsibility as well. He was so careless of his gifts, the face intent over the sketch-book was so much that of a boy.

The little island of silence they shared was suddenly invaded by the younger children, surging uphill from their play, with Lavinia flushed and panting behind them. The infants crowded upon Julius, father and uncle, for he was their hero and favourite, a magician with a pencil in the creation of lovely boats. He had tried to teach them the rigs of the sailing types, and it was a grave business sketching for these boys, for stolid young John invariably demanded a ship, full-rigged and every bit of canvas to the dizziest skysail drawing tautly, while little Ivie had a mysterious devotion to the topsail schooner.

Julius was still working to please them all when a bell ringing from the terrace before the house called the children to supper and Lavinia drove them uphill before her in a race to the table. Mark and Walter strolled across to make four on and about the garden seat.

" And how about that yacht of mine, Julius ? " asked Mark.

" Where is it now ? Those infants interrupted me. Ah, here ! " Julius found the loose sheet and handed it to his cousin, who studied it thoughtfully.

" Yes. That is pretty, Julius. Very pretty. But what," he added archly, " what if I choose to insist on a steam yacht ? "

" Ah, that would be quite a different problem ! " returned Julius eagerly. " And a fascinating one. Indeed, I've been studying it, although I'm no steamboat man. See, Mark——"

The restless pencil hovered over a fresh sheet of paper. Barbara watched the two men from under lowered eyebrows.

" The lines of the sailing yacht are fined away forward, but the keel is deep and heavy and well aft ; and that, of course, is to hold her against the wind, for I am assuming a great spread of canvas and a tall mast. That, however, does not arise with the power-driven vessel. And let me say at once, Mark, that my steam yacht—if you can imagine me designing one—will be driven by a screw."

" A screw ? " asked Mark quite sharply. Barbara saw his eyebrows lift with interest.

" Oh, yes ! " Julius dismissed the subtleties of a question most bitterly debated at the time. " I have gone into all that. The paddle is a primitive instrument. But it is more to my point that the screw will allow of a finer line in the steamboat's hull. It will allow you, in short, even with your noisy engines—even with your clumsy smokestack —to build what truly can be described as a yacht—thus—and thus, Beauty, Mark ! Beauty . . ."

A stroke of the pencil punctuated each of his vehement phrases, and Barbara saw growing under her husband's hand the sketch of something fine, something that satisfied her wholly non-technical eye as having the perfection of fitness for a given purpose. She also saw, with clarity, that Mark was excited and, at the same time, determined not to let the fact be known.

" Beauty ! " he laughed. " Don't talk to a plain Scots merchant except in terms of good hard cash ! You work away at your bit sketches, Julius," he added with a rather too-gusty jocularity. " Watty and I are going up to look at some of those books I kept out of Uncle Edward's library."

Julius hardly acknowledged this address. He was lost in his new set of sketches. He was absorbed, happy. A little whisper of warning was on the tip of Barbara's tongue, but the spectacle of his happy absorption checked the impulse. It would have been like snatching his toy from an innocent, rapt child.

She gathered her needlework and snapped it within a large bag of black satin, elaborately embroidered. She rose to her feet and stood watching her husband for a space of seconds.

" I think I shall go up to the house now, dear," she said.

" Yes, my sweetheart," he agreed with charming but distant friendliness. " This is a most interesting problem Mark has set me. The application of power from two quite different angles—angles in the dynamic sense, as distinct from sources. Most interesting . . ."

She left him to his devices. An hour later, the young children being made ready for bed, Walter had to be sent out to bring his father to Mark's formal supper table. It was heavily laden, that table, and abundantly provided with wines. Mark took this domestic rite with some solemnity.

." Your pardon, Lavinia ! " cried Julius happily, bustling into the room. " But this husband of yours set me a pretty problem, and I'm afraid I went wool-gathering."

As he passed to his place beside his hostess he tossed on to the mantelpiece a little sheaf of papers. Barbara noted the action, and her watchful eyes saw that Mark also had not failed to observe the small motion's significance. Mark was frowning. He lowered his head with some ostentation and proceeded to intone the Grace :

" O bountiful Jehovah ! For thy grace and infinite mercies . . ."

The repast and the talk across the table were as they might have been in any other prosperous house in time of family holiday, but this particular occasion held for Barbara its own special quality of excitement and suspense. With a profound sense of realism she knew herself to be engaged once again in a duel with Mark, and the subtlety of the encounter was not unpleasing. The nice estimation of its possibilities was indeed a delight to a mind fundamentally ironic except over just a small range of personal concerns. She enjoyed every nuance of the supper-table talk and, a little maliciously, took pains to address herself to Mark in such terms of intellectual equality as she knew him to loathe as coming from a woman. Poor Lavinia—Barbara reflected while Julius was in full flight on the possibilities of the balloon and the flying-machine : a subject which he declared in the face of Mark's '" Fiddlesticks ! " and " Nonsense ! " to be worthy of at least speculative study. . . . Poor Lavinia, her indifferent looks apart, was Mark's idea of what a woman should be : ready to love, honour and obey, to be used as the impulse demanded, and to leave masculine affairs to men. In the same moment of reflection Barbara made her own cool appreciation of the physical moves in the contest she saw approaching.

The moment had come when the last dish of dried fruits had been pushed aside and Julius had declined a glass of Madeira.

" No wine, to-night, Mark ! " he declared cheerfully. " You and Walter and I must keep our heads clear for this great night of cod-fishing in the Bay. I told Mackenzie we would be down by half-six ; he'll have the boat and the tackle ready ? Coming, Walter ? "

Father and son rose from the table with formal bows towards Lavinia, and at that moment childish voices from the back of the house called her to come and hear their prayers. Barbara said, as her hostess hurried from the room :

" I shall be with you in a minute, Lavinia."

Mark said to Julius :

" A moment to finish my wine, Julius, and I'll follow you down the hill."

This was the critical passage, and Barbara was enjoying its excitement. But it was too like using a long, sharp rapier against a fool with a knuckleduster ! She could wait. Could he excuse himself from going ?

Mark's capitulation was more energetic than graceful. The table-cloth was swept awry and a glass fell over as he rose from his place, his handsome face coarse with peevishness.

" By your leave, Barbara ! " he muttered.

" Certainly, Mark ! " she answered cheerfully. " I do hope it will be a pleasant night on the Bay."

Mark took two paces from his chair to the mantelpiece. He thrust his hands into his pockets. He seemed to study with a sort of acidulous indifference the sketches Julius had left lying there, but Barbara saw how his head tilted sideways and his eyebrows came down as he conned the sheets. It was even more important that he took his left hand out of his pocket and separated the three or four pages of drawings Julius had left lying there, spreading them along the mantelpiece. She watched the minute hand of the ormulu clock at Mark's elbow move from twenty-one to twenty-four minutes past the hour. Then Mark turned to her with a distant smile.

" It's a pity Julius must go back to Garvel to-morrow," he said. " But I must hurry after them."

He went away, quietly closing the door behind him. Barbara

heard the happy children still calling to her to come and say good-night in a last riot of fun. She rose from her watchman's seat and turned to the mantelpiece.

It was as she had anticipated. Julius had covered five sheets of his squared paper with sketches and drawing, each in its delicate neatness as characteristic of his personality as his smile. The first sheet was covered with free sketches of a ship under steam afloat, as it might be the imaginative fancy of a gifted boy. On a second sheet the artist turned professional, the outline of the ideal hull both under and above water exquisitely limned. The third set of plans became thoroughly technical; and on these the form of the dream-yacht was set out in elevation and cross-section, down to the details of the water-lines. There was a careful, loving note of the deck-plan, then an imaginative longitudinal section of the living ship, all its departments and amenities described in detail. The last sheet was covered with figures, calculations and small drawings in illustration thereof.

All this,' Barbara reflected with rueful affection, was Julius at work, Julius intense in the preoccupation of the moment, then spilling the results for all to see. She gathered the sheets of paper, folded them, and slipped the lot into her work-bag. When the fishermen came back late in the evening, she waited with Lavinia in the dining-room to offer them a cold supper, and she saw that, as Mark entered, he glanced at the mantelpiece and was puzzled and annoyed to see nothing there.

3

The smell of Garvel in the summer heat drifted offshore to sicken Julius even before the steamboat had touched at the Customhouse Quay. It was mainly the smell of sewage, rottenly suspended in windless waters, unmoved by sluggish tides. The sharp industrial odours from the tanworks and the kippering sheds were in the air, but the burden of the stench was cloacal. It brought into Julius's mind a revolting panorama of open sewers, clotted privies in back courts, cabbage water, rotten woodwork, bugs, rats and booze. This was the smell of Garvel, the home of the new wealth in its early development, this smell of premature death and decay. Julius was suddenly sick and ashamed, angry at his own incapacity to sweep the horror away. The perfection of the hot summer sunlight illuminating such a scene of degradation was an intolerable mockery. He thought bitterly of the privileged assumptions whereby such as Mark, whereby he himself and their people, could at any moment escape into the breezy freshness of the outer Firth.

The impact of this impression was portentous somehow, and it even seemed inevitable that Bob Rait should be waiting for him on the quay, his demeanour that of one burdened with ill news.

" What's wrong, Bob ? " Julius asked at once.

" Alan Oliphant—he's gone at last," said Bob, adding bitterly, " It's always left to you and me to clean up after the poor devil."

" Dead ? Poor Alan ! How ? "

They started to walk slowly past the mass of the great new Custom-house.

" It was yesterday afternoon," Bob explained. " That woman of his, Baxter, sent the red-headed boy with a message. . . . I suppose he's Alan's son, that one."

" I suppose so," agreed Julius lugubriously.

" It was you he was looking for, but I got hold of the doctor and hurried down to that place in the Low Vennel. God, what a hole ! I never saw or smelt the like of it in all my travels. And there the poor devil was, lying in a filthy bed in the corner, and that Baxter bitch, as drunk as a fiddler, rocking in a chair with a shawl over her head. It was no use. Drink and congestion of the lungs, the doctor said. He didn't say a word. I got a kind of a shake of the head and a roll of the eyes out of him, but he just dovered away. It would be about six o'clock he died."

" Poor Alan ! "

" So there was nothing for it," Bob resumed, " but to get Jock Simpson the wright in. I went along with him and his man in the evening, and you should have seen the place ! That besom had all her cronies in and a cargo of booze, and they were having a proper wake of it, skirling and singing, and poor old Alan lying there, not caring."

" Was the boy there all the time ? " asked Julius sharply.

" I suppose he was. Damn my eyes, Julius, I hadn't the sense to look ! The fact is, I was so blazing angry and sick, I just wanted to clear that trash out the way and let Simpson get on with his work. I had them skeedaddling in double-quick time, I tell you ! I suppose they just went down to Lucky O'Halloran's and went on with their boozing."

" Yes, I suppose so," agreed Julius emptily, appalled by this sketch of the death of an Oliphant.

" Just one thing, Julius," added Bob apologetically. " I fixed the burial for this afternoon. It looked to me . . . This hot weather ; the filth of that place . . . And is there anybody but you and me "—he asked in a burst of defiance—" to care a tinker's curse what happens to Alan Oliphant ? I wish to God our friend Mark would come and help to bury his dead ! "

." Mark could hardly know," observed Julius gently. " But I suppose we had better go up."

They had come to the tenement in the Low Vennel where one of the proud Oliphants had passed in liquor and degradation to death. Bob led the way under an archway to the back of the building. There a doorway in the base of a sort of built-on turret gave access to a turnpike stairway, narrow, dark and winding upwards like a corkscrew. The worn treads were of rotten wood. Even through the mirk Julius could discern the black mystery of rat-holes in the skirting. This dark well was thick with the Garvel stink, as it were clotted with solid filth in suspension. He could not help thinking of the passage of this dead stuff through his nostrils into his lungs ; he felt his body-clothes crepitating on his skin.

The home and death-chamber of Alan Oliphant was a single room of some twelve feet square. It was furnished with a dresser, a bare table, a bed and, in the window alcove, a metal ewer in a frame of wood. On a chair before the fire, one elbow on the table and a black bottle at her elbow, sat Joanna Baxter. Hers was a shrouded figure, mysterious in a dark green tartan shawl that hid most of her face. Only the stare of her eyes above its edge greeted the visitors ; a small sideways jerk of the head drew their attention to the coffin on the bed.

To Julius the face of the dead man seemed that of a stranger. It did not move him to personal sorrow. This was the Alan Oliphant he had once known, but older, coarser and puffier about the features, with an unkempt grey moustache. It was the face of an ageing toper, and pathetic only as a monument of waste. Julius found himself pondering the strangeness of it all—how this man had lapsed utterly into degradation but had yet kept aloof, hardly seen by his relatives about the public streets of a small town, completely absorbed in another life. And they had let him stew . . .

Julius thought of the money and wondered what, if anything, was left of Alan's fortune. He turned to the woman in the chair.

" He's awa'," she said thickly and dully. " He was no' a bad ane."

" No, he was not a bad one," Julius agreed gently. " But we'll have to be seeing about the funeral. Captain Rait has arranged all that. This afternoon, if it would suit you."

" Aye, tak' him awa', tak' him awa'," Joanna Baxter agreed. " Let the puir body hae a bit rest."·

.A nudge from Bob's elbow startled Julius then. He followed a pointing finger to see the face of a child peering at them from between the legs of the frame on which the metal ewer stood. It seemed the scared, uncanny face of a troglodyte, but the freckled features under a thick thatch of reddish fair hair were not dull. Julius seemed to get a sudden insight into an individuality that, beset by chronic squalor and violence throughout its existence, had contrived to keep itself intact in its strange hiding-place below the window.

" This boy should not be here," he said sharply. " Will you not let me take him away for the time being ? "

" Aye, if he'll gang wi' ye," replied Joanna Baxter with sluggish complacency. " He'll miss his da."

Stooping, Julius engaged the boy's attention with a smile.

" Come, sonny," he coaxed. " I want you to come and have a bit change. I was your father's friend, his cousin. I'm a kind of uncle to you really. What's your name ? "

" Duncan," said the boy stoutly.

" Good ! Will you come with me then, Duncan ? "

" Aye, will I ! " replied the child, emerging head-first from his hiding-place.

They left Joanna Baxter and Alan Oliphant, the quick and the dead, alone together. The woman regarded their going with bleary indifference. She muttered something as the boy disappeared through the door in Bob's wake, but Julius at least had the feeling of finality in the parting.

Seen in the open sunlight of the street, the boy called Duncan was not altogether the ragamuffin Julius had expected. It was nothing that he went barefoot, and that his legs were filthy. That round of freckled face, if not the neck below it, had been washed in a fashion, and the boy's clothes were neither of indifferent quality nor ragged, while his blue Kilmarnock bonnet sat his head with an air of cocksureness. Julius found himself actually diverted by the picture the little party must be presenting, and he wondered if Alan, clinging pathetically to old standards, had sought in a lazy, occasional way to keep the boy decent in his habits. At the same time, he was amusedly aware that Bob, marching along at the other side of the child, frowned at this irregularity.

" Here's a nice how-d'ye-do ! " he broke out at length. " And what are you going to do with this lot ? "

" Let us go to the yard first," said Julius equably. " I'll send Duncan up to Goldenhaddock with one of the boys. Martha will give him a bit of a scrub and see that he's decently clad. After that—well, I don't know yet. There are some things to think about."

" There's a devil of a lot to think about, if you ask me ! " declared

Bob indignantly. " If you wouldn't be so damned soft-hearted . . ."

Julius laughed, knowing securely that his wildest impulses would always have Bob's unwavering, formidable support. But what to do with the child was quite a problem when you came to think of it !

He let it pass out of his mind once the boy had been sent uphill in charge of an apprentice with a message to the housekeeper at Golden-haddock. There were matters of business to attend to at the yard and then, filling his mind with a sad wonder to the exclusion of almost everything else, the fact that Alan Oliphant had at length come out of obscurity and demanded the public ceremony of burial. This the end of Alan, who had once been a merchant princeling and a buck and now, though the dynasty was still in power, must go to the grave like a pauper, symbolising life's littleness.

Julius and Bob did not go up to the house in the Low Vennel to see the coffin lid screwed down over the features of Alan Oliphant. With a young minister Bob had somewhere found willing to take the service as a professional matter they stood, like any casual mourners at a neighbour's funeral, among a crowd of curious slatterns and their noisy children in the narrow street outside. When Jock Simpson and his men brought the coffin down the turnpike stair and through the archway the tiny procession set off without ado, ragged urchins running before it as if it were something as gay as a column of soldiers on the march. The route was up the whole length of the Vennel to the new burying ground by the Canister Kirk, and in that narrow and stinking thoroughfare through a warren of slums there was none of his own caste to see one of the Oliphants pass to the grave. Only shawled women stood at the doorways to exclaim at the sight of two leading citizens in the wake of such a lonely coffin and to assure each other, facetious and obscene, that this was a fine end to Joanna Baxter's man. The young minister and the gravediggers wasted no time over the committal of ashes to ashes.

" Lord ! I feel that we have just shovelled the poor devil away," said Julius bitterly as they walked back to the yard. " I wonder if we shouldn't in decency have told some of the family's old friends. They would have made a ceremony of it for old time's sake."

" Much better as it was, miserable as it was ! " observed Bob gruffly. " He had no friends here."

" No. He was an orphan most of his life. His father and mother died of fever within hours of each other at Mobile, away back in '98 or thereabouts. He worked abroad for the uncles most of the rest until——"

" Pity the fever didn't get him in the Chaco ! There was a curse on that damned silver," said Bob bitterly.

" Yes, perhaps. There's a curse on too many forms of wealth, Bob, I'm beginning to think."

They walked along in silence for a space, making for the western gate of the shipyard hard by the Old Kirk. As they were passing the graveyard, Julius halted suddenly and said :

" That reminds me."

" Not that Alan might have been in there with the rest of the tribe ? " asked Bob, still sardonic.

" No. That boy," Julius went on gravely. " I'll tell you what, Bob. If you can do without me for a day or two, I'll take him down the Firth to-morrow. We can't keep the child here. We've got to get him out of this—away from these filthy warrens and filthy people. Give him a chance. Get him some education. Barbara will know how to manage it . . . That's just what I'll do ! "

" Have you thought of Mark ? " asked Bob, smiling slyly at his friend's easy enthusiasm.

" Mark will understand, I think," said Julius with dignity. " It's not the old Mark nowadays. And it is perfectly clear that any Oliphant will recognise a duty towards that boy, poor wee fellow."

" I wish," observed Bob dryly, " that the Oliphant duty didn't always fall on you—and Babs. But you'll have it your own way, I suppose."

" That's settled, then . . . I think he might turn out to be a bright boy—eh, Bob ? "

" He might. But come on, man ! We've still got ships to build and ships to manage."

Julius was late home that evening and saw young Duncan only for a few minutes after his own supper. From Martha the housekeeper beforehand he had a woman's report on the boy.

" He's shy. He's feart. But he was a sight cleaner than ye might have expeckit. Noo I've gi'en him a bit scrub and an auld suit of Maister Walter's the mistress was savin' for Maister Ivie. That, and a pair o' guid worsted hose and a pair o' shoon I chairged to ye at John Crombie's. That'll dae him weel enough."

" Does he talk at all ? "

" Aye, talk ! " said the decent woman appreciatively. " Once he gets startit ; once he see's a body's friendly like. The boy's gleg enough, if that's what you're spierin'."

" Good, Martha ! Will you bring him in now ? But stay with us. I don't want to frighten him in any way."

The boy had little enough to say when he was led in by Martha, but Julius noted with pleasure that there was nothing hang-dog about him. Washed and decently clad, Duncan seemed indeed to have spirit : brightness in his eyes and a tilt to his freckled chin. Julius was encouraged to forget his own diffidence in treating with this child of unknown personality.

"I think you need a holiday, Duncan," he said after a few friendly openings, " and to-morrow I'm taking you down to the Coast. You will have friends down there, boys and girls of your own age. You have never been out of Garvel ? "

" No," replied the boy stolidly.

" And I'll take you down in a steamboat. Will you like that ? "

" Aye. I'll like that fine."

Although he replied in the vernacular, the boy's speech, thought Julius, had none of the slovenliness of Garvel's new poor ; it was as if Alan's influence had wonderfully prevailed to keep the child in some degree apart from the ruck of the Low Vennel. This, at least, Julius persuaded himself to believe, and it pleased him as he paced the garden that summer evening to think out plans for the education of the boy, the rescue of one of his own kin from calamity. Much could be made of Duncan, he was sure. Some theories of upbringing could be most usefully tested. Julius was perfectly happy and untroubled in his planning, and he walked his lawns until the sun had gone down in fire behind the hills and the ships in the stream were showing their riding-lights in the gloaming.

His vicarious affection for the boy deepened on their journey by steamboat next day. It was a joy for Julius to see a young creature come into life of his own under the stimulus of novelty. All his reserve dropped from Duncan as soon as the vessel moved away from the quay. Its motion was infectious, so that the child had to get into motion on his own account ; now running the length of the deck from stem to stern, then, his legs kicking with delight, hanging over the after bulwarks to watch the creamy churn of salt water disturbed by the paddle wheels, then standing where the beam of the engine thrust up through the deck and then dropped down again, his arms imitating the movement. He found his tongue in excitement, and Julius was delighted to answer so many eager, quaint and often intelligent questions. Indeed, Julius forgot himself as he could always do with a child of his own, forgot completely the strange new relationship he had accepted with an orphan child of the slums, and was simply happy to interest the lad in the ships and seamarks of the estuary. A teachable boy ! he concluded happily as they drew at length towards their destination. He thought innocently of the surprise he was to spring on Barbara.

She was on the quay, no doubt having brought young Ivie down to see the steamboats, and he was mildly puzzled to observe her questioning look as, his hand on Duncan's back, he urged the boy down the gangway.

" My latest discovery, Babs ! " he greeted her gaily. " Duncan, this is your new Aunt Barbara."

She was quick, as always, to grasp the essence of any situation in which her husband was involved. She bent to take the child's hand.

" I am very happy to see you, Duncan," she said. " You had a fine trip on the steamboat ? Yes. I'm sure you had. Now, run on like a good boy with Ivie here while I have a word with your uncle. Look at those fine rocks on the shore there. . . ."

The boys shot off to explore another wonderland, and Julius found himself looking into the steady eyes of his wife. It came upon him quite suddenly that he had displeased her. The little, iridescent world he had created around his discovery of Duncan was in ruins, lying like the splinters of a globe of glass between them on the cobbles of the quay.

" My dearest Julius ! " Her tone at once upbraided and appealed to him.

" Barbara, sweetheart ! What have I done now ? You must understand—you of all people ! "

He babbled his story of death in wretchedness, of burial in ignominy, of a child lost in a thicket of evil ; a child of their own kith and sort, a thicket of their own planting. A bright child, too.

Her hand touched his.

" Yes, Julius," she said patiently. " Your heart is so tender and true ; your mind so straight." Then she became her French self. " But do you not see ? It is quite impossible to take the boy up to Mount Oliphant."

" Why not ? " He was inclined to be pugnacious.

" Because, my dear, we are Mark's guests—you and I and the children. We are not at liberty to bring strangers into the house of our host."

" Mark may not like it," declared Julius indignantly, " but it is his responsibility as much as mine ! "

" That, Julius," Barbara observed with cool patience, " is neither true nor to the point. You have assumed an obligation—and oh, my dear, I do understand exactly why ! That red-headed boy . . . But there was still no obligation on you to make the child one of the family. That we should impose this boy, without warning, on Lavinia and Mark—mais, c'est tout a fait impossible ! Let me think, Julius . . ."

Now Julius was miserable, and a dull resentment mingled with his disappointment. He was acutely aware of the ludicrous character of the mere physical situation in which he and Barbara stood—arguing on the open quay while lounging longshoremen stared at them with

frank curiosity and the innocent boy, excited in a new world, skipped
after Ivie among the rocks on the shore and threw stones into the
pools.

"I know what we can do in the meantime," announced Barbara
at length. "There's a decent woman, a widow, Mrs. Macmillan,
comes to help in Lavinia's kitchen. She has a cottage up the road
behind the house. She will take him in, I am sure, until . . . Come,
Julius ! This is the best we can do."

Duncan was called up from the beach and came glowing and
reluctant, and as the quartet made its way up the track past the Mount
Oliphant grounds Barbara was at pains to explain to the boy where he
would live in the meantime. She did it kindly, but Julius was unhappy,
beholding the wreck of a fine plan, acutely fearful lest his charge should
be disappointed and afraid after his own bold promises of play and
companionship with other children. When they had dealt with the
woman of the cottage and the matter had been simply arranged, he
seemed to be aware of the boy's bright eyes on his in bewildered
question, like those of a dog that has been promised a romp and is sent
back at the very gate.

As they came away from the cottage and approached Mount
Oliphant from the back, Barbara took his hand.

"He will be perfectly happy, Julius," she said gently. "That is a
good, kind woman, and all this is new and wonderful to him—the
fields, and the cattle, and the hens, and the space and light. Please,
my dearest ! I know little boys perhaps better than you do ; I have
two of my own—and I had so many brothers ! "

Her tenderness touched him, but he could not extricate himself
from the resentful glumness of one who, innocent and meaning so well,
has been discovered in an error of judgment. He said nothing ; just
walked on, his eyes on the ground. A squeeze of Barbara's fingers on
his made another appeal to him.

"Now we shall have to make plans," she said equably. "I fear
we must assume that Mark will not accept the boy."

"He will be invited to do so," snapped Julius. He dropped her
hand then.

"If you insist," continued Barbara equably, "though I should not
while we are guests under his roof. Our position is awkward."

"He has got to take some account of a family event, hasn't he ? "

"To be sure," said Barbara, ignoring his uneasy truculence. "The
matter can be explained to him. But if my judgment is right, Julius,
he will be greatly displeased—and we are in abuse of hospitality.
Therefore," the vestigial Frenchwoman declared, "we make our
excuses and all go home to-morrow, when we can consider what is to

be done with the boy. He can be quite happy with us at Golden-haddock."

" I suppose so," he admitted listlessly.

Barbara controlled her impulses. She was angry to find herself once again in the position of peacemaker as between Julius and Mark, as between the idealist and the man of affairs, and her instinct was to upbraid her own husband for unwisdom. One glance at his stricken face, however, changed her mood completely. She must always be on Julius's side. No matter that his emotional impulses usually took the line suggested by her own intelligence. In relation to this one man she was fated to be the fool of loyalty, even when he was monstrously and demonstrably wrong. This was love. It left her no freedom. She had to be a soldier in the human warfare and, as they approached Mount Oliphant, like a good soldier she laid her plans for the battle ahead.

At the supper table, exquisitely watchful for the outbreak of strife, she surveyed the factors at play within their small family group. As it chanced, Mark was in one of his hearty moods, full of young Walter's departure to college in Edinburgh, eager in his practical way to plan even the details of the journey.

" I suppose you will go by coach," he announced regretfully, " but if I were a young man of your age, Walter, I'd try one of the night-gigs on the Canal. There's something like progress ! It is perhaps a pity that we haven't a Robert Stephenson in Scotland to lay a railway line. That's the way of the future. But my reckoning is that the canal system has still a great future before it. Eh, Julius ? "

" No, Mark," said Julius quietly, " I do not agree."

He seemed pathetic in Barbara's eyes ; his long fingers played with a silver pepperpot, and his eyes were on the damask tablecloth. His speech was slow and deliberate. .

" We are entering an age of speed, an age of iron, an age of steam if you like. I hate the idea, but there it is. The steam engine on the railways will leave your canals dead and derelict within a generation. Speed, Mark, speed ! Yes, you can have your steamboat on the canals, but you cannot have speed there. Your canals are too narrow, too shallow ; the wash of the vessels would ruin the banks. And no steamboat will ever travel so fast as the locomotive will ultimately travel. That is a simple matter of dynamics, of induction from facts scientifically ascertained."

" You'll have us all up in balloons next, Julius ! " Lavinia surprised everybody by bursting out. Mark frowned his disapproval. He was in the habit of listening carefully to Julius in his prophetic mood.

" Indeed I might, Lavinia," observed Julius patiently, " but we have enough on the earth's surface to keep us busy for a long time to come. And I have no doubt at all that the land-vehicle of the future, for a long time to come at least, is the locomotive."

" And what about the sea, Julius ? " asked Mark with a sly eagerness that did not escape Barbara.

" Why," replied Julius simply, " it must be much the same story on the sea. The steamboat will prevail, must prevail . . . No, no, Mark ! Don't mistake me. The sailing ship is not dying to-night or to-morrow night. It will last my time and yours. There will be sailing ships afloat and in use in 1932, and there will be canals in use in 1932. But they will pass ultimately, just as no doubt the steam engine will pass. But it goes on, it always goes on."

He concluded on a tone of sadness, and a queer little silence fell on the party, as if Julius's voice had spoken for an external and mysterious force. His precise assurance, conveyed on his sombre phrases, affected them all. Lavinia started to say something, no doubt foolish, in an attempt to break from strain, but a warning frown from her husband silenced her into blushing nonentity. Barbara watched and listened.

It was young Walter who, gravely diffident, took them all beyond the momentary impasse.

" But you mentioned iron as well as steam, Father."

" Yes, Walter," Julius smiled on his son. " That is only part and parcel of the process. The next source of power is steam. You cannot have steam without metal. Iron is the best metal we have . . . I think, Walter, that you can complete the syllogism."

" Syllo—syllo . . . It's all silly to me ! " giggled Lavinia.

" Lavinia ! " her husband disciplined her sternly. He turned gravely to his cousin. " You seriously think, Julius, that we are coming to the iron ship ? You really believe that a vessel of rigid iron can be built to take all the strains, let alone float ? "

" Certainly."

" That business about iron floating is an old wheeze, Uncle Mark," added Walter with youthful assurance. " A metal soap-dish floats in the bath. When we were out fishing the other night I had the metal baler in our boat floating in the sea. It's the common illusion that the weight of the material matters. Really, it's the shape of the vessel."

Mark turned to his nephew with an indulgent smile, but Barbara noted the old hint of a sardonic sneer in his :

" So you've been studying your father's books, young man, have you ? "

" No, Walter is right—up to a point," said Julius. " Weight really does matter. I should not care to build a ship of platinum, or lignumvitae. But iron is relatively a light metal. It is a simple matter of specific gravities."

At this Lavinia, whose restlessness had been confessing itself in fidgets and rolls of her eyes towards Barbara, rose in her place with a swish of silk, and a small jangle of the little ornaments she favoured.

" I don't understand a word you are all saying," she declared. " Come, Barbara, and we'll see the children to bed."

" But I am interested, Lavinia," Barbara smiled back sweetly. " In a minute or two."

This was not the moment to leave ; this, she knew, was the critical moment. Though the talk was of general things it was, in her ex-quisitely exact knowledge of Julius's temperament, leading to the very flash-point of his inevitable explosion. Barbara wondered for a moment if she should dismiss young Walter from the table on a pretext, but no—she decided ; his cool detachment and his youth would help to keep bitterness away. But the fussy departure of Lavinia was in itself an ominous clearing of the field. Even as the door closed behind their hostess Barbara heard her husband take up his argument with passion.

" No, Mark ! It goes on, and it goes too fast. A moment ago you were advising Walter to travel to Edinburgh by one of the gigs on the canal. Very comfortable, very interesting, better than the coach, I'll allow. But seven hours over some forty miles from Glasgow to Edin-burgh ! A great raft drawn along a shallow canal by horses, and a string band to play you to sleep ! Excellent ! And would that we could stop there ! But I tell you, Mark——" And now Julius was leaning over the table eagerly, his right forefinger vehemently rapping out his points on the mahogany—" I tell you that within a few years—five years, ten years—the locomotive will be pulling trains across those forty miles between Glasgow and Edinburgh within the hour ! "

Mark threw back his great dark, handsome head and roared with laughter.

" You're a caution, Julius ! You'll have me flying from city to city on my own wings in five minutes ! "

" And that, Uncle Mark," said young Walter, " does not seem to me a mechanical impossibility. Birds fly. Flight is clearly a mechanical possibility. Man can imitate and emulate the birds."

" Another of those syllogisms, I suppose ? "

The charming priggishness of the boy and the heavy, defensive scorn of his uncle thickened the atmosphere through which Barbara was peering to see the approach of crisis. She saw Julius glance round the room as if to make sure that no eavesdroppers were about.

" We go too fast, I tell you, Mark," he repeated sharply. " The machine is running away with us, and we are very ill-prepared to meet the social consequences. And now I must tell you something that has happened, bearing on what we have discussed and closely affecting the family. . . . Yes, Walter may wait to hear it. He is quite of age to understand these things."

While Julius recited the facts of Alan's death and burial and his own quixotic rescue of the boy, Barbara's mind recorded in sharp detail the elements of the scene and the play of emotion on Mark's face. That proud, dark head was framed from her point of view between the end of a heavy mahogany sideboard and one of the pointed Gothic windows of the dining-room. She would have been seeing him against the light, except that its reflection from the mirror-back of the sideboard and from the napery and crystal on the table illuminated the face with the dark intensity of a Dutch painting. Her fancy wandering for a while, she saw Mark as the subject of a picture, as a man in a critical moment of his experience. His expression was mainly one of stubborn disapproval. Now he frowned, then the heavy eyebrows lifted in sardonic contempt of human folly. But he said not a word while Julius made his urgent explanation, and he kept silence for a space when his cousin was done.

"First things first," Mark began at length, heavily. "I'll pass over your haste in this matter, Julius. I think you might have taken the trouble to consult me as—well, in a sense, the head of the family. The boy wouldn't have died, would he? You could at least have given him to one of your workmen's wives to look after, and put him to work for that matter. Time he was doing something useful, I'll wager."

"The boy had no choice between being useful and useless. That is the tragedy," retorted Julius venemously; and Barbara noted the dangerous twitch of his nostrils in anger. "We are finished forever with child labour, thank God!"

"Very well. First things first," Mark repeated. "Just tell me how you are so sure that this is Alan's son?"

"I am not sure, in any legal sense, but I shall verify the fact, of course. In the meantime, there is enough about him to make me tolerably sure that he is. But even if he is not Alan's son——"

"There you go!" jeered Mark, "I am now invited to be complacent and agreeable about any stray object of your soft-hearted charity!"

"You are not invited! You are being faced with a group of facts, with a responsibility——"

Julius was nearly shouting, and Barbara cut in quickly to avert a noisy and empty quarrel.

"No, no, Mark!" she laughed, and hoped that her laughter sounded unforced. "All the responsibility for this boy's keep and education is with Julius and me. I think Julius is mainly anxious that, if the boy is really Alan's son, you should have all the facts before you. We can, surely, take a practical problem calmly."

She knew very well that her deliberate misrepresentation of Julius's position might bring from him at any moment a violent protest, and she sought to check him with a glance. She hastened to keep the issue between Mark and herself.

" I think you will admit that is reasonable, Mark ? "

He scowled at the tablecloth, and even in the midst of her concern Barbara had the exquisite pleasure of knowing that he at once hated the fact of her intervention and was defeated by it.

" Why the devil bring that brat down here ? " he growled roughly at length, truculent as an ill-conditioned boy.

" Ah ! " cried Julius.

He had regained his calm, but now it was a calm deadly with the conviction of rightness.

" I may be soft-hearted, Mark, and I am probably soft-headed. I acted on an impulse, I'll allow. But I ask you to believe that it was an impulse born of profound horror and·bitter shame. The degradation, the filth, in which that innocent boy was existing ! Like an animal peering out of a hole to stare at Bob and me ! A body rotting on the only bed in that small room, and a drunken harridan for company ! I tell you, Mark, that any man on this side of sheer depravity could not possibly have left the child in that hell."

" Quite so," said Mark coldly. " I repeat—why bring him down here ? "

" An error of judgment, it seems," Julius's hand dismissed the question. " Forget the boy. He will not be suffered to embarrass you or yours in any way, Mark, I promise you. But this I tell you, my friend. We are storing up great trouble for ourselves, men like you and me, who make our money in and out of Garvel but let such horrors as those Low Vennel slums exist, and go from bad to worse, breeding a more and more degraded and diseased class of criminals and wretches."

" Fiddlesticks ! The old Blackneb cry ! "

" No, no ! " said Julius patiently. " Please, Mark ! Please do not take this as a matter of politics. Do not take it even as a matter of charity and patronage. Take it on those terms that appeal to your natural talents—expediency, good business. Can you really maintain that, instead of fostering a class of good, steady workmen contented with their lot, you will stand by and watch the growth—the terribly swift growth—of a huge class of malcontents and drones and drunkards, reckless and burdensome to society ? "

"We heard that from Robert Owen years ago," snarled Mark, adding with a bitter laugh : "And much good it did him or anybody else !"

He pushed his chair back and spoke with an affectation of jocularity.

"A bonnie sermon, Julius ! And if you tell me that a good man will ever stay in a slum, or that a slum will ever make a bad man, then I tell you you don't know human nature. Let the trash stay where they are and rot. Enterprise always pays."

"I wonder," said Julius sadly, seeming to consider the beauty of the silver spoon his restless fingers had picked up. "I think not. I think we are heading, all of us, for trouble. I think we may even see tragedy, and I am afraid."

Mark rose to his feet impatiently.

"Come on ! Come on ! he commanded his guests. "Out into God's fresh air !"

At the door he turned to Julius with a cynical grin and added cryptically.

"Garvel isn't the whole of the world I want, my friend."

4

The young queen was crowned. They had no doubt about that in Garvel. Even though it might be midnight, and then not certainly, before confirmation of the news would come on a chain of bonfires stretching all the way from London northwards across the Border ; although it would be days before the posts would bring printed descriptions of the great event, the town was celebrating the occasion in right royal style.

It had been proclaimed a holiday for all, even for the children in the textile mills down the new line of falls. With the accession of the girl monarch there had come even to remote Garvel, as to most communities in the kingdom, a general sense of relief, as if from the vagaries and corruptions of the old Court, and an awareness of universal entry into the brave new world of Progress and Reform. Lord Melbourne was so wise and experienced in affairs, the Archbishop so pious and dependable ; the Queen was so young and comely and modest. Novelty and expectation were in the air. In Garvel there lingered in the public mind the gallant resolution of a public meeting in the town hall to the effect that, "from acknowledged superiority and economy of railway conveyance by means of locomotive engines," a joint-stock company should be formed for the laying of a line linking the town with the great city upstream ; and it was a matter of high local pride that the Royal Assent to the Bill of Incorporation had been one of the young Queen's first acts of sovereignty a year before. Now the railway was nearing the town ; its completion delayed only by those stubborn mosses and still more stubborn lairds on the middle stretch about Dungavel.

So, on this bright though showery 28th of June, 1838, Garvel rejoiced in a grand confusion of ceremonial and merriment. The ships at anchor in the stream were splendidly dressed in bunting and, at the appointed hour of anointment and coronation, fired loud salutes from innumerable guns, starting the echoes rumbling in Highland glens and corries leagues away. The Guilds paraded with their banners and emblems and bands of music. In wig and gown the Sheriff read a Proclamation from the steps of the Mid Kirk. Above his head the big bell in the steeple under the Gilded Gabbart banged out an imperial message to the populace. Then, amid the huzzas of the populace, the Provost of Garvel, Mark Oliphant, Esquire, of Dunclutha and Mount Oliphant, led his chained and gowned Bailies and Councillors and a representative party of gentlemen across the Square to enjoy a service of cake and wine in the Burgh Chambers. The procession was headed by the Town's Drummer, Squinty Nicoll, and two halberdiers who, to the joy of the apprentices of the place, had clearly had early access to their meridian drams and marched with an uncertain elaboration of dignity that superbly parodied, as in a playhouse, the dignity of the Foot Guards in the Queen's own procession.

A great day. At four of the afternoon there still lay before the Provost a banquet in the Tontine, another procession to the Craig's Top, and the lighting there of a bonfire that would flame its message to a score of bonfires twinkling on the hills and mountains round about. But Mark was at home in his mansion of Dunclutha for a space resting from his labours, and with him in his parlour were his cousin Julius and his godson, Walter.

They had been bidden there by a special message from the Provost, and they had assumed an extension of the celebrations which they, as representing the family, should not fail to attend. Indeed, they had driven to Dunclutha in a fine carriage from the Buck's Head livery : Julius in his formal clothes with buff pantaloons strapped over high boots and ruffled shirt as became a merchant of the older school, Walter in the soberer blacks and dove-grey waistcoat befitting a young physician of promise, not long capped and doctored in the Faculty of Medicine at the University of Edinburgh.

They arrived, however, to find Mark Oliphant alone and in a strange state of exaltation. Applying a clinical eye to the problem presented by his uncle on this Coronation Day, Walter discerned that, over and above a fair amount of drink taken, the Provost was a man with a special excitement working within him. The drink was nothing. On such a day the civic head of the community must propose and honour many a toast. But, himself a little dashed to find that he and his father had come in state to what was only a small family gathering in a quiet parlour at a slack hour, Walter considered the flushed, dark face, now tending to heaviness of the lower jaw, and wondered what motive had prompted the special message to Golden-haddock. All his conscious life he had been aware of some unusual quality in Uncle Mark, something demoniac that might be near-genius. Now maturing with a scientific training behind him, he was like his mother in being unconsciously inclined to watch his uncle for sudden ebullitions that transcended the normal exchange of normal society.

Detached, cool, a little superior in his young assurance of knowledge —and always a little hurt that the expedition was apparently ending in tame formality—Walter listened to his father, that simple, unsuspecting man, pay all the proper compliments to their host, and more out of his saintliness.

" It has been a great day, Mark, and I congratulate you from my heart ! Everything has gone like clockwork. All exact and sincere and decent in honour of our young Queen, God bless her ! "

" Aye, I think it's gone well," Mark responded, setting down his glass after still another oblation to that gracious symbol. " I took some trouble, Julius, you understand ? Do these things well, or don't do them at all—that's how I see my duty as Provost of Garvel. . . . Watty, my boy, your glass is empty. Fill up ! Fill up ! "

He rose and, swaying gently, the decanter in his hand, approached his nephew.

" My dear Uncle Mark ! No, no ! " Walter protested, his hand over his glass. He laughed. " There's a long day still before us. Please ! "

His Uncle Mark stood above him, the hand holding the tilted decanter by the neck at the full stretch of his arm.

" Watty, my boy ! " said the Provost of Garvel genially, and relapsing into the dialect of the region. " Ye're a queer auld bitch, whiles. Ye're terrible like your mither whiles. But I'll tell ye this, lad —I've aye liket you. From the verra first. Come on, son, just one wee sup wi' your Uncle Mark."

The decanter was raised hopefully again, but Walter waved it away with laughing signs of protest. Uncle Mark was nearly drunk. But oblivious of the by-play, cutting through the link that so strangely bound uncle and nephew in a special sort of confidence, Julius held on about the greatness of the day.

" Yes, Mark, another of your triumphs. The town is luckier than it knows in having a man of your energy and address at the head of affairs at such a time. It would have been tragic if we had been cursed with some dull fellow. I congratulate you, Mark. I drink to the future of your Provostship."

" Ah ! But that's just the point, Julius ! "

There was a queer, sudden note of gloating in Mark's exclamation as Walter heard it. In that moment of time the young man was made acutely aware of life in the very article of changing and taking a new shape. Throughout the years thereafter he was to remember, as if it had been recorded in a painting before him, the elements of the scene —the afternoon sunlight in the small room at Dunclutha, his own father's gentle and mildly startled face, and the solid frame of his uncle, still on his feet, jocular, aggressive and defensive all at once, the decanter in his hand.

" I beg your pardon, Mark," said Julius mildly. " Did I interrupt what you were saying to Walter ? "

" No, you didn't," returned Mark roughly. " It arises . . . Something I thought I ought to tell you . . . Why I got you down here this afternoon . . . A bit of an occasion."

Walter watched the man adjust himself for an announcement. The decanter was steadily and carefully placed on the table. A chair was drawn back and occupied. The genial, hail-fellow personality of the Provost of Garvel was replaced by that of Mark Oliphant.

" The fact is, Julius," he hurried to announce, " I think I'll be leaving you."

" God bless my soul ! "

" As you know, there will be another election before we are very much older, and—well, the fact is that I am likely to be invited to go forward. For the local seat, of course."

" My dear Mark ! This——"

The Provost waved the interruption aside, but now Walter observed that the moment of restraint had passed. This strange uncle had jumped the first hurdle, and the hearty man of the world was returning to his place.

" It will be most convenient really. It forces me to a decision in a matter that has given me a lot of thought and bother. Aye, Julius," he added sententiously, his hand going out to the decanter," I've seen the change coming a long while past. You know that I took a big hand in breaking the monopoly of the East India Company."

" Indeed, yes, Mark ! Fine work, if——"

"Aye, well ! Bread on the waters, you know. Anyhow, it looks like leading to a seat on the board of the Middle and Far Eastern. That's only for your private ear, of course. I thought you might like to get the first news of it."

"And I am delighted, my dear fellow ! This is——"

"Then, of course, there is the Railway Company. That's another directorate which will call for a good deal of attention in London. In fact, Julius, the way I see things shaping now—and I think you will respect my judgment of these things——"

"Nobody more implicitly," said Julius stoutly. "Nobody ! "

"The way I see things shaping," Mark swept on, "the whole centre of British trade is going to be in London, whether we like it or no. Apart from the shipyard here—and I can put a good man in to look after my interests—my merchant business can be done better from London than from Garvel or even from Glasgow, I tell you that. And—well, there's how it is. I think I'll be moving out. I thought I ought to let you know. All these years. . . . You will be the head of the family here now, you know."

"You are thoughtful, Mark, but . . . the idea of your leaving us ! Your great interests, your influence, the loss to us of a leader. . . . Dear me, dear me ! "

There was silence in the little room for a space, and again Walter was visited by that subtle sense of a large significance in the small gathering. He suddenly saw his own father as an ageing, indecisive man, bewildered by portents and tempted to retire into the gracious ease of the past ; while the other dark man of equal age pushed his way out of an insufficient environment towards power, greater and greater power, that most alluring houri of all the ambitions. His literary fancy saw the eighteenth and the nineteenth centuries in opposition, the philosophical part of his brain thought to behold a special staging of the eternal conflict between Thinker and Doer. In his young and romantic imagination the afternoon sunlight in the parlour seemed charged with a sadness intolerably sweet.

His father sat huddled in his chair, silent and—could it be ?—stricken. Walter rose briskly to his feet.

"By your leave, Uncle Mark, but we must be going. There is still the banquet to-night. Come, sir."

"Yes, Walter, yes ! We must be going. And this great news, Mark . . . I feel most incredibly flattered by your confidence, your candour. But to leave us in the lurch and go to London . . . I hardly know what to say."

"We'll all survive, Julius my boy ! " responded Mark, himself again. " Just you go on building those sailing ships of yours, and don't worry. Not another small glass of wine before you go ? "

Father and son walked home, taking the high turnpike for it and much in the shadow of the tall sandstone walls the richer merchants of the town were building around the large plots of ground they had taken for their new villas. As they went along together, Julius was alert to point out to his son what a fine dwelling in the Italian style Mr. Oughterson, in the Newfoundland trade, had put up, and how discreetly old Jock Esplin with large interests in sugar and rum from the Antilles (added Julius with a chuckle) had adapted to the special environment the characteristics of a *château* on the Loire. He seemed to be delighted with these elegant developments of the town, but something told Walter that his father was uneasy, was talking out time, so to speak.

" The new villas of our rich men are very fine, sir," he said, " but they all seem to be escaping from something and locking themselves in. Are they afraid ? "

" Escaping ! Locking themselves in ! Our leading citizens ! What do you mean, boy ? "

" Just how it appears to me, sir. They belong to the town, their wealth is made out of the town. But surely it is as if they were running away from it and were afraid of what they have created down there in the slums ; what at least they have allowed to develop. All that beastliness of the Low Vennel and the wynds near the harbours—a stinking pit of disease as a medical man sees it. And here are the grand villas running out into the country to get away from it ! Refusing to belong to it. Why, sir, those fine high walls are symbols ! The rich putting themselves into fortresses, locking themselves in, keeping out the mob they fear and hate. They escape . . . Just as Uncle Mark is escaping."

" Walter ! This is a very strange and dangerous line of thought."

Julius was torn between alarm and pride. His gentle spirit was in middle age inclined to hive away from this very problem of inequality that had irked him all his adult life, but as a man he was superbly proud to have as a son one who could think so directly and speak so strongly about it. Out of the corner of his eye he surveyed the person of this other, surprising man who was his son. The boy was tall, dark of pale complexion, and with a profile which expressed with distinction both the calm of knowledge and the arrogance of young conviction. He was a true son of Barbara : and, regarding his near person, Julius thought foolishly of the sweet days of early marriage when he had possessed and commanded this individuality. He remembered little garments the baby had worn, quaint and foolish sayings, early and gawky exhibitions of the personality Watler was to be—all golden and sweetly sad like the memory of yesterday's sunset.

With a conscious effort to overcome his own shyness, Julius slipped his hand under Walter's arm and gave the young muscles a confidential squeeze.

" What you say about your Uncle Mark, Walter . . . Escaping was the word, I think . . . That is most interesting, though I find it difficult to understand."

" But it is really simple, sir ! " Walter laughed. " I could write a thesis on Uncle Mark. You know, of course, sir, that I am curiously fond of him ? "

" Of course, of course ! It would be strange otherwise."

" And when you are fond of Uncle Mark, you come to see that he is really rather a frightened man."

" A frightened man ! Your Uncle Mark ! "

" Oh, yes ! " Walter coolly maintained. " He is a man of great ability and quite extraordinary energy. There's something like a steam-engine inside him, driving him on. He cannot stop, and nothing is allowed to stand in the way. It is a sort of genius."

" True ! True ! " murmured Julius.

" But he is uneasy. He is not sure, never quite sure. He is frightened, as I said. For instance, sir, he is frightened of you."

" Of me ! Mark ! My dear Walter . . ."

" Not of you in any physical or material sense," continued young wisdom primly. " But he is very much afraid of your opinion, sir— I'd prefer to put it, of your brains. Why should he specially invite you down to Dunclutha, on a day like this, to make an important announcement ? "

" Why not ? " countered Julius indignantly. " Your Uncle Mark and I are cousins. We are old associates. The family interest is our greatest mutual concern. Really, Walter, I must protest."

" No, no, sir ! " said the young man patiently. " You still have to explain why I am specially invited to accompany you. My position within the family is quite unimportant. But Uncle Mark takes care that I am present when he makes his announcement. And I ask why . . . Clearly, sir, and with all respect, it is just that I may be a sort of buffer, that my presence will take the edge and drama out of what might be a difficult situation. Dear me ! " laughed Walter coldly, " It's like producing the crying baby when the factor calls for the rent ! "

" Walter ! Really ! You go too far."

He was rewarded, however, by the friendly squeezing of his hand between the boy's warm arm and side. Walter went on more kindly :

"No, father," he said reassuringly. "I am speaking purely as a scientist, clinically. Uncle Mark is a case, a fascinating case, and it was only this afternoon that I saw the truth of it. I assure you he is not a happy man, not a *whole* man. I could even argue that, so far from being a leader, he is really a sort of parasite. However . . ."

They marched on together, now across the rough square above Kilblain where the new suburb branched off from the old town, noisy in the hollow below. Julius felt himself to be carrying a load of concern. He was not wholly unhappy, but shadows beyond definition were on his mind.

"This is a very strange way of thinking you have taken to, Walter," he ventured at length.

Walter smiled over such a vague and characteristic bid for paternal authority.

"Yes, sir," he agreed, "but it is how some of us at College have been thinking lately. You might call it the science of the mind, or the anatomy of thought as distinct from that of the body. No doubt about it, this will be a real science some day, with its own ascertained laws, its own terminology. Why, sir, some of our men are already prepared to maintain that what we call physical illness is essentially a state of mind."

"God bless my soul!" said Julius.

He had always his roses. Their culture fascinated him, and their beauty was his solace. The paths of the rose-garden were his ways of escape.

He had not gone to the banquet after all. He would never be missed in that large, exuberant gathering, and there was Walter to represent the house. How much more agreeable to stay at home with Barbara and walk among the roses and, while conscious of the noises rising from the festive town, to be above it all, as serene as the summer sunset over the anchorage! And yet, even as he stooped to do a favourite tree the gentle office of nicking off a withered bud or to savour the fragrance of a deep red bloom, he was conscious of a small uneasiness in his mind. Now and again he would walk across the terrace where Barbara sat sewing by the wide open window of her drawing-room.

"No word of that boy yet?"

"Not yet, my dear," she would answer patiently. "It is hardly to be expected on a night like this. Young people want to join in the fun."

"But he must have gone with that other boy."

" We shall see, Julius, we shall see."

Always that other boy ! Julius returned slowly to his roses, ruefully considering the history of the boy called Duncan under his guardianship ; and it made him unhappy. Perhaps the error had been his own ; nay, it almost surely was. The boy should have been made one of the family from the start, brought into the house and treated precisely as a son of his own. Why had he been tempted to discriminate and sent the lad to live with old Martha in the house above the stables, apart, and then put him for his schooling to the Highlanders' instead of to the Grammar School with Ivie ? It had seemed wise and even generous at the time, but Julius sighed, remembering the many troublesome ways in which Duncan had shown himself a creature aloof and different.

Days when he had escaped to the Low Vennel and brought a gang of wild urchins up the hill to trample the garden and strip the orchard. Days when he had played truant from school and lied like a trooper when called to book, sullen and resentful. The dreadful day when Duncan had been caught in the act of emptying a purse Barbara had left lying on a table in the hall. A day—now and again—when Joanna Baxter, with drink taken, had stormed Goldenhaddock and with horrible violence of language accused them all of having stolen her boy and had had to be bought off. Oh, altogether a difficult, sullen, mysterious boy, but with his own strong personality and a fire of individualism under that red head. Old Martha was his faithful champion against criticism.

At the heart of Julius's concern was his anxiety for his younger son, the boy they had christened Ivie. Another wild, robust lad ; sandy-haired, bright-eyed and mischievous. Not an atom of evil in the boy, Julius was sure, but a worry with his bursts of lawlessness and his willingness to follow Duncan's lead. They had been in so many scrapes together, some of them touched with the grime of Low Vennel morality. To have put Ivie and Duncan on different levels of responsibility and then let them run freely together, ah ! that had been the mistake. And on a night like this of Coronation two spirited boys might fall into really sordid trouble.

In his restless state Julius was often down at the gates and even out into the road in the hope of seeing the familiar figure of his boy coming home, and then he would go to the drawing-room window to take comfort from Barbara's calm.

" Come indoors and sit down, Julius," she counselled him at length. " You cannot expect boys to come home early when all the town's on holiday. If you are worried, let us wait at least till Walter returns and hear what he has to say."

"Yes, Walter!" agreed Julius eagerly. "He may have seen those rascals about the place. Yes, Walter will know."

Walter was a pillar of strength, a great source of pride. A cool head, had Walter, a knowledge of the world. But Julius remained restless until his older son returned, pacing the drawing-room, fidgeting with ornaments on the mantelpiece, returning to stare at the sky barred in gold and sable above the Highland hills. He listened impatiently to the young man's account of the banquet, and then the question burst from him.

"Did you see any sign of Ivie down there? He is not back yet, and I fear he may have gone astray with that other fellow, Duncan."

"Not back yet!" even Walter confessed concern. "No, I saw no sign of him. The square is a solid mass of people, though they're beginning to move up to the Craigs for the bonfire."

"I hardly think you could keep Ivie away from the bonfire," observed Barbara calmly.

"Probably not," her son agreed gravely. "Still, there's a rough lot about to-night. I tell you what, sir: I'll get into old clothes and take a walk round. It will do me good after all that heavy food and all those heavy speeches. But promise me, Mother——" He rose and bent over her chair, "do not wait up. And see that my father goes to his bed early. I'll manage this. It is just one of Ivie's pranks. He'll be running like a terrier up the Craigs, never thinking, I'll be bound."

"Ah! Thank you, Walter!" Julius was gratefully relieved. "You are probably quite right. It is good of you to take so much trouble."

Walter Oliphant was a young man of naturally grave habit of mind, but as he walked down the hill from Goldenhaddock in the growing darkness he was moved by quite a sharp concern to discover his young brother and get him home. His intellectuality mistrusted, perhaps because it could not thoroughly understand, the impulsive forthrightness of the active type to which young Ivie belonged. If he could, however, have analysed his fears profoundly he would have found that behind his apprehension were a deep hatred and obsessing fear of the slums. He had seen them while he was serving an apprenticeship to Dr. Broadfoot, he had worked in them when, at college in Edinburgh, he had delivered the misbegotten brats of a score of Canongate sluts. Those fine qualities in him that made him seem sometimes a prig, those elements of the fastidious and the scientific in his make-up, were revolted by squalor man-made and avoidable. It was against this enemy that he marched in search of his brother.

He could have made for the Craigs direct across the tracks under

The Mount and above Kilblain, but an instinct directed him downhill to the seething confusion of the Square. That open space was emptier than when he had shouldered his way across it from the banquet, but it still was noisy with men and women clustered in groups and barefooted children running hither and thither. Naphtha flares blazed smokily on booths set up here and there along the perimeter of the space, and in the midst of some of those forbidding clusters of people a torch blazed or a small fire had been started on the causeways. Some of the groups danced round their pagan fires, satyrs in Walter's sober eyes. Within the square of buildings tall beyond the average in Garvel the air was filled with shouts and skirling laughter and drunken threats and cursing, so that, halting in a moment of detachment under the Mid Kirk spire, Walter was aware of a canopy of noise above and about him, confused and thick. The sense of saturnalia afflicted him. He had the feeling of a wild and dirty animal being abroad. One flash of insight gave him a horrible vision of the Mob and its stupid power.

He started to work methodically about the square, slipping between the noisy clusters in the sober clothes he had donned. In the middle of one two sailors were fighting barefisted, bloody and ugly : in the next a drunken trull, her petticoats held about her thighs, was dancing furiously. Walter was only half-way round the square, at the opening of the Cross-Shore, when he heard his brother's voice, high, clear and excited above a babel of other young voices.

He reconnoitred the group discreetly. He saw that with Ivie were one or two youths of the same order of society, sons of merchants on the loose from homes of the highest respectability, along with some who might have been apprentices from the shops and shipyards of the town —a harmless enough group of lads to be together on a gala night. What concerned Walter was that they had foregathered with a flock of young girls, bare-footed and tartan-shawled, slum-born child-slaves out of the new textile mills. Their rough voices and skirling laughter challenged the boys in the old game of the sexes.

Circling the group discreetly, Walter passed behind his brother and tugged at his jacket. The boy swung round so that his face was illuminated in the glare from a lamp on a booth nearby.

" Hallo, Watty ! " he said uneasily.

" Come out of this. You are far too late as it is."

In the boy's eyes and expression Walter could see the signs of drink taken. Experienced in student ways he did not imagine for a moment that the lad had had more than a glass or two of ale, put down with gallantry but with a youngster's distaste for the sourness of the stuff. Ivie made a small show of protest.

" I'm all right," he declared. " Leave me alone."

"You come along with me, my lad," replied Walter. "I'm not going to have Mother and Father out of their wits with worry."

Ivie obeyed, moving away from his friends without farewell, but they had hardly gone ten paces when he stopped and murmured guiltily :

"What about Duncan ? "

"Duncan can find his own way home," said Walter firmly. "Where did he go to ? "

"I don't know," replied Ivie foolishly. "He got in among a lot of people I didn't like. He shouted something about going to the Low Vennel, and I was to come along. I didn't want to." His boyishness made a sudden appeal to his older brother. "There were some mighty wild women among them."

"Yes," said Walter calmly. "Now we'll get home."

He resisted the temptation to lecture the boy. Indeed, he was mainly obsessed by the thought that the lad had perhaps only narrowly escaped a more horrifying degradation than his innocence could know to be possible. His annoyance abating, Walter began to feel tender towards his only brother. He was careful to lead him round by the back entrance to Goldenhaddock, to make him tiptoe in stocking soles up back stairs, and to see him into his room with a warning to lie late and say nothing.

His own sleep that night was broken. Into the early hours of the morning he could hear the raucousness of the mob rise in gusts of cheering and in strangely isolated catcalls from the narrow lanes of the old town below, and his sleepless mind was filled again with that sense of the horror of overcrowding which, though his medical sense could put the present concern down to the excitement of the day and a surfeit of banqueting food and wine, seemed to have come to haunt him. The air was hot and still ; and after an hour or two of fitful dozing in the brightness of midsummer's early hours, he rose and dressed even as the first of the servants was just stirring about the kitchen premises behind.

In the cobbled yard before the coachman's house he found old Martha already at the work of her small household, beating a bit of carpet with vigour against the harled gable. Her greeting told him all he wanted to know.

"Guid sakes, Maister Walter ! " she cried. "Ye're early afit the day. Have ye been gallivantin' wi' the rest o' them doon there ? That rascal o' mine's, Duncan, hasna' set fit in this hoose since he had his denner yesterday noon."

"Duncan not home yet, Martha ! " he pretended surprise. "There must have been real high jinks in the town last night."

"High jinks, I tell ye!" said the old woman with relish. "And thon ane wad be up to the lugs in it. A wee devil, he is, a red-heidit devil. But he's got spunk, Maister Walter . . . Ah, weel, Maister Watty! By your leave, I'll just step inbye and get his brose ready. He'll be comin' up the road shune enough, whistlin' like a lintie."

Walter killed time about the grounds until, as was his custom, his father came out before breakfast to look again at his roses, as if some dire fate might have overtaken them overnight. They stood together on a path hidden from the house under a pergola of brilliant crimson ramblers.

"So it was a false alarm about Ivie!" cried Julius gaily. "And he was in bed in good time after all!"

"Oh, yes! I met him coming up the hill," Walter lied cheerfully.

"He had a gallant time of it, I'll wager," said Julius, smiling with tolerance. Then his look narrowed. "But Duncan?"

"Duncan is not back—yet."

"Oh, dear! Oh, dear! Wild, wild boys! A wild night . . . But that is really too bad of Duncan. I put it to you, Walter . . ."

"If you ask me, sir," said Walter, his fatigue urging him to bitterness, "it will not surprise me if Duncan never returns. I think he tasted blood last night."

"Blood . . . Really, Walter! You mean—a weakness of the flesh—something in the poor boy's heredity perhaps?"

"Heredity has no doubt something to do with it," agreed Walter, snapping a passionate bloom off one of the trailing branches about them. "My own diagnosis would rather say environment."

He turned vehement. The rose flew from a flick of his finger on to the path.

"It's poison down there in those horrible places," he said. "An attractive, creeping poison—like alcohol. It will kill us all eventually, unless——"

"Unless what, my dear Walter?"

"I don't know. I simply don't know."

CHAPTER FIVE

WOOD INTO IRON

I

A LINE of red-coated militiamen held the mob away from the lowest step of the fine broad flight which led up to the new railway station. The officer in charge, the heavy scabbard of his curved sword clattering on the granite, came along the row to look at a white card waved in the outstretched hand of a tall young gentleman with a young lady on his arm. As he reached out for the oblong of cardboard, his hand and forearm heavily gauntleted in white leather, the dark eyes of the officer took in the facts that the young man in fawn trousers and dark blue cutaway coat was indubitably a person of social standing, and that the young lady he escorted was well-favoured beyond the ordinary. Canvassing her charms in the masculine intimacy of the ante-room, the gallant subaltern would assuredly have described them in ebullient terms.

Now, on parade, he returned the card to its bearer with a bow and permitted himself just the ghost of a hopeful smile towards the lady. (He was always conscious, that young man, of his own dark and romantic eyes under dark, rich eyebrows.) He clicked his heels, bowed again, and saluted. The lady bowed in return, the young gentleman raised his tall hat, and amid the sardonic cheers of the common folk still held outside the barrier, Dr. Walter Oliphant of Goldenhaddock and Miss Phoebe Craufurd of Kilblain proceeded, not unlike figures in a stage scene, up the flight of steps and so out of sight of the mob through the gates of the new railway's western terminus.

After the noisy huddle of the public approach to it, the station seemed to be part of quite another sort of world. The designers of the place had contrived to give it that troglodyte atmosphere which hangs about every railway enterprise to this day. The line of rails had the air of resting in an excavation. A canopy over the platform, its eaves fringed with decorative ironwork, conspired with the blank wall of a shed beyond the rails to make of the station a sort of hall of echoes. It was a day of late March, inordinately mild in the season of growth, but even the sunlight of early afternoon fell in shafts between canopy and shed as if through the windows of a prison.

Like a child at an exhibition Miss Craufurd exclaimed at everything, pointing out this and that novelty to her escort with eager motions of the parasol she dared to carry in this early week of the Scottish year.

"And aren't we the lucky ones, Walter !" she cried. "But, look ! Most of our friends are here already."

They were among the lucky ones, indeed, but not quite the luckiest of all. It was a very select company that had been cheered out of Garvel an hour before noon that day—to martial music and a booming of cannon—in the first train of twelve carriages, drawn by two engines, to depart for the city, twenty-odd miles away, along the wonderful new track laid down at vast expense and in daring defiance of natural and legal obstacles innumerable. The parents of Miss Craufurd and the parents of Dr. Walter Oliphant were of that highly privileged party which had been whisked away on the glittering wings of invention, and those of the younger generation and of the slightly lower orders who now awaited their return were in a second order of precedence, although vastly exalted above the eager, sardonic mob of the common folk that milled companionably in the station approaches.

Miss Craufurd and Dr. Oliphant were not, however, in the least affected by any awareness of subtle degradation. Their quite natural feeling, even in that age of mercantile expansion, was stoutly feudal. Their parents, representing their established families, had departed into space on a bold and possibly dangerous excursion in the van of progress. They were well content as young folk to be privileged to assemble for the high purpose of greeting the returning voyagers, pioneers triumphant. The military band was there at the eastern end of the platform, ready to strike up *See the Conquering Hero* at a moment's warning. The guns of a regiment of artillery were primed to fire a salute.

With a little bow of formality, Dr. Oliphant offered to his fair charge the oblong of cardboard which had gained them admission to this enclosure.

"You might care to have this card as a souvenir, Phoebe," he suggested.

"But how charming, Walter !" cried the young lady, who had been finished at a convent in Brussels. "Look ! It has your uncle's own signature ! 'Mark Oliphant, Director.' Oh, I shall keep this among my dearest possessions ! "

Railway or no railway, Walter would have found the company of Miss Craufurd enough for any hour. They were but a month betrothed, and this girl of nineteen, the youngest of a famously handsome family, glowed like a flower in the sun of love and triumph. Her morning dress, with its domed skirt, was of peacock green shot with purple ;

over her shoulders within the tight bodice was draped a long Paisley shawl, white with an edging to match the dress. A purple bonnet in the candid fashion of the period exquisitely framed two ringlets of her hair, and within that second dark frame the girl's lovely oval face, flawless in cream and blush, had the beauty of all the dawns and springtides of the world.

This handsome couple, for tall young Dr. Oliphant fairly matched the lady in his own masculine and faintly severe manner of looks, was warmly greeted by those already on the station platform. There were many of their own generation to salute them as having so elegantly, nay so perfectly, reached the decision proper to their age and eligibility. There were still more in the inferior grades of society—the comfortable, sentimental wives of the more substantial shopkeepers, for instance, and their uneasily envious daughters—to overwhelm them with effusiveness. As they came up with the main party the band of music at the end of the platform chose, with a nice, accidental touch of theatricality, to fill in the waiting time with a selection and burst valiantly into one of the new and nearly licentious Viennese waltzes.

So, amid a continuous chatter of female greetings and exclamations, with dark undertones of grave male prognostications as to the effect of the new railway communication on the trade of the town, the time of waiting passed quickly. A detached listener from another age might have picked up as significant such words and phrases as : coal, redingote, prosperity, pelerine, figured grenadine, screw, water, mantlet, iron, tides, three-fold linen buttons, villas, assembly, steam-boat, and again coal ; but those who uttered them had no such sense of significance, even if the men among them were cast in the grave mould of those who consciously see destiny in the shaping. They were just men and women of 1841, waiting for the first train to return to Garvel and to applaud an agreeable phenomenon.

Its approach was intimated by the murmur of distant cheering up the line, echoed from the Hillend slopes. The more observant and sharp-eyed watchers noted the gyrations of boys on trees, walls and roof-tops along the curving track to the eastward. The military band was seen to pick up and assume in readiness its formidable instruments. The company on the platform, like a company of infantry at drill, turned half-left. There the brave wreaths of smoke and steam were seen rising in puffs behind the cottages at Anglestone ; and in that single space of interminable time, no more than fifteen seconds altogether, the cheers of greeting started to rise from between thousands of lips, the battery of guns began to boom, and Mr. Handel's neat march saluted still another event more fantastic than the composer ever dreamed of.

On the people waiting at the terminus the near approach of the
train created a profound impression of might. The gleaming brass of
the two locomotives, the hiss and pulse of compressed steam, the
gigantic hoops of the driving wheels, the scream of brakes and the
jolting of carriages—all these sights and sounds conveyed an exciting
impression of enormous power successfully controlled by gifted
members of the remarkable species to which they themselves belonged.
The forward surge to greet the historic survivors of the experiment was
a miracle of happy unanimity.

To the clinically observant eye of Dr. Walter Oliphant, at least,
it did not appear that the travellers had made the journey without
discomfort. The faces of the men among them were begrimed to a
greater or less extent, their eyelids inflamed. It was to be noted that
most of the ladies descending from the train shook their mantles or
shawls with irritable little gestures or impatiently flicked fragments of
cinder from their sleeves and gloves. Those who had guarded themselves with parasols twirled them like tops on the platform.

Such small gestures, however, were largely unconscious and passed
nearly unnoticed in the excitement of the monstrous event. The air
was loud, even above the hiss of steam, with cries and greetings and
congratulations and prophecies.

" Prodigious ! Only 65 minutes from the city—24 miles ! We
shall be flying next ! I declare I had to hold my bonnet on all the
time ! The trees seemed to *fly* past ! It seems like a year since we
left Garvel this morning ! I declare I'll waken up and find it
is all a dream ! Now we can count on unlimited supplies of coal
at a really reasonable rate ! This, sir, spells the end of riverborne
traffic ! "

The Craufurds and the Oliphants, both travellers and attendants,
found each other in the crowd and formed their own group.

" There you are, my dear Phoebe ! " cried Julius, happily greeting
his son's betrothed. " As pretty as a picture ! I think I can say . .
my little joke, Walter ! . . . that you are really a sight for sore eyes.'

Walter laughed, but poor little Phoebe blushed and pouted a little
and looked puzzled.

" I am sure you are teasing me, Mr. Oliphant."

" No, no ! Of course not ! "

Walter's intervention was both swift and ever so slightly impatient.
He bowed over the hand of his mother-in-law-to-be, then over that
of his mother.

" You are none the worse of the journey, Mrs. Craufurd, I hope ?
It must have been wonderful. And you, Mama—you did wrap up
well, as I told you ? "

Barbara's distinguished chin tilted upwards in the most obvious defiance of the obvious. Both her husband and her son were suddenly nervous, awaiting a pronouncement of such a forthright nature as the Craufurds of Kilblain might not wholly understand.

" If that is what they call a journey nowadays——" Barbara began.

The exclusiveness of their group was suddenly broken by the appearance of Mark Oliphant : director of the new railway, their host. In Walter's eyes he seemed to loom very solid, coming down upon them out of the ruck, a posse of official-looking persons on his heels. He dominated the small occasion, even if, as Walter observed, his distinguished nose bore the dirty smears of smuts hastily wiped. The directors' carriage, it also appeared to Walter, had not lacked refreshment. But it was still Uncle Mark with his own special gift of large command.

" Well, Julius ! How was that for an adventure ? Barbara—I am delighted to see you could join us. Mr. Craufurd, Mrs. Craufurd—the railway company is honoured. Watty, my lad ! And this must be Miss Phoebe."

They were all watching him, closely. He was the great man down from London for a day or two. They were all, with the mild exception of Julius, either hostile or envious or critical. They saw how the dark eyes and Byronic features seemed to possess the innocent person of Phoebe.

" I must have you know," Mark confided to the girl roguishly, " that Watty is my favourite nephew. But upon my soul, Miss Phoebe, this is the first time I have been really jealous of him."

The high, successful man had spoken. Except Barbara, everybody in the group contrived a laugh. Mark waved a hand.

" But I must go now. Meetings, conferences—you know what it is ? I might manage up to Goldenhaddock to-morrow forenoon, Barbara, but don't count on it, don't count on it. These are busy days. Good-bye all ! Thank you for coming. . . ."

The voice of the successful man departing in haste, and the dutiful trot of the small officials behind his urgent person, seemed to leave the family group in a sort of vacuum, helpless.

" I think, Mrs. Craufurd," Julius diffidently contrived to suggest at length, " if the carriages are outside. . . . You ordered the carriages, Walter ? "

" Yes, sir. They should be waiting. Mama——"

Barbara Oliphant, *née* Rait, held her ground. It appeared that she had still her mantle, her parasol and a large workbag to arrange to her own satisfaction.

" There is one thing to be said——" she announced.

"Yes, dear," Julius temporised. "But I think that Mr. and Mrs. Craufurd would like a cup of tea. Or a glass of wine."

"If that Mark would wait for a civil reply," continued Barbara relentlessly, "I would have told him that his railway is an outrage. Never," continued the daughter of Sophie Rait, "never have I endured a journey so odious ! If it is not noise, it is cinders in the eyes. If it is not cinders in the eyes, it is draughts. From beginning to end the experience was beastly, humiliating. *Alors . . .*"

"Yes, yes, my dear," her husband agreed.

"I quite understand, Mama," Walter added hastily. "But—the carriages."

"I shall be delighted to ride in a reasonably civilised vehicle," said Barbara. "Phoebe, my dear—your arm, if I may."

Among the last to leave the station, the Craufurds and the Oliphants made their way in a group down the fine flight of steps Phoebe and Walter had ceremoniously ascended an hour before. The red-coated militiamen were gone. The mob had melted away. Bits of paper drifting on the winds of March uneasily marked where they had been.

"And that," Mrs. Julius Oliphant concluded, "was the most barbarous experience I have ever been called upon to endure."

She grew more and more like her mother as she aged, thought Julius in the wake of the family procession. She was—what would it be now ?—in the middle fifties. They were all getting on ! She was the finest woman in the world. Once, a gay girl, she had whirled into his arms along the windy deck of a ship at sea, and had surrendered there and then.

2

Where once old Edward Oliphant had paced the terrace before The Mount, brooding in princely aloofness on the affairs of his mercantile kingdom, the young men of the technical college his grandnephews had endowed in his honour crowded at the railings to watch a great ship come up the Firth to anchor. With them was their preceptor in marine architecture, a black-bearded, faintly shabby man called Forbes, and young Dr. Walter Oliphant, the latter outstanding in the little gathering by reason of the long white laboratory coat he wore over his ordinary clothes.

The ship on which these twenty-odd pairs of eyes were fixed was of a size and character remarkable at that period. The smoke curling from her tall black stack and the white churn of water under her monstrous paddles as she manoeuvred for position against a brisk sou'westerly wind suggested such power as none of those present had ever before imagined to be capable of confinement and control within one of man's creations. To these men of a sailing-ship port she seemed at once grotesque and majestic in her ominous dimensions.

The prim, faintly old-maidish tones of Mr. Forbes sounded comically inadequate to the occasion.

" As you know, gentlemen," he piped to his class, " we now see the steamship *Travancore* of the Middle and Far Eastern Steam Navigation Company. As you also know, our patron, Mr. Mark Oliphant, is a director of that great company, and we may be sure it is to his influence we owe this call, promising a notable new addition to the trade of the town."

" Now as to the vessel—and please make notes, gentlemen. The *Travancore* was built on the Thames by Messrs. Brierley & Oakes. She is 230 feet in length, with a moulded depth of 37 feet. Her tonnage may be reckoned at 1180. The nominal horse-power of her engines is 520, giving her an estimated speed—confirmed in practice, I understand—of twelve knots."

A whistle of appreciative surprise from the young men testified to the profound interest of this intelligence.

" Now let me call your attention, gentlemen," Mr. Forbes proceeded, " to certain features of the vessel as illustrating the present trends of design. You will observe first of all that, in spite of her powerful engines, the *Travancore* is rigged as a ship—masts, spars and sails complete. . . . I wonder if they cannot trust those fine engines of theirs ! "

A titter from the youths acknowledged the force of this legitimate and topical sally.

" As for the vessel's shape," proceeded Mr. Forbes in a tone markedly patronising, " you will notice that, although constructed of iron, she is bluff at the bows and full along the water-line like any old-fashioned ship-of-the-line. I cannot think that our English friends have got far beyond their Wooden Walls, and I am quite sure that they could learn something from our patron, Mr. Julius Oliphant, our good friend Dr. Walter's father."

The class dutifully cheered this pronouncement, but faintly. Walter was suddenly visited by a sense of frustration he could not immediately analyse. He could only wish that Mr. Forbes would drop the sycophancy from his manner.

" Later on, gentlemen," that specialist concluded, " I shall have something to tell you of the method used in this vessel's construction. Naturally, it differs greatly from our practice in wood. But now, gentlemen, back to the class-room ! I shall be with you in a moment."

He turned to Walter while the youths, chattering, moved in twos and threes across the terrace to the door of the house ; and then Walter saw in the man's face something his unctuous lecturing manner had not confessed, a personal and puzzled concern.

" That will do for my young men, Dr. Walter," he said, " but I don't like the look of this at all."

" The look of what ? " asked Walter, quite failing to take the sudden allusion.

" That new ship," replied Mr. Forbes; nodding his head lugubriously towards the anchorage. " Steam—iron—and a success ; no doubt of that. We're seeing changes, Dr. Walter, big changes. This school itself was founded on an old set of principles—wood, sail, design, workmanship. And already we're falling off—not half the number of pupils we had five years ago. And why ? Iron, steam, everything in a hurry. Sometimes I'm worried, Dr. Walter, thinking of the money your good father has to pay out every year to keep us going. Will we have to start teaching engineering, do you think ? This new-fangled iron shipbuilding ? "

" I'm sure I don't know, Mr. Forbes," answered Walter gravely.

" Nor do I ! " the good man sighed. " However, sufficient unto the day. . . . By your leave, Dr. Walter, I'll get back to my young hopefuls."

The man made for the house, and Walter suddenly saw him as shabby, superannuated, undecided. For the first time, in that moment of illumination, he saw that the very fabric of The Mount was in need of attention—the roughcast on the walls fallen in round patches here and there, the paint and putty of the window-sashes dull and fissured.

It had never occurred to him before—and now it troubled him sorely—that he had assumed so much of security without question. All his life, he and his mother and brother had been surrounded by the assurances of ample means. That dear, gentle man, his father, had been a giver and provider without question ; and now it was alarming to be reminded by Forbes's words and gestures that even on his father's resources the new order of economics might be having its delayed but inevitable effect, to the tragic extent of the decay of this place of learning, the most tangible of his dreams.

Walter went indoors and up the finely curving stairway to a great room that had been fitted up as a laboratory. Its hard, cold emptiness depressed his spirits still further. Once it had been a classroom, but now the room could be spared ! And herein did he, Walter Oliphant, at the age of twenty-five, choose to dwell apart from the world and pretend to be usefully engaged in research ! Yes : his old teacher in

Edinburgh had urged him to these investigations into the new and fascinating Germ Theory. Yes : his father had eagerly applauded the intention, provided him with the room and equipment, and had been as happy as a boy in superintending the work. Walter did not doubt for a moment the ultimate worth of his experiments, but he did in that unhappy hour doubt his own capacity and his own right to take so much and give so little back. A sort of honorary post as medical man to his father's carpenters and seamen, a healthy breed, did not merit such an abundant fee. And he had even dared, in his wholly dependent position, to claim the hand of Miss Phoebe Craufurd of Kilblain, the beauty of a wealthy line !

The young man's mood of self-criticism had one special cause. He was in the condition which comes often to those who traffic in ideas, when certain favoured notions stubbornly refuse to arrange themselves in support of a speculation. Walter's most recent experiment, conducted over a period of time, had gone wrong or would not, certainly, come right. Cultures in his test-tubes, preparations in his oven, the readings of instruments—all made less than sense in relation to his theory. It seemed to him then that his array of glass containers and balances and burners stood for so much waste and futility. He could almost believe that his talents might find their proper level in prescribing cough mixtures or, at the best, superintending a confinement.

Surveying his hollow kingdom thus, Walter decided to do what men more experienced in the battle against frustration accept as the right technique of warfare with intractable fact—to abandon the field and return in a more hopeful hour. He stripped off the long white coat and threw it on the table that was his desk and experimental bench in one. He reached for the tail-coat and tall hat of outdoor formality which he had thrown carelessly on a chair by the window. He would go down to the shipyard and rediscover his vision of truth in the sight of honest men building an honest ship. He could call in at the gatehouse and see Mrs. Phemister, the wife of his father's foreman carpenter, who had taken to queer fits of giddiness and alarming falls without apparent cause. His scientific interests stirring, Walter's intention bent towards Mrs. Phemister and her troubles. This might be indeed his first encounter with that strange affliction known as Meunière's Disease.

As he went down the hill there broke into Walter's self-absorption the sounds of cheering, rising to the height of the Gilded Gabbart itself from the square below. He had to struggle out of his own little world before he could recall what it was all about. Ah, yes ! Nomination Day in the new General Election, and Uncle Mark a candidate.

. . . This would be interesting. Test-tubes and the details of notes faded out of Walter's mind, and his step quickened.

It excited him to find that the Square was packed, and that with more than the riff-raff and the loungers of a seaport town. Groups of men in aprons, many of them bareheaded, declared the new and ominous interest in politics of shipyard craftsmen, coopers, tinsmiths, sugar-boilers, carters, shop-hands and even fisherfolk from their exclusive colony about the mouth of the West Burn. Here and there a banner held aloft on poles proclaimed the faith of a progressive sect. As he came down by the corner under his Uncle Mark's office Walter heard a voice raised in public speech and noted that the crowd's responses were not altogether the flippant, sardonic comments of a mob amused by its own growls and murmurs and occasional cheers. This was a mass of people seriously interested in the day's business.

A hand grasped his arm from behind, and he turned to look into the hearty but ageing face of his Uncle Bob.

" You are just in time, Watty," said Captain Robert Rait gleefully in his ear. " There's going to be fun here to-day, or I'm a Dutchman."

" Where are they now ? "

" Oh, Uncle Mark has been proposed and seconded, and has delivered himself of a damned lubberly speech, promising the Kingdom of Heaven. This is the other hypocrite, Aitken of Kellybank, who cares even less for the good of the town than Mister Mark Oliphant, if that's possible. But just wait a minute."

Walter grinned. Uncle Bob, the complete independent, still a bachelor in his fifties, was specially licensed in the family as the forthright seadog, the uncompromising enemy of sham, and in particular the grim and sardonic critic of all Mark Oliphant's enterprises. And there was the great Mr. Oliphant himself, smiling among his supporters on this easterly side of the hustings that had been set up before the Mid Kirk. Mr. Aitken of Kellybank at the westward end remained only a voice from that viewpoint, for the figure of the Sheriff in wig and gown and the ample outlines of the gowned Magistrates on the platform intervened.

The voice that was Mr. Aitken of Kellybank perorated, but the lively breeze carried his words away from Walter's ears and over the roofs, and the applause from his supporters on the hustings seemed even more substantial than anything of approval that came from the solid mass of working-folk before him.

" Bilgewater ! " Uncle Bob dismissed the candidate's claims. Then his powerful elbow drove into Walter's side. " But listen to this now, boy ! Now the fireworks are going to start."

There had suddenly appeared at the front of the platform, in a central position hard by the Sheriff, a small man of the artisan sort. He had donned his Sunday suit for the occasion, but his squat, wiry figure was stamped all over with the marks of toil and dependency. His first word, delivered on a rough, strong voice through thin lips, seemed to fill the Square.

" Brothers ! " he began.

" But who is this ? " whispered Walter urgently.

" Joe Tolmie, a sailmaker with Drummond's," Bob Rait explained curtly. " A Chartist. Duly proposed and seconded. Had it all arranged. Look at your Uncle Mark's handsome mug—grinning like a sick cat. He would shoot the fellow out of hand if he could. And— O my God, Watty ! Look at Alan's bastard ! "

Before the crowd in the Square the young man who had once been the boy called Duncan was acting like a Dervish. He waved his arms to lead the cheering for Joe Tolmie. He danced up and down in the narrow open space before the hustings, calling on the folk behind to cheer for the Chartist. He waved his arms and, at the same time, with a sort of devilish and not wholly ill-humoured assurance of popular support, threw gibes at the eminent and respectable on the hustings. The vitality and exuberance of this sandy person confessed his part as a prime-mover in the people's demonstration. Laughter and cheers saluted a solo performance of the sort that any Scottish crowd, always eager to mock pretentiousness, most dearly loves.

" Brothers ! " cried Joe Tolmie again, and a hush fell on the Square.

" A broadside now, boy ! " chuckled Uncle Bob appreciatively.

Whether or not the sailmaker had ever had the opportunity of practising the art of oratory Walter did not know, but his own fine feeling for quality told him, after but half a dozen sentences had been uttered, that here was the demagogue born, the true and natural genius in one sphere of activity. His fastidiousness was revolted by much in Joe Tolmie's manner—the mouthing, slovenly speech of the West ; the flailing, extravagant gesture ; the sneering, sardonic vulgarity of the man's attacks on his opponents. Unlike his Uncle Bob, Walter could not laugh at the exuberant candour of the display ; his own sense of purely social form was too subtle for that. Ever and again, however, he forgot the crudity of the voice and language that filled the Square in the sheer interest of the man's meaning and saw in the squat, artisan figure an embodiment of the sacred passion of an otherwise mute mass of human beings.

" It would be all right," commented Uncle Bob in a shrewd mutter at Walter's ear, " if those people and brothers of his weren't

just as damned a collection of selfish rascals as all the Tories in
Parliament ! ''

Walter was moved to argue the nice questions of education and
opportunity implied in Bob Rait's cynical aside, but again the vehemence of the sailmaker engaged his attention. Now, to the delight
of the crowd, he had moved into a passage of that edged and scathing
humour in which the Scots, with their introverted taste for denigration,
have always rejoiced.

" Men and women of Garvel," he bawled. " Take a good look at
this Queen of ours, wee Victoria—take a good long look ! ''

The mob yelled its delight. The Sheriff was seen to frown.

" Have you ever studied the Civil List of the monies at her disposal ? No, you havena ! —for it would take from now to Doomsday
to read it through. But I'll tell ye something about it. I'll tell ye to
begin wi' that her auld mother has a fine fat pension. And for why ?
Juist because the bit lassie—and it was nae fau't o' hers—had the
misfortune to be called to a throne ! ''

Boos, hisses, and some cheers for the adroit little sentimentality
of the reference to the young Queen greeted the sally. This was meat
and drink to the crowd that filled the square, gall for the few on the
bustings.

" And do ye know how much Her Majesty draws from the public
funds ? No, ye don't, but I'll tell ye. Twelve hundred pounds a day
—one thousand, two hundred pounds for every day in the year ! ''

This intimation caused commotion. The senior Bailie looked
anxiously at the Sheriff. The Sheriff shook his head.

" And at that," roared Joe Tolmie, " the poor lassie canna'
support a husband. She's got to get a salary for him as well ! ''

Had he been the most renowned comedian on the stage the sailmaker could not have commanded such delighted applause, nor from
an audience so large. Walter watched and appreciated the artistic
cunning with which he held up a minatory finger, waited for the
tumult to subside, and then, before it had died to create an anti-climax,
cut in with a nippy joke at both his adversaries and a wave of his hand
at each in turn.

" The Whigs wanted to make it fifty thousand pounds—a mere
fifty thousand pounds. But the Tories—great men the Tories for
economy !—cut it down to thirty thousand. Think of it, brothers—
only thirty thousand pounds a year for a braw new Prince Consort,
made in Germany ! ''

" He's pulled it off, by God ! '' cried Uncle Bob above the tumult
of amusement and anger that followed the jibe. " What did I tell
you, Watty ! ''

"He should stop now," said Walter tersely.

And Joe Tolmie did stop. A few sentences restating the points of the People's Charter, and the sailmaker stepped back, having spoken for forty minutes and made public history in Garvel under the noses of the very men accustomed to regard that as their exclusive function.

The Sheriff stepped forward and the shouting died. Walter noted that his putative cousin Duncan was still in the forefront of the crowd, his sandy head bare, his face raised cheekily in defiance of authority on the platform. The lad had the wild look of one ready for mischief.

"I will now take a show of hands," announced the Sheriff.

He called the names solemnly and one by one. Oliphant of Dunclutha—and some sixty arms were raised sporadically over the area of the Square. Aitken of Kellybank—and perhaps half as many arms shot up. Joseph Tolmie, sailmaker in Garvel—and the Square suddenly became a miraculous plantation of uplifted arms and waving hands while red-headed Duncan Oliphant took to dancing up and down again, his arms waving, his yelping voice leading cheer after cheer of triumph and defiance.

These noises subsided as Joe Tolmie was seen to step forward again.

"Brothers!" he began, but quietly now. "As you all know very well, I canna' continue the contest. Not being an Oliphant of Dunclutha nor an Aitken of Kellybank, I havena' the money to do so. But I'll tell you this"—and his voice rose imperatively—"and I'll tell these two gentlemen, whichever is returned, that I am still the true representative of the people of Garvel."

"And the man's right, by God!" said Captain Rait. "And just look, Watty, at that bloody uncle of yours grinning like an ape, knowing that he's going to walk in when it comes to a poll. Aye, I thought so! There he is—demanding one. A fly brute that!"

Uncle and nephew waited on their corner until the bulk of the crowd had drifted away along or down the intersecting streets.

"I'll walk down to the yard with you, Uncle Bob, and pick up my father," said Walter. "He wasn't here to-day, was he?"

"Not he!" chuckled Bob. "He's got more sense—buries his old head in his drawings. The trouble would be to keep him from proposing Mark and seconding Tolmie within two minutes of each other."

They started to thread their way towards the Cross Shore opening among the groups that still argued vehemently on the cobbles of the Square.

"But it's all an abominable farce, Uncle Bob!" exploded Walter, the recent proceedings still on his mind. "Thirty-five thousand people living in this town to-day—with proper accommodation for about ten thousand!—and there aren't twelve hundred voters all told. That show of hands for Tolmie means nothing in effect. The poor fools have no influence at all ! "

" Haven't they ? I wonder. Perhaps we'll see queer things happening before you and I are dead and gone," Bob Rait spoke grimly. Then he laughed sardonically. " That's about the size of it, all the same. When they close the poll to-morrow afternoon Mister Mark Oliphant will be Garvel's Member of Parliament by a big majority. Three cheers for Reform ! And do you see what a cunning devil it is, Watty ? "

They had turned the corner on to the East Breast and the sea was before them, its brightness and its brackish flavour in their eyes and nostrils.

" How do you mean, Uncle Bob ? "

" That damned great iron tub of his out there, the *Travancore*. Nearly the biggest and most powerful steamship in the world, pride of the god-almighty Middle and Far Eastern Fleet. They trade mainly in opium from India to China, Watty, and you're a doctor and should know what that means. Never mind ! Business is business, and Britannia rules the waves, and Governor Mark Oliphant goes off to make the laws of the nation. Hell ! It would make a dago stevedore spew ! "

Walter glanced at his uncle's face. He had never realised the depth of thoughtful passion within this man ; he had accepted the convenient family legend of a hard humorist with a stocky frame and a slightly comic, slightly empurpled face.

" And still, Uncle Bob," he demurred with a smile, " I don't see what the *Travancore* has to do with the election."

" Good God, boy ! " Bob blew up. " And I thought you were the one of my nephews with some title to brains. Damme, don't you see that that ugly brute of a floating boiler, cruising up the Firth at the right moment, is a confounded piece of bribery and corruption ? A big new trade coming to the town ! Garvel to build iron leviathans for the high-and-mighty Middle and Far Eastern ! Wealth, happiness and plenty of booze for all ! Mister Mark Oliphant is the man to guarantee you a hell of a good time on Earth and a high place in Heaven when the time comes ! Lord, Watty," he concluded ruefully, " I wonder I haven't murdered that man before now ! "

Bob ended on that deliberate anti-climax and chuckled over his own violence. Then he was for a moment serious again.

" You know, of course," he seemed to explain his outburst, " your Uncle Mark's shipyard is going over from wood to iron."

" Oh ! "

But Walter's reception of the news was casual. They had crossed the quay to where a sizable crowd was milling and peering above one of the flights of granite steps leading down to the tidal water. Through this they made their way to find that a ship's gig of singular smartness lay by the landing place. As trig as if she had come off a royal yacht, the boat was painted black with a white bottom, and there was a carven emblem in heraldic colours on each bow. The internal woodwork was scrubbed white ; so were the ends of rope that lay in neat coils on gratings fore and aft. The eight sailors who held aloft oars painted black with white blades, and the leading seaman who held the boat to a ring in the harbour with a painted and polished boathook, were uniformly dressed in something very like Navy style. The braided lad in the sternsheets, though obviously under a strong internal pressure to appear indifferent in face of the crowd's stares and observations, would have passed any day for a midshipman off a crack vessel of Her Majesty's Fleet. The remarkable nature of this unusual visitant to the East Harbour of Garvel was emphasised by the fact that, whereas the boy in command was of a type as fair as East Anglia can produce, his crew were to a man thin-faced, brown-eyed and dark-complexioned.

" Come and see the niggers, Sandy ! " cried a small boy on the quay to another, loudly.

" That's the way they do it in the Middle and Far Eastern," explained Bob Rait to his nephew, and not without grudging admira-tion. " White officers and Lascar crews ; Lascars being cheap and easily dropped overside, and no awkward questions asked. Upsides with the Navy they reckon themselves, if not better. It's the old John Company tradition. I'll admit they do it in style. But just wait till those Karachi water-rats get loose along the Vennel."

The edge of Bob Rait's violence was suddenly turned by a com-motion among the crowd. The loungers swung in a trice from the strange spectacle of the smart, Lascar-manned boat to a new and equally exciting phenomenon on land.

" Good God, Watty ! " whispered Uncle Bob in his nephew's ear. " Dip that high tops'l'e of yours for the Lord's sake ! Here comes the Almighty High Admiral himself ! "

Deliberately merging themselves with the mass of the crowd, uncle and nephew watched Mark Oliphant cross the quay to the boat that waited, as they realised now, to take him off to the *Travancore* on a ceremonial visit. He came in something like state, the big ship's captain in blue and gold by his side and a small army of officials and politicians behind him. Occasionally he waved a regal hand in acknowledgment of a servile greeting or a small cheer ; and with him, thought Walter, came an indisputable aura of influence, authority, power. The crowd of hangers-on about the steps divided to let him through. He was part of their spectacle. But they did not cheer.

" Uncle Mark was not looking in the crowd for common relations like you and me," laughed Walter when the tall silk hat of the Member-elect for Garvel had disappeared below the level of the quay. " Come on, Uncle Bob ! I ought to be picking up my father."

" Aye, come on ! " his uncle agreed sourly. " The place stinks. Opium—opium pretty well every way you look at it ! "

They made their way westwards, Uncle Bob rapping the cobbles with the ferrule of the cane he always carried nowadays, much as if he were smiting and spearing the enemies of his own conception of decency ; and as they came round behind the Customhouse they had to halt while a procession passed them.

It was an unhappy procession and it was, in the vision of any reasonably observant person, indubitably made up of persons from Ireland, mainly males and just a few ancillary females, newly landed off one of the steam-packets at the Customhouse Quay. The dumbness of serfdom was in the look of every one of them, an impression heightened by the briskness of the shipping agent who shepherded them on their way up to the new railway station. A few of the younger men were upstanding and ruddy of countenance, but high cheek bones and fixed blue eyes betrayed their slave condition. The majority were slight of build and dark, with long melancholy faces and eyes that one might imagine to have been saddened by long brooding on the sterile bogs of their native land. Only one or two of the young women among them seemed to have vitality ; their black eyes glinted from within the hood of the shawls they wore over their heads. Two young priests with heavy grey faces led the procession.

" There they go ! " said Bob Rait sadly. " The hewers of wood and drawers of water. Forced and blarneyed and bribed to come over here—and it might as well be Greenland for all they know—to dig sewers and build railways and lift potatoes——"

" And live in slums and beget children as fast as their women can produce them ! " Walter added with bitter swiftness. " I can only see them as a medical problem—a factor in public health. We haven't decent room for our own people, Uncle Bob ! How in Heaven's name are we to escape some sort of catastrophe with thousands of these— these foreign rabbits pouring into the country ? "

" Ask your Uncle Mark."

" And that's our tragedy ! " Walter retorted passionately. " The men in power don't seem to understand. One side of their minds is open and receptive to the general notion of progress, but that prospect is so dazzling that the other is utterly blind to the consequences of their way of managing it. Power . . . By God ! That's a horrible illusion, when you discover that money is an easy substitute for the real thing. And it's no more the real thing than a crown piece in payment of a doctor's fee is the real measure of all the study and experience and anxiety he has to go through before he can begin to diagnose."

Bob Rait glanced at the face of his nephew and accurately measured the hardness of thought that was freezing those young and singularly handsome features into a sort of mask of suffering. It also occurred to him that the kerb of a dockside pavement was a queer place for a violent discourse on social economics. But he said and did nothing to check the young man's exuberance.

" The trouble with men like Uncle Mark," Walter swept on, " is lack of education. If it takes five or six years to make a doctor, who is only a sort of plumber when all's said and done, why should the men who deal in human destinies by the hundred thousand be free to order humanity about without even an elementary training in science or political economy or anything else except book-keeping ? "

" I don't know, Watty," replied his uncle gravely, " but in my experience of life there are always the three sorts of men. . . . Come, boy, we'd better be getting along to the yard to meet your father. . . . Just the three sorts of men, Watty. I've never had much beyond a sailor's education myself, but I've worked it out this way. You start with men like your father, aye, and like yourself—the men with the ideas ; the Dreamers I call them. Then you have plain chaps like myself—active, ready for adventure, not very brainy but good at managing men and things ; and I call them the Doers. . . . Does all this sound a bit daft, Watty ? "

" No, Uncle Bob, it doesn't," said his nephew heartily. " But what's your third sort of man ? "

" Ah, that's a new lot, and I'm dashed if I can think of a right name for them ! " cried Uncle Bob with the simplicity of a hearty schoolboy. " But it's men like your Uncle Mark I mean. They haven't any great brains, and they'd run a mile if you fired a pistol in anger near them. But they're keen, man, keen ! They have just that damned rogue's trick of picking up the ideas from clever men like your father; and then getting plain chaps like me to do the dirty work for them. They're not clever, Watty, I'm telling you, but they can twist the rest of us round their little fingers, and I'm damned if I understand it. What is it, think you, they have got and the likes of us haven't ? "

"A love of money and an understanding of money," said Walter primly, "and the new knowledge that money means power."

"And what name would you put on them?"

"A name? Exploiters. . . ."

"Exploiters? I could find another name for the likes of Mister Mark Oliphant," said Uncle Bob grimly, "and it wouldna' sound very polite in your mother's drawing-room. . . . But there's the man himself coming towards us, your father. And the best of the lot of us!"

And there indeed was Julius approaching them through the yard gates, smiling, simple, unenvious.

"Ah, you two!" he greeted them affectionately. "Playing truant! What's been happening to keep you from your work? What have you been doing?"

"Just talking, sir, I'm afraid," said Walter.

"Aye, but talking to some purpose!" added Bob.

"Dear me! You must tell me all about it," observed Julius, delighted that they had been happy and interested together.

3

The first case of the cholera occurred in Drummer's Close. The victim was a strumpet, but a young girl of singular loveliness, and Dr. Broadfoot, called in only at the end of the woman's short journey, was shaken out of his professional detachment to see such a terrible shrinking of the human form, such a sad discoloration of a pretty face, and such a gross incontinence of a beautiful body.

The encounter had indeed an unfortunate effect upon a practitioner so experienced and responsible. He saw Peerie Kate (as the girl was strangely nicknamed) at about two o'clock of the afternoon. He then went on to complete his round of calls, having automatically promised to return in the evening. As he told Dr. Walter Oliphant later on, the curious and lethal nature of the girl's affliction clouded his thoughts throughout the afternoon. It was not until five o'clock, however, in the burdened heat and brassy light of a thundery afternoon, that he set his pony to the hill and made his way to The Mount.

"But it sounds like asiatic cholera!" cried Walter, having heard his senior's story.

"That's what I was thinking," said Dr. Broadfoot lamely. "But what possible source of infection——?"

"You had a ship in from the East a week ago, with a Lascar crew," snapped Walter, throwing off his white laboratory coat.

"That's your possible—probable—source of infection, doctor. And
if it is cholera in this town—in this weather—God help us all! Can
I come with you to see the girl?"

"That was my idea, I confess. Your special experience in these
matters, Walter. Hardly in the general practitioner's line. . . ."

"Cholera is cholera," said Walter harshly, hurriedly arranging
the test-tubes and papers of the day's experiment. He broke every
rule of etiquette in speech to his senior. "There's not a moment to
lose. Isolation. . . . We'll have to organise a team of men. . . . If
this stuff breaks loose . . . I tell you, doctor," he shook his colleague's
arm, "pray for rain! Water—water to wash away the filth! Come
and we'll see this girl."

They were just in time to witness the end of Peerie Kate. The
cold, emaciated and foul-smelling body almost visibly collapsed into
death under their eyes.

"Poor lass!" said Walter; and then, his voice hardening:
"That's the asiatic cholera beyond a doubt. The smell's enough.
Everything that's been near her must be burned. Now we have to
think quickly and act quickly. Doctor—can you be at The Mount
at eight to-night? I'll take the whole responsibility of getting the
Faculty together."

"My dear boy!" said his colleague, surrendering seniority,
"anything you can do will have my full support. Your position in
the town. Fresh from College. All the latest ideas. . . . This looks
bad."

"Bad!"

Walter realised himself to be in a state of the highest excitement.
The state of fear into which he had suddenly been plunged had even
a pleasing quality of the theatrical. It was as all his thinking had
foreseen; the experiments in the laboratory at The Mount were
justified. The living conditions in the low quarters of Garvel were
ripe for the dramatic onset and rapid spread of contagious disease;
a ship from the East had brought in asiatic cholera. Another bitter
syllogism for Uncle Mark to complete!

For all his ability and poise, Walter Oliphant was a reasonably
modest young man, but now he had upon him the cool, happy assurance of predestination. Of the nature of the harsh problem represented
by the putrescent corpse of Peerie Kate he knew that he knew much
more than his senior colleague; it was right that he possessed through
his father the social power to act effectively and to be beyond all the
limitations of a professional etiquette.

"The Mount at eight, then, doctor," he repeated. "I'll have
some sort of scheme worked out."

Up at Goldenhaddock the summer evening, though clotted with heat, was passing pleasantly. It was a Friday, and Aunt Sophie was up from Kempock as usual on her weekly visit. Walter's absence from the family dinner-table had been noted, but without concern.

" Oh ! He'll be busy among his test-tubes and have forgotten all about us," Julius had answered Barbara's question.

" That," Aunt Sophie had agreed decisively, " is a young man of intelligence and industry. Walter is the grandson of whom I am most proud."

And then, when they were sitting in the bay of the drawing-room window and Aunt Sophie was discoursing on the education of the young in general and the feebleness of the girl of 1841 in particular, they saw Walter staring at them from the terrace outside. He had the look of a visitant, haunted and tired. His face was grey and strained. The air of unhappy aloofness he wore stilled even the voice of his grandmother in mid-sentence.

His mother was first on her feet. Her intuitive comprehension of his distress was complete.

" I can't come in," he answered her plea brusquely. " We've got cholera in the town. I have been in contact with a fatal case. Please stay where you are. Father——"

" Cholera ! " Three voices echoed the fatal word.

" But, my dear boy——" Julius began, rising to his feet.

" I am not afraid of cholera ! " Barbara cried simultaneously.

" If it is cholera," said Aunt Sophie, " that is a matter I understand. In my childhood in Louisiana . . . *Alors*. . . . That is right, Julius ! Let him not escape."

For while the women exclaimed, Julius had slipped out of the room and through the front door and was now bearing down on his son. They saw the boy backing away from his father, making agitated and even peevish gestures of protest ; but they cried on Julius to go on, and on Walter to listen to sense, and at length they saw Julius lay a hand on his son's wrist.

" But there is no cause for alarm, my dear boy," Julius was heard to say gently. " This is something we must all talk about, do our best about. Your mother and I, your grandmother—we are not children. Come, Walter. . . . It is very terrible, this news of yours, but we must take it as calmly as we can. Come. . . ."

Her persuaded the young man indoors. Even so, Walter would not budge from the far end of the drawing-room. Barbara started to approach him.

" If you come near me I'll run away," he said harshly. " This is no joke."

"I do not consider it a joke at all, Walter," said his mother coolly, though halted half-way by his vehemence. "I merely want to be sure that you have something to eat before you start your work."

"That doesn't matter." He was still brusque in his excitement.

"And that, *mon cher Gaultier*," observed his grandmother drily, "is the statement of an infant. You are a man of science and, I trust, of sense. You bring us news of a calamity. It is obvious that you, of all people in this filthy town, are most competent to meet and deal with it. That you should be in a proper condition to go about your duties is obvious. . . . *Eh, bien!* If you persist in behaving like a child, stand in the corner there and let your mother pass to the kitchen. It is clear that you have *not* eaten!"

"But this is *urgent*!" the poor boy cried, spreading his hands in a gesture of appeal against feminine triviality.

"Precisely," agreed his grandmother. "The more reason that we should now take ten minutes of time to discuss the matter thoughtfully and with calm. Your father and I are neither children nor fools, as he has observed. Now, Walter—proceed."

Comedy, as always, intruded on the realm of tragedy. The old lady's precise and sensible arrangement of the meeting brought a smile to the young man's tired face.

"Very well, grandma," he agreed. "I think I know, not all that should be done, but all that can be done. Father"—his anxiety broke out again in rapid speech—"you must realise that this is a dreadful situation. The disease is horrible in itself, swift and agonising, and most damnably contagious. What has already started from that poor girl down in Drummer's Close I can't bear to think. Her clothes, her bedding, her—everything! Carried by flies and rats and dirty people everywhere through those filthy warrens. And this stifling weather! Hardly a breath of air and not a drop of rain, open sewers, stagnant . . . If you do nothing else this evening, grandma, pray for rain!"

"Yes, yes, Walter!" his father demurred. "But——"

"I have never observed," added Aunt Sophie, "that prayer, however admirable as an exercise, could put out a fire. *Moi*, I am realist. . . . See, Walter! Your mother has brought you something to eat. *Manges, mon cher enfant!* Barbara, pray be seated. My grandson has something of great interest to tell us. *Alors . . .*"

A plate in his hand, Walter ranged the shadowed portion of the drawing-room and blocked the sketch of his plans in abrupt sentences.

"Father, I want to have The Mount as a base. All of it. Clear out the students for the time being. I have already sent to Glasgow and

Edinburgh for volunteers—senior students and young graduates. A great clinical experience for them. The first should be here to-morrow."

" You mean," asked Aunt Sophie shrewdly, " to make The Mount, as it were, a fortress or camp for those excellent young men who will come to help us ? "

" Precisely, grandma ! " cried Walter happily. " A base for what you might call a combat team. The local doctors will have their hands sufficiently full. The rest of us will tackle the one job—isolating, checking the spread. It is all quite clear in my mind. The system will require to be almost military. And we shall have to be segregated."

" The Mount is yours, my dear boy ! " said Julius, his voice breaking with happiness and pride. " And all the support in money you may require. Do not think for a single moment of expense. . . ."

" The idea is intelligent, Walter. It does the greatest credit to your heart and brain alike," observed Aunt Sophie. " But may I ask how six, or seven, or—it may be—a score of young men will contrive to look after themselves in The Mount ? "

" Oh, that's a trifle ! " Walter dismissed the problem airily.

" It is not a trifle, Walter," said his grandmother severely. " It is a matter of the first importance. Your plan is otherwise foolish. And I now intimate that I, who understand these matters, will take charge of The Mount in person."

" *Maman !* "

" Aunt Sophie ! "

" Grandmother ! "

The three voices protested simultaneously. The old lady smiled tolerantly from face to face.

" *Mes enfants,*" she said, " you agitate yourselves excessively. I am now in the seventy-fifth year of my age. I have enjoyed a varied and interesting life, happy for the most part, if not without its sorrow. All my sons and daughters have settled themselves satisfactorily— except that Bob, who is a fool in being a bachelor. I have the honour " —and she bobbed an odd little bow in Walter's direction—" to be the grandmother of a young man of intelligence and courage. Cholera, illness, death—of such things I am not afraid. So it is clear that if some small risk must be taken—and that I do not admit—it is equally clear that it must be my privilege to take it."

" It is my duty to look after Walter ! " cried Barbara angrily.

" Your duty, Barbara, is first to Julius and to your home."

" I wish my mother and father would agree to close this house and go away," interjected Walter despairingly.

" And that I shall not do ! " Barbara blazed at him.

" My dear boy ! " His father protested more mildly.

" *Alors*," said Aunt Sophie, " the matter arranges itself. Your part, Barbara, is clear. No doubt I shall send across frequently for household supplies. I beg of you, for instance, to have an ample supply of bed linen always ready. Julius, I shall rely on you and Bob to send me up such heavy supplies as I may require. A means of communication will suggest itself."

She rose from her chair. She was not tall, and now she was a little bent, but she commanded the room and the small group of her relatives.

" If I could have the carriage now, Julius. There are many things to which I must attend to-night. To-morrow early, Walter, I shall be at The Mount. Barbara, Julius—I shall no doubt have several lists of articles required."

" You will have all the help, all the supplies you need, Aunt Sophie," Julius promised with emotion. " Either Bob or I will be there first thing. But if I can suggest, even at the last moment, Aunt Sophie . . . Professional help——"

" *Chut !* " The old lady dismissed the protest. " Now the carriage. Barbara—my things."

" I'll get Semple," said Walter, disappearing from the room in the wake of the womenfolk.

Julius was left alone for five minutes, and he had no mind for thought. His being was a welter of fear and exaltation. He found himself staring without sight across the leaden surface of the anchorage when Walter's footsteps sounded on the steps outside.

" The carriage will be round immediately," the young man announced. " I'll get grandma to take me as far as The Mount. I have that meeting at eight. Then I'll try to be back soon to report. But you know, of course, father, than I can plan nothing ? We may hear of a dozen fresh cases before midnight."

" Yes, yes. I understand, Walter."

But he spoke emptily, and silence fell between father and son. It was broken at length by a petulant kick of the lad's foot on the gravel.

" Heat ! Thunder ! But no rain ! " he muttered viciously. " No water, sir ! And only water can save us now. Uncle Mark could find water for his mills and factories, but not a drop to run through the sewers or into the houses ! "

" No," agreed Julius dryly. " It is a tragedy."

The return of Aunt Sophie with Barbara stirred him into awareness again.

" And that is now all arranged," the old lady was declaring cheerfully. " Walter has the carriage ordered ? Good ! Barbara, my dear, Julius will see me to the gate. I ask you to be calm. This affair will arrange itself, I have no doubt. I shall be in touch with you continually. *Courage, ma chère fille !* "

She kissed her daughter tenderly and took Julius's proffered arm. As they passed through the hall he whispered to her.

" You are a brave woman, Aunt Sophie."

She halted and gave him an affectionate and confidential smile. She even patted his hand.

" *Jules, mon ami*," she said with a softness strange in her. " My own children apart, you have always been the best beloved of my relatives, for you are at once a man of distinguished intelligence and of the most delicate sensibility. Imagine, then, the satisfaction I have in getting through you and my dear daughter, Barbara, a grandson so exquisitely intelligent, so courageous, so fine as that Walter. On that account I am, at my great age, the proudest woman in the world to-day *sans doute*. If these things could be measured, it might be discovered that I am also the happiest. . . . And now let us find the carriage."

Julius returned to Barbara. They looked at each other and silently admitted to each other the completeness of their desolation. The wheels of the carriage, grinding on the dry surface of the road outside, might have been those of a tumbril. Their first-born was gone into battle. They faced the possibility of a loss that must make a wound raw and jagged beyond repair, an agony never to be forgotten or otherwise escaped until death, tantalisingly slow to strike, should bring release from a world of mockery. Barbara fell into Julius's outstretched arms, and they wept together in the fecklessness of middle age.

4

Garvel's cholera epidemic of 1841 is now a matter of medical history, amply documented though familiar, in the nature of things, only to specialists in the tortuous and daunting history of public health organisation.

The standard account of the affair in its more personal aspects is that of Peter Lusk Leishman, M.D., one of the survivors of the gallant and devoted band of young medical men from the Universities of Glasgow and Edinburgh who volunteered to fight the epidemic and so, incidentally, acquired such experience as stood every one of those who did not die in excellent stead through the years that followed. General Leishman's volume of reminiscences is dated 1882 and prefaced from an address in Tunbridge Wells, to which town he retreated on his retirement from the Indian Medical Service. The General had lived to see in the Madras Presidency epidemics of cholera much more devastating than that which had afflicted Garvel in the 'forties, but his chapter on the battle in the slums of a Scottish seaport is (as reminiscences of impressionable years are apt to be) by far the best in the book and sets a standard of clinical experience by which all his subsequent, and more devastating, experiences of epidemic are measured.

The statistical facts of the visitation are fully set out in Oliphant and Ferrier's *Public Health : A Study of a Particular Case with General Applications* (University of Edinburgh Press, 1854 ; 3 vols.), but General Leishman had access to this standard textbook on his return from the Indian service in 1877, and his simplification of the details, backed by his experience as a participant, is more acceptable to the common reader. *Pages from an Indian Doctor's Diary* is long out of print. It was, in the most charitable view, the amateurish work of a man of affairs : a literary waste of splendid material ; and only a few copies now survive on the bookshelves of old houses and in just a few old-fashioned subscription libraries. Therein, however, repose not a few memories and bones of events and people that a happier civilisation than that which created the Garvels of this world would have taken care to cherish for reverence and warning at once.

General Leishman seems to have remained a bit of a boy all his life long, but so much the better. His account of the Garvel episode has at once the vividness of a healthy boy's recoil from the sordid and a boy's open admiration of a hero.

We can still read in this chapter that, of a population of some thirty thousand people, fourteen hundred odd died of cholera between mid-July and mid-September, most of them in the first three weeks of that period.

" The heat was oppressive," says General Leishman. " I have known great heats during my Indian service, but the heat of that exceptional summer long ago is still with me. I conclude that the atmosphere of humidity in suspension, or, as it were, of a thundercloud which refuses to burst, burdened our souls as well as our operations."

The General's memory, which was still the boy's, allows us some gleaming flashes of photographic realism.

" I remember one lad, he could not have been more than fourteen, who carried his little sister, a child of ten, to the place that had been set aside as an isolation hospital for the very poor. The girl was in an advanced stage of the disease, comatose and already blue in the face ; her rags of clothing were soaked with her own discharges,

nauseating and highly infectious as all familiar with this loathsome
fever will readily appreciate. Angered by the boy's disregard of
elementary precautions, which we had been at pains to impress on the
common people through advertisements in the newspapers and by
word of mouth on our visitations, and no doubt suffering from the
strain of our long exertions, not to mention the burdensome nature
of the meteorological conditions ; I asked him rather sharply why he
had not come for us in the usual way to arrange for the patient's
removal by the special service of vehicles Dr. Walter Oliphant and
his father had inaugurated with a foresight and energy I now realise
to be beyond all praise. Standing up to my impatience like a little
hero, the boy proceeded to outline one of those domestic situations
which continually arise to unman the most detached practitioner of the
healing art.

" *This gallant child—and I use the epithet advisedly* "—continues the
General in generous italics—" *had that morning witnessed the death of
his widowed mother. He had, in an orderly fashion, made due arrangements
for the disposal of the body according to the decent rites of his class ; and only
then, perceiving the straits his little sister was now in, he had taken, at the
gravest risk to his own life, the quickest means of bringing the child under
professional care !*

" ' I couldna' wait, could I ? ' said the boy defiantly. ' Thae
Cholera Carts o' yours '—(for so our primitive ambulance service was
popularly known)—' Thae Cholera Carts o' yours tak' a lang time.'

" The boy then braced his shoulders and looked me in the eye.

" ' I'm no' feart ! ' he declared, meaning in his doric fashion that
he was not afraid.

" Alas ! The boy's care for his little sister was in vain. She died
within two hours of admission to our hospital, and never will there be
erased from the tablets of my memory the sight of that lad waiting
prayerfully on the open space outside, nor the distress of his sobbing
when, as it chanced, it became my sad duty to convey to him the
grievous tidings.

" It has been well said," the General continues, " that every cloud
has its silver lining. Every medical man, no matter the strength of
his inclination towards Science and even the doctrines propounded by
Professors Darwin and Huxley, is halted at least once in his career by
an arrangement of facts so strange and wonderful that it can be
attributed only to the intervention of a Divine Providence. In the
case under review "—the chronicler returns to italics—" *the boy escaped
infection despite the risks to which he had exposed himself in carrying his little
sister to our headquarters.* I understand that, thanks to the good offices
of Mr. Julius Oliphant, the lad was cared for and educated at the

charge of that enlightened merchant and subsequently enjoyed—and
may still enjoy, for all I know—decent prosperity as a skilled operative
in the shipyards of his native town. This thought, I may add, has
been to me a constant stimulus, a beacon of hope in the darkness of
suffering and ignorance, throughout my professional career."

Other human details, naturally omitted from the Oliphant-Ferrier
survey of the epidemic, are to be found only in General Leishman's
belated reminiscences. The plans of segregation, incineration and so
on, to which the team of doctors worked, are set out in detail in the
extended study, but only in *Leaves from an Indian Doctor's Diary* is there
to be found a really full acknowledgment of public services rendered
by individuals. The local newspapers of the period were either
incurious as to the facts, or, more likely, were denied them. General
Leishman writes :

" I tremble to think what might have happened in Garvel had
not the community been able to boast two citizens so selfless and
enlightened as Dr. Walter Oliphant, our leader, and his father, Mr.
Julius Oliphant, the eminent marine architect.

"The latter was, at the period of which I write, in his fifties, of
good height though slightly stooped by long addiction to study,
still wonderfully fresh of complexion, well featured, and of a cast of
countenance more benevolent than I remember to have seen in any
other fellow creature. It is not too much to say that this benevolence
was the *fons et origo* of the bulk of the equipment required by our little
army of healing in its campaign against the fell disease. The muni-
cipality was at that period ill-equipped with sanitary appliances and,
it may now be said without uncharitableness, almost totally lacking in
any general understanding of its obligations in matters of public
health to the commonalty. In the later stages of the epidemic Government stepped in, though none too soon, notably with a hulk which
was moored in the Bay of Tweek and used as a place of isolation for the
milder type of case, and well suited as such on account of the fresher
sea air and the scouring motion of the tides. I do not hesitate to assert,
however, that if our work in Garvel saved these islands from a wholesale spreading of the plague, as is now generally recognised, much
of the credit must go to Mr. Julius Oliphant, whose generosity and
intelligence never failed, even before the most exorbitant challenge.

" *Integer vitæ, scelerisque purus,*
  non eget mauris jaculis, necque arcu. . . .

" I was to learn from his own lips during the height of the campaign, if the phrase be permitted, that Dr. Walter Oliphant had

foreseen the possibility of a visitation of epidemic disease to a seaport so exposed to foreign and unquarantined influences as Garvel then was, and had tentatively sketched a plan of campaign, though only in pursuance (as I understood him) of his specialised studies at Edinburgh. He had clearly foreseen the need for the strictest isolation of contacts, for the ruthless burning of all contaminated material, and for the swift sterilisation of all fæcal matter associated with a patient : though the latter precaution was in practice, thanks to the abnormally protracted spell of thundery weather, impossible of complete achievement. The idea of a body—or team, as Dr. Oliphant preferred to call our sodality—living apart, ready for any emergency on something like the system of watches obtaining in Her Gracious Majesty's Royal Navy, was entirely his.

"*The best-laid schemes of mice and men gang aft agley*, Scotland's national bard, the Ploughman Poet, wrote in his telling verses, which I have often heard repeated in the garrison towns and cantonments of India on St. Andrew's Night and on the anniversary of the Poet's Birthday, with all the fervour the exile brings to the recital of the language and customs of his ' ain folk,' but no such disability—if the gentle reader will forgive the digression—attended Dr. Walter Oliphant's intromissions during the period under review. Mr. Julius Oliphant was prompt to put at his son's complete disposal the mansion-house called The Mount, which he had previously maintained as a technical college and Mechanics' Institute for the advancement of scientific knowledge among the less fortunately endowed of his fellow-citizens. There the ' team ' was comfortably lodged and conveniently segregated. Adjacent to Mr. Oliphant's shipyard was a large space of waste ground running down in peninsular form to the Bay of Tweek, and on this promontory stood a group of buildings previously occupied, as I was led to understand, as kippering sheds and stores for the gear of the local fishermen. These were rapidly and easily transformed into the reception station and the isolation hospital which, with the appropriate offices, including a huge bonfire for the necessary purposes of incineration the genius of Dr. Oliphant had envisaged.

" These amenities, and many others," continued General Leishman handsomely, " were made available to us only through the enlightened generosity of our leader's father. Drugs, rare stimulants, a special service of repair, or transport, or even personal convenience— the youngest of us had only to say a word, and this rare and saintly man invariably obliged with more than mere competence ; with—if I may hazard the phrase—the sweetness of one of the Lord's Anointed."

Then the General's record of a fading episode flashes suddenly into lurid reality.

" For a mortuary we used the shed nearest the sea and farthest from the more substantial erection set aside as a temporary hospital, and the interior of this makeshift dead-house would, near midnight of any day during the early, virulent stages of the epidemic, present such a scene as I have never seen equalled for sadness and desolation in the course of a long life devoted to the practice of medicine. Wholesale burnings of the fever's myriad victims on the torrid plains of the Deccan had never what I can only describe as the *lonely horror* of that small and shabby place of death by the seashore. In the dim light of a stable lamp suspended from a beam as many as eight corpses, even ten on one occasion, lay shrouded and covered in double rows on the bare ground, so many mortal journeys suddenly interrupted and now over for ever. On the stillest nights the odours of the disinfectant fluids we used copiously contended in vain with the stench of putrefaction, though Dr. Walter Oliphant was a martinet in the matter of the thorough washing of all corpses. When the door was open and the fitful flames of the bonfires outside were reflected on the inner walls of this chamber of death, the general effect was eerie, even horrific, in the extreme.

" Even so, the beloved figure of Mr. Julius Oliphant was occasionally to be seen at a late hour of the night, contemplating from the door of the mortuary this ghastly demonstration of the frailty of the flesh. I have since surmised that the spectacle afforded material for reflection to a mind so notably cast in the philosophical mould, but I have also thought that his visitations to the uttermost chamber of horrors were the measure of his pride and sympathy in his son's work and, if I may so express it, a mystical sharing of his risks and responsibilities. Certain it is that neither the mildest remonstrance nor the most peremptory instruction could persuade this saintly gentleman of the grave dangers he ran.

" ' At my age,' he would say with his sweet smile, ' safety is not a matter of great account. After all, gentlemen, I am your agent with the outside world and must be allowed to know how the work goes on.'

" Then came a night, however, when the tragedy of death by cholera became personal to the Messrs. Oliphant with an intimacy almost beyond endurance and with a dramatic force that moved the most hardened among us to the deepest emotion and, I trust, a sharpened sense of the inscrutability of the Divine Purpose.

" Only a few weeks before the onset of the epidemic Dr. Walter Oliphant had become engaged for marriage to a Miss Phœbe Craufurd, the only daughter of one of Garvel's most distinguished citizens, a gentleman who had at once inherited landed property in the western district of the town and subsequently improved his fortune in the Newfoundland trade. Miss Craufurd was a young lady of quite singular loveliness of face and form and, I was assured, of the gentlest disposition ; and while the why of the infection of such an innocent creature is a question we must ask in vain, the wherefore was made all too clear by our medical investigations. A servant in her father's house had taken to loose living and frequenting the lower parts of the town and had been dismissed, but not before she had conveyed on her person to her young mistress the seeds of the disease. Again I pause to make the clinical observation that the sources and courses of microbic infection are among the more baffling problems always present in the mind of the medical man concerned with the treatment of fevers. In this case the servant girl, though afflicted, escaped with her life, while Miss Craufurd was the only other member of a household of twelve to attract the fatal germs.

" In the ordinary course of things, the size of Mr. Craufurd's establishment would have allowed ample room for the segregation and treatment of his daughter's unfortunate case, but the gentleman in question was a person of the highest public spirit and, in a courageous accordance with Dr. Walter Oliphant's appeal, decided that even his beloved child must go into isolation in the appointed place. We were able to accommodate this patient in a cubicle apart from ordinary members of the public, and I had the delicate honour of having the young lady placed under my care. Her case was, alas ! hopeless. The disease had taken a thorough grip of a delicate and refined constitution, the process of collapse was of alarming rapidity, and at seven o'clock on a stifling evening, only seven hours after her admission, death put what may fairly be described as a merciful term to her sufferings. To all of us working in the hospital at the time, wearied and harassed as we were, it seemed intolerably sad that a disease so wasting, so revolting and even humiliating in all its symptoms, should destroy such a lovely flower of a distinguished family and an elegant culture.

" For some hours at least that evening, the body lay in our mortuary with those of persons from humble homes, and I recall that one of her neighbours in death was a little girl of perhaps seven summers, a pretty child before the wastage and discoloration of the fever ravished her fairness. Mr. Julius Oliphant paid us one of his visits that night, and though I was not a witness of the scene I learned later that, instead of lingering by the door and peering into the house of death as was his custom, on this occasion he pushed past the attendant, despite the latter's protest, and walked between the rows until he stood above the sheeted form he persuaded the official to point out

as that of his son's betrothed. Then, though the body was heavily
shrouded and the face covered, he stood for a long time in silent and
reverent contemplation, and when he passed out again—so the
attendant informed me with the most respectful emotion—the frame
of this fine gentleman was shaken by his sobbing.

" I may now, after the lapse of so many years and since almost
all the actors except myself have now quitted the scene, be permitted
to describe what I myself was by force of circumstances privileged, nay,
obliged, to witness of a scene even more heartrending in its sacred
intimacy.

" At a late hour that night, I had occasion to seek the urgent
advice of Dr. Walter Oliphant and was directed to look for him in the
vicinity of the mortuary. Perhaps thoughtlessly, I entered that gloomy
chamber only to find myself the unwilling witness of our leader's last
parting from his bride that might have been. The undertakers
employed by her family had arrived to coffin the body, and there,
standing a little apart in the lamplight, was the bereaved lover, a
silent and motionless spectator of the scene. His complexion had a
deathly pallor, but his fine features were as immobile as if carved out
of marble, and his eyes were dry. Only when the men had placed
the body in the coffin, which they had raised for convenience on
trestles, did he suddenly step forward and lift the cloth that had
covered the wasted features of his beloved. This he held from her face
for the space of only a few seconds, but in those brief moments his
dark eyes directed on the sleeping countenance a gaze in which a lifetime of grief and surmise seemed to be concentrated. He then replaced
the napkin and, turning abruptly from the coffin, strode out of the
chamber of death. It is a singular circumstance that though I stood
almost in his path and in the full light of the lantern, this sorely
afflicted man brushed past me without, I swear, being in the slightest
degree conscious of my presence.

" I have often been asked to give some account of the singular
character of my old colleague and leader, and on such occasions have
usually proffered a brief sketch of this distressing scene. Dr. Walter
Oliphant's singleness of purpose in a given situation, his indifference
to extraneous detail, his very refusal to display the slightest signs of
emotion are, I think, well illustrated even in my halting account of
the incident. While he was admired for his distinguished talents to
the point of idolatry by all of us who worked under him during the
Garvel epidemic of 1841, it would be idle to pretend that he commanded our human affections in any notable degree. Of his great
scientific virtues he had the defects of intolerance with our most venial
faults even if the outcome, as they were as often as not, of fatigue.

He drove us hard—as, indeed, he drove himself. Some of the weaker
brethren among us, wearied out as the rainless weeks went past, were
sometimes tempted to rebelliously and openly discuss the cold sarcasm
of which he was occasionally capable in moments of stress : a fault
which some were oddly inclined to contrast with the distinction of his
physical form. A great physician, it is strange to reflect that Dr.
Walter Oliphant could never have acquired ' a bedside manner ' or
controlled a general practice with acceptance to his patients. The
new-fangled term ' specialist ' is most properly applied to this remarkable character. He was a man of science. That he was a great man
of science in the department of public health is beyond any doubt.

" It gives me particular pleasure in my declining years to recall
yet another episode which displays, however briefly, the other side of
the medal. For a second time it was my privilege to be close to him
in a moment of emotion, and, on this occasion, to feel the glow of the
inner warmth his customary demeanour concealed from the outer
world.

" This was when, on the 27th day of the visitation, the rain for
which we had prayed so long began to fall in earnest. Such a prolonged spell of drought is phenomenal in a notoriously wet district
and conduced, no doubt, to the virulence of the epidemic. Except
during the first week it was not a phase of clear, brilliant sunlight as
we know in India. The meteorological conditions constituted rather
an agglomeration of elements in which a thundery and windless atmosphere and an overcast sky latterly predominated. Throughout the
last week the signs pointed clearly to rain, if not to a positive cloud-
burst, and that period of strain seemed on this account all the more
intolerable to those of us who, already struggling against fatigue, knew
the importance of water and the copious flushing of drains and sewers
to the success of our operations.

" It came upon us quietly, however, that ' gentle rain from
Heaven.' I was myself snatching a hurried meal with some of my
colleagues in our common room at The Mount, when one of my
companions called out : ' Rain ! Look ! ' In a trice we were crowding
at the window, watching those precious raindrops as children watch
the dancing flakes of winter's first snowfall, patting each other on the
back and exchanging joyous congratulations. The first drops of the
downpour seemed painfully tentative, but as we watched they gathered
in strength and numbers, and soon the Heavens were emptying themselves in a steady, heavy fall on the parched earth. I recall the delight
with which one of our number—he was Dr. Ludovic Hall, latterly the
esteemed Superintendent of the Midland Counties Fever Hospital at
Loughborough—drew our attention to a rivulet forming and cutting

its own bed through the gravel outside the window at which we stood.

"Duty then called me to return to my post at the hospital for the night watch, and I was down in the entrance hall or lobby, searching among the garments hanging there for some sort of protection against the rain, when Dr. Walter Oliphant entered from the outer world, dripping.

" 'Rain, Dr. Oliphant!' I could not help offering him a joyous greeting.

" 'Yes, rain!' he agreed with a faint smile. 'The rush of it in the gutters is the loveliest music I have heard in all my life.'

"With this pretty conceit, surprising on those austere lips, he passed me towards the rear of the building, but when I opened the door to go out and paused for a moment before braving the elements, he turned back and stood beside me, his fingers closing round my arm in a gentle and (I dare to believe) affectionate pressure.

" 'Yes, I think we may soon see the light,' he said. 'It should not be long before you can arrange to return to your work in Edinburgh, Dr. Leishman. You have done well; you have all done so very well. My sorrow is that so many good men will never go back to work again.'

"This he delivered in a voice so charged with emotion and in a tone so profoundly reverential, I dare to believe that, of all those who worked under him, I was the fortunate recipient of the most intimate confidence Dr. Walter Oliphant exchanged with any one of us in the whole course of the campaign. It is also to be reckoned a singular circumstance that I had not until that moment, such being the depth of my absorption in the work and the pressure upon the faculties of us all, paused to reckon with exactness the casualties among those who had gone into battle against the disease. Of our team of eighteen senior students and doctors alone, seven, in fact, paid with their lives for their fidelity to the Oath of Hippocrates.

"It may finally be mentioned in brief that the loss of his betrothed was not the only personal bereavement suffered by our leader through the epidemic; and though I have often been called upon to describe the severity of his methods, I have never failed to give due weight to the fact that, if he asked much of his colleagues, he never spared himself nor was he spared by Fate two grievous personal losses.

"The second of these afflicted him through the death of his maternal grandmother, Mrs. Sophie Rait, the widow, I understand, of a master mariner. At the very outset of our operations this remarkable person, although well advanced in years, had volunteered to act as housekeeper at our campaign headquarters in The Mount. She was a lady of eccentric manner and a tongue not a little sharp, much

given to the use of French phrases, which seemed singular in respect
that we understood her to be of American origin. Hers was a downright and realistic personality, and I have little doubt but that Dr.
Walter Oliphant inherited the more austere traits in his temperament
from this unusual female. Be that as it may, I must confess that her
management of our bachelor establishment left nothing to be desired,
and that the old lady showed no lack of indifference to danger in her
inevitable contacts with men and wearing apparel that were in close
daily contact with a lethal infection. If she failed through her masterful
ways to command the complete sympathy of her charges, I must
testify that we were provisioned with taste and in abundance, and that
her care of our bed and body linen touched the highest standards of
particularity.

" I had left Garvel and the strange experience that seaport had
held for us behind when Mrs. Rait was gathered to her fathers. It
appears that she was the victim of an infection as it were subsidiary
to the prevalent cholera but related, obviously, to the insanitary state
of affairs then prevailing in the town. She was, indeed, in the act of
surrendering her important office at The Mount when she was taken.
The disease appears to have been in the nature of diphtheria ; indeed,
I was led to understand that Dr. Walter Oliphant had Professor Meikle
down from Glasgow and that a tracheotomy was attempted, but
without success. This aged and redoubtable lady succumbed to simple
cardiac failure after, as is common in such cases, notably in the
scourge of pneumonia, a sudden subsidence of the earlier fever.

" Such, then, is some account of what Dr. Walter Oliphant suffered
in his personal attachments during the period under review and of the
motives which moved him to undertake his monumental life-work. To
me, so long as life lasts, his memory will be sacred. It is my most
profound source of pride that my name is, among those of the original
' team ' of eighteen young men, inscribed on the dedicatory page of
the noble work which bears his name. Indeed "—concludes the
General on a quaint note of antiquity—" I have always ascribed my
perhaps not negligible professional success to the fact that I was one
of Oliphant's Men in the famous Garvel epidemic of '41."

5

On a gusty and fitfully wet day of November that year, there passed
through the town of Garvel from east to west a procession of some
eighty men and boys. It was a procession entirely lacking in military
colour and precision, but it had a strangely austere quality of its own.

It was made up of working men. They marched in their working clothes, many of them in the white aprons of their craft, and not a few carried symbolically one or other of the tools of their trade—a mallet, a rule, or an adze at the slope on the shoulder. The apprentice boys in the rearward files appeared to take the occasion with some levity and jested blithely enough with the spectators of their passing. One single touch of heraldic gaiety was provided by a Guild banner in blue and gold, carried along in the middle of the procession and in the teeth of the westerly wind by two stout young men at the poles and four others on the guy-ropes. The forward section of the column, however, was of grave dignity compact. Here marched older men, journeymen of long standing, many of them bearded and bespectacled, and most obviously not of a kind to be taking part in an outing with a frivolous purpose. In front of them all strode a patriarch, a tall lean man with a white beard and the unmistakable look of a master crafts-man, as indeed he was. He had the air of a prophet leading, though without undue elation, an austere sect out of bondage towards a potentially better land.

That was what the procession did, in some sort, truly portend. Its appearance in the streets of the town, with the Guild banner cere-monially borne above it, was an act or demonstration of faith. Though it proceeded through the main streets of a small seaport town, and did not attract witnesses in any considerable volume from the com-monalty of that insignificant place, it was a cavalcade much more significant as a symbol of human torment than a hundred State funerals of a hundred field-marshals and of a meaning more profound than the coronation of the mightiest emperor that ever ruled.

One shipyard was going over to iron and steam, and these were the shipwrights of the old order, the skilled and loving craftsmen in wood, demonstrating according to their lights against heretical inno-vation. In his exhortation to his followers before they set out, the leader had indeed referred to Scripture and reminded them that the Lord Jesus Christ himself had been of their craft. Now, a tribe of Israel, they were bearing down on another shipyard which, notoriously faithful to timber, might be their destined refuge.

From the windows of his shipyard office, called from London to deal with crisis, Mark Oliphant watched them form up outside the gates and march away from his sphere of influence.

" Pig-headed bastards ! " he directed a rough, angry comment out of the corner of his mouth to his manager, Gavin Semple.

" Yes, sir," agreed that squint-eyed accommodating man. " But they'll learn their lesson pretty quick."

At the other yard, nearly a mile away, Bob Rait burst a few

minutes later into the room where Julius sat, the fingers of his left hand drumming nervously on the table.

" They've started," he announced, " and they are making for here all right."

" Damnation ! " said Julius with surprising violence. " And what do we do now ? I don't want to be involved in a trade dispute with Mark on the other side."

" You'll meet them, my friend," answered Bob firmly, " and you'll speak to them. Lord, Julius ! We've had this out time and again these last six months. These men look to you. It's a big responsibility, but you can't escape it. It's not Mark Oliphant on one side and Julius Oliphant on the other. It's iron or wood. It's the new or the old. Dammit, Julius ! It's men or machinery."

" Dear me ! " sighed Julius. " Perhaps a deputation, Bob——"

" Better see the lot of them. I'll clear the moulding loft."

" Dear me ! "

The grave procession wheeled right at the Square, passed down the Cross Shore, turned left along the West Breast, and halted at the gates of the old shipyard. It had not carried a train of enthusiasts or even children with it, for it was not a joyous parade. Men and women were grave-eyed as they watched it pass, as it might have been a funeral, and there were a great shaking of heads and much weighty argument on the sidewalks. The few urchins and loafers who trailed along with the marching men hoped either for an outburst of music or (as some wiseacres had prophesied) a collision with the constables. The carpenters neither provided nor provoked any bit of fun likely to appeal to the idle.

A man alone came through a side-gate of the Oliphant yard to meet them and ask their business. The lean old man with the white beard explained that he and his followers begged the favour of speech with Mr. Julius Oliphant. The man from the yard withdrew, and the main gates then slowly opened to let the procession in. They were closed behind the tail of apprentices and in the face of the hangers-on. A few of these hung about for a space, as if they hoped that explosive and pleasing noises might still issue from within. The high, flat gates outstared them, and they went away one by one until no stranger lingered outside except a seedy man who, with a drip on the end of a long pink nose that seemed to embarrass even its possessor, was the owner-printer, editor and reporter of the *Garvel Herald*, not long set up in hopeless opposition to the established *Courier*.

From a platform rigged up out of planks on trestles in the echoing loft, Julius looked down on the shipwrights from the other shop. The sight of them assembled in their patient decency and their antique

faith brought a lump to his throat and tears to his eyes, but he knew
his own emotional weakness and strained his faculties to take in what
old John Fenwick, their spokesman, had to say to him. The patriarch's
Scots speech was of the eighteenth century. Phrases of it stuck in
Julius's mind like lines of poetry.

"The feck of us'll no' be haulden wi' thir new-fanglet weys o'
daen'. . . . Airn's no' canny gear for auld-farrant chiels the likes o'
me. . . . I wrocht wi' your uncle syne, and his faither afore him,
that's deed it'll be saxty year come Candlemas. . . ."

John Fenwick's message, like his vocabulary, came out of the past.
He appealed to ancient gods and hopeless loyalties. Julius found himself shaking his head over many of the old man's arguments and, for
fear of offending these decent craftsmen, had to check himself. When
the time came for him to speak he rose with a great feeling of sadness
in him.

"Men," he started quietly, "I have listened with sympathy to
what John Fenwick has said on your behalf. If I were one of you, I
would have done as you have done, no doubt. I am a shipbuilder in
wood. I am a believer in sail. I rate the craft of the carpenter as high
as any man could. But "—and now he shook his head deliberately—
"I think you are mistaken in what you are doing."

He held up an appealing hand as a murmur of protest and disappointment passed through his audience.

"No, no! Hear me out. I am giving you the best advice that is in
me to give. . . . But let me say this one thing first. You come here
seeking work—what is it? eighty or a hundred of you. Lads, there
isn't work for you all in this place or anything like it. As you go out
again you will meet my foreman shipwright, Sandy Mackinnon, and
he'll take on all the hands he can. There may be jobs for a score of
you, and I hope they will go to the older men. For I must tell you
bluntly that this is my advice to the younger men—go back where
you come from, swallow your pride, *and learn the new trades in iron.*"

The protesting mutter of the crowd had now an angry note in it.
A young man at the back forgot himself so far as to shout out a word
which suggested treachery and betrayal. But he was hushed by his
mates, and Julius went on.

"You don't like it, and I hate to say it, but a fact is a fact, men.
Iron has come to stay, and nothing you or I can do will stop it, any
more than we sailing ship men could stop the development of steam
these last thirty years. I'll tell you more than that "—he challenged
his hearers sharply with a wagging forefinger—"I tell you the day
is coming when we shall be building even our sailing ships of iron!"

For the men who listened to him this was heresy, shocking in its novelty. It puzzled them and angered them. Their ancient suspicion of the Masters afflicted even the older men among them. Some shouted their protests ; some laughed sardonically. Old John Fenwick shook his head as over the stupidity of a good man misguided.

" That is a prophecy, if you like," Julius allowed, " but there is solid reason behind it. Already some builders are using iron in sailing ships—iron frames, strong and easily shaped to take the planking, instead of our good old oaken ribs—and I cannot say that they are wrong. We'll all come to it, no doubt. But there is more than that, and now I speak to you as a man who has wrought his life long to keep this yard in full employment and pay good wages to decent tradesmen."

. . . And his hearers, being of the old, fair-minded Scottish race, applauded him then, though with a faintly grudging discretion. . . .

" The Americans."

Julius saw that he had at length the complete interest and sympathy of these men. Here were facts and ideas, rich meat to men of their breed. His own heart warmed to their ready intelligence, and he seemed to confide professional secrets to fellow-workers in the same field.

" America has unlimited supplies of native wood, cheap and handy in a degree we can never understand. She has ship-designers of genius —men like Donald McKay of Boston : a very great man indeed. She has a great reserve of fine seamen, bred on the coasts of New England. I tell you, lads," Julius warmed to his congenial thesis, " unless we can find a good commercial answer to the Americans they will sweep our sailing ships off the seas. . . . Not our steamships—mark that point ! They haven't, as yet, the iron and the engineering resources we have. . . . But isn't the conclusion staring us in the face, whether we like it or not ? Why, it's just that we shall—almost that we must —build our sailing ships of iron ! "

He paused, and his audience regarded him with a sort of stupefied hopefulness.

" That is all I have to say," he concluded gently. " As many hands as can be taken on here will be taken on. To the rest—you younger and middle-aged men—I say as your friend : Go back and don't be too proud to work in iron."

His voice began to falter in a resurgent wave of emotion.

" So long as it doesn't enter our souls. . . . God bless you all ! "

Julius stepped down from the little platform and seemed to seek concealment among a pile of planks that stood against the wall. Most of his audience remained staring blankly in front of them, comically immobilised by surprise and disappointment, but the elders among them gathered in a muttering group to confer with agitated beards and wagging forefingers. At length the patriarchal Fenwick stepped forward and with grave formality announced that they had heard what Mr. Oliphant had had to say, that the gist of his advice had been disappointing, but that they allowed it to contain matter for serious discussion. They thanked Mr. Oliphant right heartily for giving them a hearing, which was more than they had got in another place, and now begged leave to withdraw.

As they crossed the yard to the office, Bob said thoughtfully :
" That's given them something to think about."

" Yes," agreed Julius warmly, " and I wonder what the poor fellows will make of it. They'll be thrawn, I doubt. Your old-fashioned craftsman may be a Chartist or a Revolutionary by conviction, but he's at heart the greatest Tory of them all. I'd dearly love to overhear their debates."

The same thought, though with an angrier urgency, filled the mind of Mark Oliphant, fuming at the window of his room overlooking the Square. He had sped the shipwrights from his yard with a contemptuous oath. He had pretended to his office people that their going was a triviality of indifferent concern to a man capable of large and drastic decisions. He had even hinted at a belief that they would return before the evening, like whipped curs, their tails between their legs. Now, seeing them come up the Cross Shore to the Square in small groups and stand there in vehement knots of argument, he burned to know what they were saying and what had been said to them.

He had, in fact, been wounded in the two most sensitive parts of his being. His power, in him an appetite as strong as the craving for drink in a weakling, a necessary adjunct of his way of living, had been flouted. A pack of rapscallion carpenters to defy Mark Oliphant ! Fools ! Trash ! Pig-headed bastards ! But though his conscious mind despised and defied them, another and basic part of him feared and hated the demonstration and its consequences. And they had gone to Julius with their grievance ! That damned, soft-hearted fool, always cropping up with his hare-brained ideas and Blackneb politics ! But again the anger represented a fear, and this the subtlest and most daunting of the apprehensions that lurked, like rats within the walls of a palace, behind the grandest success of a shining public career. If a man could only understand Julius, get the hang of that crazy mind of his ! The fellow was so damned shifty. . . .

Allowing himself in the circumstances to break a prudent vow, Mark unlocked a cupboard, filled himself a glass from a brandy bottle, and tossed it off. Even into the act of seizing his hat from a peg he put the tempestuousness of his mood, and his passage through the outer office was like that of a tornado. Indeed, one of his captains who waited there and was hurt by being quite ignored, saw fit to address the clerks bending over their accounts.

" Blast my eyes ! " he cried, for he was of a ripe generation of seadogs. " Here's me ready to go to the notary to register my protest in common form against the Act of God in the Bay of Biscay, but damme if I won't have to put in a word about the governor's storms ! "

He spoke lightly, but a grey-haired clerk replied for his colleagues with a bleak bitterness.

" That ! " he spat the word. " That's only an animal ! "

As Mark strode across the Square the discussions within the few remaining groups of working men were suddenly hushed, and discontented and uneasy artisans watched his passage among them from under lowered and unfriendly eyebrows. The gatekeeper at the old shipyard stood aside more than respectfully as he swept in ; draughtsmen in the office looked up to see him pass without ceremony into the room where Julius and Bob were closeted.

" Aye, Julius ! " Mark began belligerently, tossing his hat on a window ledge. " So you think you're going to steal my shipwrights, do you ? "

The partners looked up at this stormy invasion ; and then :

" Here you ! Belay there ! "

That was Bob. He had risen in wrath, his face purpling. He thumped the table. He seemed to shout from a poop as through the rising gales of yesterday.

" You may be a Member of Parliament, Mister Mark Oliphant," he roared. " You may be a Governor of the Middle and Far Eastern. But, by God ! you needn't think you can come crashing in here without a by-your-leave and start scolding like a fishwife. Pipe down, Mark Oliphant, pipe down ! Or by the Lord Harry, I'll take you by the seat of the pants and the scruff of the neck and heave you through that window."

Mark stared at this angry man ; and before he could conjure up a retort Julius spoke with an iciness unusual in him.

" Yes, Mark. I think you might drop this trick of making wild accusations before you hear a jot of evidence. It's a bad old habit of yours, and it seems to grow on you. And Bob and I were discussing confidential business."

Mark was defeated and knew it. The gambit on which he had relied throughout his adult life, and which had indeed become habitual as power grew in his hands, was now checked in the opening moves. He had not reckoned with Bob Rait ; and what had happened to Julius to put this nip into his voice ? Raging inwardly, Mark shifted his ground.

"A joke, a joke!" he protested genially. "Surely——"

"Pipe down there!" growled Bob Rait. "It was no joke. It was your usual bluff."

"It hardly appealed to me as a joke," Julius confirmed dryly. "And now, Mark, sit down and tell me what is it you wish to know?"

"You're damned stand-offish to-day, I must say," Mark laboured to improve his position with a heavy laugh. "You know very well, Julius, what I want to know—and have the right to know. These shipwrights. This is a serious business."

"It is, Mark," Julius agreed, "very serious. It is a crisis of the first magnitude within the industry, and I think it may even be a social—nay, a political—crisis."

"And I suppose you gave those fools of mine a rare Blackneb speech?"

The fatal sneer, though jocularly delivered, had Bob on his feet again in a trice.

"One more dirty word out your face, Mark Oliphant——" he began, but Julius motioned his cousin to be quiet.

"You always seem to jump to the basest conclusions, Mark. What is your conscience like, I wonder?" he asked with an irony that was all the more cutting for the mildness of its delivery. "If you will now be so good as to listen without interrupting, I shall gladly tell you what passed between me and your men. Bob was present at the meeting and can confirm my report."

"Go on," said Mark sullenly, settling himself back in his chair.

"Your shipwrights came to me, of course," Julius began, "without invitation. Indeed, I would rather they had not involved me in the dispute. However, they asked to interview me—to seek my advice, was their own phrase—and to that I agreed."

"All very fine. But——"

Julius held up his hand.

"They explained their determination not to work in iron. They told me that they had walked out of your yard in protest after some discussion with your manager. And then they offered me their services."

"The bloody trash! And you?"

"This is my story, Mark," Julius insisted calmly. "I told them, what is obvious, that I could not give employment to eighty new hands or thereabouts. A few experienced hands at any time, yes. I told them to see my foreman shipwright. Nothing in that. Men keep moving from yard to yard up and down the River."

"Quite, quite!" Mark eagerly allowed. "But——"

" And then," said Julius, " I advised them as a friend to swallow their pride and go back and learn the new trade in iron."

Mark stared, and his lower lip dropped.

" You what ? "

" You heard what he said," growled Bob Rait. " He advised them to go back and learn to work in iron. I would have advised them to go back and throw you into the nearest dock."

" Good God ! " cried Mark, and his astonishment was genuine. " Are we all going crazy ? "

The gentle opening of the door seemed to supply a mystic answer to the question. It was Walter : tall, elegant, his fine face pale, his personality seemingly chill and withdrawn. He bowed formally to his father, but kept his grip on the door handle.

" I beg your pardon, sir. All the people outside have gone to dinner. I am intruding."

" Come in, Watty ! Come in ! " cried Bob Rait, his high spirits restored by the sight of a young friend. " Take a seat and listen to this. It'll make you laugh."

His Uncle Mark looked up to grin at the young man, but uneasily and briefly. Walter's bow to his uncle was curt and aloof. There was no shaking of hands. Julius watched his son as he took a plain chair from under the table, set it in the shadows by the inner wall, and sit down to be an aloof but interested spectator. He understood the meaning of every one of these deliberate motions on his son's part.

" I have been telling your Uncle Mark," he explained to his son, " what happened when his men waited on me this morning, and I have been at pains to make it clear that I advised them to go back and learn how to work in iron."

Walter bowed a formal acknowledgment of the receipt of this information, but Mark fidgeted on the edge of his chair, his heavy eyebrows working. The discussion absorbed him.

" This is all very fine ! " he announced. " Like a damned meeting of a kirk session ! But what the devil was in your mind, Julius ? What are we going to do ? "

" No, no, Mark ! " retorted Julius easily. " What I have done and propose to do you know. Now the question is—a very important question—what do *you* propose to do ? "

" What do I propose to do ! Do I need to do anything ? I can afford to sit tight, those fools can't. I'll give them a week to come to heel."

" And if they don't ? No, no, Mark ! That is not a hypothetical question. My own belief is that they will go on refusing to work in iron."

" Then they can starve, and be damned to them ! "

" No, they won't starve," said Julius thoughtfully. " All your iron will still not put the shipwrights out of work. These men will sort themselves out in due course. And you know, Mark, shipbuilding in wood is not finished yet."

" You seem mighty cocksure about it all ! "

" And you, Uncle Mark, seem to be in a state of complete confusion and impotence. So far as I can follow the discussion, the shipwrights have you completely beaten."

The voice was Walter's—a little pedantic, dry, cultured, and as clear as a bell. It was a toledo blade against his uncle's bludgeon. It was a gout of acid dropped into a beaker of frothing salts. Mark's face again coloured deeply with anger, but Walter's dark and black-ringed eyes did not move their frigid gaze from the empurpled countenance, and he saw that his opponent was incapable of a retort. The anger came out in an untidy sneer.

" So you're an expert on shipbuilding too, are you ? Very well," and Mark thumped the table, " I'll show you if those damned carpenters have me beaten ! I'll tell you, Julius, what I propose to do. Mark my words." And now he pointed a challenging finger at his cousin. " I'm not done because a handful of confounded idiots are too proud to dirty their hands. They're not the only pebbles on the beach. I've got labourers there, scores of them—aye, the dirty Irish, as your fancy shipwrights call them. *They'll* handle the iron for me. *They'll* learn. They'll take my wages. Every builder on the River will follow my example ; every builder in Britain. And then, by God ! you and your skilled craftsmen will maybe learn what's what."

His vehemence and his meaning won him the satisfaction of silence. Without seeing clearly into the prospect thrust upon them, the three men who listened knew that there was something dire in the threat. It portended revolution and a changing of orders. Its implications most darkly menaced the established frontiers of nationality and religion. It promised to exalt the crude, cheap unskilled over the fastidious and devout skilled. They knew it to be, in a word then still uncoined, anarchy.

" But you can't, Mark ! " pleaded Julius.

" Can't I ! You'll see," swaggered his cousin.

He won another brief space of silence ; and then Walter's voice stated a conclusion with icy detachment.

" Your irresponsibility, Uncle Mark, seems to me to be almost criminal."

" Irresponsibility ! Criminal, be God ! Here . . . Damnation,

Julius ! " Mark pushed back his chair as if to rise. " Have I come here to be——"

" Pipe down, pipe down ! " Bob advised him grimly. " You came here to bully and bluster at everybody in sight, and you'll stay here till Watty's finished with you."

" Ah ! It's an arrangement, is it ? " Mark returned to the sneer. " Something seems to have come over you all. It seems damned unfriendly to me."

" Yes ! "

The affirmative from Walter was a serpent's hiss. The stigmata of pain appeared in his blanched face and in a twist about his lips.

" Yes ! " he repeated. " We have all not long survived a very terrible experience, an epidemic of cholera—a very virulent and foul disease, I assure you, Uncle Mark. My mother, my father, Uncle Bob and I have all suffered bereavements of an almost unendurably painful kind. The town was in a state of shocking chaos for several weeks on end ; my father gave much of his personal fortune to help my colleagues and me to clear up the mess. Perhaps that is what has come over us, Uncle Mark—an awareness of horror, shall we call it ? "

" Yes, yes ! I would understand that. I wouldn't suggest for a moment . . ." Mark was mumbling not too convincingly.

" It was observed that you—our Member of Parliament and one of our leading citizens—did not visit the town during the course of the epidemic, and that will probably be remembered in the public mind. To the scientific mind it appears only a symptom—and a minor symptom at that—of the irresponsibility I have mentioned."

" Dr. Oliphant's free advice ! " Mark fell back on the sneer again, but only after a glance at Bob. " This is good, Watty. I like this scientific mind of yours."

Walter glanced towards Julius, but his father's face was impassive, neutral, patient. Walter's cold voice went on.

" But the fundamental irresponsibility is that you helped to create the conditions which favoured the plague and have done nothing, less than nothing, either as a leading citizen or the elected representative of the townsfolk, to improve these conditions."

" Go on ! This is good ! "

" It has the virtue of being true. You were Baron-Bailie of this town. You were Provost of this town. You are now its Member in the House of Commons. But ever so much more than that, Uncle Mark, you have made a great deal of money out of this town. Your energy, your foresight—these things are not in doubt. But that irresponsibility—the doing nothing for the people in general, the deliberate refusal to do anything, the careless creation of horror through that refusal, the sort of horror in which my grandmother died, in which my . . . No! This is science, Uncle Mark." Walter allowed himself an empty little laugh. "I beg your pardon. I merely wanted to point out that you are creating the very circumstances which will swallow you up, and all decent people with you, you and your Irish labourers and your discontented craftsmen. Irresponsibility! But it's so stupid!"

Mark was listening to all this. His heavy torso was bent over his arms splayed on the table. He had had time to recover his self-possession.

"A grand speech, Walter!" he commented, with a belligerent chuckle. "I've heard it from the Radicals in the House many a time. It never stops to explain who provides the ideas and the capital for expansion, who pays the wages, who gives you the convenience of railways and steamboats. Never a word about that!" His voice rose to anger again. "Just this yaw-yawing bloody Blackneb nonsense I've heard from your side of the family till I'm sick of it! Now I've had enough."

He rose, pushed back his chair and reached for his hat, and nobody said a word to stop him.

"And you sit there, my friend," he swept on, pointing a finger at Julius, "and let me be insulted by this whippersnapper—me, his uncle!"

Julius's head seemed to droop a little with weariness.

"Walter owes no responsibility to you, Mark," he said sadly. "He is an individual who has suffered greatly. Can you not understand?"

"He never could and never will," Bob surprisingly answered the question in a low voice.

Mark laughed with the assurance of one who has scored a dialectic triumph.

"You're mad, the whole damned lot of you!" he asserted. "You for a Blackneb, Master Walter—and you know what happened to Chartism? You and your shipwrights, Julius—I'll break them and I'll break you. I tell both of you: if it's a war you want, by God! you'll have it."

Mark left them then. By one of the silly little tricks of circumstance his sweep from the room was not so effective as he had probably hoped, for the door was old and he had to labour at the knob before it would turn. Mark made up for this with a violent slam of the door, and he would have been pleased to know that he had left his relatives thoughtful and silent.

He had spoken of open war, and Julius at least was oppressed to think of all the meanings of the word as his cousin had used it—war within the family and war within the industry. Walter thought of war within the body politic and of the long, apparently hopeless struggle of goodwill against self-interest. Bob Rait thought of war as a man's physical concern.

" The swine ! " He broke the silence at length. " Why didn't I heave him through the window ? "

Walter smiled faintly to see his Uncle Bob's comically frustrated expression, but it was a bleak visage he turned to his father.

" The tragedy is that he really does not understand the strength of the forces he is playing with. Like a bad boy mixing chemicals to blow up his father's house."

CHAPTER SIX

THE SIXTH DECADE

I

IT WAS with amused detachment that Barbara analysed her own state of mind. Here she was at the Great Exhibition, the complete and grandiose expression of British aspiration in the sixth decade of a wonderful century, and she found the whole affair tedious in the extreme.

True, she reflected ruefully, she was not getting any younger. Getting on for sixty in fact ; and if *le bon Dieu* had of His mercy allowed her to preserve a slim figure she was, like countless women of generation after generation, most painfully aware of the hot, swollen, aching feet which afflict all who pace the inordinately hard pavements of a strange city in fashionable footwear. She also reflected, but without resentment, on the burden of clothing she was called upon to carry through the heat of a London July as the well-dressed wife of a man of substance.

It was very wonderful, this Exhibition within the great glass-house so cunningly devised by Mr. Paxton to enclose even the living trees of Hyde Park. The red-carpeted passages ; the gleaming glass cases ; the model engines in shining brass that miraculously and ingeniously worked ; the displays of a nation's infinitely varied manufactures in metal, from pins and fish-hooks to cotton jennies and colliery pumps ; always a band playing somewhere, loud in brass or discreet on strings ; palms, indiarubber plants, geraniums, fuchsias and begonias everywhere ; the clatter of cups and glasses in refreshment places ; and the enchanted, triumphant peoples of Britain—broad Lancashire vowels competing with Welsh sibilants, Cockney diphthongs contrasting with Scottish gutturals—streaming along the avenues, peering, explaining, exclaiming, arguing, but with never a voice or tone to suggest anything but a complete, unquestioning acceptance of this display as the perfect expression of a great nation's greatness. . . . It was all very wonderful, Barbara confessed to herself, but like so many things in human experience, loudly proclaimed, carefully prepared for, eagerly anticipated, there was a something not quite . . . a something lacking, which was all in yourself and which you would never confess to your most intimate companion in the adventure.

Julius—dear Julius !—seemed to be so enraptured by it all. They had planned the expedition so carefully together. It was to be their great outing of the middle years. Julius—that foolish, sweet man !—had invented a private festival, their Mahogany Wedding. Foolish, private jokes round the fireside that was once again wholly their own. . . . Two grown-up sons gone away on their devices ! And *le bon Dieu* be kind to all fathers and mothers of men-children ! . . . Mature, kindly and yet coquettish jokes when the lights were out and they were warmly in bed together. One evening he had come home and poured into her lap handfuls of golden sovereigns. It was to buy her *trousseau* for the Mahogany Wedding. Julius always knew instinctively what was near the heart of a woman ; not the fat sovereigns but the lovely compliment of devotion behind them ; and Julius never failed in his wooing. Barbara remembered one of her mother's wild speeches years and years ago.

" That Jules is one man in a million to understand what passes in a woman's mind, what of distress is always in her heart. His chosen woman, it follows, is likewise one in a million. If you were of an age to have wisdom, *ma chère fille*, such as I now possess, you would be on your knees each night to thank *le bon Dieu* for his great favour."

And here was Julius, getting old, but eager to dart about the main halls and innumerable wings of the Great Exhibition, the red-bound catalogue open in his hand. So many things to see, and he so anxious to appreciate everything.

" Prodigious ! " he would exclaim. " There's rare ingenuity for you ! The range, the variety, the wealth ! God bless my soul, but here's a clever man with a device for threading needles ! Did you ever hear the like of it, Barbara ! They'll be putting our clothes on by machinery next."

And yet she knew in her subtle understanding of her husband that Julius was not utterly happy amid this fantastic efflorescence of the mechanical instinct. He was living up to the pitch of excitement ordained for the occasion by the national chorus that had Francis Charles Augustus Albert Emmanuel of Saxe-Coburg-Gotha, the admired if hardly beloved Prince Consort, as its leader ; he was paying lip-service to the shining triumphs of a sort of flashy skill in which his artist-craftsman's soul could not fundamentally believe.

The confession came from him after he had spent ten minutes about a gleaming case in which were displayed the plans and a tentative model of that ship the British people believed with sentimental honesty to be the peerless expression of their own mechanical ingenuity and their maritime predominance ; the ship that was to be the ship of all time ; the *Great Eastern.*

" No, no, no ! " said Julius, as if scolding himself. " This won't do at all."

" It seems to me a very bold project," said Barbara artfully.

" But absurd, my dear girl ! " retorted Julius, all his true instincts surging to meet a portent that threatened their integrity. " Look at the design of that enormous hull ! It is as if marine architecture had made no progress since the days of the Flood. An apprentice draughtsman in my office would not dare to show me such a clumsy sketch. Look at the rig and the engining of the ship ! They give her five masts and a full suit of sails. They give her five funnels, powerful engines and these huge paddles. If that is not enough, they must give her a screw propeller. Why not throw in a couple of wings and make her a flying-boat ? "

He took Barbara's arm and led her away from the offending display.

" Come, my dear, you must be tired. A cup of tea, yes ? I seem to remember a refreshment room down this passage."

When they were seated at a marble-topped, iron-pillared table in the shade of a giant aspidistra and had given their order, Julius dabbed his brow with his fine red bandana and expelled his breath in an explosion that quaintly suggested weariness and disgust at once.

" That *Great Eastern* of theirs is a portent," he returned to his favourite subject. " It is the product of men who do not know where they are going. They are like children with too many toys to play with. They are in love with power, but they do not know where or how to apply it justly. I wonder where we are going ? Perhaps we shall learn from the fate of that preposterous vessel. . . . God bless my soul ! What hideous din is that ? "

This agonised question was forced from him by the impact of a burst of music in enormous volume. It filled the great glass-house, rolled along the vaulted roofs, and slapped back in echo from every corner and protuberance of the lofty building. The piece was recognisably the march from *Athalie*, but delivered with such force that it constituted a brutal assault upon the nerves. With a smile about her lips Barbara watched Julius riffle through the leaves of his catalogue to discover the origin of these remarkable sounds. He had to shout in her ear.

" A steam organ ! *Steam !* They must make their music by sheer force. All iron, steam—and they cannot control the valves with moderation ! This country is being carried away on a jet of steam, and it does not know where."

It was useless to attempt a discussion against the enormous bellowings of the steam organ, but while they waited for the storm to abate, Barbara reflected that Julius had put into words exactly what had irked her about the Great Exhibition as a whole—its hardness, its deification of the mechanical, its uncritical prostration before the flashy wonders of mere ingenuity. It made her think of high factory walls in red brick, of dirty, sunless streets and of myriads of pale-faced people streaming to work through a haze of smoke.

The marching tune of the bellicose priests came to an end in a series of terrorising chords, and the ensuing peace, broken only by a ripple of hand-clapping and the tinkle of cutlery on china, seemed a blessing.

" That was a formidable performance," said Julius with a smile. " And now I suppose we must get ready to dine with Mark and Lavinia to-night. I think, dearest, we might drive back to Albemarle Street and have a rest first."

" Yes, indeed ! " Barbara agreed. " I fear that Mark's friends may be as dull as they are important."

" Sir Mark Oliphant ! " chuckled Julius. " A baronet now, if you please ! He will be my Lord Oliphant in due course, no doubt. We are honoured."

" And no love lost on Mark's side ! " snapped Barbara. " I would very much rather see our son Ivie. Are you sure his ship is in the Thames ? "

" Quite. There was the note from Bob yesterday. I sent our message to Millwall through our agents. But," concluded Julius with a fond chuckle, " you know what our Ivie is ! "

" He is a very exasperating young man," said his mother severely. Then she laughed fondly in her turn. " The scamp ! "

The phenomenon represented by Ivie within the Oliphant family had long been accepted with intelligent resignation by Julius and Barbara ; and like every wild boy since women have borne men-children he still commanded an admiring and anxious affection such

as the austere, self-contained personality of Walter never seemed to
require. A wild lad, he took after the Raits except in his fair, fresh
complexion. His truancy as a schoolboy had been a chronic heart-
break to Julius as a young father. Two attempts to stowaway were
to his credit before he was sixteen, and one of these ended only after
a hectic chase down the Firth by his Uncle Bob in a hired steam-tug.
As he came to manhood the escapades tended to be wilder and occasionally nearly scandalous in terms of the new respectability that had
developed as the overwhelming domesticity of the Queen and her
Consort affected their prospering subjects. But his Uncle Bob Rait
was always his stout champion.

" There's nothing wrong with the lad, Julius, I tell you," he would
argue," unless high spirits are criminal. It's you and Barbara are
wrong with your tutors and putting him to the University and trying
to make a student of him. Put him to sea for a couple of years, and
then you'll see a real man ; and we'll need him in the business when
I decide to buy a farm. Nothing wrong with Ivie. High spirited—
and the cheeriest, kindest-hearted boy I know."

Ah ! That was it. Whatever the scrape, you could never feel that
there was the slightest instinct of viciousness behind those open,
grinning features. The small boy who came home from his wanderings
dirty and weary, while the search-parties still scoured the moors and
ranged the beaches, had always, wrapped in the corner of a filthy
handkerchief, a sticky sweetmeat saved for his mother. He could never
understand the alarms created by what to him were his natural proceedings, and he knew no need to lie himself out of blame.

So, in due course, Ivie Oliphant sailed one autumn day, supercargo in the ship *Constant Heart* bound for Pondicherry, and before he
was home again he was a sailor confirmed. His blithe spirit needed
the world for elbow-room. He came and he went, and sometimes he
would remember to write his mother a long, amusing letter, and
sometimes for her there were agonising periods when he would simply
forget, his approximate whereabouts known only through the despatches Bob Rait would receive from his various skippers. And when
he came home, he was always burdened with the sort of treasure-trove
that eternally seems most desirable to the mind of a boy—it might be
a coloured and virulent macaw, or a whole herd of small elephants
carved in ivory, or a waspish green monkey, or a tiny compressed
human head from the Americas. He grew a fair beard, was romantically tattooed on forearms and chest, and developed a talent for the
fiddle. In the year of the Great Exhibition, in his early thirties, he
was still a bachelor and first officer of the four-masted ship *Constant
Watch* under old Jack Hatterick, commodore of the Line.

That ship lay in London River as Julius had reported, and it was Ivie's honest intention to wait upon his father and mother at their hotel as soon as might be, but on the first day in after a 100-day voyage from Fremantle he did not feel the pressure of time upon him and, as it chanced, there came to him an opportunity for what he regarded as a bit of sport. Even as Julius and Barbara were smiling over his casual ways within the great glass-house in Hyde Park, Ivie and his cousin, Edward Oliphant, were sitting at another table together little more than a mile away—to be precise, in a tavern near Temple Bar.

"Cheer up, Bart!" Ivie was saying, almost shouting jovially. "And drink up. Gin again? Or try rum, Nelson's blood. One glass and you'll forget it all. Ahoy there, waiter! *Garçon!*"

"I wish you would stop calling me Bart, Ivie," said the younger man petulantly. "You know perfectly well that John's the heir, and he's welcome to it! It has been worse than ever since father got his title. I can't do a thing right. I'm supposed to understand book-keeping and banking and rates of exchange and things, and I want to get away like you and see the world. He's a—a brute!"

"Who? Uncle Mark? Belay there, young Bart, and talk sense," Ivie advised his cousin. "Do you mean to say, you young devil, you think I'm going to smuggle you on board one of my father's ships and have Uncle Mark down on me for press-ganging, barratry, baby-farming and God knows what else? Pipe down, Bart, pipe down!"

"But what can I do?" wailed the young man.

"Have a drink," said Ivie promptly. He smacked the table. "You there, waiter! Ahoy!"

Edward Oliphant took after his mother. He had her foolish, good-natured face, with a prominent nose and a comic little button of a chin set well back beneath a slack lower lip. This countenance was smooth and of a bright pink that supplied a rather startling background to protruding eyes of pale blue. He had carroty hair that waved naturally from a central parting and was always copiously oiled. As he sat with the silver nob of his cane pressed against his mouth, his fine and slightly too fashionable clothes outstanding in this dark tavern at the wrong end of the Strand, the young man might have served as a model for the booby of stage tradition.

Perhaps only his mother and his cousin Ivie knew he was not that. Assuredly his tragedy was that his father and brother so regarded him. Edward Oliphant was, in fact, that not uncommon product of wealth—the child unfortunate at once to be less able than his father and the joy of a foolish mother's heart. She knew at least the kindness of her youngest's nature ; and Ivie, of whose wild and cheerful personality poor Ned had been the slave throughout his conscious life, knew there was spirit and to spare within that apparently foolish figure.

Their second round of drinks set before them, Ned returned to his obsession.

" I wish you'd talk sense for a minute, Ivie," he pleaded gravely. " You're always making jokes and getting away from the subject. You don't know what it's like at home, and . . . and hang it, Ivie ! You're the only man I know who *does* anything."

" All right, old Bart ! " agreed Ivie cheerfully. " Drink up. Here's hair on your chest ! And now, my hearty, I'm ready to talk to you like a Dutch uncle. Right away I'm going to tell you what you ought to be. My son, you ought to be a soldier."

With his clenched fists in line before his mouth the first mate of the *Constant Watch* gave a hearty rendering of a bugle call. The goggle eyes stared at him.

" A soldier ! I say, Ivie, really. . . . I wish you would——"

" Stow it, Bart, stow it ! I'm serious, truly. Now listen, and for Heaven's sake stop looking like a grampus with the bellyache ! You'll never make a sailor, son," Ivie was suddenly kind and serious. " I know it by the cut of your jib. The merchant service is only for rough tykes like me, and Her Majesty's blooming Royal Navy is about twenty years out of date. But if you are so dam' well determined to get away from home, Bart, why not the Army ? Your old man can afford to buy you fifty commissions. Ensign Oliphant of the Scots Guards. Ensign Oliphant of the Dragoon Guards. Murder that damned brother of yours, and you'll end up General Sir Edward Oliphant, Bart., in command of the British Army. What's wrong with that, old cock ? And I mean it."

This proposal, though so expansively sketched, had a stimulating effect on Edward Oliphant. The generous lips parted more widely still in wonder, the pale eyes goggled more candidly than ever. He called for another round of drinks and plied his cousin with questions to which the answers must fortify his own assurance. Ivie was in trim to support the most wavering resolution.

" Fighting, my son ! " he cried, his sea-voice filling the tavern with healthy noise. " Take the first transport to India, and you'll have your bellyful of it. There's all sorts of blackamoors out there will fight you for your shirt. Get yourself out to Canada and have a cut at the Redskins. But if it is just getting away from the respected dad and that longshoreman brother of yours, why, Bart ! there's Hongkong, or the Straits Settlements, or the Bermudas, or the West Indies. It's a big enough world even for you, my bonnie boy ! "

The prospect expanded as the refreshments circulated and worked. Ivie was in the mood to brush aside difficulties, poor Ned in the mood to discount his own timidity in the home of a baronet member of the House of Commons.

" We'll fix it to-morrow," Ivie declared. " We'll have the articles all signed, sealed and delivered before you're a day older, old Bart, you slab-sided old sodger. I am seeking my old dad in the morning. He can work the oracle with Uncle Mark. Or my mother ; she'll do the trick. . . . Cheer up, my hearty ! Ensign Oliphant—'*shun* ! "

The young man's eyes were beginning to lose their always indifferent power of focus. He stared hopefully at his empty glass.

" I've just remembered, Ivie," he remarked lugubriously. " They are dining with us to-night, your father and mother."

" And that, Bart," returned his cousin largely, " ain't going to spoil a bit of fun for you and me. You and I are going to bite a chop at Stone's. Then we are going to get ourselves a cab and drive in style to the best music-hall, with the fattest chairman, with the largest moustache in Town. We're going to ogle the prettiest girls, Bart, and we're going to . . . D'you hear me, Bart ? Don't fall asleep now, you pie-faced son of a sea-cook. . . . We're going to have *a night*. Waiter ! Waiter ! "

The programme so bravely sketched by Ivie was not carried through after all. Potations on the scale and in the style of the merchant service ashore worked in with the mood of cheerfulness engendered by Ivie's suggestion of a career until poor Ned was in no fit state to face a chop, or even to be one of the audience in the most tolerant music-hall. On his first day ashore after three months across three oceans, Ivie himself was in no condition to be either a model of decorum or a judge of the proprieties, but even his exuberance became tinged with concern for his cousin's state. He exhorted him reproachfully.

" Ahoy, there, Bart ! Carry your drink like a man. Damme, Ned, we're only *beginning* ! You're not going to spoil the night for me ? Show a leg there, or the sun'll scratch your eyes out ! "

Ned contrived to open his weighted eyelids and to shake an unhappy head.

" Enough," he announced. " Finish."

" Finish ! " cried Ivie. " Not on your life, Ensign Oliphant ! You'd be cashiered from the Guards for less. Come, Bart, I know what you want. A nice drive through jolly old London up to Stone's in a growler, a noggin in the taproom to set you up again, and then a nice crunchy chop inside. You'll get your second wind all right, my hearty. I've seen it happen many at time. Come, Bart, show a leg ! "

He contrived to shoulder the unfortunate young man from the tavern, to prop him up until a cab appeared at the kerb in response to his hails, to heave his cousin into the vehicle, to wake him up again when it stopped before the chop-house, and even to persuade the nearly comatose figure into the crowded taproom. There he left him swaying against a wall for a moment while he himself sought a waiter, but he was immediately recalled by a sort of slithering thump behind. Ned had collapsed incontinent into the sawdust, and a friendly Cockney was bending over the sagging red head.

" Friend's 'ad a drop too much, capting," the Cockney suggested tolerantly.

" Can't carry it, blast his eyes ! " said Ivie indignantly.

" Better get 'im 'ome—if he's got an 'ome to go ter," advised the friendly one. " Never can tell, can yer ? I'll fetch a keb."

It was one of the new hansoms the Cockney brought to the chop-house door, and the driver, wise in metropolitan experience, obligingly got down to assist Ivie and the Cockney with the unresponsive and extremely heavy carcass of Mr. Edward Oliphant.

" Where to, capting ? " he asked cheerfully.

" Damned if I know," said Ivie. " Belgravia way."

" Soon see," said the cabby.

Expertly he rifled the various pockets of the indifferent Ned until he found some papers, including addressed envelopes.

" Seems to be name of Olip-hant," the driver decided. " Rummy sort of monicker, too. 'Undred and ferteen Eaton Square. Bit of a swell, your pal 'ere. Jump in, capting."

The hansom sped along Piccadilly, and Ivie was so exhilarated and entertained by what had happened that he sang as if his companion was with him in spirit as well as in the too solid flesh.

> *Farewell and adieu to you, fair Spanish ladies !*
> *Farewell and adieu to you, ladies of Spain. . . .*

Elderly bucks from the clubs of St. James's and shopmen putting up the shutters turned to see who possessed a voice so remarkably powerful and a nerve so brazen as to offend the West End with bawling and brawling at this discreet hour of a summer evening. When the clopping of the horse's hoofs echoed along the austere streets of Belgravia it was to an obligato supplied by a voice which yearned in fo'c'sle style for the Rio Grande.

As, however, the cabby reined in to scan the numbers on the yellow pillars of Eaton Square the first officer of the *Constant Watch* set to pummelling his companion, slapping his face, forcing his eyelids upwards, blowing into his nostrils; and Ned revived sufficiently to allow himself to be dragged, instead of carried, out of the cab when it drew up before the portals of No. 113.

" Wait, you ! " shouted Ivie urgently to the driver.

He manhandled his cousin up the gracious steps of the house, left him to sway or collapse as the laws of nature might allow, took one mighty pull of the bell-handle, and bolted back to the obscurity of the hansom's cabin.

" Out of here like the hammers of hell ! " he commanded the driver, who was in fact waiting with all the Cockney's intelligent and sympathetic interest in such human proceedings to take precisely that course of action. The whip cracked, and the horse with the light chariot behind it bolted towards Sloane Street.

The noises incidental to these proceedings were heard by at least some members of the dinner party seated within the house. They were mercifully spared a view of the scene, for the shutters were closed and the heavy curtains drawn against the vulgar view; the gas-jets in their glass bowls threw a warm and intimate light on the napery, the crystal and the silver of the table. But Barbara at least thought to hear her younger son's voice from the outer world and controlled herself not to cast a questioning glance in Julius's direction; while Lavinia, startled by the clangour of a bell on springs, imperative even from the backward and below-stairs recesses of the mansion, had to be her foolish, frank self.

" What's that ? " she demanded to know of the company at large.

" Hibbert will attend to it," said Sir Mark Oliphant curtly. " As I was saying, Lady Grace, if Lord John could only keep Palmerston in order——"

Barbara noted that Hibbert, the butler, was absent from the room for a considerable length of time and that, on his return, he showed signs of considerable strain on his professional suavity.

2

Dr. Walter Oliphant was kept waiting a long time in the anteroom of the office in Leadenhall Street. If it was his Uncle Mark's intention to impress him, he completely succeeded in his aim. At forty, after ten years of lecturing to university students on the new science of public health, Walter had perhaps more than his share of cynicism, but this mercantile world was not his, and he was duly awed to see so many worried and important-looking people pass into and out of the inner sanctum with important-looking books and bundles of documents. When, at the end half an hour, a clerk motioned him into the presence he was aware of nervousness.

His Uncle Mark, his back to a large window, sat behind a table at the far end of what seemed to Walter a very long room, heavy with panelling and portraits in oil. It was not pleasant to march so far towards a face of which he could not discern the expression against the light. He halted before the table and bowed gravely.

" Good-morning, Walter ! Take a seat. I can give you ten minutes."

" Good-morning, sir ! Thank you. I shall not waste your time."

It was to be a formal interview, and no love lost, no pretence at cordiality. Walter was relieved.

" I represent my father, sir. My business is to inquire if you could consider the charter to him of a steamship of at least a thousand tons."

" Good God Almighty ! "

Sir Mark Oliphant's businesslike reserve suddenly broke down. Walter saw the familiar sneer ripple across the now heavy and dull red features. His medical intelligence recorded the probability that Uncle Mark had become fond of his pint of port wine of an evening. The blood pressure was high. There was a wheeze in the older man's sardonic laugh.

" So your father wants a steamship, does he ? Giving up his old windjammers at last ? That's rich ! "

" Let me explain, sir," said Walter patiently. " The ship is required to carry medical supplies to Scutari for the sick and wounded from the Crimea. I understand that a sailing ship cannot use the Mediterranean easily and could not get through the Dardanelles without a steam-tug."

" You're damned well right there. But what's this about medical supplies ? What have you and your father to do with Army affairs ? "

" Nothing. Perhaps we are only trying to succeed where the Army has tragically failed. That responsibility is mine."

Walter saw the frown and the other stigmata of a sour disapproval come over his uncle's face. He proceeded calmly.

" Before she left this country, I was in touch with Miss Florence Nightingale about certain technical problems of hospital sanitation ; my specialised subject, as I think you know. Some weeks after she arrived in Constantinople, I had a letter from a mutual friend, detailing at length the deplorable facts of the hospital situation at Scutari."

" Facts ! " barked Sir Mark. " But go on. Only, I haven't all day to listen to this newspaper story."

" Shall we say—what I, and *The Times*, believe to be the facts ? "

continued Walter suavely. " These things can never be taken into
the laboratory and tested by delicate scales and exact measures. The
fact is that I communicated to my father what I believe to be the
facts. He immediately made himself responsible for the raising of a
public fund in our part of Scotland to assist Miss Nightingale's purposes and, of course, to ease the sufferings of the British soldier. It has
been a great success. With the result that I have been able to buy
large quantities of those medical supplies I happen to know are most
desperately needed at Scutari, and that we are well able to charter
a steamship to carry those supplies, if we can get one."

" You won't get one," said Sir Mark Oliphant promptly.

In spite of the sharpness of his comment, he leaned forward in a
pose that Walter knew to be characteristic of the ageing, his forehead
resting on the palm of a hand that was, in its turn, held up by an
elbow propped on the table. The thick fingers harrowed through the
nearly white hair.

" That's your statement of a case," said Uncle Mark, seeming to
address the sheet of blotting-paper before him, " and I suppose you
believe in it. We'll not argue about that. Now I'll give you what
I believe to be some facts."

The heavy face was raised from its support, and now it challenged
Walter's cold scrutiny.

" Your Miss Florence Nightingale is a damned interfering bitch,
poking that sharp nose of hers into matters she doesn't understand,
and Aubrey Herbert was a damned fool to let her get out there. As
for shipping, we have a good deal more to do than set aside tonnage
for linseed poultices and doses of cascara. We are much more interested—*much* more—in sending our soldiers muskets and cartridges,
guns and cannon balls, food and clothing. In fact, I tell you—and
you can pass it on to your father—that this project of yours is perfectly
gratuitous and thoroughly irresponsible."

Irresponsible. . . . That was the word. So it had rankled all
these years since the affair of the carpenters away back in 1841 or
thereabouts ! There was also that authoritative, gubernatorial " we "
. . . Walter rose from his chair.

" That is perfectly clear," he said, " and I am obliged to you, sir,
for being so precise. I apologise for taking so much of your time.
Good-morning, sir."

" Good-morning."

3

" And this is the tub I've got to take to the wars ! " asked Ivie Oliphant through a roar of laughter. " What knacker's yard did you pick her up in, Uncle Bob ? "

" Real old-timer, isn't she ? " agreed Bob Rait with a grin. " But she's as sound as a bell. She'll get you there, and she'll get you back again."

" I'm jack-easy," Ivie assured his uncle. " This trip ought to be fun."

They were standing on the edge of the East India Quay, Ivie and Bob, Julius and Walter. Below them, for the tide was low, were the flat decks and squat outline of the wooden paddle-steamer *Freeman.* In the seaman's eye her appearance told of the early 'forties. Two stumpy square-rigged masts and a thin, black smokestack almost as tall sprang from a hull that sat remarkably low in the water, and the fact that the bulwarks had been built up to take a deck-load of coal did not improve her appearance. The old *Freeman* had the unmistakable air of a relic or a veteran resurrected for service. Bob had found her plying sketchily from the Bristol Channel ports coastwise to London River and back, and Ivie had been recalled from a statelier ship to carry out a task the Services seemed unable to perform for themselves.

" She's in thorough repair now," Bob explained. " Engines overhauled, your victuals, water and coal all complete, the best crew I could find. I've arranged with our agents to serve you at Gib. and Malta—and the Piræus, if you feel like it. She'll get you there."

" And all your medical stores are carefully classified and stowed," Walter added gravely. " I took special trouble with the bill of lading, and I have left a detailed sketch-plan in your cabin."

" God ! You're like a pack of mourners at a funeral," cried Ivie happily. " It's just that I can't help laughing when I look at the old packet."

He did laugh again, and Julius interrupted him anxiously.

" If you feel any doubt at all, my dear boy . . . Any risk that your judgment tells you is beyond the point of absolute safety . . . Then I would have to insist . . ."

" My dear old dad ! " Ivie threw an arm about Julius's shoulders and squeezed him affectionately, as if his father was a spirited wench. " I was only joking. Don't worry your old noddle for a moment. I'm as proud of my new command as a dog with ten tin tails ! Now, Uncle Bob——"

He dropped the arm from his father's shoulders and became the responsible ship's master.

"If we can get that old copper-bottomed chief engineer—what's-his-name . . . Mackintosh? Good! If he can get up steam now, I'll take her down the Firth this afternoon and get the feel of her. I expect she'll yaw about a bit with that flat bottom and so much damned coal for top-hamper. If she behaves reasonably like a good girl, I'll anchor off the Tartan Buoy and be ready to sail to-morrow forenoon. How's that?"

"She's ready for you," said Bob Rait solidly.

"I certainly think the business should be put in hand as soon as you can manage it, Ivie," Julius added mildly. "Those poor lads . . ."

Ivie slapped his brother's shoulder.

"Eh, Watty? Why not forget those drains of yours and sail with me? I could be doing with a pill-pedlar in this craft. Come and see the glories of the Near East—and smell the smells. Right in your line, Watty! Gorgeous smells."

Walter shook his head and smiled patiently.

"They have refused me already, Ivie. I'm too old. I haven't got the qualifications the British Army requires. The War Office is not interested in sanitation."

"Ah, well! It's a pity. And about noon to-morrow, Uncle Bob, if everything is shipshape."

Next day the *Freeman* started to slip down the Firth at the hour appointed. It was one of those soft, clear days which the northern February sometimes borrows from April. The sunlight laid a golden dust over the near woodlands and cultivated slopes of the southern shore but, away to the northward, the Highland peaks were etched in steel-blue on a clear plate of cloudless sky that was like a faintly-tinted glass. The wind was easterly, but so light that even the antique paddler outstripped her own smoke and left it in a dark smear over miles of smooth water. Great sailing ships that might have made the anchorage under their own canvas in normal sou'-westerly conditions went past in the wake of tiny tugs, their sails furled, flying creatures with their wings clipped. Some saluted the house flag, silver star on a ground of horizon blue, Ivie had had hoisted at the main of his ship.

None of these phenomena, however, held any æsthetic interest for the master of the *Freeman*. As gay a dog ashore as you would meet in any port, Captain Ivie Oliphant was transformed into the rigid and anxious professional when his ship was under way. For him the splendour of the estuary resolved into a series of so many landmarks and seamarks—the white pillars of the Knock and Lamont lights, the

bell buoy on the Tomont patch, and the lift of a mountain on one
island above the mild hills of another, which told him that he had
laid a proper course for the outer spaces of the Firth. The melodrama
of the jagged peaks, faintly coloured against the clear sky, was for the
sailor no more than an indication that he might stand a fair chance of
getting across the Bay in a fine spell ; he thought also of fog off
Finisterre and of crowded traffic lanes on the steamship routes. He
left the bridge only once in five hours, and then to confirm his weatherly
impressions by the glass in his cabin and to have.a word with his chief
engineer who, in the manner of Scots chief engineers, complained that
his machinery was twenty years out of date but allowed, on being
pressed, that it might, under God's providence, last out the voyage
and no more. So back to the bridge by way of the tiny chartroom
below it and to ask of his first officer if all was still well.

This seemed a decent, competent man, older than himself, but in
these first anxious hours of the voyage he was only a remote official
figure. All about Ivie Oliphant, Barbara's merry baby, was now the
loneliness of command : the responsibility for twenty-odd lives and a
small fortune in shipping and cargo, the sovereignty under God and
the Queen over one detached piece of British territory, the obligation
to defend it against mutiny, the acts of the Queen's enemies and the
fury of the elements. Was she steering fairly enough ? Was she lifting
lightly enough to the swell coming in from the deeper seas ? How did
she take and throw off every seventh big one that smacked into her,
now from the sou'-east ? Had she the healthy groan of a proper,
buoyant ship as she heaved her mass over a sea and sank into the
trough ?

There were a thousand-and-one such things to be seen to, noted,
registered, added, subtracted, and summed up to make a proper
seamanlike estimate of the *Freeman's* worthiness. But the process was
of a subtlety beyond mathematics ; the ship is not female in the minds
of men without reason. Ivie was in these first hours like a wooer,
mature and cautious, who considers a stranger woman as a possible
mate.

They passed under the western cliffs of the lone Craig as the dark
was coming down. Instinctively pursuing the quest of his ship's secret,
Ivie reached for a lanyard at his shoulder and pulled it to release one
long and surprisingly hearty blast from the siren. From the sheer
cliffs above his head the seabirds tumbled and fluttered, white and
nervous like the petals of the wild cherry in an April breeze, and the
boom went rolling and echoing down the length of the rocky islet.

Ivie turned to his first officer with a smile.

" I think she'll do. What do you think, Mister ? "

" She'll do," the mate agreed, adding with the caution of his race, " I've sailed in a sight worse."

" Good ! " said Ivie. " I'll go below now and have a bite. I'll be obliged, Mister, if you will keep the bridge for an hour or so. We'll get into our proper routine of watchkeeping to-morrow. The second officer can take over at eight bells, once we're clear of the Isle of Man."

" Aye, aye, sir ! "

The ship *Freeman* was in being.

Ivie was up on the bridge again before the lights on the two Mulls were dead abeam to port and starboard respectively. A messenger from the bridge had reported Corsewall, Pladda and Rathlin and their bearings as he ate alone. Now the horizon ahead was alive with flashing lights like a lightning storm in summer, the galaxy bewildering to the longshoreman but each flash of a clear and sustaining proven-ance to the seaman on the bridge of his vessel. For him these incan-descent explosions marked an avenue through the darkness and amid the besetting dangers of indented shores. Out there on the starboard bow, on Irish soil, were the beacons of The Maidens, New Island and St. Johns, under the Mourne Mountains. Fainter on the port bow, on English land, St. Bees blinked its assurance of safe passage. Dead ahead, in red and white, the light on the Point of Ayre proclaimed the barrier of Man.

The wind was freshening. The paddles of the *Freeman* were now skidding and then burying themselves deep in the short but vicious seas that come up with any brisk air out of the west. But for all her tophamper the old ship rode her element nicely and gave out a healthy groan or shudder from time to time, and the sting of the spray over the port bow felt good on Ivie's face. This was the ship in being, in motion. The phosphorescence of the paddles' creaming trail was to the master of the vessel as good as the sight of a fresh-cut loaf to a hungry man.

His staid first mate was still beside him, silent, on the bridge.

" She'll do, Mister," Ivie repeated.

" Aye, aye, sir ! " the older man repeated. " She'll do. Once the stokers get through this deck-load of coal . . ."

" Then she'll be a bird ! " laughed Ivie, gripping the bridge-rail in the pride of possession and mastery.

" I've seen worse," the mate allowed again, then turned gruffly on the steersman. " Watch your helm there ! You're not a bloody ballet dancer."

From the crow's nest, faint and scattered by the wind, came a hail that had the quality of a pronouncement from another world.

" Eight bells ! And all's well ! "

The last glorious word stretched itself out in long but manly vowels, merging orchestrally into the thinned strokes of the actual thick-lipped bell at the break of the deck below the bridge.

Eight bells, and all was well. Ivie felt himself braced by the assurance, as by the force of a tonic medicine. The first bad twelve hours of his ordeal were over. The ship lived, floated, moved, fought, carried its given burden, obeyed. She would do.

The second officer had been on the bridge ten minutes before his time. He was tall, young and sandy of complexion.

" Now you can take over," Ivie addressed him. " You have your course—due South. Call me if you need me. You shouldn't.''

" Aye, aye, sir ! "

" Good-night, gentlemen ! "

" Good-night, sir ! "

The ship was in being, and all was well ; yet Ivie lingered at the foot of the ladder, tempted to remain on deck more by the sheer happy excitement of starting a new voyage than by the anxieties of command. He passed into the chart-room and stood there pondering the Admiralty sheet, although the region it mapped was as familiar to him in every feature as his father's garden. He glanced at the rough log, made some desultory notes on a pad and considered a selection of signal flags in their pigeon-holes. Only the instinctive need to see how the barometer was moving took him below at length.

He was halted in the door of his stateroom. In a comfortable chair before the stove, reading a newspaper and apparently very much at his ease, sat a tall man in plain clothes.

" Watty ! "

" Hallo, Ivie ! " His brother turned with a smile. " What do you think of your stowaway ? "

" God help us ! How did you get here ? "

" That was easy—a little arrangement with Uncle Bob. But I don't want another twelve hours in your paint-store in the forepeak, thank you. And I'm hungry."

" Well, I'll be . . . I'm hungry too. Where's that steward ? We'll have a drink to begin with. . . . But Watty, you damned old pier-head jump, that is all very well, but——"

" Don't worry, Ivie." His brother rose and laid a hand on his shoulder. " I made up my mind long ago to get out there somehow, for I know I can help. I've left letters for the old folk, explaining it all. They'll understand. This was the obvious way ; and I must say your *Freeman's* not a bad old hooker after all."

" That's all very well," Ivie protested, his fresh face covered with

and the Cabinet as well, a middle-aged doctor who happens to be in Scutari at a time of crisis might—entirely at his own charges, altogether on his own responsibility—undertake an independent survey of the sanitary arrangements at the base hospital and be permitted to lay his observations and suggestions on the desk of the Lady Superintendent? I notice that her office equipment includes a sizable wastepaper basket."

The Lady Superintendent cocked a shrewd and not unfriendly eye at the thin, intelligent face of her interlocutor. The little mouth blossomed like an apple-bud in a wry, masculine smile.

" To be sure, I am not officially aware of Dr. Oliphant's presence in Constantinople. At least, the advice has not reached me through the usual channels. "

Walter rose then, and the Lady Superintendent also stood up. She moved with him towards the door of her little office.

" May I say one thing, Dr. Oliphant? " she suggested. " Not an impertinence, I trust. But you do not seem to me very robust. The conditions here . . ."

Walter turned to look the Lady Superintendent full in the eyes. He answered her with passionate gravity.

" I have already seen thousands of much younger men than I come down from the Crimea in a state much nearer death than I am ! I have been taught, and I have learned, that my calling implies a duty. I know that that duty——"

" Yes, yes ! " the Lady Superintendent interrupted him. " I see that you are one of those few who do understand. So difficult to put into temperate words, is it not ? "

Still, she lingered in the doorway for a moment while Walter in the corridor bowed himself out of the presence.

" You might care to get into touch with Mr. Macdonald of *The Times*," she suggested casually. " Not being an official, he is very well informed as to our needs."

Ivie was waiting for his brother in the embrasure of a window some ten yards down the corridor from the Lady Superintendent's door. He emerged from this cover with the distinct air of one who has concealed himself in the presence of a major and possibly hostile force.

" So that's the Great Acid Drop, is it ? " he whispered irreverently. " Thank the Lord I'm not a private soldier in one of her wards ! "

Walter shook his brother's elbow affectionately, but he spoke quite sharply.

" Some day you'll be boasting to your grandchildren that you once saw that woman. It will be something to boast about, I promise you. But I admit that she frightens *me*."

" Lord, she must be a Tartar ! " said Ivie, but with indifference.

They came out into a courtyard that was filled with harsh sunlight but also with little clouds and columns of dust set up by a northerly wind with a Balkan nip in it. Three rows of convalescent men on pallets under the arcades that filled three sides of the square seemed cheerful enough, and two soldiers on crutches, one lacking a leg from the thigh, were merry in North Country chaff as they sought to lure and catch the pigeons that strutted about the fountain in the middle of the paved enclosure. There was nevertheless something faintly rotten in the air, for though the acrid odours of chemicals predominated, it was as if they had been poured out in quantities to overcome an underlying and overwhelming stagnation of filth.

" Better get back to the ship," Ivie suggested curtly. " Some fresh air out there. And better food than you'll ever get in this town."

" Yes," Walter agreed automatically.

They passed through the archway and turned down the street leading to the landing-stages.

" There's something I want to talk to you about," said Walter out of the blue.

" Oh ! "

Ivie glanced at his brother's face out of the corner of his eye. It was clouded over with thought, that fine and delicate face. Queer chap, old Watty ! thought Ivie patiently. Always worrying about something ; bent on setting the world to rights. But he was content to await the unfolding of his brother's thought. Perhaps it was only about those stinks up at the Barracks. Old Watty worried himself about stinks.

They were waiting for the *Freeman's* boat on a wooden jetty when Walter at length expressed himself again.

" Ivie," he said, " I'm not coming back with you this trip."

" Oh ! That's a pity," returned Ivie patiently. " And I was looking forward to a grand voyage in early summer weather. Thought of putting in at Algiers or Oran and letting you see a bit of Africa. However——"

Ivie held his tongue, beyond the trivialities, until they were on board ship again. He had dealt with the sea for some eighteen years of his life and he had learned patience. Watching his brother, he realised that he did not know this man very well after all. A difference in years and long separation in quite different pursuits had denied both of them a complete knowledge of each other. On board the *Freeman*, however, Ivie was king. It was his duty to take his ship and his ship's company home to the immediate disposal of Her Gracious Majesty, Victoria Regina, Defender of the Faith. He had waited until the grinning steward had served them each with long drinks of gin and lime and soda to wash the Ottoman dust from their throats.

" So you're thinking of staying behind, Watty ? " he began.

" Yes. That's what I meant to talk to you about." Walter seemed to be startled out of a private dream. " I'm staying here, Ivie, to give what help I can. You see for yourself what a mess it is, medically. That woman alone is fighting the Devil himself and all his Asses. It so happens that I have one little bit of knowledge and another little bit of experience that can possibly make all the difference. And I can *learn*, Ivie. . . . So I have decided to stay."

" I can understand all that," returned Ivie equably. " But there are one or two points you forget."

" Such as ? "

" You have no standing here—no passport, no credentials."

" The Lady Superintendent herself had very few," Walter smiled.

" You are a member of my crew. I've got to take you out of here again. That's in the rules, and they're not easy on merchant skippers."

" The stowaway," Walter smiled sweetly again, " will have to perform another pierhead jump."

" There are still the old folk."

" I'll have letters ready for them. They will perfectly understand."

" Oh damnation, Watty ! " cried Ivie, his dignity breaking down. " Your health, man ! In this bloody shambles ! A man of your age. . . ."

Walter looked sharply at his brother but spoke mildly.

" To talk about health, Ivie," he said, " always seems to me the confession of a sick mind. Health is always in the spirit, believe me. As for my age," he added with his smile, " can't an ancient gentleman such as you make me out to be go to the grave on the route of his own choice ? "

" Hell ! " exclaimed the master of the *Freeman* roundly. " You're just too damned clever, Watty. Making rings round a simple sailor. I could put you flat on your back if I had only your gift of the gab. However . . . Steward ! Where's that confounded steward ? "

Ivie spoke heartily in the seafaring convention, but he was not happy within himself. Walter's frailty seemed more obvious than ever. He had taken no colour from the middle-eastern sun, and his thin face appeared indeed to have gone whiter and more peaked during their few days in harbour. Ivie was aware of more than his own responsibility as brother and ship's captain. He had a quite subtle understanding of the iron will, the scientist's restlessness and the bleak fatalism that conspired together to energise a frail body into significant action. He had the healthy man's anxious fear of frailty, and he had the instinct to protect his brother. But behind every concern that reason could explain, he was possessed mainly by an uneasy, brooding, mystic sense of something decisive in the parting Walter now insisted on.

The brothers ate together, all the other officers of the ship being ashore, under an awning that had been rigged over the after-deck, but they did not linger long over the meal. The sun set behind the Thracian hills, the dusk deepened quickly, and an evening wind began to blow from the east across the Marmara, causing the old *Freeman* to start snubbing at her cables. In his shy concern Ivie thought to see his brother's face more pinched than ever.

" Better get below," he said, rising. " The night wind is treacherous in these parts. Unless you'd like to go ashore again and have a last stretch of the legs ? "

" I don't think so," said Walter absently. " I was really wondering, Ivie, where I could lay hands on a big quantity of chloride of lime."

" Chloride of lime ! Well, I suppose I could get a cargo shipped out to you, though how it's packed or how it's stowed or how it keeps I'm shot if I know. I'll see Uncle Bob."

" No," Walter demurred, still in his private world of public health. " There ought to be ample local supplies of lime. I think, Ivie, if you were to send out, or bring out, a good number of carboys of the acid. . . . However, I'll put all that in writing before you sail."

They were standing at the mouth of the companion-way for a last look at the land before they went below. Ivie engaged his brother's eyes with deliberate intimacy.

" You have really made up your mind to stay behind, Watty ? " he asked.

" Oh, yes ! That was why I stowed away at Garvel. My dear Ivie, you don't imagine I was interested in taking an ocean trip for the good of my health ? "

" No, I suppose not, now I come to think of it," said Ivie unhappily.

" I had to abuse your rights and your good nature, I'm afraid, and I apologise."

" That's all right between you and me, Watty. Dammit, I'm all for a bit of sport ! But——"

Walter gave his brother's arm a little squeeze as they went down the ladder. " This is my business in life, Ivie," he confided in an almost passionate whisper. " How would you feel if you were told you must not go to sea again ? "

5

The words, the tones, the intensity, the very voice of Walter were in Ivie's ears as he conned the *Freeman* towards the Golden Horn in the August of that same year, 1855. The Fund had been able to provide a second cargo of stores and a second charter for the wooden paddler. Walter had sent home by privileged despatches, franked by the Lady Superintendent herself, the strangest demands. Once there had come through Government in Whitehall, by the most special privilege, a new and surprising suggestion sent by the electric telegraph. And here was the old *Freeman* once more bumbling her way across the Marmara with Heaven alone knew what in her holds—bandages and old cotton shirts, new woollen shirts and socks, chemicals of a dozen kinds in a dozen shapes of container, patent stoves and paraffin for the stoves, phials of chloroform, sheets that could be used as shrouds, stationery, toilet paper, books, pencils—Heaven alone knew what ! Then there were those carboys of acid, stowed away from the water tanks and secured against leakage, down in the forepeak where old Watty had hidden last voyage, the sly old devil ! And Ivie heard the calm voice again : " However, I'll put all that in writing before you sail."

From the bridge Ivie watched the hills behind Scutari loom into sight, and as they came towards the anchorage he watched again for the Admiralty cutter coming out to meet them. He had made his signals at Sedd-el-Bahr and knew that Walter would find ways and means of finding a place in the first boat. But when at length he stopped his engines to let the tender come alongside, none of the faces that looked up to him from her deck was his brother's.

The fact was suddenly alarming. He could most reasonably argue with himself that there was a score of good reasons why Walter had not come out to meet him, and he did have to occupy himself for two hours in the detailed business of going through the formalities and preparing the ship for her stay in harbour. The concern lingered with him, however, a disappointment and a sudden angry glowing of those ashes of apprehension that had smouldered ever since he had seen Walter's pale face set in the lines of a dangerous determination.

It was late afternoon before he got ashore alone to hurry to the Barrack Hospital. The porter on duty recognised him ; the man spoke as one who had been expecting him.

" It's you, Captain Oliphant," he said in his persuasive Highland speech, for he was of the 93rd and the Thin Red Line and had lost an arm at Balaklava. " The Lady Superintendent said you were to go up to her office right away. It's a great pity, sir. He was a very fine gentleman."

" Thank you, sergeant," returned Ivie automatically.

He was dead. Watty was dead. His own second sight of a sailor had spoken sooth all these months past. Ivie went along the corridor in a daze, living in a numb little world of his own, an agonised small world that was the battered plaything and satellite of the larger planet wherein other people seemed to be happy and careless.

The Lady Superintendent rose from her chair and came from behind her desk to meet him. She took his hand ; and Ivie maintained throughout his life thereafter that she gave it a furtive stroke of her disengaged fingers. Then she abruptly pointed to a chair and returned to her place of command behind the desk. The wide brow, thin nose and puckered lips of her authority rearranged themselves.

" I see that you have heard the sad news, Captain Oliphant," said the Lady Superintendent. " I sent a message by the electric telegraph, hoping to advise you before you left home, but I seem to have been too late. I am very sorry."

" That is kind of you, ma'am," said Ivie quietly.

" He died three weeks ago. It was on a Sunday night about seven. I was able to be there. He went very quietly, without pain."

She spoke so softly that Ivie raised his eyes to study this woman's face, but the bold nose was still held high, the expression was official. The Lady Superintendent had witnessed so very many deaths.

" Enteric fever was the last cause, but the doctors seem sure that his lungs had been affected for some years past. He was not strong, poor—poor Dr. Oliphant."

" No, he wasn't strong," Ivie agreed limply. " I tried to persuade him not to stay."

" I took it upon myself to make the same suggestion," retorted the Lady Superintendent, her small mouth puckering. She was not used to being interrupted. " However, he stayed. Your brother had a very high sense of duty, Captain Oliphant, and I have said so in a report to the War Office. His work here was invaluable. I thought I knew a good deal about hospital organisation, but I learned much from Dr. Oliphant. He had the gift of comprehending and analysing and replanning the fundamental structure of my system. He improved upon my system greatly."

The Lady Superintendent's tone confessed surprise. She was clearly not used to meeting men who could improve upon her ideas. The thin, curved nose rose high in a just assertion of her own authority. Then she remembered that the occasion was not official.

" I rather think," she said quite gently, " that his devotion to his cousin's case was the last straw. He had no need to be so much in the fever wards, but——"

" Our cousin ? " asked Ivie, lifting his eyes quickly.

" Oh, I am so sorry ! Did they not tell you ? Yes, Ensign Edward Oliphant of one of the Guards regiments, I forget which. So many names. . . . And one gets so used to the fact of death, so terribly used."

The Lady Superintendent's gaze fell from Ivie's face to the surface of her desk.

" They are buried side by side, up in the cemetery at Pera. I arranged for headstones to be put up. I have written to their mothers."

Ivie rose from his chair.

" Thank you, ma'am," he said. " You have been extremely kind and you have so many worries of your own. I am still a little dazed ; you will understand that. But . . . But Walter died at his work."

" Yes, and such valuable work ! So modestly done ! "

In the cemetery, in the officers' plot amid the acres given over to the thousands of common British men who died for a cause they understood only a little less than their rulers, Ivie found the two small, white headstones side by side. One inscription recorded curtly that Edward Wedderspoon Oliphant, Ensign of the Foot Guards, born on September 17, 1827, had died on July 23, 1855 ; the other marked the grave of Walter Rait Oliphant, M.D., born March 20, 1815, died July 29, 1855.

The empty finality of it all left Ivie desolate. He was afflicted for a moment by the sharp onset of the thought that the price of Admiralty was high to this one merchant family ; two decent men out of his own generation dead so far from home—and for what ? But the sense of desolation was more powerful than the emotion of anger. He thought of familiar scenes, and of the sorrow of women, and of humanity's endless and apparently futile struggle to live reasonably.

A bunch of withered flowers at the foot of his brother's gravestone caught his eye. It had once been a bunch of red roses, but now the crimson petals had rusted into decay, and little but the thorny stalks remained of an emblem of somebody's emotion. They lay across a crumpled and weathered card, and Ivie stooped to pick the bundle up. On the card was an inscription in a woman's bold Italianate hand—

In Memory of a Gifted and Gracious Colleague, from
the Lady Superintendent.

From the Lady Superintendent had come this, the only wreath

on Walter's grave. She had not written down her own famous name.
The Lady Superintendent must always be aloof, official. But Ivie
wondered in what degree exactly she had cared. He wondered if she
had sent the flowers, conventionally, by a deputy, as she might send
flowers for the funeral of any one of her assistants. Or had a woman
alone climbed the hill one evening, a bunch of roses in her hand and,
with a little sigh for a warm possibility vanished, saluted the interesting
passer-by ?

Ivie thrust the dead stalks of the roses inside his uniform jacket.
He had untied the stained and faded ribbon and put the card away
in his wallet. His mother would like to have these small relics of her
first-born, even if the Lady Superintendent had chosen to remain just
the legendary Lady Superintendent.

Then he made his way back towards the landing stage, planning
just how quickly he might get his ship turned round again, and set
out on the voyage home, and escape from this place where there was
so little beyond frustration and emptiness.

CHAPTER SEVEN

A GAME OF POKER

I

" I never could stand the sight of those guns ! " .

Coming from Barbara, the declaration seemed to Julius a strangely
vehement confession of sentiment.

" Yes, it will be a pleasure to get away from them," he agreed.
" And all those great tenement buildings crowding in upon us. The
poor old place has entirely lost its character."

" As a house for two old people," concluded Barbara practically,
" it is quite absurdly large. We should have been out of it long
ago."

They were in the act of leaving Goldenhaddock. The great
furniture vans were at the door. The familiar pieces that had seemed
so right in their established domestic setting took on a queer air of
pretentious shabbiness as they stood about on the gravel, waiting to
be packed. The smells of straw and dust and old carpets filled the
air with the aroma of failure.

" And the climb uphill was getting rather too much for me,"
added Julius on a belated inspiration.

But they were leaving Goldenhaddock, and no amount of ration-alisation could get the sorry meaning of the act out of his mind.

It had been a gradual retreat, a long rearguard action. First of all, the Town Council had approached him to sell most of the great garden on the seaward side of the house for a public park. It was represented to him that the sale would be an act for the public good, and Julius's spirit was genuinely touched by the appeal. He could argue, easily and soundly, that it was wrong for one man to withhold for his private use so much space in the very heart of a growing com-munity ; and he could gently explain to Barbara that he was losing with the relentless years some of his pride in the garden, some of his interest and much of his physical capacity to supervise that array of greenhouses and rose-plots and pergolas and what-not. Good old-fashioned gardening labour was not so easily come by as it used to be. All the good men had as much as they could do about the great new villas springing up everywhere and forming new streets in the West End.

Barbara gently agreed with all his arguments ; and now a twenty-yard strip of lawn in front of the old, harled house was separated only by a tall iron fence from the asphalt paths of a public park, within which ragged, barefooted, clamorous children played on the iron swings and roundabouts and see-saws of municipal pleasure-making or under and over the iron guns that were the community's proud share of the trophies of a meaningless war in the Crimea, but were to Barbara and Julius ugly and inveterate reminders of Walter's fate.

Then, two years later, the railway company came seeking stables for the horses and lorries of their growing delivery trade. There were the old stables up at the back, where that queer boy Duncan, poor Alan's brat, had lived with old Martha. Nobody ever went near those outhouses these days, now that the boys were grown up and gone on their ways. No carriage now ; no coachman and stablemen ; no shining, nervous horses. Why, Julius reflected, he had last been in these outbuildings to see to the storage of poor Walter's books and small possessions, away back in '55. He had, in his grief, put them away in a wild access of vain hope that the report of his death was not true, that Walter would still come back ; and now, at the instance of the railway company—with Sir Mark Oliphant, Bart., as Chairman of its Directors—it would be an agreeable idea to send Walter's books to the library of his University. The stables had ceased to be either interesting or useful, and now there was behind Goldenhaddock, some fifty yards of drying-green and kitchen-garden intervening, the blank wall the railway company had seen fit to build to the height of twelve feet, topped with broken glass, to protect its property.

Another year, Sam Downie the builder had pointed out that the strip of beeches on the eastern side of the grounds, properly cleared, could take a row of good working-class tenements. Forbye, as Sam emphasised in his rough way, those beeches were getting old and were tricky bastards in a winter storm ; you never knew how the brutes would fall with those shallow roots of theirs. Then Canon O'Reilly, the soft-spoken and adroit priest-in-charge of St. Roch's, had come to speak for his Church and its wish to build a new school for the town's growing Catholic community ; and so, after some subtle negotiations with sundry Irish-spoken persons, Julius had found himself parting with a half-acre in the south-western corner of his land.

Thus the old mansion-house of Goldenhaddock was gradually hemmed in, surrounded, beleaguered. Shrill children from mean streets played almost on its doorstep, and working men's wives could look into its rooms as they washed clothes and dishes at their kitchen windows. The mass of the old house became too great for the diminishing lands about it, and these suffered from the ever-increasing slatternliness of the district—dirty papers blown on every wind, the agonised amours of innumerable cats, garbage cast over walls, cloacal smells, flowers trampled and vegetables stolen from the remaining bit of garden, and the incessant shouting and crying and bickering of overcrowded and impoverished humanity. Barbara complained that she had no privacy now, that the house could not be kept clean.

" It's no place for a gentleman in your position, Mr. Oliphant," Sam Downie argued. " It's just a damned anachronism. But it's a rare good building site, and I'll give you a rare price for it."

And now the old furniture was coming out of the home that had been his and Barbara's for more than forty years and Granduncle Walter's for forty years before that, and to-morrow, no doubt, Sam's men would be tearing down the fabric of a fine Scots building of the early eighteenth century to make room for the flatted barracks of mid-nineteenth speculative building.

As he stood in the sunshine, ruefully considering his household goods, Julius made no effort to shut out from his private mind the truth of this retreat. He saw with bitter clarity that the gradual fall of the house of Goldenhaddock perfectly symbolised his own feckless rearguard action against the new economics. All very well for Barbara and him to pretend that their desertion was a sensible move of convenience ; that truth was only too convenient. He had needed these ten years past all the monies the piecemeal sales had brought in. Now the departure from the old house was but an act of prudence enforced.

It was strange how something like a fortune could dwindle in forty years ! So much spent on the dream of the technical school at The Mount, now closed after a sad period of obvious decline. So much put into the Improvement Trust that had been one of the happier consequences of the cholera epidemic. So much given to subsidise Walter's work in public health, then to endow a Chair in his memory. Not a penny of all these thousands of pounds had he grudged or would he ever grudge, but it seemed a pity that the good causes somehow did not prosper in this brisk age of iron and engineering and what they called Progress.

Pacing the terrace and, to the amusement of the removal men, threading an eccentric course among serried chairs, rolled carpets and oddments of crockery, Julius peered through the mist of his not un-happy regrets to discern the grim shape of the central economic truth. The Yard. Not the shipowning business of Oliphant and Rait, the men of the *Constant Star*. That, as dear, old, faithful Bob kept saying, could always wash its face for all the ups and downs of trade ; and, as Bob was also fond of saying, it would last their time. But the Yard he had inherited, and the traditions of the Yard he had maintained in the face of the advice and the laughter of shrewd men like Mark. Craftsmanship ; fine, slow, careful, loving work ; the best of materials, whatever their cost. . . .

Colliding with the end of a sofa and skirting its squat shape, Julius hereabouts discerned the flaw in Bob's easy philosophy. The shipping business in sail could wash its face, but it was losing the earning power to maintain the old-fashioned shipyards. It was in a state of uneasy balance. What were the phrases these new economists were using ? A wasting asset ; the law of diminishing returns. Then those Americans, with their inexhaustible supplies of cheap wood and brilliant designers like McKay of Boston. A very great man, this McKay ; a genius, Julius allowed to himself with pleasure.

His last uncomfortable thought was that Mark had been right in his downright way. This was the age of iron and steam. America was the country of wood, but this Britain was assuredly the land of iron and smoking stacks and hissing jets. But wait ! Why not sailing ships of iron ? His own old idea. No doubt some bright young fellow would seize on it soon.

But it was too late. Barbara came out of the house, dressed for the road. Still tall and slim and handsome, wonderfully so, but Julius saw that his beloved had become an old lady. They were getting old now, and it was too late—even if he could ever have dreamed of lowering the flag ! And he chuckled to think that, after all, he never could !

" Why laugh, my dear ? " Barbara asked kindly.

" A foolish little thought. But shall I not send down to the Buck's
Head for a carriage ? "

" No, let us walk. I should enjoy that."

" And so should I, on such a fine day, and "—with a small, old-
fashioned bow—" in such company."

Barbara chuckled with pleasure. She took Julius's proffered arm.
Without a word of sentiment or a backward look they passed down the
drive and through the gates into the public street.

A workman, looking up from a crate of cups and plates, followed
them with his eyes as they went.

" That's a right couple of auld warriors," he remarked to one of
his mates.

The house to which Julius now conducted his lady was, though
small, a place of character and charm. A low house, dormer windows
lighting its upper rooms, with something of classical grace about its
deep eaves and well-spaced glass, it sedately faced the sea. A Virginia
creeper on one side of the porch and a luxuriant clematis on the other
provided points of colour to blend pleasantly with the roof of purple
slates, window sashes in white and a front door in bright green. From
this door, with shallow, broad steps before it, a lawn of wiry seaside
turf ran down almost to the water's edge and should indeed have
merged into the shingle except that a former occupant had had built
there above high-water mark a sort of platform or small esplanade of
concrete surrounded on three sides by a chain and stanchions of a
proper maritime kind. From one end of this platform rose a flagpole
or mast with gaff and halyards all complete ; at the other was a
small cannon of the sort used for firing signals and salutes.

The house bore the odd name of Guatemala Lodge, and this, with
its physical peculiarities, confessed the calling of its founder. Old
" Boxer " Buchanan had retired from the sea some forty years before
with a small fortune gained by bold privateering and, some whispered,
still more discreet slave-trading. He had laid out his property with
the neatness a master mariner learns on shipboard, and it was the
commonplace of town talk for many a day that he continued to run
his domestic establishment according to a discipline. All eyes could
certainly see that he flew his old house flag daily from the gaff, and
that if he ever hoisted an ensign on special occasions it was with strict
regard to the niceties of the sunrise and sunset ceremonies. Most ears
could hear that it was Boxer Buchanan's agreeable custom to salute
the incoming of one of his old company's ships or the arrival of any
old shipmate with a blank shot from the carronade. There were a few
specially great days in the summer months when, a number of friendly
ships in at the same time, Boxer would organise a regatta for cutters'

crews (and a party of considerable splendour for his friends) and in beaver hat, nankeen trousers and a blue cutaway coat with gilt buttons act as commodore, timekeeper and bombardier all in one.

" A nice place," said Bob Rait, looking round with a smile. " I like old Boxer's private quarterdeck. I'll wager the old boy's very happy in Heaven—or it may be Hell—to know that people like you and Barbara are in charge."

" It brings us back to the sea again," said Julius.

It was the evening of the removal day, and they had been sent to pass the time out of doors while Barbara and her sole remaining maid-servant struggled within to establish some sort of order in the new house. They paced the concrete platform from signal mast to carronade and back, up and down, up and down, two ageing gentlemen taking the air, enjoying the scene and spasmodically conversing. The late evening was dull and still. Smoke lay in dirty billows over the un-ruffled waters of the estuary. Outlines of mountains beyond were muffled, and peaks were lost altogether in the mist that heralded rain before morning. Between the two shores, however, the anchorage held a vast amount of shipping, impressive by dint of mere numbers, even in the doldrums of the night's oppressive stillness.

" Busy days," observed Julius casually. " I haven't seen so much shipping at the anchorage for a long time."

" War," explained Bob curtly.

" Ah, yes ! This American business. Bad, bad ! "

" Always the same," Bob pursued his theme. " Give us a good-going war, and the Port of Garvel makes big money. We saw it in Boney's time. We saw it during the Crimea. We saw it even during the Mutiny. And we're seeing it again, now that those Americans are cutting each other's throats for no good reason that I can see."

" The issue is perfectly clear, Bob," Julius protested sharply. " President Lincoln——"

" Yes, yes, yes, Julius ! I was talking loosely, I'll admit. Yet I will say that it is no *immediate* concern of ours, though," Bob laughed. " I wouldn't dare to repeat that in the cotton districts of Lancashire !

" I mean this sort of war," he continued. " Civil war—cutting your cousin's throat. I mean war in which our country is not engaged. In fact, a war in which British neutrality is of the first importance. And yet we are in it or, at the least, a lot of our people are. What I said holds good. War—war anywhere—and the Port of Garvel makes profits far beyond the decent, legitimate profits of peace. It's insane ! "

" You are becoming a philosopher in your old age, Bob," Julius chaffed his cousin. " A philosopher-economist. And I can't even admit your premises. You offer me no evidence of this new profit-making."

" You'll have it," said Bob morosely. " You'll have it within the next half-hour, or I'm a Dutchman."

" Bob, you speak in parables ! "

" Wait, Julius," Bob chuckled now. " Just a bit of a hint I picked up in Liverpool the other day. Oh, you are going to have your eyes opened before the year's out ! Profit ! Steamboats ! International morality ! International fiddlesticks and spillikins and bilgewater ! "

" I'm sure I don't know what you're talking about, Bob."

" Wait ! "

The night thickened and was so still that the slow heave of the swell through the weed on the shore and over the shingle produced little waves of crackling sound. It was so still that the bark of a farm-dog on the hillside four miles across the water came to their ears with ghostly clarity and the scream and puffing of a railway engine away beyond the Port ran echoing round the long escarpment of the nearer foothills. At length the tension of silence was broken by a steady note of water-music, familiar to the ears of the elderly men listening from Boxer Buchanan's promenade. It was coming down-river out of the ship channel ; it persisted with a pleasing beat ; it announced the approach of a paddle steamer moving outward-bound at the top limit of her considerable speed.

" Here she comes," said Bob cryptically.

The beating of paddles waxed in loudness, and soon they were able to discern through the gathering mirk the shape of a little steamer passing close inshore towards the waters of the outer Firth. The course her skipper was taking alone suggested a furtive purpose, and this impression was strengthened by the uniform greyness of the hull, merging into the evening shadows, and by an air of eccentricity about her outline and features. To the landsman she might have seemed just any small steamer built for pleasure traffic in estuarine waters, passing out of the River on her lawful occasions, but Julius's experienced eye noted how all her ports and saloon windows had been boarded up and how, as in the old *Freeman* of unhappy memory, the long saloon deck had been built up with iron plates to take a deck-cargo of coal. It most astonished Julius that she showed no navigation lights on a night so heavily overcast.

" But that's Henderson's *Diamond* ! " he protested to Bob. " What the devil is she doing at this time of night and in that rig ? And no lights ! "

" She was once Henderson's," Bob agreed morosely, " but now

she belongs to the Emperor of China, and God alone knows what her new name is ! She cost Henderson's about four thousand to build two years ago, but the Emperor of China paid eight thousand for her last week. Aye, it's a proper game ! "

" Emperor of China ! What on earth are you talking about, Bob ? I can take a joke, I hope, but what's it all about ? You have me bewildered. I don't hear these things nowadays."

" Sometimes it's the Emperor of China," Bob chuckled sardonically, " and sometimes it's a Spanish merchant. Sometimes it's the Confederates buying through their own agents, and sometimes it's speculators in this country. I believe the rate of profit is running into hundreds per cent. And you and I could," he added bitterly, " be doing with some of it ourselves."

" Blood money, no ! " cried Julius. " Never ! But tell me, Bob, tell me about this traffic. It is—I must suppose it is—the running of the Northern blockade of the Southern ports."

" It's just that."

" But little ships like this *Diamond* ! Small things, built for pleasure sailing on the Firth, mere cockleshells—to cross the Atlantic and then run the gauntlet of the Union forces ! Why, one small cannon-ball would sink any one of them ! One lucky shot."

" They are fast, Julius, that's the point," Bob explained patiently. " You and I never liked steam, never would have anything to do with it. But the other chaps up and down the River have done well in their own way, we must admit it. If it has to be steamships, there's none better than they build hereabouts."

" And you mean to tell me—— ? "

" I do tell you, my dear Julius, that these little ships are being sold out of the River by the dozen, at enormous profit."

" And only cockleshells, built for coastal waters ! "

" Yes, they'll be wrecked by the dozen, swamped by the dozen. They'll be sunk, and they'll be captured. But some of them will get through, and the rate of profit is so high that the speculators will still get a big thing out of it. Never mind the loss of good ships. Never mind the loss of good lives. Never mind the needs of our own traffic. The British merchant—mentioning no names—does well. And that's war for you ! "

" It is a hideous thought. The greater our mechanical advances, the more powerful and efficient the engines we produce, the easier it seems to be to make war of a more and more horrible kind. Perhaps there was reason behind our decision to stick to sail, Bob, after all. When I think——"

Julius could no doubt have continued at length in this strain, but his eloquence was checked by a familiar authority. The beat of the small ship's paddles had died away beyond the Battery point, and Barbara's voice sounded clear through the stillness on the garden.

"Are you never coming indoors, Julius and Bob? You will get your deaths of cold. Come, I have prepared coffee."

2

It was the legend of Nassau in the Bahamas that the poker game in Greek Charlie's tavern had been going on without a break for more than a year, night and day. The longshore gossips could tell of a hundred quickly-made fortunes, more quickly lost at the table in the back parlour. They could explain virtuously and wisely how just a few sharp men, professional in the card business, had made fortunes overnight and could, at the worst, always bank on the steady plucking of the innocent and foolish sailormen who crowded the port. They never failed to emphasise that Greek Charlie—who was a Venezuelan christened Enrico—was the steadiest winner of all, with his percentage of the kitty and the prices he charged for his concoctions of Bacardi rum.

The most reckless of the tale-tellers, however, could not chronicle a suicide on account of gaming losses. Suicides in the madness of drink, suicides and murders for the love of island girls—these by the score, taken for granted. But no man in Nassau of the Bahamas in 1863 dreamed of taking the gold itself seriously. It was easy come, easy go, for any lad of a little spirit. North and South were at war over on the Continent and the beleaguered South was crying out for goods. One successful run into Wilmington and out again meant a fortune for the meanest member of a runner's crew. In this island port, therefore, were concentrated most of the scamps and rascals and romantics and adventurers of a civilisation ; and therefore such as Greek Charlie and the big men of the Trade prospered vastly.

And the poker game went on and on, one man dropping out at midnight with empty pockets, only to reappear on a hot afternoon a month later, throw a handful of Mexican dollars into the pool, and take up where he had left off ; another to cut in for an hour or two each day over a period of weeks, to sit impassive over the cards, to pay or rake in his losses or gains and then, without a word to the company, to step out of his chair and disappear into the limbo. At any hour of day or night there was somebody waiting for the first vacancy, even to fight for it. Hundreds of men, coming and going like their sudden small fortunes, sat round Greek Charlie's table in

the course of any month. All that was permanent in the back room
of the tavern, its jalousies drawn against the fierce sunlight and idle
eyes, was Greek Charlie himself with his smile and his watchful eyes,
with the gun in his pocket and the knife in his armpit, its hilt not far
from the open neck of his pink shirt.

Ivie Oliphant had been in the poker game for a week off and on
before he knew that he must pull out and return to sanity. He had
decided more than once during these eight days that he ought to do
so, but the sense of duty to himself at least had never weighed greatly
with Ivie. There would be a long run of bad luck, and the decision
to quit and admit himself a fool would gather in his mind, then a
straight flush heavily backed and a brimming jack-pot thrown in
would change the picture and he would be off again, all the other
players his good friends once more, the cards bright with magic.

Now, however, it was a case of compulsion. As he had known from
the beginning, no honest man could hold out long against the run of
the cards and their manipulation by the professionals. A nice packet
of cash gone west ! It was not in Ivie to grudge a penny of it. You
had your fun and you paid for it ; and fun it had been. He would
not for worlds have missed this glimpse of Nassau at the height of
war-time lunacy. Sheer curiosity and an infallible nose for mischief
had brought him across the Gulf from Belize where his ship, the
Constant Tide, battered and dismasted on the edge of a cyclone in the
Yucatan Channel, was being repaired on his own bond of bottomry.
A damned fool to have left her, a damned fool to have come so far
to gamble away six months' pay ; but then he had never been able—
as old Walter had said years ago, reflected Ivie with a grin—he had
never been able to resist a bit of sport.

Now the issue was purely practical—how to get back to Belize in
the Honduras on the few dollars and oddments of small change left to
him. His gold watch and chain would fetch big money in this daft
town of flowing gold, but they had once been Wattie's, and he would
sooner have pawned his ship's chronometers. The alternative was
clear and hard, as alternatives are apt to be. He would just have to
go down to the harbour and look for a ship bound Belize way. All
the decent Gulf traders were short-handed, thanks to the lure of the
Trade, and even if the passage must be worked before the mast, little
did Ivie care.

The gaming rooms in Greek Charlie's lay discreetly to the rear
of the tavern and could be reached only through a *patio* in the old
Spanish style. This courtyard was so beautifully shaded against the
harsh Caribbean sun by an ancient bougainvillea cunningly trained
that the whole area of it, as well as the verandas, could be arranged

for the accommodation of a floating population which, as rich as it was motley, set no store by the siesta or any other of the sub-tropical graces. Greek Charlie was not the man to neglect this source of easy revenue, and as Ivie set out, blinking in the mottled sunlight, to thread his way among the tables and find the freedom of the public streets he had to pass under the scrutiny of scores of eyes in the knowing heads of the spies, pimps, agents, sailors, whores, confidence men and money-lenders of a lawless community who crowded the tables.

Ivie knew that they knew what he was. Nothing out of the way ; just another fool well and truly rooked at the endless poker game ; and he was as tolerant of their curiosity as they were of his plight. Such things happened in Nassau while, over on the Continent, men of the same tongue and race killed each other in large numbers, and with bitterness, over the academic case of a bunch of niggers. Ivie walked the thirty paces across the courtyard with a smile on his face and a jaunty carriage of head and shoulders, but as he passed one table near the outer veranda his eyes focused on one face that was familiar and, also, most obviously challenged his special attention. It was for him the one significant face among hundreds of blurred, sallow-pink ovals, like so much pink caviare in the lump.

Ivie had been seeing that face at intervals throughout his stay in Nassau. More than once it had been thrust round the edge of the gaming-room door to regard the poker game and to challenge him in particular. It had been familiar from the first, but he had not troubled to place it until, at the third encounter, he had recognised his cousin John, Uncle Mark's precious son. A damned stupid, coarse, brutal face it was too, thought Ivie—Uncle Mark all over again, but without the dark distinction the father had had in his early days. He hardly knew the fellow ; hadn't spoken to him since John was a big, loutish boy and he himself a youngster in Garvel the best part of forty years before. And our John was in the Trade, was he ? Nothing in that. A lot of queer fish were floating about the Caribbean these days, and where big money was to be made quickly in the shipping line, there one of Uncle Mark's agents was bound to be.

Ivie ignored the challenge of the face and passed out of the tavern into the blinding glare of the waterfront. The strike of the afternoon sun on white walls, blue water and the coloured sails of sponge-boats was almost unbearable on eyes strained by peering at playing cards in an atmosphere thick with tobacco smoke. Ivie blinked even at the lurid turbans and shawls on the heads and shoulders of black mammies among the foot-passengers now thronging the sidewalk as the cool of the evening approached. He stood at Greek Charlie's door until his eyes could bear to stay open, and then, spying a likely schooner berthed a little along the quay to his right, he sauntered across the road.

He was standing on the edge of the quay, looking idly for signs of life aboard the ship, when the sound of footsteps approaching from behind made him turn round in a swift, defensive reaction.

" I'd like a word with you," said his cousin John abruptly. " Come across to the little café over there."

A crude devil, but the fellow seemed to know his mind and to mean business. Over the drinks he came straight to the point.

" I guess you could do with some ready cash."

" Your guess is right, Cousin John," returned Ivie just as promptly but much more cheerfully.

" Well, there's a job going," the other continued. " It's to run a cargo in and another out. You know what I mean ? "

" Through the Blockade, I suppose. Good old Uncle Mark was bound to be in the Trade. He's got a nose like a pointer for cash."

" Leave my father out of it," John warned him, scowling. " This is my own private enterprise, and no damned sentiment about it either."

" No names, no pack-drill," Ivie agreed blithely.

He was almost taking to the fellow with his rough realism. This was better than being confused by polite family sentiment in a practical affair. If John disdained the value of the relationship, that suited Ivie down to the ground. He just didn't like the big, thrusting, coarse-faced chap.

" What is the proposition exactly ? " he asked.

" To be master of one of my ships for the round trip. To keep order among one of the toughest crews you have ever handled. To navigate the ship from here to ten miles from the mouth of the Cape Fear River, and back again from the same point. In between times the Pilot is in full charge. Wilmington's your destination, of course—nearest port to Confederate headquarters at Richmond."

" And this ship ? "

" You ought to know her," laughed John sardonically. " Used to be the *Diamond*, plying on the Firth to the coast towns. Hundred and ninety feet overall, a couple of haystack boilers, ninety horse-power——"

" That tub ! " cried Ivie, smacking the table and laughing so that people at the other tables looked round. " Dammit, you might as well offer me a canoe ! "

" Shut your mouth, for God's sake ! This isn't a joke. . . . The point is that she's fast. The fastest packet on the run. She's been in and out of Wilmington five trips, and never a hitch. Your pilot's Colborne, the best man in the game."

Ivie observed with malicious delight that his companion was eager. The eagerness kept breaking through the façade of business realism. He was beginning to admire this downright lad. This was fun. And he had always been one for a bit of sport.

" And what's in the proposition for me ? " he asked, dropping into the vernacular of the region.

" Two hundred and fifty pounds. You can have it in cash now, or we'll go up to the Bank in the morning and put it to your credit. But I want that ship out of this harbour before ten to-morrow night."

Ivie whistled.

" There's money in this game ! "

" Of course there is. Big risks, big profits, and no damned sentiment. I'm not bluffing you. My regular man has bilked me—gone off to Cornford's without a by-your-leave. Two hundred and fifty— and I'll throw in a dollar commission on every bale of cotton you bring out. Dammit, I've got to pay your pilot seven hundred ! "

" Hm ! "

Ivie's demurrer had no commercial motive. It was just that a spasm of responsibility had cut across his amused excitement over the prospect his cousin dangled before him. The ship awaited him at Belize and he was his dear old father's agent. There was no hurry about the ship ; it would be another month before she could be fit to sail ; and his first officer was a good man. Still . . .

" It won't take you three weeks," John pursued his argument, " probably less. And I'll guarantee you a steamship passage back to the Honduras when it's all over. Add that to your two-fifty and the commission. What about it ? "

Ivie drained his glass and laughed.

" I'll do it," he said.

He was a damned fool, but he never could resist a bit of sport. He called loudly for the waiter.

3

It was like being on the bridge of the old *Freeman* again.

It was good to have the feel of a ship under one's feet once more, even if she was a steamer. The *Diamond* had her own pretty turn of speed and was a handy craft, even if she was painted a dirty white and was so heavily laden that Ivie could hardly bear to look overside and see that she had barely two feet of freeboard. Otherwise it was much as it had been on that voyage to the Golden Horn, down to the deck cargo of coal : a small ship speeding towards a seat of war

with goods sorely needed by one of the belligerent powers and himself,
poor idiot, in half-willing command.

They were three days out from Nassau, and somewhere under the
declining sun lay the coast of North Carolina beyond the Frying Pan
Shoals. Pacing the bridge alone, Ivie thought of the embattled armies
over there and of the men and women of the South nearly beleaguered
in their small cities. It was queer what they needed, or wanted, in
their extremity. The old *Freeman* had carried only medical supplies,
and now the *Diamond* bore her share of these ; but he had been
through the ship's manifest with the supercargo, and Lord ! it was
an eye-opener. Cloth, buttons, boots, stockings, thread, wool. A man
could understand the need for these things in a country almost without
manufactures. But then case upon case of the latest in Parisian
fashions, silken underwear, lace, the finest Irish linen, rolls of silk,
cosmetics. You could never change a woman, and Ivie allowed that
the Southern girls would need a lot of cheering up before it was all
over, poor dears. Still, there stuck in his forthright mind the uncomfortable thought that there was a basic indecency in this Trade. He
saw why John could afford these fantastic wages—fifty pounds for the
round trip to the meanest member of the crew ! But that was always
the way of it in war, Ivie had observed : easy money for some, easy
come and easy go, even if the lives of good and skilful men were freely
pledged in the making of it.

There was neither bitterness nor morbidity in Ivie's consideration
of this problem. It created only a vague wonder in the mind of a man
of action ; it was not the business of a shipmaster with an expensive
vessel, a fabulous cargo and a highly-paid crew in his exclusive charge.
He glanced at the compass. He scanned the sea and the sky. He hailed
the masthead.

" Lookout, ahoy ! Ahoy, there ! "

" Aye, aye, sir ! "

" Anything in sight ? "

" Nothing in sight, sir, and all's well."

Ivie chuckled to himself to think of the queer custom of the Trade
whereby the lookout-man earned a dollar for every ship he sighted—
and was fined five if it was seen from the bridge first. But all was
peace on the Atlantic, the sea smooth over the slow heaves of a ground
swell. It seemed incredible that perhaps only forty miles away in
the haze over the land the Yankee cruisers were lurking to shoot the
Diamond out of the water if they could catch her !

He kept the bridge alone until, about an hour before sundown,
the Pilot climbed the ladder followed by Shefford, the first mate.

Mr. Colborne, the Pilot, cut a figure that Ivie found entrancing.

He was immensely tall and thin, with a long American face that terminated in the little goatee beard of tradition. He wore a uniform cap, a long frock-coat and striped trousers tucked into high boots. His speech was a sort of crackling drawl charged with the cool humours of his race. The three days since they had left Nassau the Pilot had spent mainly in bed in his cabin reading *Ivanhoe*, between his lips a cigar as long and thin proportionately as his own body and seemingly inexhaustible. At meals he questioned Ivie interminably on the similarities between Sir Walter's world of romance and contemporary England. He was grieved to learn that jousting was of the past and reckoned that it must have been a mighty fine game to watch.

Now his demeanour on the bridge suggested that he had arrived at the point of business. Crisply he asked Ivie for the ship's exact position and then, stroking his chin, requested that she be stopped and a sounding taken.

" Sixteen fathoms and a sandy bottom with black specks, eh ? " he repeated the leadsman's report. " Too far south, mister, too far south. I've gotta get this landfall just right. Give me full speed ahead, mister, and port two points."

The *Diamond* shuddered into life once more, rolling gracefully over the low hills of the swell. Mr. Colborne motioned Ivie into conference apart on the starboard wing of the bridge.

" This is your first trip, Captain," he began, " and now it's time I gave you the set-up. From now on I'm in charge. What I says goes. Got that ? " And when Ivie nodded. " You and Shefford will have plenty to do. You ain't gonna know one moment from now on when your knees won't be knocking holes through your pants."

" Now, sir, I'd have you understand how the Yankees have their fleet disposed—and you may thank your lucky stars that it ain't bigger. The mouth of the river is blocked by Smith's Island, and that makes two channels inwards towards Wilmington, sixteen miles upstream. Waal, at each entrance they've got a regular squadron of ships, anchored by day but on the prowl at night. Pretty tough, eh ? Yes, but we have one ace of trumps left to us. On the point covering the northern channel is Fort Fisher, still safe in Confederate hands, Major Lamb in command, and one hell of a fine fellow. You can put your shirt and pants on Lamb giving you covering fire and a signal now and again that's usually worth having. And that's that bit of it."

" Perfectly clear," said Ivie, visualising the disposition from the chart engraved on his mind by hours of study.

" But that's only settin' to partners," Mr. Colborne proceeded with a dry chuckle. " Wait till the band strikes up. That ain't nothin'. Lookit, Captain ! Outside the ships watching the channels there's a cordon of cruisers on the move all the time, and outside them again there's a cordon of fast gunboats. The Yankee ain't makin' no allowances."

" In fact, he's got two half-circles of defence outside his main defences at the river-mouth," Ivie resumed. " And we're supposed to get through all that ? "

" Yes, sirree ! And just consider the fact that these fast gunboats on the outer ring are placed at exactly the distance that can be covered between the hour of high water on Wilmington bar and sunrise. Get me, Captain ? "

" To catch the blockade-runners coming out. That's clever."

" You said it," agreed the Pilot, adroitly rolling his long cigar from one corner of his mouth to the other. " So we just got to be a sight cleverer, see ? Now, to get in first. I aim to get round the gunboats north-about and to hit the coast about fourteen miles up from the mouth of the river. Then we'll run down it, close in, when it falls dark. Guess it will be dark enough ; that cloud is spreading against the wind. But I warn you, Captain, I'm gonna hug that coast so close—and a darned ugly coast it is—that you'll thank the Lord twice a minute it's me and not you that has the responsibility. Say, we'll be runnin' the shoals so close you could toss a cracker from the bridge here and hit a rock ! "

Mr. Colborne chuckled at his own conceit. The long cigar rolled between his lips from port to starboard. Then the air of amusement dropped from him and the Pilot took charge.

" Now, Captain, if you'll get your first officer across we'll talk turkey. We've gotta strip for action right now."

With that he took the cigar from his mouth and threw it overside.

" Gentlemen," he announced, " that's the last smoke in this ship until we've over the Wilmington bar. Any son of a bitch smoking or lighting a match from now on gets the gun," and he tapped a hard lump in the pocket of his frock coat. " You know the ropes, mister. Not a light to be shown. Tarpaulins over every port and rigged abaft the funnel to shield the glare of the fires. Yes, Captain, you've gotta screen even your binnacle light. And now, mister, get to it."

" Aye, aye, sir ! " responded Shefford, and as he clattered down the ladder the Pilot called after him :

" And say, mister ! Better get all your deckhands into their white clothes right now."

He was turning back to speak to Ivie when a hail from the masthead reached their ears, thin and forlorn in the gathering darkness over the indifferent sea.

" Ship on the starboard quarter," it announced. " Can't see much more than smoke, but I reckon she's headin' this way."

"Aye, aye!" the Pilot acknowledged the report. "Bully for you, son! Keep your eye skinned."

He took the glasses Ivie offered him and scanned the seas behind them.

"Just smoke," he confirmed; "but I reckon from his course that it's one of the Yankee gunboats all right, all right. I'll have a trifle more speed, Captain, if you'll give your engineer the word. And tell him we're gonna need a big head of steam from now on, even if he's gotta have a couple of niggers settin' on the safety valve. Yes, sirree! And look, Captain! Our landfall."

The coast now looming on the port beam was so low and feature-less that even Ivie's experienced eyes might have taken it for a low cloud over the sea, and he wondered how Mr. Colborne could discern any sure landmark. The Pilot, however, was chuckling again.

"Reckon we've done a very purty bit of navigation, Captain. Three points to port and we'll close the shore just where I calculate to put about. Yes, sir, this is where the band begins to play, and there's gonna be one hell of a lot of fun before it's Home, Sweet Home!"

Exactly as Mr. Colborne had reckoned the *Diamond* came in to the shore with the very last of the light. The darkness was thick when he gave the order to put about and the little ship started on her desperate run southwards for the mouth of the river. Ivie felt himself taken, as never before in all the crises of his life at sea, with a sort of paralysis of apprehension. It might have been different had he been in com-mand, but this hour was Mr. Colborne's. He was forced to be the watcher of a performance that was superb but hazardous in the extreme. To pass orders to steersman and engineer and to see the compass needle held to a precise bearing was automatic seamanship that could not distract him from his obsession with the fantastic risks of the commerce of warfare.

Ivie's very knowledge of the sea gave the Pilot's proceedings, for him, the character of lunacy. In that seamanlike concern he could almost forget the wall of Federal fire inside which they were running. A sailing ship man, he distrusted the engines that maintained their speed and mobility in these shoal waters. The same habit of mind forced on him a horrified apprehension of the nearness with which Mr. Colborne skirted the shallows and shoals, changing course abruptly every minute or so. The man's jocular boast of narrow shaves was being only too fully implemented for Ivie's peace of mind. That near crash and surge and rattle of the swell on the rocks sounded horrible to a deep-sea man. He could only thank God that the lethal noises probably neutralised the beat of the paddles on a night so still; and for the rest, he could lose something of his alarm in sheer admiration of this eccentric American's knowledge of the smallest indentations of an apparently featureless coast. It was like that of a fisherboy who knows every rock and eddy in the bay before his father's house.

For the first ten minutes or so their progress southwards had a sort of mechanical monotony. The noises of ship and sea apart, it was a taut silence broken by Mr. Colborne's clipped orders, by Ivie's whispered relays in the steersman's ear, and by the man's quiet acknowledgment. At length this tension was broken by a subdued hail from the masthead.

"Ship on the port quarter, coming up fast," reported the lookout. "Reckon she ain't much more than a mile behind."

"That's our friend we spotted before nightfall," commented Mr. Colborne easily. "Doesn't mean he's seen us. These Yankee skippers often cut inshore at the end of their beat. Jumpin' Jehoshaphat ! He has spotted us ! "

A flash and a roar leapt on them from out of the sea behind. The scream of the ball arched behind them and then was lost in the darkness and the noises of the sea.

"Two cables short, brother," Mr. Colborne calmly addressed the unseen gunner. He explained to Ivie. "Means he cain't exactly see us. Just gotta kind of an idea in his head. Still, I reckon I'll have to shave the North Breaker Shoal mighty close. More speed still, Captain, if your boilers can stand it, and one point to starboard."

"Starboard a point."

"Starboard a point it is."

"Hold her there. Engine-room . . ."

Palpably, like a willing dog, the *Diamond* surged forward still faster. Out of the night behind came three more flashes and three more crashes, but the whine of the balls had a distant and feckless sound.

"Lost us ! " chuckled Mr. Colborne. "Reckon that Yankee gunlayer is shellin' ole Ez' Price's barn."

The voice from the masthead, thin but ominous, broke into his amusement.

"Bridge, ahoy ! Ship dead ahead. Guess she's two mile distant and a mile offshore."

"Okay, lookout ! " Mr. Colborne acknowledged calmly. "Well done, son ! "

He turned sharply on Ivie.

"Stop everything ! "

A yell from Ivie and the *Diamond's* engines ceased their hissing and churning. The floats of the braked paddles sheered through the water.

The ship ran about a hundred yards thus and then lay wallowing in the swell, and Ivie, hearing again the boil and gurgle of broken water near at hand, knew a prudent master's alarm for her safety.

" Guess that's one of the inshore gunboats layin' off the mouth of the river," said Mr. Colborne calmly, " and I reckon it's now or never, Captain. He won't fire until he's sure of us, else he'll have the Port Fisher guns scarin' him off Lamb's doorstep, and mebbe Lamb will spot the Yankee before the Yankee spots us. Purty set-up, ain't it ? Jest the same, I guess we'll run for it. That O.K. by you, Captain ? "

" I'm ready," said Ivie steadily.

" Shoot, then ! " ordered the Pilot briskly. " Back on your course, and every darned ounce of steam the firemen can raise. Yes, sir ! I guess this is where the rockets start goin' up."

And no sooner had the *Diamond* shivered and plunged into life again that three white flashes rent the darkness and three crashes, a few seconds later, had their ear-drums tingling. The shots were heavier than the vessel behind had loosed off at them. They came from ahead but slightly to starboard.

" That's Lamb ! " cried Mr. Colborne. " He's spotted the Yankee, and he'll be lookin' for us."

Another flash and crash ahead pointed this observation, but they came from seaward, and now the scream of a shell bore down on the *Diamond*. On Ivie it produced an icy certainty that this was the end ; his imagination endowed the ball with a malignant precision. His instinct was to duck behind the plates that protected the bridge, but while his brain conducted a split-second argument with his instinct, a detached part of his mind registered the fact that the shell was in fact flying wide and high. It passed at mast-height above the *Diamond's* creaming wake, more than a cable behind.

" Now for the shootin' match," announced Mr. Colborne calmly, " and my money's on Lamb. He's got the heavier metal and the steadier platform."

The *Diamond* raced on under the archway of the cross-fire, and Ivie began to find the triangular duel exhilarating. He took to reckoning coolly the angles of the shots from the gunboats, and through his night-glasses he sought to spot the fall of the heavy shells from Fort Fisher. At the back of his mind always was that treacherous lee shore and the Pilot's hair-raising gamble with its hazards, but there was a blessed distraction in the excitement of battle firmly joined. He had the impression of a protracted fusillade while they covered these last two miles to the river mouth, but the gunboat in fact fired only nine shots, of which only one passed dangerously near. With a metallic, frightening clang it nicked a rent out of the after side of the ship's funnel only four feet above their heads.

" Good shootin'," observed Mr. Colborne with approval.

It was the last shot aimed at the runner. Three thunderous salvoes from Fort Fisher, nearly above them now, and the guns ceased. The noises of the sea filled the night once more.

" Lamb wins," said the Pilot, " and let's us in. Can you see the hill to the left of the fort ? Good. I'm makin' for the bar now. Wheel, there ! Hard a-starboard ! "

The *Diamond* seemed to pivot within her own length. The sea about her boiled and swirled. She swung nervously in the eddies.

" Hold her ! Hold her ! " was the Pilot's warning, sharp with excitement now. " A point to port ! Steady as she goes. . . . Two points starboard ! Ah ! "

The little ship appeared to surmount an obstacle. Under Ivie's feet were the clear sensations of a rise out of the cauldron over the bar and then the fall into placid waters.

" Stop her now, Captain, and anchor right here," said Mr. Colborne quietly. " This is where we go through quarantine. And quite a nice little trip."

Mr. Colborne drew one of his long cigars from the breast pocket of his long frock-coat and lit it deliberately.

" The darn thing is," he smiled at Ivie through the flame, " we've gotta get out again."

4

Wilmington danced. The guns were thundering up North in Virginia and away down South around Vicksburg. The city's hospitals, and cotton and tobacco warehouses crudely improvised as hospitals, were packed to overflowing with the gaunt, weary wounded and sick of the Confederate armies. In any street at any hour of the day a sharp eye could discern a tall figure with a furtive expression slinking along the crowded sidewalks and mark it down with certainty as that of one of a stream of deserters from the uneasy cause of the South, looking for a way across the Alleghanies. The Yankee cruisers, their power gathering every week as their numbers increased, lay across the mouth of the river only twenty miles away, a noose closing slowly round the neck of the Confederacy. One well-aimed shot from their guns, and hundreds of men in those stinking hospitals must die from gangrenous wounds for lack of bandages and disinfectants. Still, Wilmington danced, the Southern ladies lovely beyond belief in the

dresses of European fashion brought in by the blockade-runners, their
exquisite bodies sheathed in the underwear of silk and fine cambric
delivered to them at the dire risk of men's lives : adorable textiles
that might, in another dispensation, have been swabs for wounds.
The excellent string band in Nash's Assembly Rooms was playing a
Viennese waltz. Everybody who was anybody in the exclusive official
life of a sub-capital at war had a girl in his arms, her hair fragrant
in his nostrils, the light, occasional rub of her body against his a flint
to the fire in his loins.

Seated alone at a table on the low balcony that bordered the ballroom floor on three sides, Ivie Oliphant glumly, and even bitterly,
contemplated the spectacle of the *élite* of a people at war dancing the
hours of destiny away. Eight days in Wilmington, and only now,
sober as a judge in the early second hour of the ninth, was he realising
in what a crazy, vulgar, hysterical small world he had been living.
It had been an experience without boundaries or points of space or
time—drink going at all hours of day and night ; half a dozen invita-
tions to dinner delivered at his hotel every morning ; a ball or a
grandiose poker game in what could be only vaguely apprehended as
the evening and early morning hours ; apparently cordial and then
immediately forgotten encounters in saloons and over mint juleps with
drawling, cynical Confederate officers ; conferences in the office of a
smooth Greek person called Andreados—conferences at which the
neurotic, boastful talk of money in thousands of dollars (as if in their
hearts they despised the currency of their own vulgarity) flowed as
freely as the liquor. It was all free, disordered, unhappy—the free
drink, the free money, the free love : the desperate South throwing
the sanctions aside as the clumsy but ruthless fingers of the North
closed about its throat.

As he biliously considered the scene in the ballroom, and more
biliously its implications, Ivie's eyes now and again followed with some
concentration of interest the figure of one girl notable among much
more dazzling beauties for the sobriety of her dress. She was in black,
relieved only by a large red flower above her left breast and by a
smaller flower of the same plant in her dark hair. She seemed, so far
as appearances went, very small and modest among the mainly tall
and fair and flamboyant daughters of the Southern aristocracy, but
she had taken Ivie's notice among so many and more brilliant girls
on parade. The Greek called Andreados had presented him. What
was her name, now ? . . . Miss Harland. Miss Kitty Harland. . . .
She had seemed a quiet sort of girl, not one of those flaring, talkative
febrile girls of a nearly-besieged town. Ivie said to himself that she
seemed to have some sort of sense . . . what was the word—reticence ?

integrity ? At all events, watchful at his lonely table on the balcony, he found himself faintly resenting the fact that, for the third dance running, she was in the arms of Andreados. His damned, greasy, egg-shaped face smirked possessively over her bare shoulder.

Well, it was no business of his own, thank God ! If the silly little fool chose to cling to a greasy Greek for his money and the power of his money, that was the crazy, indecent sort of thing which happened in time of war. The inherent fineness of women was all my eye and Betty Martin. Give them money and excitement and drink and a yard or two of silk to wear against their silken skins, and they were the damndest fools, wreckers of the pious legend of purity they and besotted men had created about a body rather shapelier than that of any man. But, when you come down to brass tacks, it was just the old business of a womb desperate to be filled and pointing the way with blossom and perfume and all sorts of reckless allurements.

No : that wasn't fair to the child, Ivie told himself. He was, at this early and weary hour of his ninth day in Wilmington, transferring to the girl. . . . What was her name again ? Miss Harland. Kitty Harland. . . . He was throwing around the person of this girl the mud of his own disgust with himself. That was the real beastliness of his situation. It was not the reckless folly of a people at war. It was not a pretty girl in the possessive arms of a Levantine profiteer. It was the folly of a nearly middle-aged Scots shipmaster in blundering like an intemperate boy into a crazy world that was none of his business.

In his candour of self-communion Ivie reflected that his feelings were exactly those of a boy caught in wicked folly. The track of his descent was crystal-clear in his mind's eye ; he was sullenly conscious of guilt and could find no way of rationalising his impulses. Always fond of a bit of sport ? Too damned fond. . . . Leaving his own and his father's valuable ship with a pack of dago workmen ; travelling nearly a thousand miles to mess himself up in a poker game ; falling for a bribe from Uncle Mark's precious heir ! He had let himself be bluffed all along the line, and his failures of skill and judgment were criminal. Now he was, justly, the prisoner of his own follies and could see no way of escape. It would be a good thing, thought Ivie bitterly, if the *Diamond*, seeking at length to run the blockade outwards—and when might that be ?—were hit by a Yankee shell and blown out of the water. It would be at least something to die in action ; perhaps the most he could hope for.

His thoughts thus unhappy, his eyes focused closely on a pallid pink stain of spilt wine on the tablecloth, Ivie did not observe the approach of a friend until a hand fell on his shoulder. His head jerked upwards.

" Hallo, Mr. Colborne ! I'm sorry . . . I was thinking."

The Pilot was as he had been on the bridge of the *Diamond*. He still wore his long frock-coat. As a concession to social formality he had donned a black bow-tie, all too obviously made-up, and a laundered collar, but he was still an amphibian, slightly ill at ease among these landlubberly ongoings. In a flash of illumination Ivie saw Mr. Colborne as a ship's mast that had been temporarily and unhappily seconded for duty as a flagstaff in the garden of a gentleman's villa.

Mr. Colborne jerked the wet end of his long cigar towards the mazing throng on the dance-floor.

" Purty, ain't it ? " he observed lightly.

" It has been making me think," said Ivie.

" Yeah ! " agreed Mr. Colborne, folding his length into a chair on the other side of the table. " Gives you the heeby-jeebies, one way of looking at it. Still——"

Mr. Colborne turned round to call for a waiter and would not return to his subject until he had engaged the certain attention of a large Negro.

" Still," he resumed his discourse, the butt of his cigar again indicating the dancers as a special subject of study, " what can the poor devils do ? Draw down the blinds and mope ? No, sir ! These folk are beaten, and they know it, and they're having one hell of a good time so's they can forget. Guess it's been the same in every war since Judas Maccabæus."

" Beaten ? "

" Yes, sir. Beaten," Mr. Colborne repeated decisively, " and not a hope in hell for the South. Lookit ! This General Grant from the North—Ulysses S. Grant—has got his armies right down the Mississippi and is shapin' to take Vicksburg. Oh, says these folk here in Wilmington, that's miles away out West, and General Lee will see to Grant. Says they ! What the poor boobs don't see is that this Ulysses S. Grant is gonna get right round them from the South. There won't be no stoppin' General Grant. The poor old South just ha'n't got the power, the men, the money, the factories. No, sir ! "

Mr. Colborne expressed his views vehemently enough, but Ivie felt uncomfortably that they sprang from a cool and detached mind. He was suddenly moved, however, to defend the cause in which he had involuntarily become engaged, and which he had only a few minutes before been condemning in his private mind.

" I don't think the South is beaten so easily as all that," he said.

" Sure ! " Mr. Colborhe agreed lightly. " The South ain't beaten yet by a long chalk. It may take a year, two years, three years, to beat the South ; for those guys up North are sure a bunch of political bums. But the South is going to be beaten, Captain Oliphant, and you can bet your bottom dollar on that. The South is goin' to lose its ports one by one when this guy Grant gets goin'. . . . Savannah, Charlestown, an' then Wilmington. Why, son ! You saw for yourself the trouble we had to get our little ship right here ! This is—what do the professors call it ?—this is a bridgehead. This is, will be, the South's last bridgehead, with a lot of damned Yanks lyin' across the turnpike, and a derringer in each hand ! You're settin' on the jugular vein right now. You and your li'l ship, sir, make one small clot of Southern blood. Cut off Wilmington an' where's Richmond, where's Lee and his armies, where's the South ? Why, this outfit ain't got no more prospect of survival than a bunch of niggers in an up-country race-riot."

Mr. Colborne was violent in expression but still detached in his attitude. Ivie found that the older man's dry tone and cool self-possession were irritants to the raw patch in his own conscience. He spoke sullenly.

" That greasy Greek, Andreados, seems to be enjoying every minute of it."

Mr. Colborne smiled drily. With a long forefinger he carefully tapped an inch of fine, grey cigar-ash into the saucer on the table between them.

" Let a guy like that get up your back ? " he quizzed gently enough. " Sure, it's vermin, that sort of thing. You'll find an Andreados around every sort of seat of war. They like the big money, these dagoes ; can't keep away from it. And that, my son, is why the Jews are persecuted—can't stop rootin' around like hogs for the titbits, dirt no objection—an' the Christians don't like it. Say, son—were there Christians around when old Judas Maccabæus was busy ? Forgotten my Bible history."

Ivie was still not to be chaffed out of his dull anger.

" Dagoes ! Jews ! " he cried bitterly. " And every girl in the place seems to want to dance with Mr.—bloody—Andreados ! "

There had been an interval, but now the excellent band had struck up again, and the small girl called Kitty Harland was once more in the arms of the smoothly-smiling Greek.

Mr. Colborne engaged Ivie's look with a twinkle.

" Say, son, you've got this wrong," he observed kindly. " The Greek ain't interested in the little girl's pretty face. Why, he's got a fat wife and six kids of his own back in Whitesville, and proud of 'em too. It's the thought of old Grandpa Harland's dollars that's biting him."

" Who is she exactly ? " asked Ivie, slightly mollified.

" Kitty Harland ? Why, that girl's heiress to one of the tidiest tobacco fortunes in the South ! And," added Mr. Colborne gently, " she's one of the tragedies of the South at that. Lost her father at Bull Run, lost her only brother at Shiloh. Old man Harland just don't know what to do for the kid, and that's where Andreados comes in."

" But what's his game ? "

" Search me," said Mr. Colborne dryly. " Your guess is as good as mine. Reckon he'll do whatever Ole Man Harland wants done— and sting him good and hard."

" It beats me," growled Ivie, and he added violently : " But why the devil should I care ! The sooner I'm out of Wilmington the happier I'll be, and I don't care if I never see it again ! "

Mr. Colborne leaned across the table. He spoke quietly.

" I reckon you'll have your wish purty soon, Captain. Within the next twenty-four hours is my guess. But sst ! Here come our friends."

Ivie looked up to see Andreados and the girl advance towards their table through the throng of couples dispersing after the dance just ended. The face of the Greek was proprietorially radiant, but Ivie thought to see in Kitty Harland's expression the signs of a fretful bewilderment at least.

" Ask the kid for the next dance," he caught Mr. Colborne's whisper. " A little kindness don't cost much."

5

It was good to have the feel of a ship under his feet again, even if it was only a steamboat. Ivie whistled softly out of sheer pleasure as the *Diamond* paddled against the rising tide in the Cape Fear River towards the Wilmington bar. The sky was cloudy and the evening light was failing in a manner to cheer the blockade-runner's heart. The pilot had spoken truly. Eighteen hours ago he had been cursing himself in that hot, scented ballroom in Wilmington ; now he was a shipmaster alive and alert again, liberated, happy to be taking his ship out to sea. A vision of the puzzled face of Kitty Harland floated across his mind now and again. That was a queer case, if you please, but just part and parcel of the tragic mess that was the South at war. It was good to be getting away from that shabby imbroglio.

Ivie glanced aft and saw how the bales of cotton had been piled so high on the main deck of his little ship that their top level was in line with his feet on the raised bridge. That, too, was good. It was light stuff, and an honest shipmaster liked to have his vessel carry a profitable pay-load. Quite a lot of work here for some poor devils in Lancashire, and if his cousin Oliphant took a whacking profit, he also took risks and paid big money to the fools willing to do his dirty work for him. So Ivie whistled, and the waves of her passage rolled graciously away in smooth curves behind the speeding *Diamond*.

" Yes, sir ! " said Mr. Colborne in a sudden explosion.

" What's that, Pilot ? "

" Just been figgerin' out our chances," replied the tall man, " and they're good."

" Glad to hear it."

" Yes. The light's right, and I can hear a nice sea boilin' up beyond the bar to kill the noise of these darned paddles. Not that I ever had any great trouble gettin' out. Reckon the Yankees have enough to do keepin' their eyes skinned seawards. But here's the shoal water comin' at us. Ease her, Captain, and we'll stand by to slip over on the last of the ebb."

The water about the ship now boiled muddily in the surge of the tide over the bar, but a few curt orders from Mr. Colborne took her into the slack along the southern bank of the river, and there she lay awhile, checked against the influences of the stream by an occasional touch of the paddles. At length the butt of Mr. Colborne's cigar went overside in a fiery arc.

" Guess we'll darken the ship right now, Captain, and get out with the last of the light," he suggested. " The drill as usual, and as strict as the last time, only stricter. Lookouts posted right now. Full head of steam down below. I'll take the bridge while you have a look round."

Within ten minutes Ivie had satisfied himself that the elaborate ritual of precaution had been observed, and shortly thereafter the *Diamond* was under way. Over the bar into deep water, she began to dance in the short seas kicked up by a northerly wind from which they had previously been sheltered by the hill above Fort Fisher, and Ivie was happy to feel the buoyant life in her once more. He heard the Pilot pass an order that faintly surprised him, but he was content that it took the ship away from the mouth of that dull river.

" Reckon we'll try south-about this trip," Mr. Colborne explained in his ear. " I gotta hunch that some of the boys will be tryin' the run-in from the north, and that should keep the Yankees on the hop. Masthead, there ! "

" Aye, aye, sir ! "

" Anything in sight ? "

" Not a darned thing."

" Good. Keep your eye skinned to port."

" Aye, aye, sir ! "

The *Diamond* drove on into the darkness, and Ivie was content to leave her and his own fate to the Pilot. He was mildly surprised to find that there was upon him very little of the tension that had bedevilled his first approach to Wilmington. For one thing, Mr. Colborne had laid a course which, though it must take them close by the Frying Pan Shoals, and these forming a lee shore at that, involved none of the hair-raising dashes through rocky shallows which had made one hour of his life a year of purgatory on that first night. Nor had he called for an excess of speed ; the engineers had still a knot or two in hand. But, Ivie reflected, the roots of his queer contentment lay not in these considerations. They were going away, away from Wilmington, and he was himself in the act of escaping from a folly and of recovering his self-respect. That was everything. Just a little bit of luck now, and in a day or two he would see the sunlight on Nassau's white walls. Then by the very first vessel to Belize and his own ship, and then his private, personal fight to con her across the Atlantic and up the familiar Firth to the grey northern town where his mother and father awaited him by their fireside.

Ivie hummed a little tune, enchanted by the pleasantness of his own thoughts, but it was cut short by a boom, flattened by distance and the surge of the seas, then by another and still another. The voice of the unseen watcher at the masthead came thinly against the wind.

" Gunfire away to the nor'ard ! Guess by the flashes it must be five to six miles away."

" Good enough ! " Mr. Colborne shouted his acknowledgment between cupped hands. " There'll be more. Report every flash yon see, and give me your reckoning of the distance."

" Aye, aye, sir ! "

The Pilot crossed the bridge to where Ivie stood alone on the starboard wing, peering into the blackness astern.

" Mine wasn't a bad guess, eh ? " he boasted. " Reckon there's a regular party startin' up there right now. This looks like lettin' us out, Captain. We'll be sure when we hear Lamb openin' up with those big wallopers of his."

Soon enough the heavy crash and brighter flashes of Fort Fisher's salvoes filled the night. They did not silence the Yankee gunboats, however, and shortly the exchanges developed into such a cannonade as made Ivie reflect that their own run-in must have been a miracle of good luck. Every report from the masthead confirmed that the *Diamond* was heading swiftly away from the scene of action.

"Yes, sir, I guess there's more than one li'l ship aimin' to make the Wilmington bar to-night," Mr. Colborne remarked. "Only a chance now that one of the Yankees will be lyin' so far south as this with that party goin' on up there. We'll risk a point or two to port and let her run."

The course changed to make a shorter bid for deep water, the masthead warned to keep a strict look-out ahead and ignore the diminishing noises of battle to the northward, the little ship seemed to resume her own identity in remoteness. She became the pleasantly familiar small world of Ivie's contentment. He stood apart on the wing of the bridge, humming again. The shame of the unhappy adventure was passing like the terror of a bad dream in the light of a summer morning. He was no longer on edge for a warning hail from the masthead and was strangely sure that none would come to disturb his peace of mind. The tune he hummed took its time from the slow strong beat of the engine, and his eye took pleasure in the white breaking of the lively seas on and away from the ship's bows.

An hour must have passed before Mr. Colborne found occasion to speak again. Both booms and flashes of the guns, if they had not ceased altogether, were quite out of hearing and sight.

"I reckon we're out all right, Captain," said the Pilot. "We'll want a sharp look-out at dawn, and I guess you and I had better be on deck then. But we're headin' well clear of the Frying Pan, and if you care to leave your first officer in charge I think you and I could go below and have a drink on our luck so far."

"No, thank you, Pilot," Ivie returned. "I'd like to hang on here for a bit."

"Oh!"

That little ejaculation had an unusual emphasis of significance. It was as if Mr. Colborne, rarely at a loss for words and rarely put about, had suffered an unexpected rebuff. Ivie thought that he had perhaps transgressed some curious code of American or blockade-running manners.

"Just forgive me this once, Pilot," he urged warmly. "But I'm in a queer mood to stay up here and think out some little problems of my own. My own ship, for instance. . . ."

"Surely," Mr. Colborne agreed readily.

But he did not move. Ivie was awkwardly aware of a slightly uneasy presence at his shoulder. Neither spoke during the passage of minutes.

"Say, Captain!" said Mr. Colborne suddenly.

" Yes, Pilot."

" Reckon I've got to tell you something right now. Reckon I've got to go through a purty bad passage with you, and I won't blame you if you take it hard and bawl me off your bridge. But it's a fact, son, and it ain't no good bluffin' any more, but we've got a passenger on board the ship."

" A passenger ! "

" Yes, sir, right now. Say, son ! I knew this would get your dander, but——"

" To hell with your buts ! What damned dirty shenannekan is this now ? "

Ivie shouted his protest. His hands seized the rail before him and shook it, lest they be tempted to the Pilot's throat. The anger in him was a trembling and a sickness.

" Am I the master of this ship or not ? " he roared. " Do you damned Americans not know. . . . I don't care whether you're North or South or plain nigger. . . . Dammit, that I'm responsible for this ship, and for everybody on board ? Lord, I knew from the word Go that this business was rotten from the keelson up ! "

The first wave of his anger broke in those incoherent waves. The backwash of them was a flash of human curiosity, just a little less truculent.

" And who's your passenger ? Or have I got to go below and clap him in irons ? Our beautiful Mr. Andreados, I suppose, clearing out with the loot ? "

" No, sir," said Mr. Colborne quietly, and with a nice suggestion of penitence in his tone. " Why, I thought you would have guessed, Captain Oliphant. It's that li'l girl, Kitty Harland. You couldn't be sore on a poor kid like that."

" She has no business to be in this ship," retorted Ivie, still angry. " If she knew nothing about it, then it was just a damned dirty put-up job, arranged behind my back by you and Andreados. I'm master here, and I'm in the mind to turn about and put back into Wilmington."

" Sure," agreed Mr. Colborne drily.

" Go to hell ! "

The Pilot drew one of his long cigars from his breast pocket and bending into the shelter of the dodger, lit it between his cupped hands.

" I know what's bitin' you, Captain," he resumed calmly, " and I sympathise, but there are still one or two things you don't understand, and I'm going to tell you them right now."

He spat forcefully and decisively into the sea.

" First of all, this was no put-up job between me and Andreados.

First I knew of it was three hours before we sailed, though I had a hunch. The gal was to come on board in a sassy officer's uniform when you were up at our Greek friend's office. She was to be locked into my cabin. And that's just what did happen. Guess the kid's down there right now, bein' as sick as a puppy and wishin' she'd never seen the sea."

" And you fell in with all this," said Ivie bitterly.

" Sure," agreed Mr. Colborne unabashed. " It was good business for the folk who pay us good money. There's a fat bonus in the job for both of us. I guess old man Harland has had to part with ten thousand bucks at least for the li'l girl's passage-money."

" A lot of damned roguery ! " cried Ivie, his disgust with himself poisoning his speech. " They can keep their money."

He turned on his heel and stalked across the bridge to the other wing. Mr. Colborne followed him at a more leisurely pace.

" No, Captain," he insisted, " I ain't goin' to let you ride off in no tantrum. I ain't goin' down on my rheumaticy old knees to apologise. I'm just anxious to see that you get all this business straight."

" Straight ! "

" Yessir—straight. That's the word. Straight between two fair decent seafarin' men, you and me. I told you I knew what's bitin' you ? You weren't consulted. Your owners are givin' you the dirt, and your pilot is in with the owners in givin' you the dirt. It's lousy, son, but if I had come to you with this proposition—well, what, son ? "

" I'd have told you to go to hell. And I tell you again."

" Fine, Captain ! " agreed Mr. Colborne, still patient. " But you don't get it yet. You'd have told me to get to hell, and I'd understand that. What you don't get is that you have no darn' business to tell me or anybody else to get to hell. Son, you ain't got a leg to stand on."

" I am master in this ship."

" Yes, brother. And under what flag ? "

The sharpness and cogency of the question had Ivie nonplussed, and while he searched his mind for a retort the American voice pursued its theme with relentless calm.

" This ain't the British merchant service. You ain't sailin' under any Red Ensign. You ain't carryin' the Queen's authority into these here waters. Why, son, you're a rebel, even against your own flag ! You're just a plain, hard-bitten pirate like the rest of us, and you ain't got a leg, moral or legal, to stand on."

Now it was Mr. Colborne's turn to walk away in dudgeon from his companion of the bridge. Ivie was left to stare at the phosphores-

cent churn of the waters overside and to consider a new and still more
terrifying aspect of a situation that had seemed sufficiently bleak
before this issue of authority had arisen. He felt very lonely. He felt
that his old, familiar world and all the accepted sanctions of his
conduct hitherto hàd suddenly fallen into a void below his feet. He
had the feeling of ageing in years within the space of only an hour
or two.

. Mr. Colborne's tall form reappeared at his shoulder and leaned
over the dodger beside him.

" Reckon we're as safe as the Bank of England now, Captain," he
observed professionally. " If you feel that way, why, you could safely
alter course due south or just a point or two to the east'ard. The
Frying Pan can't scare us now. An' if you're in any hurry, waal, you
could risk another knot of speed. But it's your own judgment for it
now."

" Thank you, Pilot."

Ivie was still stiff within his shell of resentment.

" Not one li'l drink together—just for a break ? "

" No, thank you. I . . . I'm in the mood to stay on deck."

" Sure, that's O.K. by me," said Mr. Colborne.

It was something to be alone : not much, but something. Ivie had
this square yard or two of deck for his own and the enigmatic leagues
of the Atlantic to brood on. Near midnight his second officer reported
briskly, but Ivie pointed to the other wing of the bridge where the
first officer stood aloof, sedulously minding his own business. The
change of watches was an incident outside the captain's ken. The
professional part of his mind noted that the formality had been carried
through, but the real Ivie Oliphant was trying to project himself far
ahead of the time and place of his ship's position. Say, three days to
finish his miserable business in Nassau. Allow another week—perhaps
ten days—to make Belize. He would have been away from his ship
for just a little more than a month, and those dagoes could never
possibly have her repaired in less time. Probably have to kick his heels
in the Honduras for still another month. Meanwhile, he had seen a
bit of life, had enjoyed a bit of sport.

The effort of projection outwards was not enough. The small
steamship under his feet, the loom of the cotton bales against the
creaming white of her wake, his sense of the nearness of Mr. Colborne
and a female passenger, smuggled aboard in defiance of his authority
as ship's master, and even of his decency as an individual. . . . All
these immediate images and resentments were at hand to smother his
dreams of escape and of a return to decency. Damn the whole trip for
a folly beyond belief and toleration ! And how to remain decently

aloof throughout the long hours of the run to Nassau ? Or how, more like a man, to shake himself out of this peevishness ; to rise above the personalities, and get the ship to port, and take his wages, and go his ways ? It was a damned queer business if Ivie Oliphant, who always had been one for a bit of sport, should now let himself be huffed by a pack of confounded American rebels and a girl.

He heard footsteps on the ladder behind him, and the tall figure of Mr. Colborne appeared again by his side. It was followed by a much smaller figure, comically rotund and vague within a seaman's bridge-coat.

" By your leave, Captain," said the Pilot, " but Miss Harland here was feelin' a bit queasy, and I guessed that a mouthful of fresh air would do her a power of good."

" Certainly," Ivie agreed. " Sorry there isn't more room for the passengers, but I'm afraid that it's all taken up by cotton. Use the bridge by all means, Miss Harland."

" Thank you, Captain Oliphant," returned a voice out of the dark ; a voice at once polite and dignified. " Sure I won't disturb you ? "

" Not at all."

This was the torment all over again. Could that old busybody Colborne not have had the decency to keep his precious passenger down below and out of sight ? This was his idea of a joke, no doubt. Now he had walked away to the other end of the bridge and was chatting with the second mate.

The girl stayed beside Ivie, her head just above the top edge of the dodger, her gaze apparently fixed ahead. She was still a comic small figure in the borrowed reefer, but pathetic too. She had the air of a lost, unhappy boy, and through Ivie's defences there crept insidiously a feeling for her loneliness.

" You must find this a very strange experience, Miss Harland," he ventured.

" I do," she agreed, but without animation. " You understand that I had no choice."

It was a challenge—or an appeal ? Old Colborne had been talking. Or she had sensitively divined his hostility to her presence.

" I was given no choice in the matter," he replied gently enough. " If I had been, you wouldn't be here—or I wouldn't be here. It's probably all right now, but it was a quite fantastic risk, and it was all—well—irregular, to put it mildly."

(And why should he be so anxious to explain himself, or she so quick to defend her position ?)

" I understand how you feel, Captain Oliphant," said the girl.

Her tone was still sombre, but he noted the soft, drawling charm of her Southern speech. It reminded him of his mother.

" Is it any use telling you that my grandfather wanted it this way ? " she broke into vehemence. " They almost had to carry me on board your ship. I didn't want to leave the South ! "

" Oh, please, Miss Harland ! If I ever had any grievance—and I think I had a good one—it was never against you personally. It was just that you got sort of mixed up in something . . . well, something I didn't like."

" Yes, I guess we're both in the same boat. . . . No, I'm not trying to make a bad pun. . . . Both just messed around. . . . War ! "

(There is was again. It seemed that they were under some odd compulsion to explain themselves to each other.)

" It's not my idea of fun," flashed the Southern girl.

" Nor mine," Ivie agreed.

Kitty Harland fell silent then. She was still the small, rapt bundle of feminine humanity, her head just above the upper selvedge of the dodger, her eyes levelled dead ahead. In the sheen from the breaking seas, and with his sight accustomed to darkness, Ivie could see her face and its expression. The latter was one in which sadness and stoutness of intention were subtly mingled, but her eyelashes were long and dark and seemed to fall over a sweet curve of cheek beside a fine, small nose. You could not but feel tenderly for such a gentle child in such a situation.

" It's no business of mine, of course," said Ivie, " but I suppose these people—Andreados and that lot—have got you properly fixed up in Nassau. It's a queer town these days."

" I suppose there's an hotel can take me in for a day or two," said Miss Harland. " Mr. Colborne's in charge of all that. Next thing is to get a passage to England."

" England ? "

" Near the city of Bristol," the girl explained calmly. " All our folks have business connections there. Tobacco, you know. I guess I'll manage somehow. What does it matter ? "

" If I can help in any way——"

Mr. Colborne rejoined them.

" Perhaps you feel like goin' below, Miss Kitty," he suggested. " My cabin is at your disposal. Not feelin' like joining us in the saloon, Captain. I guess you can forget all about the Yankees now."

" No, no ! " Ivie protested warmly. " Miss Harland must certainly have my cabin. I feel like standing by till dawn, and the settee in the saloon is perfectly comfortable."

" Have it your own way, Captain," said Mr. Colborne, and Ivie suspected a chuckle.

" Thank you, Captain Oliphant," murmured Kitty Harland.

" A pleasure, Miss Harland. Good-night ! "

" Good-night ! "

The tall figure and the short disappeared down the ladder, and again Ivie had the feeling of the girl being helpless and nearly apathetic in her helplessness ; a victim of circumstance, her life arranged and managed for her even in the hour of escape. And a nice thought it was that she would now no doubt pass into the tender care of his cousin, John Oliphant, another of his little speculations in property.

6

Bob brought the news in the forenoon.

" That rascal of yours," he announced to his sister Barbara, " is coming home at last. And he's bringing his ship with him, thank God ! "

Bob Rait was ageing quickly now. He had grown thick about the neck, and the tinged red of his face was reflected in an explosive irascibility of temper. His hair was all white in this seventy-sixth year of his life and stood up in a shock that gave him, in conjunction with his old-fashioned mode of dress, an air at once comic and endearing. Receiving him in her garden, where she was cutting the roses Julius was cultivating once more in his plot by the sea, Barbara feared for Bob's health on this warm, clotted day of August. He so often got so excitable and violent. But it was like her dear brother, Bob, to toddle through the heat with his good news. His affectionate loyalty to her and her children had always been her great joy.

" He has been such a long time away," she remarked of Ivie.

" You never know what that young devil is up to," Bob complained proudly. " Young ! Not so devilish young either. Must be in his forties, God help us all ! We're growing old, Babs ; that's the devil of it. But that limb of Satan, young Ivie, never grows old. Buckets about the world ; smashes up a ship here, another there ; lands his old father and me in monstrous great bonds of bottomry—pawning his blasted ship in every port in Christendom ! But there it is. He'll be coming up the Firth now. I've sent a tug down to pick him up ; might as well be in the Doldrums in this damned flat weather. Anyhow, you'll tell Julius when he gets back from the city ? "

" But you'll stay for a bite of food, Bob ? A slice of cold tongue, a fresh lettuce. . . ."

" Can't manage, Babs. We're up to the ears. Just thought you'd like to know. I'll look in and see the young devil in the evening."

Then, when Julius came home in mid-afternoon, he was so boyishly excited by the news that Barbara was concerned for the health of another of her menfolk. Unlike Bob, Julius was growing thinner. He stooped, and sometimes she saw how his hand would tremble when handling a small object, as a salt-cellar at the table. There had been another hot evening three years before when he came in from his work among the roses and stared at her with a ghastly expression and pointed with a shaking finger to his mouth and she almost scolded him until she realised, with dread, that the power of speech had deserted him. It was a slight shock, said the doctor, adding something about blood pressure, but he would have to be careful ; at his age, you know. Dosed with sedatives, he was out and about again in three days, but the fear instilled by that alarm signal and the help-lessness of him in his palsy was never far from Barbara's mind.

Now Julius wanted to climb the Craigs to look down the Firth beyond the islands, and when she quite flatly forbade that he must think of all sorts of exciting things which could be done to watch and welcome Ivie home. Finally he hit on the idea of having a boat and an oarsman sent down from the yard to take them out to the ship the moment she should cast anchor.

" We shall see her coming round the point at Kempock," he explained eagerly. " Then we'll row out and be alongside as soon as he has his hook down. That will be a surprise for the young rascal ! My hat and stick, darling."

" Yes, my dearest," agreed Barbara, " but you will now go and have a rest in your chair in the garden. Margaret can run with a message to Bob ; that child loves any excuse for a trip into the town. Later on I shall bring out a tray and we can have tea together. Go now, Julius, and do as I tell you."

Delighted to be disciplined to such an admirable end, Julius made off to the garden, carefully arranging his chair so that it should com-mand the view downstream, and when Barbara came out again a little less than an hour later he was sleeping like a child. What a fine face ! she thought, pausing to look down on her husband ; the features seemed to have been ennobled and refined by age, and his white hair, grown rather long nowadays, enhanced her own impression of him as a poet of a sort.

The small crash of the tray on the garden table wakened him, and he smiled at her.

" But we haven't missed the ship ? " he asked anxiously. " No sign of her yet ? "

"No, no!" she assured him, "and here is our tea. Try one of the small sandwiches, Julius—our own apple chutney and heart of lettuce, as Maman used to make them for you."

Julius happily surveyed the anchorage, the surrounding hills, the garden, the tea tray, and his wife's face.

"This is splendid," he announced. "There is Tom Aitken and his boat, waiting for us. My favourite sandwiches. Capital! You are a wonderful manager, my dear."

But still he fussed. He must have his coat and hat at hand; you never knew the moment the ship would come round the point. Was she ready to make for Tom Aitken's boat at a moment's notice? His gaze was continually upon the point of land two miles away, with the spire of the new church rising on its spine, and Barbara was filled with pity to see how nervously eager he was. It was sometimes believed of fathers that they had little care for their grown-up sons, but Barbara knew better than that, and she also knew that this fretful concern over Ivie's return spoke of his many and growing apprehensions, however subconscious, of advancing years and dwindling fortune. So little time left, so little left of the old Oliphant glories within wide margins of security.

At length the ship came into sight. Her sticks were bare, and she dragged along in the wake of a tug-boat which, from a funnel painted in broad bands of black and white, chose at the moment of appearance nearly to smother her in banks of oily brown smoke.

"Here she comes!" cried Julius.

He leapt to his feet and took both of Barbara's hands in his. She could feel his emotion throbbing through her fingers.

"Our boy is coming home, Barbara! We have been a long time without him."

"Yes, my dear," said Barbara calmly, "but there is ample time. Julius, you must have patience, *je te demande!* Your coat—yes, I insist. Your hat. *Alors.* Now, Julius, *doucement, doucement.* We must approach the ship with some dignity."

But even while the cable was being slipped and the tug-boat had paddled away, and before the anchor went down in a clatter from under the ship's bows, Julius was standing up in the sternsheets of their wherry, wildly waving his red bandana kerchief.

"There he is!" he cried jubilantly. "Ivie waved. That was Ivie waving."

"Yes, I saw that, my dear," observed Barbara. "But is that not a woman I see beside him?"

"A woman? God bless my soul! Nonsense!"

" Aye, it's a wumman, nae doot aboot that," remarked Tom Aitken helpfully.

" But how ?   A woman ? "

" Julius ! " said Barbara severely. " That we shall learn shortly. Pray sit down or you will have the boat overturned."

A woman it was. As they closed the ship there were Ivie, grinning over the rail, and, beside him, a young female smiling. When they made the ship's deck their son was waiting for them at the break of the poop, and the girl stood in an unconsciously picturesque pose on the ladder beside him.

" Mother !   Father ! " cried Ivie happily. " Look what I've brought home—my wife, Kitty ! "

" Your wife ! . . . My darling boy ! . . . . My dearest girl ! "

The four persons concerned closed in a happy confusion of embraces and exclamations, from which old Julius emerged at length, nearly breathless with excitement.

" But what a day ! What a day ! This is prodigious. Capital, Ivie, capital ! And you, my dear child. . . . But still I am in the dark. This romance . . ."

" It's a queer story, I assure you, sir," Kitty laughed, a chuckle for the first time betraying the gurgling charm of her exotic speech.

" Come, we'll go below and have a glass of wine on it," added Ivie. " Mother, my arm."

" Kitty, my dear," said Julius, bowing to his new daughter.

And so, with a nice old-fashioned formality, the dignity of the Eighteenth prevailing into the Nineteenth Century under the spars of a tall ship, the two generations passed into family council.

Until late that evening Julius remained full of the wonder of the day. Even as they were preparing for bed he kept chuckling and exclaiming to Barbara over the incalculable wildness of their son.

" The rascal ! Running himself into that bees' byke of knaves and rebels and pirates, and coming out with a charming wife ! I never heard the like of it. But tell me, my dear," he said, suddenly and comically turning serious, " you understand these matters much better than I. Tell me—are you satisfied that these two young people are likely to be happy together."

" My dear Julius ! " Barbara laughed lightly. " What a question ! As if an affair of the heart were a matter of drawings and calculations, like one of your ships ! "

" No, no ! " protested Julius tetchily. " Any ship is the outcome of drawings and calculations, my dear, but the very strange thing is that you may build twenty ships from precisely the same specification and yet each one will differ from the other, and each will have its own little ways and crotchets and virtues. This is a subject to which I have——"

"But Julius !" Barbara patiently stopped the flow. "Is that not precisely what I say ? If two ships differ, any two human beings must differ still more exquisitely. Therefore I cannot tell you whether Ivie and this Kitty will or will not be happy."

"So like her mother !" murmured Julius, confiding in the universe at large.

"This I can tell you. When I had the girl in my room this evening I found her to be of good breeding, good education and, what is more to the point, good sense. I could not have chosen better myself—*moi, qui te parle.*"

"Capital ! Capital !"

"This allowed me to advise her," Barbara pursued her Gallic theme to its logical conclusion, "that it would be most pleasing to you and me, as to herself and Ivie, if a child were to be born. Preferably a son, *bien entendu.*"

"Barbara !"

"But it is obvious. That child would have a valuable heritage of brains and character. . . . Ah, perhaps I grow old ! But it is my deepest thought that the fight against the Mark Oliphants of this world must proceed."

"Fight ? My dear girl . . ."

"Fight—even war. The war which never ends. *Allons !* It is near midnight."

7

Round the mahogany table sat eleven solid men, five on each side and Sir Mark Oliphant in the armed chair at the top, the baldness of his head brilliantly reflected in the great mirror above the sideboard. For the company had gathered in a private dining-room of a discreet Liverpool hotel, and the room was perfectly of the period of its creation, the year of the Great Exhibition ; from that expanse of mirror above the monstrous sideboard to the marble, gilt-faced clock and glassy windbells on a marble mantelpiece : all that above an iron fireplace which, this being a day of August, still suggested the warmth of a hearth with fans of crinkled scarlet paper set within the bars.

"Well, gentlemen," said Sir Mark Oliphant, "you know why we are here."

Only one among them was not quite sure, but he did not say so.

He was a youngish, fine-drawn sort of man, representing his father, old Tom Manifold of Silloth. He observed that Sir Mark Oliphant was growing alarmingly choleric in girth, complexion and manner. He recalled how his father, himself no sluggard at the table, would boastfully regret that the great Mark Oliphant, his trusted colleague in the shipping business and his friend (he dared to assert) was good for three bottles of port a day. Young Mr. Manifold, a student and follower of Mr. John Ruskin, merely observed to himself that old Oliphant was a rough and relentless man of the exploiting type running to seed physically.

But the old codger was able—no doubt about that—and it was a part of young Mr. Manifold's æsthetics to recognise perfection in its own kind.

Sir Mark coughed and wheezed, the veins straining in his thickening neck. Young Mr. Manifold duly observed the curious sheen, as of a surface much washed with soap, which comes on the skins of a common type of elderly, full-blooded alcoholic. So far as freshness of complexion went, old Oliphant was the heartiest man in the room. But how much craftiness was not behind that rubicund frontage ?

" My first duty, gentleman," Sir Mark Oliphant resumed, " is to apologise for my son's continued absence. He is still held up in Nassau, representing your interests—not unsuccessfully, I think."

" Hear, hear ! " agreed everybody heartily.

" You also understand that my presence here is as his representative, and that only. I hold no shares in your company. I cannot be concerned in this particular branch of the trade, for obvious reasons. I think that should go on the Minutes, Mr. Palmer."

" Agreed ! Agreed ! Perfectly understood ! We appreciate your courtesy, Sir Mark."

The brazen old liar ! thought young Mr. Manifold with amusement ; and these other fools, kowtowing to wealth, half-believing it all, certainly would not examine the facts. That would not be good business.

" Well, if that's understood," Sir Mark went on through a wheeze in which he seemed in danger of losing his breath entirely, if not of bursting all his veins, " I can outline the results of my boy's operations on your account in just a few words."

" During the financial year ended June the thirtieth we—I mean you, of course. Just a habit—lost two ships, and their cargoes, in or out of the Southern ports."

(And their crews ? young Mr. Manifold asked himself but dared not put the unbusinesslike question to the meeting.)

" Wages and every other oncost have risen. I don't conceal from you, gentlemen—that is, my son asks me to report to you—that it becomes increasingly difficult to secure officers and men for the run from Nassau to Wilmington, short of bribery and corruption. It's a pity, but that, however, I think you will agree, is a commercial factor we have got to accept in the regrettable circumstances of civil war. And the fact remains that the profits on our shipments inwards. . . . I keep saying ' our,' but you know what I mean, I'm sure—the profits on the little bits of comforts your company is able to send to the Confederate Government, also the profits on the cotton brought out, are not to be despised."

The shareholders applauded these sentiments. Only young Mr. Manifold was left puzzling over certain gaps and assumptions in Sir Mark's process of reasoning.

" On her last trip, for instance," the baronet went on hoarsely, " the *Diamond* brought out 500-odd bales of cotton as well as a consignment of tobacco as ballast. On the tobacco alone, just ballast, freight was paid at the rate of £70 a ton. The profit on each bale of cotton was £50. Over and above that, a very special passenger was brought out at a fare that would take a lot of us sitting here across the Atlantic in first-class comfort."

The appropriate whistles of pleased surprise greeted this information.

Sir Mark concluded his oration with some consciousness of drama.

" Therefore, gentlemen, my son, with all the papers before him in Nassau, recommends a dividend on the year's working of one hundred and ten *per centum*, and I need not remind you that you still have in the fleet of fast ships an asset of growing, and not diminishing, value. I hope you find these results satisfactory."

This the company did. It was too intimate a meeting for cheering, but young Mr. Manifold sardonically remarked to himself that for two pins his colleagues would break into a song of praise and self-congratulation. He had to endure a long and heavily-phrased speech in almost abject admiration of the Oliphant acumen by a Manchester alderman, and he cynically amused himself by watching the signs of basic contempt in the crafty eyes behind old Sir Mark's professional smile.

" Thank you, gentlemen," the latter curtly acknowledged the vote of thanks. " Now you see what's on the sideboard behind me. Help yourselves, sirs ; there's more in the cellar if we need it."

When all were furnished with brimming glasses, he stood up among them, smiling coldly.

" I give you a toast, gentlemen. It comes to me in a letter from my son, who says it is to be heard in every club in Nassau. Gentlemen,

I give you—The Confederates who produce the cotton ; the Yankees who maintain the blockade and keep up the price of cotton ; the Britishers who buy the cotton and pay high prices for it. Here's to all three—and success to the blockade-runners ! "

This sentiment was greeted with laughter and honoured with enthusiasm.

CHAPTER EIGHT

THE SETTING OF A STAR

I

" THERE HE GOES ! " remarked old Tam Tulloch the caulker to the apprentice working beside him. There was a chuckle of affection in his voice.

" He can fairly sclim a ladder yet," said the boy.

" Aye, and him seventy-wan, if he's a day," agreed Tam proudly.

Their eyes followed the slight figure of Julius as it climbed a forty-foot ladder to a staging under the stern of a ship in the building. It made the ascent with the ease of one long accustomed to tall ladders and with the spring of a man much younger in years. It was only when he had gained the staging and stood looking along the lines of the new vessel that his advanced age became apparent in the stoop of his shoulders and a charming antiquity of dress. The apprentice giggled at his master's tall beaver hat.

" You may laugh," said Tam Tulloch, " but he's a rare auld-farrant gentleman that. I mind the day . . ."

Tam launched himself on a series of reminiscences designed to demonstrate that he had attended the building of ships more splendid than the apprentice boy could ever hope to see and lived through days more romantically glorious than could ever come the way of a lad born only yesterday, in the rattling, mechanical year of 1854. The child was content to let old Tam meander on. It filled the time and distracted his senior from hard work in hand. The whistle would soon be going for the dinner break at noon.

The thoughts of Julius, standing under the skeleton of the ship, ran along much the same lines as the spoken memories of Tam Tulloch. Indeed, they were also spoken, for the habit of talking to himself was growing on him with the years. His communications could not be heard, however, for now, in this temple of the art of wooden shipbuilding, the harsh and ringing sounds of metal-working outdid the drone and rasping of saws and the thud of axe and adze. But if there had been an intelligent listener by the old man's elbow at that moment he would have heard Julius chuckle and say :

" It's droll, when you come to think of it."

He was regarding the curved ribs of iron up which the wooden planking was only now beginning to rise, and he was thinking whimsically of the old days when he and his cousin Mark had differed, sometimes violently enough, over the merits of wood and metal, steam and sail.

" The days of long ago," old Julius said to himself. " Dear me ! "

Mark had been in the rights of it up to a point. Iron had thrust its way even into the making of a sailing ship. Composite—that was the new-fangled word. You wove your web of supple wooden planks round the skeleton of iron ribs, the living flesh over the hard bones. Even Oliphant's yard had had to move with the times and set up a shed in which long lengths of oven-heated iron were laid out on an iron floor and, still white-hot, beaten against iron pegs into the subtle curves limned by cunning hands in the drawing office. The names of the old craftsmen, cunning with saw and adze and axe, had gradually vanished from the fortnightly paysheet with the coming of the new methods. Some, Julius reflected with a pang, had walked out in dudgeon, just as Mark's shipwrights had walked out and across the town away back in the 'forties. A new breed of hard and grimy men, mostly Highlanders and Irish by origin, had taken their place, and the stink and smoke of their fires were apt to overwhelm and stain the odour and sheen of the fine woods—oak and yellow pine and teak, mahogany and ash and lignum vitæ.

" Composite," said the old man to himself. " Transition. Ah, well ! "

His sigh was the measure of a certain resignation. The listener by his elbow might have thought it defeatist, the expression of an old man content to mark time, without thought for the future, until death should solve the problem abruptly and completely. Then Julius could have been heard to say with decision :

" No doubt about it ! Speed. Pliability. The race is not decided yet ! "

He was at once admitting the validity of the new and proclaiming the virtue of the old. The new composite technique of building sailing ships had been proved to be good. Sound wood on iron frames was giving the wind-driven vessel a new lease of life and a new elegance. The British Clippers, whether out of the Mersey or the Clyde, or Hall's of Aberdeen, were meeting and defeating the Yankee fliers.

They dominated the rich China tea trade. If sail was dying, it was in a blaze of glory.

"And I think we have done our share," said old Julius mildly to himself. "That fine run aft was a happy thought."

He cocked his head sideways to consider the lines of the ship on the stocks, and they pleased him. Just as, many years before, he had taken a poet's and discoverer's delight in the gracious hollow curve of the *Barbara Rait's* bows, now he rejoiced in the elegance of the new ship's lines toward the stern. His own drawings had so refined her shape in this region that, from almost amidships, the hull began to take the form of a fine wedge, with the underwater parts forming something like a racing yacht's long counter. Julius knew as well as any man that this was a great sacrifice of carrying capacity, that it horrified his friend and partner, Bob Rait. They had argued about it again and again.

"They're just skiffs, these new ships of yours!" Bob would explode. "They're about as fit to carry a decent pay-load as the Coulport Ferry!"

"But, my dear Bob, they do pay!" Julius would retort. "They are built to carry tea from China to the London market at enormous freights, up to £7 a ton. They are built to carry a light, valuable and perishable commodity. The demand is for speed, a fine and profitable demand as you will admit, I hope. Therefore I and my fellow-designers give them speed. My dear Bob, it's a naval architect's dream come true!"

"It's a lot of damned decadence! It's the sailing ship dying of inbreeding!" Bob would shout, his face colouring deeply, his fist thumping the table. Rheumatic nodules were forming on the knuckles to make it a formidable fist. "Your Tea Race from China is just a confounded regatta. You're littering the trade routes with a fleet of blasted yachts!"

That was the word of truth : the Clippers were yachts. Looking up at the hull of the latest of them, Julius rejoiced in the fact. He rejoiced in the lithe beauty, already showing through the patchwork of iron ribs and wooden planking, of the vessel into which he had dared to put a refinement of line aft never hazarded before. He thought warmly of fine woods, of the deck of teak that would be put in this ship, of the manipulative skill and cautious minds of his Scots artisans, of the three long tapering poles that would be so carefully selected and stepped into the hull as masts, and of the radiant flights of canvas sails that would drive her along faster than sailing-ship had ever been driven before—from the great ventripotent mainsails to the airy top-gallants, lone and free flying like seagulls near the masthead.

The listener at Julius's elbow would then have been surprised by an announcement, spoken loudly.

" It was very civil of Mark, I must say."

Sir Mark Oliphant had ordered a yacht, a racing yacht, from his cousin Julius. Sir Mark Oliphant, Bart., Chairman of the Governors of the Middle and Far Eastern Shipping Company, Governor of the Bank of England, was tending in his old age to match his commercial dominance with a position among the landed nobility. Titled gentlemen owned estates, and Mark had bought a stretch of land in Argyll with a fine name. He had become Sir Mark Oliphant, Bart., of Tullich ; the master of some 4000 acres of rock and heather, with a shooting lodge in the one green glen, and of a dwindling native population of some 300 souls. The next necessary symbol of his position was a steam yacht, and the graceful, yellow-funnelled *Nagara*— 168 feet in overall length, with a natty crew of thirty : officers, deckhands, cooks and stewards—was the admiration of half Britain's longshoremen. The racing yacht followed as the sport became that of princes and gentlemen and a leader of dignified commerce could now decently aspire to see his ships wear the White Ensign of the Squadron. An occasional accommodation to a Prince of the Blood was a small fee to pay for such a distinction.

Mark had come to Julius with a nice blend of patronage and deference to his cousin's renown in design for sail, and Julius was simply unaware of the former and enchanted by the latter. Mark was hard about what he wanted ; no expense was to be spared, but the new yacht must be the fastest thing in her class afloat—must be, and no nonsense about it ; and that was a challenge Julius could embrace with joy. Here was the glorious opportunity of putting a new theory into exquisite practice. Speed ; the long, exquisite line towards the stern, as suave and shapely as the muscles and angles of a greyhound's driving legs, as daring in design as the wings of the swift, the bird so fast in flight that it cannot walk.

With the boldness natural to him, Mark chose to give his new yacht that very name—the *Swift*. Even in a mere symbol he had to challenge the world, roughly and confidently. But it is true that to this day knowing men talk of the *Swift*, the legendary yacht of the '60's and '70's : the yacht that was like a snake on the water, as some put it, or a tern in her flashy flight in a breeze. Men still exclaim at the height of the mast Julius dared to plant in such a shallow shell of a thing, and they pore over old, faded Victorian photographs that show her carrying a pyramid of canvas loftier than man had ever dared before to impose on a vessel of her type. There are even a very few old persons still alive, who say that the *Swift* could glide along on airs so light that the rest of the racing fleet were ships becalmed, static and flapping and feeble against the dark pull of the enamelled tides. And in the newspaper files of that period there are even to be seen the grubby hints of the still lingering legend that Sir Mark Oliphant, never a popular man, had had a steam engine and propeller (of microscopic proportions but remarkable power) secretly installed in his triumphant craft. Thirty winning flags fluttering from her halyards at the end of her first season, and that out of thirty-three starts—well, the triumph had to be explained somehow !

Thinking that over, still considering the fine lines of the new ship, old Julius did not smile. Indeed, an observer near at hand would have seen a frown of irritation pass swiftly across his features and heard him mutter to himself :

" I suppose we must pay a certain price for speed. Not that I think the problem insoluble. . . ."

This was the memory of one of those small, chill winds of self-mistrust that blow ceaselessly over the surface of the artist's complacency. Julius was remembering an autumn day when, at the end of her first glorious racing season, he had gone down to the basin to see the *Swift* brought in to be laid up for the winter. He had taken her skipper, old Jock Maclachlan from Lochfyneside, up to the office and, over a dram, questioned him closely as to the yacht's performance. He could still hear every soft inflexion and delicate nuance of the man's Highland speech.

" There was never the like of her in light airs ! Slipping along on a fairy's whisper while the rest of the fleet would be rolling like a pack of dead whales, never a yacht was launched that could touch her ! The loveliest gurl that ever I knew ! *Slainte !* "

The skipper flicked his long moustache, the colour of beech leaves in autumn, with the base of his stubby left forefinger, drained his glass and set it down with some ostentation.

" Yes, skipper," Julius had agreed. " Another tot ? "

" If it's your pleasure."

" A great pleasure. . . . But I am interested to know how she behaves in weather."

" Weather, is it ! " cried the hairy man.

He had been about to make a staggering pronouncement, but his Highland sense of delicacy in the personal relationships restrained him.

" Well," he said judicially, holding the whisky up to the light, " she could mebbe be handier in a bit of weather than she is."

" Oh ! "

" The weather coming up from behind, I mean," the sailor

hastened to refine his generalisation. " A bit of a breeze abeam or a head sea, and she's not so different from any other yacht. But if the wind is coming up on the quarter, man, but it's bad, bad ! There was a time there, coming round Ardlamont and a dirty swell dead astern, and I thought our last day had come. It's that long counter, by your leave, sir. It gives her the speed of a deer in the light airs, but it seems to hold the water most lamentably in a following sea. She'll just not raise her tail to the sea, and them chasing you, and that's the God's truth. But a fair topper in light weather. There was never the like of her ! "

" Quite. . . . Another glass, skipper ? "

" If it's your will, and thank you, sir ! "

That was it. The yachtsman-fisherman, with his empirical and perfect knowledge of the ways of a ship in a seaway, had put his finger on the defect inherent in the new design. That fine run aft had caused a lack of buoyancy in certain conditions, and in his artist's heart old Julius knew it and was troubled. He considered again the lines of the new ship and wondered.

" But those fuller lines amidships will surely be ample compensation," he might have been heard saying to himself ; and, as he turned away at length, he added decisively : " We shall see."

Old Tam Tulloch and the apprentice boy watched him come neatly down the ladder from the staging, backwards.

" A rare auld warrior that ! " said Tam sentimentally. " I mind when we wis workin' on the *Swift*. . . . Ye'll have heard tell of the *Swift*, laddie ? "

" Aye," said the boy automatically, but he was still thinking of the broth in the can and the oatcakes in the red cotton handkerchief his mother had prepared for him.

Julius crossed the yard from berth to office, his feet now and again bumping on a baulk of timber, his hand raised in salute to friendly smiles on faces he could not place. There were so many new faces nowadays ; and he really must see to his eyes.

Bob Rait was puffing and blowing over papers and books in the room they shared, overlooking the yard. He merely looked up when Julius entered, then dropped his head again to his affairs. The old man crossed to the window and stood there looking across the yard.

" She shapes well, I think, Bob," he said.

" She would need to," said his partner roughly. " She's all we have on the stocks, and a bad debt at that. And here's another of those damned long letters from old Barclay, arguing about his rights this, his rights that. What the devil rights does he think he possesses ? "

" I'm sure I don't know, Bob," replied Julius mildly ; adding hastily : " None at all, of course. The man hasn't a leg to stand on. We assumed all his obligations."

" Much good may it do us ! "

" My dear Bob ! I have every confidence . . ."

But there it was again. The new ship was another challenge to fortune. Captain Barclay—" Bloody Bob " of the China trade—had ordered her, and no expense to be spared. She was to have the measure of Mackay's *Lightning* and of *Ariel, Taeping, Serica, Sir Launcelot* and *Fiery Cross*. Teak and yellow pine and mahogany were to go into her. Her hull was to be sheathed in beaten copper ; her spars and canvas were to be of the rarest and most delicate. And one morning, the keel laid and the frames in place, Bob had opened a letter from a firm of Writers to the Signet in Edinburgh, which regretted that their client, Captain Robert Barclay of Granton, had suddenly and unhappily found himself unable to meet his financial commitments and was applying to the Courts for relief in his unfortunate condition of bankruptcy.

Julius turned from the window and sought to engage his brother-in-law's eye and confidence.

" It may be very foolish of me, Bob," he said wistfully, " but that ship means a great deal to me. A point of honour, if you understand me—the honour of our yard and our duty to our own men. I have great faith in her. I think she may do very well in the China Trade and bring us good profits and a new reputation. Don't you think so, Bob ? "

" Yes, yes ! " his brother-in-law replied patiently but without conviction.

" When is Ivie due home again ? "

" Can't be before March next year, more likely April."

" That will suit capitally," said Julius. " The ship should be finished and ready for her trials by then. You agree that Ivie should have her, of course ? "

" That suits me. He's the best man we have."

" Good ! " cried Julius, warming up again. " Now we must find a name for her. Do you know, Bob, I should very much like to go back to the first of our names, the name of our first ship, the *Constant Star*. Now what do you think of that ? "

" Excellent ! " agreed Bob.

But he really did not care very much. Whether it was his age or the state of his health or his closeness to the financial side of the business, Bob Rait had little left to him of faith or hope. Glumly he saw Julius and himself as two old fools, doddering through the last years to failure and death.

2

The Court of Governors of the Middle and Far Eastern Shipping Company was in full session, and eighteen men—some of them anciently titled, most of them portly, all of them elderly—were giving close attention to the remarks of their Chairman, Sir Mark Oliphant.

" And now, my lords and gentlemen," he perorated, " I call your attention to a development that is bound to affect our policy closely. I refer to the cutting of a canal across the isthmus of Suez from the Mediterranean to the Red Sea."

The lords and gentlemen cleared their throats expectantly, and their Chairman indulged in a small fit of wheezing that brought up the colour of his face and neck.

" This, as you know," he resumed, gasping a little, " is a French enterprise. My information is that the Khedive's national interests have been bought off with a block of shares, and it will occur to you that there is some danger of all Egypt becoming a French colony or dependency."

" Shame ! " cried an earl whose Norman ancestors had occupied a considerable tract of English soil by force of arms.

" But we are not here to discuss politics," Sir Mark soothed him. " We can imagine that the Cabinet has the facts. Our business is to realise that this French engineer, de Lesseps, is assuredly going to succeed in his project, and it is my duty to point out to you that the successful completion of the canal will revolutionise the world shipping situation. I use the word advisedly—revolutionise."

His colleagues, most of them bankers, sat up in their chairs and leaned eagerly towards their mentor.

" It's as plain as a pikestaff ! " cried Sir Mark, seeming to scold them for their slowness in the uptake. " A canal at Suez will shorten the voyage to India and the Far East by a great many days—how many we cannot know yet. No more long and expensive voyages round the Cape. No more expensive coaling stations up and down the African coast. How the canal dues will be calculated I cannot tell you, but what I can tell you with certainty is that, on the most conservative estimate, our Company must at once save a good many thousands of pounds each year and be in a position to vastly increase our carrying trade."

The split infinitive passed unnoticed in a burst, discreet but hearty, of hand-clapping. Recovering his aplomb, the earl emitted a peculiarly loud " Hear, hear ! " Sir Mark quelled the applause by raising and shaking a plump forefinger.

" I don't know if you see the end of it, my lords and gentlemen,"
he warned his hearers, who promptly returned to attentive silence.
" It will not have escaped your notice that the canal can only be
used by steam-driven vessels."

" Ah ! " ejaculated the earl intelligently.

" And that means that the days of the sailing ship, on one of the
great trade routes, are numbered."

Sir Mark paused to let the point sink in. A banker coughed.

" It means that this Frenchman is ridding us of a competition that
has latterly—and let us be frank about it—become quite serious.
Those Clippers, as they call them, those new and specially-designed
sailing ships, have been cutting deeply into our China Trade, and
very fine and beautiful ships of their kind they are."

The earl obliged with a sportsmanlike " Hear, hear ! " Sir Mark
was taken with a second spasm of wheezing.

" But they're finished now," he pronounced, recovering. " Our
duty as a Board, my lords and gentlemen, is now to decide the policy
of building or whatever it may be that will bring us the best advantage
of the new situation."

He took a fat gold watch from his waistcoat pocket and consulted
it deliberately.

" Before we next meet I'll be in the closest consultation with our
managers here and our agents abroad, and I think I may have some
good news and some constructive proposals to put before you. And I
think that that, my lords and gentlemen, is all for to-day. Unless
somebody has something to say ? "

Only the earl had something to say by way of proposing a hearty
vote of thanks to our Chairman, whose foresight and acumen, he
dared to assert, were among the most valuable of the Company's
assets.

3

Where it opened out to an estuary the waters of the Min River
gleamed under the eastern sun but stank most abominably. In western
nostrils it was as if all the sewage of Foochow and every town and
village for a hundred miles into the interior of China hung in turbid
suspense in the slack tides. There was a coppery haze over the
anchorage, and the heat had the weight of metal on the European
body.

Ivie Oliphant was burdened by a headache ; the burden of his
topee was an affliction. He thirsted, but his stomach revolted at the

thought of drinks, hot or cold ; it was weary of working only on liquids that simply oozed through the pores to stain the third white suit of the day. His eyes were hot balls within the aching head, and even the back of his neck was stiff, for he had spent much of that day in staring aloft to where his own men and a nimble squad of Chinese artisans were rigging new spars and reeving fresh halyards carried away or merely chafed on the voyage out. For her first trip home with the new season's tea the *Constant Star* must be in trim as perfect as a rich man's yacht at Cowes. Both his father and Uncle Bob had made that point, the one eagerly, the other rather dully and reluctantly. In the rich China Trade, in the most grandiose sailing race the world had ever known, there could be no spoiling the ship for a ha'porth of tar.

Ivie leaned on the rail and stared up-river to the clotted mass of Foochow. He supposed that folks at home would think it a beautiful scene. Well, it would look mighty fine in a coloured picture that did not stink, no doubt, but it was not a seaman's notion of paradise. He could discern the picturesque values of bronze gleaming dully in the afternoon sun on the arabesques of a pagoda in green porcelain and the huddled charm of the go-downs on the water's edge. The junks and sampans that crowded the anchorage, like water-beetles on a stagnant pond in June, made a proper picture, if you could forget the conditions of living in those floating homes of a people who regarded water as other folk regard their native fields. No, said Ivie to himself, give me Sydney Harbour or the Golden Horn or Vigo or the Rock, rising out of clear, green northern seas.

He turned to look downstream, and then he crossed the deck to take his spyglass from where he had left it lying on bearers under the rail at the break of the poop. (And that confounded cabin-boy had again forgotten to polish the brass !) He directed the telescope towards a vessel lying some five cables out in the estuary and scrutinised her for the space of a minute or more. He closed the instrument with a snap and tucked the tube under his left arm.

The ship he had inspected over those thousand yards was much as his own, rather small as sailing ships went, but with the same fine lines and three masts of almost reckless height, with horizontal spars of great width.

Ivie raised his head and hailed the main-masthead.

" Bos'n, ahoy ! "

" Aye, aye, sir," came the faint response from aloft after a pause.

A figure came tumbling down the ratlines like a monkey, as it seemed, and landed on noiseless bare feet on the deck beside Ivie. He was a short man with the bow legs and long arms of a gorilla, and his face had the texture of polished leather. He wore on his head a round cap of blue worsted.

" Nearly finished up above, Cristie ? " asked Ivie.

" An hour, sir, and we'll be fit for anything," replied the man in the thin, exotic accents of the Orcadian.

" Keep them at it," the captain ordered. " The *Sultan* looks as if she is nearly finished loading. We may signal the tug any moment between now and eight bells. Then I'll want all hands to jump to it. You're watching that none of them slip ashore in the sampans ? "

Magnus Cristie from Stromness grinned.

" They will not go ashore," he said. " There's hardly a dollar left among the lot of them. And they know there's a bonus on the first cargo of tea into London River. You would not know, sir, but the lot of us have a month's pay on the result against the *Sultan's* lads."

" That's the spirit ! " laughed Ivie. " Well, keep them at it, Cristie. I hope we'll be piling on the canvas before this time to-morrow."

" Aye, aye, sir ! "

The little bos'n sketched a salute, dived to the rigging, and disappeared into the upper regions like a tree-creeper. Ivie smiled to hear him exhorting his men and threatening them with an outrageous account of their captain's fuming wrath. He felt better now. The ship was coming to life even in this reeking furnace. He started with pleasure to hear a salvo of healthy oaths boom from the fo'c'sle ; that was Mr. Mackersie, the second officer, instructing his working-party in the business of getting spare canvas up from the sail-locker. He thought of his first mate, Mr. Cutler, sweating and cursing in the holds below, seeing to the proper stowing of the tea-chests in the face of Chinese indifference and Chinese prejudice. The work was really going on.

His eye settled at length on the figure of the Comprador. It was a figure that had amused, puzzled and baffled him for days on end. He had once phrased it to himself that the Comprador looked like a walrus with a yellow face above his drooping moustache and slit eyes. That conceit, however, did not away with the fact that the life of the ship in port was dominated by this functionary. There he sat from early morning till late evening beside the hatch which happened to be in use for the time being. He always brought a stool with him. He wore a round black cap and a blue silk gown, and his feet, the gross belly sagging between outspread legs, were encased in sandals with thick soles of felt.

The Comprador seemed to Ivie a completely static figure. Only occasionally did he utter, in a high, chattering voice, a command, instruction or objurgation to the coolies sweating among the tea-chests below. His chief function appeared to be that of presiding over the work of others ; he apparently earned his keep by the simple act of watching. The decorated umbrella he kept lashed to the struts of his stool and under which he sat like a mandarin, proclaimed a philosophy of life that Ivie found maddening, comic—he could never decide which.

Ivie shinned down the ladder from the poop and approached this imperial figure, now presiding over the after-hatch, and on his way he paused to look down into the hold. For some minutes he forgot his special interest in the Comprador while he admired the native method of loading this queer, light valuable cargo ; this dessicated leaf that nowadays made the favourite brew of an island people on the other and northerly side of the world.

A bed of shingle had been laid in the bowels of the ship, clean and speckled gravel from the Min's estuarine beaches ; and Ivie reflected on the narrowness of a peasant economy that could look for a living to the washing and carrying of the sea's jetsam. On this base the square cases of thin wood, queerly stencil-marked, were set out in regimented order, the spaces between them exquisitely packed with matting. The hold was filled with the musty smell of China, but it was a wholesome smell, and it gave Ivie pleasure to think that his ship carried such a rare cargo, dry, light and scented. At the same time a small cloud of concern passed across his mind, and he stilled the chatter of coolies in the twilight below with a hail down the hatch.

" Mr. Cutler ! Are you there, mister ? "

" Aye, aye, sir ! " came a faint response, and shortly the first mate's face, red and wet with sweat, was staring upwards.

" You aren't putting too much load aft, are you, Mister ? " asked Ivie anxiously. " It looks to me as if this hold has just as much as is healthy."

" Don't think so, sir," the mate replied. " I wanted that old mandarin up there to stow more amidships, but this was his way of it. Still, I don't think we're overdoing it."

" The Comprador doesn't know this ship as I do," replied the captain grimly.

He turned to the placid figure on the stool under the coloured umbrella, and the Comprador smiled. Ivie had not yet mastered the pidgin English of the Coast, and his effort to explain his small anxiety about the loading was not made any easier by the mask of utter non-comprehension the Chinese chose to assume.

" See, Comprador ? " Ivie concluded desperately and with many

gestures. " Too much piecee weight aft. Want piecee more amidships.
See ? "

The Comprador smiled again. " No savee," he remarked placidly
and relapsed again into aloof Confucian calm.

Ivie looked round as if desperately seeking aid, and his search
was miraculously rewarded by the appearance over the rail of a
white topee on a head with a long, brown, lantern-jawed face. This
apparition elongated itself into the tall figure of a European in white
ducks, which dropped noiselessly in roped-soled white shoes on to the
deck in the waist.

" And hoo are ye the day, mannie ? " the newcomer hailed the
shipmaster exuberantly in an outlandish accent.

" I'm in a fair mess with this Comprador of yours, Mr. Dyce,"
returned Ivie with a wry jocularity. " I think he's putting too much
of his load in the after-hold, and I would rather have more amidships.
But I'm hanged if I can get him to understand a word I'm saying,
or he just pretends not to understand."

" I'll deal with the falla," said Mr. Dyce bluffly.

Mr. Dyce was apt to be hearty both in and out of season, Ivie
reflected quietly while Agent and Comprador wrangled in the absurd
common tongue of the coast. The lean and mobile jaw of the man was
always capable of a smile, apt to be excessively enlarged by the display
of long yellow teeth within a big mouth. It tended to be the automatic smile of the marionette, and its apparent munificence was always
belied by the steady coldness of the man's protruding grey eyes. Mr.
Dyce's heartiness, his deliberate and elaborate use of the tongue of
Buchan—a district he had left, an ambitious grocer's boy from
Inverurie, some thirty years before—were items of a specialised
stock-in-trade.

Leaning against the rail while Mr. Dyce harangued the Comprador, and the Comprador retorted without moving from his throne
under the coloured umbrella, Ivie's thoughts strayed from his immediate anxieties and considered the odd fact that Mr. Dyce had become
an almost symbolic figure in his own life. There was Mr. Dyce, the
highly efficient shipping agent of the Constant Star Line, and agent
also for the up-country growers of tea. There was the sentimental
Mr. Dyce, who read and could copiously quote from his twin bibles—
the *Works of Robert Burns* and *Johnnie Gibb of Gushetneuk* ; the Mr. Dyce
who had founded the Caledonian Club of Foochow and had organised
in Ivie's honour a dinner of that foundation, at which the whisky had
flowed freely and the speeches to innumerable toasts had got more and
more lachrymose as the night wore on ; the Mr. Dyce who, with
much drink taken, had insisted on seeing Ivie to the boat that awaited

him on the waterfront and entertained him on the way to an account
of his commercial successes and a statement of his ambitions to retire
in due course to a wee bit hoosie in Inverurie and take to himself a
snod bit wifikie for the comfort of his old age.

As he stood waiting for the colloquy to end, Ivie vaguely wondered
why the personality of Mr. Dyce should interest himself so much. Was
the creature not just the average Scot in exile, his elaborate dialect
and his sentimentalities the most obvious symptoms of his nostalgia?
But no; there was more than that in the puzzle. There was the
hardness behind Mr. Dyce's mawkishness, the falsity of his wide,
yellow-toothed smile under the unsmiling eyes—something, something
. . . What was it?

The tall man turned from his argument with the Comprador, and
his smile was large.

"It's a' richt, man," he said. "He's an auld rascal, that Ah
Lung, but he kens his joab. No," Mr. Dyce dropped the dialect, "it
seems he's got his main load well amidships, and what's going aft is
just the tail-end of the cargo. I'd trust Ah Lung, captain. He kens
ships and he kens tea, mebbe better than you and I do."

"He doesn't know this ship as well as I do," retorted Ivie.
"However——"

Mr. Dyce's cold eyes took his keenly.

"Ye're no' sayin' she's cranky, eh?"

"No, not cranky," Ivie demurred slowly. "But she's tender.
It's that fineness aft. Sometimes she's damnably slow to pick up from
a big sea coming up behind."

"Slow!" cried Mr. Dyce, recovering from a transient concern.
"You that made the passage out in eighty days! Man, ye've got the
nippiest Clipper in the Trade. Ye've got the feel of her now, have ye
no'? Have I spared a penny in repairs and renewals? Come on,
man! Ye're aboot to start the race of yer lifetime. That reminds me,
twa-three things I've got to tell ye. . . ."

"We'll go below," said Ivie curtly.

"Aye, a drink afore we pairt and a wee chat aboot our bittie
business. There's yer tug comin' doon the river. I doot the *Sultan*'ll
have the better o' ye by an hour mebbe, but fit's that in a race to the
ither side o' God's world? Wait you till I tell ye somethin'!"

To Ivie's faint annoyance Mr. Dyce held his arm above the elbow
until they reached the companionway; it was a pulsating grip that
sought to convey a perhaps deeper emotion than Mr. Dyce was capable
of entertaining sincerely. In Ivie's cabin, however, the papers before
him and a pair of steel-rimmed spectacles on his nose, Mr. Dyce was
a changed man for a while. Facts, figures and explanations flowed

from his mouth in a lucid stream and good plain English. This and
that had to be done in London. Bills of lading, Customs clearance,
receipts for repairs and harbour dues and tugboat charters ; a consignment of Manila cigars with his compliments to old Mr. Julius
and Mr. Bob ; a bolt of silk in a cylindrical case of zinc—for your own
good lady, Captain ; a teaset in Japanese porcelain—with my compliments to your mother, Captain, and ye'll notice that every single
piece is packed separately in bran in a bonnie wee cardboard box ;
and these odd boxes and parcels to be forwarded to my ain folk in
Inverurie, if ye'd be so good, Captain. . . . In such matters Mr. Dyce
was a precise realist, moving with assured accuracy about the material
province he understood thoroughly.

"That's all perfectly clear, Mr. Dyce," said Ivie sincerely
"Couldn't be clearer. As for those presents, well, really——"

Mr. Dyce became again the founder of the Caledonian Club of
Foochow.

"Ha'd yer tongue, mannie, ha'd yer tongue ! Naethin' ava' ! A
wheen ferlies for oor ain guid fowk at hame in Bonnie Scotland."

His eyes sought Ivie's earnestly.

"Juist trash, Captain ! " he explained candidly. "Juist trash
compared wi' the profits we're like to mak' on this trip. I didna' tell
ye, but I've contrived the record freight—eicht pun a ton ! Eight
golden sovereigns a ton, man, and a bonus if ye get yer ship into
London River wi' the first o' the season's crop. And fit div ye think
o' that ? "

"It's—it's phenomenal ! " cried Ivie, groping for a word to please
the author of such a commercial triumph. "Your glass, Mr. Dyce."

"Aye ! " said Mr. Dyce sententiously, " a wee drappie o't. Rabbie
aye had the richt word for it. Your health, Captain ! "

He sank his tot neat with a ritual finality, and his protruding eyes
again engaged Ivie's with solemnity.

"There's a fortune in't ! " said Mr. Dyce. " There was never the
like o't ! See you and drive this ship o' yours as fast's she'll go. See
you and win this race. And ye'll dae it, man ! Ye'll dae it ! "

Once more his excitement gave sudden place to a practical concern.

"Well, I'd best be getting ashore," said Mr. Dyce.

It was a relief to see him over the side and to turn to the working
of the ship. Now he and his men had it to themselves again. The
Comprador was gone, stool, umbrella and all, and Ivie did not waste
time scanning the scores of sampans on the river for a last glimpse of
that redoubtable figure. Lingering and no doubt light-fingered coolies
were being kicked off the lower decks by hearty British seamen. The
carpenter was busy at the hatches ; the second mate had a squad on

the fo'c'sle clearing gear from about the capstan ; in the waist Mr. Cutler and the bos'n and the sailmaker formed a knot of disputation. His kingdom was regained.

While he awaited the final All Clear from his officers, Ivie fretted happily on the poop. At one point he saw through his telescope that the *Sultan* had passed a line to her tug and was starting slowly downstream. A minute or two later he was below in his day cabin getting out the charts. Then he called the cook and the steward and had anxious, unnecessary words with them about supplies and rations. Anon he was on deck, again ruefully watching the smoke of the *Sultan's* tug go thinner and smaller in the distance, and irritably now he asked Mr. Cutler if he was not ready to go.

" Just two shakes now, sir ! " his first mate cried cheerfully. " By your leave, I'll start them easing up the pick."

" Yes. Get on with it."

A shout relayed forward, and the group on the fo'c'sle stirred into brisk life. Straining abreast on the bars, the sailors up there started to take in the slack of the cable. The clacking and clanking of the machinery sounded finely in Ivie's ears, and better still was the ship's little lift forward until she felt the strain against the embedded anchor. More shouts and some oaths, and finally the pick was off the ground and the men were moving rhythmically round the capstan, their great chests heaving, their brawny arms corded with tensed muscle. Out of this clot of labour rose a voice in slow, slightly falsetto song :

" *O, Sally Brown, she's a bright mulatto.*"

The chant was answered by a rumbling chorus :

" *Way-ay, roll and go !* "

The cantor gave tongue again :

" *O, she drinks rum and chews tobacco——*"

And the chorus thundered gladly :

" *Bet my money on Sally Brown !* "

Ivie laughed with pleasure. So *Sally Brown* was their chosen shanty. Not a song for the polite drawing-rooms of Garvel, but a real man's song, the proper choice of a happy crew homeward-bound.

Meanwhile, the *Constant Star's* own tug had slipped alongside, and

Mr. Cutler's language was of extreme but picturesque violence as he superintended the passing of a line and then the yellow hawser of the finest manila hemp. It seemed that everybody on board the ship was now in excited and positive action ; even the galley funnel was smoking thickly ; and Ivie leapt into the fray with shouts of his own as a shrill whistle from the fo'c'sle indicated that the anchor was up and clear and the tug paddled slowly ahead to start the vessel on her long voyage.

The tow-rope shuddered and threw off a shower of water as it took the strain, but the jar was of the slightest as the gracious shape of the *Constant Star* obeyed the pull. The tug increased speed, and in a couple of minutes they seemed, after the stagnation of the last few weeks, to be flying down the waterway. Junks, sampans and pagodas, all bright and foreign in the livid evening light, appeared to fly past, the evanescing figures in a dream. The stinks were all behind, left to fester in the slack water before the city of Foochow. A little north-easterly breeze came up the estuary to abate the heat and riffle the yellow waters about them. The canvas, now being hoisted under the vociferous direction of officers and bos'n, with a great bellowing of " Heave ho, my hearties ! " from the happy shellbacks, slatted and drummed most cheerfully against spars and braces.

Ivie was humming the vague air of *Sally Brown*. The little breaths of happy excitement were coming and going in whistles between his teeth. On the way downstream he had noted that no other ship of the Clipper fleet was ready to go within a day or two at the least. Probably they had not a Mr. Dyce to drive their Compradors on. It was the *Sultan* and the *Constant Star* in the van of the annual race, and by God ! the older, more famous ship, now a little triangle of creamy canvas about ten miles ahead, would get a run for it.

A feeble toot from the tug-boat's whistle indicated her skipper's intention to cast-off. They were well in the open now, some twenty miles of sea-room between shore and shore, the emptiness of the East China Sea ahead. The hearties on the fo'c'sle bawled again as they hauled the slack hawser inboard. The tug made a turn to port and passed upstream, her whistle busy on a prolonged series of Chinese salutations. Ivie waved an acknowledgment, then turned quickly from that last earth-bound symbol to rap an order to the steersman and shout an order to Mr. Cutler in the waist.

The quality of the steersman's voice, acknowledging his command, was strangely reassuring. Ivie glanced at the man's face. It was dark, bearded and eagle-nosed, a face bold and assured. Lord ! It was good to be among real men again.

The steersman spun his wheel with an apparently casual flicking of hands, but Ivie knew with a profound satisfaction that this was the skilled professional in charge. The *Constant Star* heeled slightly as her masts took the shock of the wind's impact on a modest spread of sail. Her body began to rise and fall ever so gently. Ivie felt her living under his feet on the waves that were her proper world.

The first mate came up to the poop, hot and tired and contented from his manifold labours and anxieties.

" All ship-shape now, sir," he reported formally. " Shall I take over my watch ? "

" Right, mister ! " Ivie agreed. " Hold her gently on this course till I've had a bite of food and another look at the charts. Don't give her any more sail for a while yet. We'll be running into the currents and among the islands soon enough. Steady as she goes. I'll be up soon again."

" Aye, aye, sir ! " responded Mr. Cutler. He added humorously : " But all hands are in great fettle to have a go at the *Sultan*."

" They'll get it," said Ivie, grinning. " But full and bye just now, mister, full and bye on this tack."

" Aye, aye, sir ! "

The steward was ready for him, but Ivie lingered in his cabin. He was almost conscious of being enchained by the perilous interest of those charts of the China Seas, with their unwritten warnings of currents, typhoons, unlighted rocks, pirates, waterspouts and head-winds. They forced him to see himself as a man charged with the task of breaking through a thick cordon of wary and remorseless enemies, the fates of a fine ship, a priceless cargo and some thirty human lives resting on his skill and courage. The fact of sheer distance filled his mind. It would be a thousand miles of sailing through the Formosa Straits and past the Pescadores to Hong-Kong, and that only the first short leg of the long course round the world to London.

He turned from his charts to an atlas he had left open during the afternoon and morosely considered the stretches of responsibility before him—Hong-Kong to Anjer Point in Java ; the passage of the Sunda Straits ; the long beat in the teeth of the monsoon across the Indian Ocean ; then into the dirt and fog of the Agulhas Stream, south of Table Bay, with perhaps a beat away into sub-antarctic waters. Even so, the *Constant Star* would still be far from home. There were hundreds of miles upon miles of the South Atlantic. There must be many days of slapping in torrid heat and futility through the Doldrums. Then the Bay still lay ahead, with mountainous waters, a dirty grey, blowing up from the sou'-west and a delicate ship under his feet. (No, not cranky, but tender, tender in following seas.) Inexorably before Ivie Oliphant there stretched at least a hundred days of hazardous travel and, except for such hours as he might snatch in the sleep of fatigue, not a minute in all those many thousands of minutes before him free from care.

The steward, a privileged person, poked an elderly and toothless head round the edge of the door and spoke unceremoniously in the lingo of Glasgow.

" Did ye no' hear me sayin' yer meat's ready ? "

" Yes, yes," Ivie impatiently responded.

But the man was right. This was no time for brooding and delay. The ship awaited him. Ivie had no illusions about the jollity of the seafarer. That was all very well for the folks at home, but they could not know, happy souls ! what it was to be a ship's master or even what it was to be just an able seaman ; underpaid, overcrowded, usually wet and dirty, and momentarily in danger of his life. Sailor-men were romantic only by reason of their gawky simplicity among the safe distractions of life ashore. He recalled the bitter observation of an old skipper of his, who had said : " My owners will never understand that Atlantic weather is three months' fog and nine months' storm." Yet men kept going to sea, escaping from one drudgery into another. . . .

Still, dammit ! that old steward was right. A man must have his meat. Least of all should the man in command stand over maps and charts, pondering his lot. He must remember to warn the mates against those eddies to the southward of White Dog Island. . . .

Ivie found himself in his sleeping cabin, washing his hands and considering his own reflection in the mirror above the copper basin. So he was really getting old. Although a Chinese barber had nearly shaved the hair above his ears, he saw that he had gone white along both sides of his head. Had it happened, he wondered, all in that moment on the outward journey when the *Constant Star*, chased by heavy seas in the monsoon, had yawed and sagged in a canyon between two heavy seas and had come up again only by a miracle, pouring water, heavy with the load taken in, unresponsive to the wheel : as sullen as an old bitch in pup ?

And was that somebody looking over his shoulder ? A long and plausible face with a false smile on a big mouth with yellow fangs of teeth ? Our Mr. Dyce, and all the Dyces of this world, driving the simpletons of the world along its trade routes at a rate of profit beyond the wildest dreams of any honest seaman ?

Ivie heard the old steward fidgeting again outside his door.

" Have you not got that grub on the table yet ? " he shouted.

" Aye, aye, sir ! " the steward responded to the voice of command he could alone respect.

He toddled forward and observed to the galley-boy :

" The auld man's in a rare tirravee the nicht. See you and no' jaup the lip o' his plate."

His officers stood up as Ivie entered the saloon.

" Sit down, gentlemen ! " he said easily. " There's a long road before us now, and we needn't stand too much on ceremony. . . . I think we might have a glass of sherry on this first night out."

" Thank you, sir ! " chorused the young men.

Up on deck, Mr. Cutler considered the sea, the sky and the set of the sails. He felt the *Constant Star* pulling eagerly under his feet.

" She'll do," he observed to the eagle-nosed helmsman.

" She's a daisy to steer," replied the man at the wheel.

" Keep her full and bye," said the first mate.

4

Julius pottered among his roses, a perfectly happy man.

He had made a new garden for just a selection of his old favourites under the high wall of yellow sandstone that bounded the grounds of Guatemala Lodge on the eastward side.

" You see, my dear," he had carefully explained to Barbara, " the wall has at once the properties of holding the heat and sheltering my little bushes from the cold winds. At the same time, the plot is open to the sun until the late evening. I think we may expect some very charming results."

" That will be delightful, my dear," Barbara had replied equably. " Your roses have always given me great joy."

This year, however, they were a worry—" a real bother," as he gravely phrased it to Barbara. Whether it was the wet, close weather of the spring months or some sort of spore in the load of manure Tam Warden had sent down from The Dowries, the blooms would not flower clean and in the rolled perfection he required. It was not a trouble of budding, nor was it his old, familiar enemy, the green fly. It was a canker that took the flower as it was opening, withered its lovely promise, and left it a browned and stunted ball of uninteresting vegetable matter on the stalk. Most alarming and disheartening. Julius went up and down the paths, snapping off these failures and absent-mindedly stuffing the diseased blooms into the tail pockets of the long coat he still affected.

" Tch, tch ! " he might have been heard to exclaim continually. " Even my beautiful Madame Legrand ! Too bad, too bad ! "

He paused, feeling the ache in his back induced by this fond bending over the bushes, and stretched his shoulders backwards to ease the strain. It suddenly occurred to him that he might write to the people at Kew Gardens, explaining this distressing and inexplicable intrusion of disease. Two or three specimens in a box and the people at Kew (Julius was quite sure) would be deeply interested and completely competent to solve his problem. That must be done first thing in the morning. He must remember to ask Barbara to remind him. Barbara never failed to remember these things. His own mind was just a broken sieve, and getting worse than ever, but it seemed that Barbara could always miraculously master this sort of detail.

" A very wonderful woman," he confided thoughtfully to a rambler he had trained over a pergola of larch poles.

The old man, holding to one of the pillars of the arch, surveyed the scene about him and forgot his disappointment in the roses. The notion came to him on a warm flood of awareness that he was one of the happiest men on God's earth.

The July evening was one of supreme loveliness, and the picture of sea and mountain before him, the familiar prospect of sixty years, was as splendidly fresh as if he were beholding it for the first time. The elements of the scene, Julius reflected, were unchangeable, inveterate, static, but at no moment of time were they ever as they had been before. States of wind and tide and subtle conditions of atmosphere kept them in a flux as cursive as the play of sunlight on a waterfall. One day of the Scottish summer the Ardhallow peninsula, seen through mist or fog, was a sullen, aloof and dreary thing, a chunk of flotsam on dead waters, a dull extension of a lost continent ; and then, with a change of wind, it came near and alive and green, till you might think to hear the hens clucking and the dogs barking and the children crying about the gables of its cottages among the crimped foliage of the Duke's woods ; and then again, in fine weather utterly settled, it was still green but had receded into a remote serenity of its own, like a pretty conceit of landscape in an Old Master's background.

So it was with the sea—now grey and dull and flat ; then green in a sort of bright anger ; then blue and sparkling and young ; and then, as on this night, serenely flat and pale blue shot with olive green and a ripple, as of a smile, on its face. So with the hills—so often aloof and ominous, the mist streaming over wet and cold and barren rockfaces, and again, as to-night, when they stood up in decent majesty against the northern sky, neither braggart nor humble, their summer colours of green and bronze and blue and purple enamelled with utter certainty on their great flanks.

Julius, still clinging to the arch of the pergola, deliberately considered his good fortune in having been suffered to live so long in the face of so much beauty. He humbly considered also the blessing that had come to him with Barbara : a woman intelligent and personable (he could dare to think in the detachment of his old age) far beyond the dreams of his youth, far beyond his deserts. He thought of their joint loss—Walter, dead long ago in Stamboul, his brilliance wasted on a political folly, but still splendid in his intelligence and detachment, his course completed.

"Now the labourer's task," murmured old Julius, addressing the candid petals of the American Pillar against the large pole, "is done."

His nearer self heard the words and considered vaguely whether they applied to himself or to the son on whose grave the Lady Superintendent had laid the red roses.

"Old fool!" chuckled Julius, and moved to bear down on a clump of chickweed he had suddenly discerned flourishing about the roots of one of his noblest standards.

The small instinctive act released him from his trance. He called himself an old fool because he lingered so readily in the golden past, whereas the true source of his fundamental happiness was in the active present. At Anjer Point in Java, the cable had reported, the *Constant Star* was leading the *Sultan* by eighteen hours in the great Tea Race.

Two thousand miles from Foochow, and only eighteen hours between two fine ships ! It was prodigious. To Julius the fact spoke of a poetic perfection of both design and seamanship. He had no wish to think of the *Sultan* as a ship inferior to his own *Constant Star* or of Ivie as the superior in seamanship of the famous Captain Billy Fylde of Liverpool. He was too much the artist, beyond self-delusion in the affairs of his craft, and he most sincerely rejoiced to think that in this late flowering of the sailing ship, in this gritty age of steam and canals and trade wars, two vessels could simultaneously demonstrate the achievement of near-perfection. Only as a fallible human being and a father did he take a little special pleasure in his own ship's lead and in Ivie's fitness to stand against Billy Fylde ; and he knew that any small trick of weather, a little mishap among intricate and delicate rigging, might at any moment reverse the position.

Julius was happily pondering this exciting state of affairs and pacing the little platform that had been Boxer Buchanan's private quarter-deck when a hail brought him up short. He turned to see Bob Rait approach the house along the path that was a short cut from the turnpike to the shore, and Bob was waving his cane in the air. More news ! Could it be ? Yes. There might be—should be—

word now from some remote and rocky signal station in the Indian Ocean.

"Ho, Bob !" cried Julius in a comically crackling falsetto of age and hurried to greet his friend ; and Bob likewise hastened to the glad encounter, bellowing in a short-winded blend of hoarseness and huskiness : "Great news ! We're still leading ! Ivie has got Bill Fylde fair beaten !"

Julius's fine face was pale, and Bob's broad and coarsening visage was empurpled, as they met and shook hands violently.

"Word from Mauritius !" Bob panted. "Just in ! *Constant Star* leading *Sultan* by a day and a half ! God help us, but the boy's a sailor !"

"Mauritius ! Five thousand miles, and only a day in it ! But this is beyond belief. . . . Bob, my friend, come indoors and we'll tell Barbara and Kitty. . . . Mauritius, and Ivie's ship still in the lead ! God bless my soul !"

The two elderly gentlemen stumped up the gravelled path leading to the porch of the house, and they made between them a great deal of noise. Julius kept calling "Barbara !" and "Kitty !" and Bob was swearing roundly that he had always known Ivie could give old Bill Fylde a flying start and still knock the head off him in the plain, damned, honest business of sailing a ship.

Barbara appeared in the porch, tall and still slim in a severe gown of black silk with a gold chain round her reck and the locket that held a tinted miniature of Walter's aloof and inscrutable features ; Barbara with her hair nearly white now but uncovered by the lace bonnet of current fashion for old ladies ; Barbara with a wrinkling skin ; but still Barbara poised, serene and sensibly kind.

"Julius ! Bob !" she upbraided her menfolk reasonably.

"The most astonishing news, my dear !" Julius cried.

"That lad of yours," Bob added, "has got old Billy Fylde sewn up in a bag with a real sailor's knot round the neck of it !"

"Mauritius !" Julius insisted. "Thirty-six hours ahead ! The scale of the thing has to be understood. It is much as if——"

Julius launched into a discourse on the enormity of the race between two small ships across thirteen thousand miles of incalculable ocean.

"That is glorious !" Barbara interrupted him kindly. "I am proud and happy. But you must not shout so loud, you two. Have I not an invalid on my hands ?"

"Kitty !" said Julius penitently. "A very charming girl. A great joy. . . . But do you mean to tell me, my dear," he added with vast gravity and concern, "that she is now—I mean, in this minute ;

for that would be a most extraordinary circumstance—in pain? I really mean to say—why not face it?—in labour."

Barbara laughed softly and understandingly in her French way.

" *Mais, comme tu es charmant, cher Jules!* " she said. " It must be at least a fortnight before you see our grandchild and you, Bob, your grandnephew, as I hope. But do you not understand that a young woman, carrying her first child, is sensitive in the extreme to the welfare of her husband, the child's father? It would unduly excite the girl to hear you two roaring about Mauritius and ships and this Fylde. Surely you appreciate the circumstances? "

" My dear Barbara! " said Julius handsomely. " I am sorry. Truly sorry. Not to have thought of Kitty! About a fortnight, you said? That will be a day! Just the excitement of Bob's news. One thing and another."

" We'll pipe down, Babs," growled Bob. " Sorry. How's the girl taking it? "

Barbara laughed again.

" Into your study, Julius," she directed. " No doubt you and Bob will have a glass of wine, and I may join you shortly to drink a little toast to my dear Ivie. Then you will have supper with Kitty and me. But I forbid this roaring about Mauritius and hours and this Fylde. I will not have my son's wife excited unduly."

" Certainly not, Barbara," Julius agreed. " You are perfectly right, as usual. Eh, Bob? A glass of wine in my study? Such an occasion! But we shall keep quiet. When Kitty comes down, we shall make a point of being discreet. And there is a little trouble among my roses this year I'd value your advice on. It appears that . . ."

The old gentlemen were not alone in their excitement. Their little colloquy in a back room of Guatemala Lodge was one of thousands at which, in taverns and clubs and homes, men argued the merits of two ships racing neck-and-neck from Foochow to London River. Ahead of the main fleet, brilliantly matched, their past deeds and present doings chronicled in the newspapers, the *Sultan* and the *Constant Star* assumed in the sentimental minds of the British peoples the character of racehorses. They became the objects of partisanship, the symbols of a vast system of gambling, from dockside sweepstakes and the artisan's shilling to the pontifical wagers of solid men on the Exchanges. " An English peer and a Scottish nobleman," even *The Times* reported, " are credited with having pledged themselves in £10,000 a side on the outcome of the China Tea Race now proceeding." It was altogether the most stimulating event the country

had enjoyed since the Derby, and it had the peculiarly pleasing quality
of appealing to patriotism and confirming a nation of seafarers in the
conviction that Britons never, never would be slaves.

The excitement grew as the summer weeks passed. Societies were
formed. A group of Garvel ladies pledged themselves to the making
of a new ensign and house flag for the *Constant Star* in anticipation of
her victory ; and a still larger group of Liverpool ladies undertook
to do the same for the *Sultan*, adding to their effort the organisation of
a collection of funds for a service of silver plate to be presented to
the invincible Captain Billy Fylde. Garvel's prompt retort was to
form a committee for the organisation of a banquet of welcome and
congratulation to Captain Ivie Oliphant and his officers ; and the
Chamber of Commerce promised a solid gold loving cup to be handed
over at the function.

Old Julius found himself a public figure, prised by a universal
curiosity out of his cherished privacy and plucked from among his
roses. The flag-sewing ladies sought him to give them an address on
Ships and Shipbuilding, and only Barbara's firm way with the leader
of the deputation had saved him from that embarrassment. One
newspaper actually sent a person from London to interview him, and
Julius feared afterwards that he had perhaps bewildered the young
man with his eager, allusive talk of hollow water-lines and midship-
sections and sail areas. However, the young man had displayed an
intelligent interest in roses, and Julius found himself duly displayed
in the young man's periodical as a rose-grower in the first place and
a naval architect in his odd moments. But no doubt the young man
understood his own business best. . . . A gentleman describing
himself as " a frequent exhibitor at the Royal Academy " wrote from
Luton, proposing a full-length portrait at the special reduced fee of
thirty guineas.

It was all very exciting and pleasing ; and then there came the
day in August when, in what seemed to Julius the just moment in
the crescendo of delight and fulfilment, Guatemala Lodge was roused
to life in the early morning, and Barbara leapt out of bed and disappeared from their room in a whirl of flying dressing-gown, and there
was a great running of women's feet about the upper parts of the
house.

Julius was dismissed after a scratch breakfast, eaten alone.

" You must arrange to stay out all day, my dear," Barbara warned
him, " and eat at the Club or with Bob in his lodgings. And I may
not be able to attend to you in the evening. These first confinements
are often extremely tedious."

" Certainly, my darling, certainly ! " Julius was eager to agree.

" I should be in the way. Let me leave everything till the evening. The dear girl is not in too much pain, I trust ? "

" She is in great pains at intervals," said Barbara equably. " Labour cannot be anything but agonising. But Kitty is a girl of courage and good sense and I "—she added in a quaint echo of her mother's imperial manner—" I shall be with her throughout."

As he walked to the yard Julius had upon him a lively and exhilarating sense of occasion. It was a dull morning, with mist down on the remote hills, but he whistled softly as he went along and was so relieved by his inward delight from the consciousness of his age and its physical burdens that he swung his cane merrily and cut with it at weeds by the wayside : thinking what a fine and even miraculous circumstance it was that a grandchild should be coming into the home of the Oliphants in the very hour of Ivie's separate triumph in an Oliphant ship. After all those long years, this blessed apotheosis !

He was in no mood for work and in the office discoursed largely to Bob Rait of the uniqueness of the circumstance in which they found themselves, of the interesting variety of Christian names that might be given to the child, male or female, and of the propriety of giving the workers a holiday and a bonus.

" They're having a holiday, for there's next to no work for them," said Bob, sourly humorous. " As for your bonus, tell me where to find the cash and they'll get it."

But Julius was not to be abashed by gloomy demurrers, and at noon he made his way to the Merchants' Club and there foregathered happily with hearty old gentlemen like himself : solid, prosperous men in sugar and shipping and engineering, who were secure in the prosperity of their times and could safely leave their office affairs to their sons while, over noggins of sherry or spirits, they praised the past, deplored a great many tendencies of the present, and enjoyed themselves thoroughly in a ripe autumnal fashion. To-day their talk was all of the progress of the *Constant Star* ; and when Julius added the information that he was about to become a grandfather, it seemed to these old parties that life could never be more interesting than at that given moment, and that a celebration was the imperative logic of the circumstances. Old Tom Kennoway of the Felt Works was heard to call for a magnum of the Mumm—a jereboam if they had one in the cellars : not that he thought much of the present committee's taste or courage.

And then there was the appearance of Bob Rait, waving a sheet of paper above his head ; Bob transformed from the worried merchant of the earlier forenoon into a gruffly proud uncle and nearly jovial sailor. The clatter of male voices within the low-ceilinged room ceased under the fierce " Whist's ! " and peremptory " Silence, there's " of the older gentlemen.

." It's news from the Cape of Good Hope," Bob announced. " *Constant Star* leads by more than two days. Made her signals on the morning of the 5th. *Sultan* didn't show up until the afternoon of the 7th."

Cheering filled the room to bursting-point, and Julius was suddenly aware of discomfort behind his great happiness. It was too stuffy ; all this smoking nowadays ; not used to so much wine. He wished they would not slap him on the back and shake his hands so heartily. Good friends, fine, generous gentlemen all ; it touched the heart, this solid cordiality among his contemporaries. But this heaviness of the head, those friendly faces growing large and then dwindling in his foolish eyes.

Bob noticed his distress and, shouldering his way through the throng, led him into the quiet coolness of the dining-room. They ate simply, and Bob had a cab waiting to drive them to the yard.

" Very thoughtful of you, Bob," sighed Julius. " I confess I feel most desperately tired. That wine . . ."

" Just too much excitement," said Bob gruffly. " No good at our age. Now you'll have a rest. Lie down on the couch in your own room, and I'll have a cup of tea ready for you after your nap."

" Yes, a little rest. We may have a long wait for news. Extremely good of you, Bob. But what a day ! What wonderful news from the Cape ! "

" Yes, yes ! But off you go now. I've got work to do."

An excited girl from the Guatemala Lodge kitchen came flying with a message near four o'clock, and Bob gently opened his partner's door and peeped in, but Julius was asleep and he had not the heart to waken him. His stillness was of death, even to the parted lips ; the thin, fine features seemed pinched and remote. Poor old lad ! thought Bob tenderly of his friend ; he had given so much to life and got so little back, and his present happiness was no more than a sunset gleam. They were both growing old, and their strength was nearly exhausted, and it could not be long now for either of them. Even the success of the *Constant Star* could be no more than a modest chance for Ivie to take up where they would leave off—and smoke lay thick across the horizon.

Bob closed the door again, but he reflected an hour later that the whistles might waken the old man with unpleasant suddenness, and he went in again and patted the white, veined hand that lay outspread on his friend's chest. Julius blinked and smiled in response to the broad grin on Bob's face.

"Come along, grandfather, show a leg! There's a small boy waiting to see you at home."

"A boy! Kitty! Ivie's boy!" cried the old man, sitting up with a jerk. "Why was I not informed?"

"Message came just a minute ago," Bob lied cheerfully. "And all well."

"God bless my soul! But Bob!" He seized his friend's hand and pumped at it vigorously. "What a day! What a day! And now I must hurry home. Barbara will be expecting me, looking for me."

But he would not think of taking the cab Bob suggested. Look— the evening had brightened. It would be a pleasure to walk home through its mildness and think of the wonderful events of the day.

The sentimentality that was his refuge in old age spurred him so eagerly towards Guatemala Lodge that his breath was coming fast as he hurried up the path to the front door, his old feet kicking the gravel on to the lawns to right and left. It was completely gratified by the picture he saw through the open front door.

Barbara was coming slowly down the suavely-curved stairway. She had attired herself for an occasion in her finest black silk gown with a deep collar of cream lace and a gold chain about her neck. She had put on a lace cap with primrose ribbons through it, as if she had at length and within an hour or two accepted a matriarchal position. She wore stockings of fine black silk and shoes of patent leather with small gleaming buckles on their pointed toes ; and, moving thus. voluminously but with a commanding rhythm down the stairway, her person suddenly suggested to Julius a full-rigged ship under steady sail. She held firmly but comfortably in her arms a bundle within a most gracefully trailing shawl.

Barbara paused on lowest step and smiled radiantly on her husband.

"See, Julius!" she said. "Here is our grandson."

Julius tiptoed forward. He felt a clumsy masculine thing, incapable of the right actions and statements. He looked down into a small face most comically pink and disgruntled : gnarled, little, womb-puckered features that suggested disapproval of these formalities. Julius bent awkwardly and kissed the wrinkled forehead. He raised his eyes to meet Barbara's triumphant gaze.

"Kitty?" he asked.

"She is resting now. She was brave and sensible."

"And would you believe it, Barbara? We had word to-day that Ivie's ship was still leading at the Cape of Good Hope."

"Ah!" cried Barbara. "Then we are well content!"

"We have many blessings indeed, my dear."

5

The South Atlantic was in one of its sullen rages. In the region of Lat. 10 E. and Long. 30 South, the visible world was but the trough between pairs of mountainous waves sweeping at speed from the sou'-west under a low ceiling of scudding cloud. Between any two seas the *Constant Star* was as a chip of wood in the wash of a great steamer, no larger relatively than a peasant's hut on one slope of a deep valley. Each great wave was a moving mass of ocean in itself, furrowed by waves that would be breakers on the coasts of home ; these in their turn riffled by eddies of a gale that seemed to have a malevolent and powerful mind behind its fury. The ship was a little thing trapped and overwhelmed by an inscrutable tyranny. When she topped the great waves, all her spars and timbers creaking under excessive strain, the few men on her deck, lashed for safety to her stable parts, could see no more than an extension of their own inferno, limited only by the pall of scud about them. It was nearly dark all the time. The least of it was that it rained continually ; that was not noticed at all in a ship incessantly drenched by tons of sea-water lifted and thrown in stinging sheets along her decks by the sheer force of the gale. The *Constant Star* and her ship's company lived in their own hell and had done so for two days on end, ever since her master, his heart breaking, had given orders to heave to and put her head to the wind, with oil and sea-anchors and all the devices he could think of to mitigate his vessel's travail.

Captain Ivie Oliphant shouted to his first mate, who had braced himself three feet away on the other side of the binnacle, his form and face lost within oilskin coverings.

" It doesn't get any better, Mister ? "

" No, sir ! "

" She's taking about as much as she can stand ? "

" Yes, sir ! That foremast's worrying me."

Clinging as a monkey might to the wheel and the shoulders of the quartermaster, Ivie edged round until he could shout into Mr. Cutler's ear.

" How are the men ? "

" Pretty poorly. Most of them seasick."

" Like ourselves ! "

" Yes, but they're restive since they saw the *Sultan* pass us yesterday evening, going strong."

" Restive ! What about me ? " cried Ivie bitterly.

" Yes, sir," said Mr. Cutler automatically.

But Ivie knew that this was the decisive challenge. It was the opinion of his officers and his men that they should run for it, accepting all the known risks of escape from this vortex of misery. Accept the challenge of the great seas chasing them from behind or cling to the rules of prudence, even if there was danger in prudence itself? Ivie's heart was heavy as he stared at the sea in its malignant tumult. This was the burden of command weighing upon him intolerably. He thought of his beautiful ship and of his fine men and of the couple of hundred lives at home bound up with their fate. He saw old Julius illuminated with pleasure in the beauty and speed of his last creation, and he thought on the prize he could win for his crew and his people, and of pride and love and honour.

He knew that the decision must be fatal, and he made it on a gust of emotion that was an orgasm of release.

" Mister ! " he shouted in the mate's ear.

" Aye, aye, sir ! "

" We'll run for it now. Get your flying jib set. We'll see if she can take a trysail later on. Get all your gear inboard. I'll stand by the wheel here. There's enough light left to see what we are doing."

" Aye, aye, sir ! "

Mr. Cutler dropped on all fours to crawl forward to his tasks, and Ivie never saw him again. Perhaps twenty minutes passed before the ship, rid of her encumbrances, took the pull of the small triangle of canvas above the bowsprit and sped ahead with the wind like an arrow released, but she was hardly three minutes under way when, with a dreadful simultaneity, the tiny jib broke from its lower fastening and flew and threshed like any baby's napkin on a clothes-line on a gusty day, and the master wave came racing up from behind to overwhelm the vessel that had now lost both anchorage and power.

Watching its approach over his shoulder, Ivie knew what the wave portended, this fatal seventh wave of legend. It came after them like a heavy machine with a cutting edge, all the blind fury of irresistible power in its surging mass. It was a mountain range suddenly erupting and curving over and collapsing on the plain below. His ship went from under him, and he was in a boil of water. Before a heavy spar was torpedoed from a minor wave to pierce his skull, Ivie's mind held an irrelevant picture of the Comprador, that placid agent of a relentless commerce, secure under his coloured umbrella.

At home they never knew how to break the news to Julius. When Bob Rait had the word from St. Helena that the *Sultan* had made her signals on August 9, but that there was no news of the *Constant Star*, the old man had petulantly dismissed his partner's apprehensions.

" This is not a hard mechanical business of steam and the electric telegraph," he had said defiantly. " This is art."

" Nevertheless, my dear," Barbara had demurred, " it would be agreeable to have word of Ivie's ship."

" Naturally it would, my dear," the old man had snapped with such force that Barbara and Bob looked to each other. " That is hardly worth saying—if you will forgive me. Why should we not surmise that Ivie had taken a course of his own ? He may have chosen to hug the African coast, or even—we must allow for it—to pass the island widely to the west. . . . And how well I remember the fuss about Boney and Sir Hudson Lowe ! A pitiful controversy."

" Yes, *mon cher Jules*, but——"

" No, my dearest ! I simply insist that we must consider certain imponderables. Ivie's skill as a shipmaster is universally acknowledged. He has under him—and I declare this as a matter capable of scientific proof—what may decently be described as the finest and fastest sailing ship ever launched. It is wrong of me to make such a claim, no doubt, but I speak as a humble student of these matters. Some sixty years . . ."

" That, Julius," said Barbara promptly, " is perfectly understood. *Alors*, Bob ! We shall be patient until further word reaches us."

But the days passed, and the days passed, and no word came of the *Constant Star*. One afternoon Bob made his way to Guatemala Lodge, his gait heavy under the burden of the tidings he carried. The *Sultan* had made her signals at the Cape Verde Islands, but of her rival not a syllable. There was separate intelligence of storm in the South Atlantic, and Bob contemplated tragedy and an end as he plodded his way westwards.

It was too late to harm Julius, however. Barbara had seen Bob approach the house by the short-cut across the riparian fields and was out to meet him, and sister and brother exchanged a stricken look. Julius, in an alarmingly listless mood, had chosen to sit in the afternoon sunshine beside his roses, and she had brought him out a cup of tea and arranged cushions behind his head ; and he had said he would sleep a little, and she was only at the door when the crash of the cup among the things on the tea-tray told her that he had been taken by another stroke. She had run back to his aid, but there was only that trembling hand pointing to a speechless mouth ; and then he had collapsed, the lower whites of his eyes up-turning. It had been a heavy task for the womenfolk to carry him indoors.

Bob heavily followed Barbara up the stairs and into the room where Julius lay in a coma.

"Aye, Julius!" he murmured, as it were apologetically, the speech ending in a broken gulp.

Next day, as quietly and gently as he had lived, Julius Oliphant, shipbuilder, died without recovering consciousness in the seventy-second year of his age.

6 .

A four-wheeled cab took Sir Mark Oliphant all the way from the railway station to the cottage at Kempock, his years, figure and dignity demanding the hire. Moreover, as he stated frankly to himself, he had no wish to be seen on the streets of Garvel and have a pack of damned spongers and nosey-parkers after him. At the core of the man's mind indeed, unacknowledged, was the firm decision to make this his last physical contact with the filthy place. As for the yards, John's second boy, young Ned, would soon be through Cambridge ; it would do him a power of good to come up here, learn the business and protect the family interests. That was all arranged in the old man's autocratic mind.

But, by God, it was a filthy place on this day of teeming rain ! This narrow main street, a dark glen between rickety tenement buildings, with muddy rivulets and puddles all over the uneven pavements and the cobbled carriageway ! Dammit, the very windows of the cab were splashed ! Those sullen, dirty people daundering along purposelessly, their shoulders hunched against the rain—the same glum-faced men in greasy caps and knotted woollen scarves instead of collars ; the same fat and shapeless women in greasy tartan shawls, raddled with drink and haphazard child-bearing ! A pack of damned Radical trash, no good to the country or themselves or any-body else !

At the foot of the Auld Kirk Wynd the cab had to pull into the kerb and halt while a procession wheeled out of the side road. It consisted mainly of dark weasel-faced men in cheap serge suits and high bowler hats, but among them were two priests and half a dozen young women with tempestuous eyes. The two priests flanked a banner on poles, the green banner of some Hibernian order with a paschal device upon it and the legend : "God Save Ireland ! "

Sir Mark dropped the carriage window with a slam and leaned out to harangue the driver, while the dark eyes in the procession stared at the great red face of the stranger.

"Drive on, man ! " the baronet roared hoarsely. "Let those b——'s get back to Ireland and save it for themselves. Drive through them ! I'm in a hurry."

Fully alive to the lethal possibilities of this speech, the man on
the box cut at his sad horse with the whip and wheeled round the
tail of the procession so briskly that Mark's heavy body was thrown
back on the worn leather padding of the vehicle.

" Damned Irish trash ! " he puffed indignantly to himself. " And
this damned fool of a driver doesn't know his business."

He was not aware that the small episode had been observed from
a corner by an ageing man with a lean face so distinguished even under
the roughness of drink as to contrast strangely with his poor clothes
and bursting shoes.

" That's my bluidy fine uncle ! " said the man at the corner to
the bearded lounger beside him.

Without taking his hands from his trousers pockets, and moving
only a few inches sideways to dodge a small cataract of water pouring
down from a leaking gutter and sensitive in its flow to the winds of
an early winter day in West Scotland, Duncan Oliphant added from
between bitterly twisted lips :

" That's the old bastard that's done more to make this place the
mess it is than anybody else. Julius was just a bluidy old soft fool
with his head in the air. But this bluidy bull . . ."

" Jesus ! " said his friend indifferently and spat into the gutter.

No sense of his own degree of responsibility for the degradation
of Garvel troubled Mark, but as the cab took him behind the Glebe
into the region of villas a lively satisfaction with his part in that
development filled his mind. The sight of these solid stone houses,
with their slate roofs, lace curtains and large gardens running up the
slopes, or down to the sea, gave him great satisfaction ; they were
property : tangible, realisable, assessable. That had been a right good
idea and a rare bargain with old Sir John, even if Lavinia had never
been aught but a doited fool and was now in her second childhood.
It was a damned nuisance that Barbara had left the district and gone
back to that hen-coop of a cottage at Kempock where she started
from, landing him in for this damned long drive, but Mark allowed
that the woman would need every penny she could lay her hands on.
Anyhow, he had arranged to take over the old yard from Bob Rait
at a figure that would keep them from starvation at least. Not a big
figure, but fair in the circumstances. How Barbara would get on
was no business of his.

She received him in the small white sitting-room in which they
had first met nearly sixty years before. It had changed little enough
in all that time, but Bob had sentimentally cherished the house and
much of his mother's furniture, and Barbara at least did not feel that
she and Mark had changed much in their fundamental natures for

all the burdens of experience and knowledge that had fallen upon them in their different lots. She was indeed stimulated by the feeling of meeting her ancient, predestined enemy once more, and on a familiar battlefield.

Alert for every nuance of his approach, she apprehended at once that Mark had chosen to appear to her as the mourning relative, the sympathetic cœval laden with sentimental memories of the past.

" Aye, Barbara ! " he replied to her greeting, settling himself with a grunt in the low chair she indicated. He spoke heavily in a partial return to the doric of his youth. " It's a pleasure to see you again. Bob will have told ye that we've settled that bit of business about the yard. I just thought I couldn't go back without looking in to say a word and have a bit talk about poor Julius."

" That would have been appropriate at the funeral," returned Barbara with dangerous sweetness, " but, of course, Mark, you could not find it possible to attend."

She watched the shaft go home and the sting acknowledged by a new reddening of the great face. It was strange, she reflected, how the presence of Mark, the very idea of Mark and all he stood for, brought out the devil in her. But she also saw that he was determined not to be provoked. The last victory was his, as he saw it ; he could contrive to tolerate a woman's tantrums for half an hour.

" No, no ! " he agreed, hesitantly bluff. " It was a disappointment, but just one thing and another cropped up—this Suez Canal business ; evidence before a Royal Commission—you know what it is. But you'd see my son John ? "

" Indeed, yes," agreed Barbara, in her French manner this time. " A man of great ability and force of character, I am sure. But not naturally sympathetic to our small provincial interests, bien entendu."

" No, John has his own responsibilities," said Mark gravely and proudly. " Still, I'm glad he was able to pay our last respects to his Uncle Julius."

" To be sure. You were admirably represented, Mark."

" Aye ! " agreed Mark, easing up a heavy thigh from among the cushions on which he sat. " Poor Julius had a sudden call. All these years of honest work, and his troubles never far to seek, but determined to stick to his sailing ships ; and then that Clipper of his and poor Ivie ! Aye ! It's a pity he didn't slip out quietly before he knew the whole business was bound to be a failure."

" Failure ! "

The sharpness of her protest surprised Barbara as much as it did Mark. It was wrung from her in angry resentment of this heavy false and sentimental parody of mourning over a tomb. She disciplined herself to be calm.

" Failure ! " she repeated quietly. " Success ! What is in a word, Mark ? Perhaps you and I do not speak the same language in these matters. If you mean money and power——"

Her thin, white hands fluttered in her eagerness to make the point that most seriously concerned her.

" But failure ! Of Julius and of his children ! *Regardez, mon ami.* . . . I was going through some papers this morning. They are here on the desk."

She rose, slenderly brisk even in her old age, and took from a high-backed bureau in the corner of the room a sheaf of documents.

" See, Mark ! Of poor Walter this letter from the Secretary of the Royal Society, dated two months after his death, to commisserate with us and to say that it had been the Society's intention to award a Fellowship to our dear son in recognition—this I read from the letter—' of his distinguished contribution to the science of public health and municipal sanitation.' Failure ! Success ! I take it that to be a Fellow of the Royal Society may be counted an achievement."

" Surely. Of course. But——" Mark wheezed through one of his beefy fits of coughing, but Barbara ecstatically swept on, holding out another document.

Then she withdrew it with slightly awkward haste. In her eagerness she had proffered Mark the yellowing letter from the Lady Superintendent. Ah ! but that was between two women, a secret inviolate from such as her cousin-by-marriage. Her long fingers riffled through the papers on her lap, and she held out a letter most beautifully engrossed on a fresh quarto sheet.

" And this from the Principal of the University of Glasgow. Again a most gracious letter of condolence and to say that it had been the Court's intention to bestow on Julius the degree of Doctor of Laws *honoris causa* ' for his most elegant and enlightened work '—you observe that I quote again—' in the fields of ship-design and marine architecture.' And I dare to fancy, *mon ami*, that the University of Glasgow has some title to judge in this matter."

" Certainly ! " agreed Mark heartily enough. " Nobody deserved it better than Julius. You don't understand what I mean, Barbara."

" No, no ! I understand you perfectly, Mark ! " insisted Barbara in a spate of cold passion. " I now read you something about Ivie. This letter came only last week. It has given me great pleasure. It is dated from Liverpool. I now read it to you."

She held her adversary helpless while she intoned :

" *Dear Madam,*

On behalf of myself, my officers and my ship's company in the Clipper Ship Sultan *of Liverpool, I beg leave to offer you sincere condolences on the loss of the Clipper Ship* Constant Star *and of your gallant son, her commander, Captain Ivie Oliphant, also on the consequent death of your eminent husband.*

" *It is our sincere regret that the* Constant Star *and her gallant crew did not survive to make a race of it, but the gales then prevailing in the South Atlantic were something furious, and I reckon that the much-admired fineness of the vessel's lines may have been her undoing in the fearful conditions then prevailing.*

" *I had the honour of meeting your gallant son on various convivial occasions in Foochow and adjacent ports and formed the highest opinion of his character as I previously and since had occasion to admire his remarkable gifts of seamanship.*

" *Again, madam, on behalf of self, officers and men of the Clipper Ship* Sultan, *I beg leave to offer you this expression of our profound regret and sympathy.*

" *Believe me, Madam,*
" *Your obednt humble Servant,*
" *Wm. Fylde, Master.*"

Barbara let the sheet fall into her lap.

" That," she insisted, " is a letter of great charm and honesty."

" It's a nice letter," Mark agreed.

" And it answers our question, Success and failure ? For here I have, even for my wild sailor son, the admiration of a master in his own profession. No, no, Mark ! I have been a woman blessed far beyond the ordinary in my menfolk, in their great distinction in the world of affairs, and in their qualities as gentlemen. Their names will live when—when others that are apparently more powerful are quite forgotten. And I, having been Julius's chosen wife and the mother of Walter and Ivie, am well content to have shared so much honour and happiness. In the mercy of *le bon Dieu* I now await the end with calm."

She stopped there, and Mark had apparently nothing to say in the face of her poise. The small silence was torn by the healthy cry of a hungry infant upstairs. Barbara turned to Mark with a smile.

" There it is, Mark ! There is still work for me after all. That is Julius's grandson, Walter's nephew, Ivie's boy. I have great hopes of him. He and his charming mother fill my days with much happiness."

" Oh, yes ! The wee boy." Mark seemed to brighten with sincere interest. " That crossed my mind, Barbara. I was thinking about his keep and his education. Now, if you'd allow me——"

" That is thoughtful of you, Mark," she interrupted him. " As it turns out, the fortunes of Kitty's family have been completely restored. It appears that the demand for tobacco is growing. . . ."

" I should think it is," grunted Mark with professional passion.

" And so the child's future is assured. And now, Mark, let me offer you a glass of wine, a cup of tea."

" No, no ! I should be going."

He pulled a large gold watch out of its narrow prison in a waistcoat pocket tightly sealed by the protuberant mass of his stomach.

" Aye, I must be going," he announced. " I'm due at the Municipal Buildings in half an hour's time, and I've got the cab waiting. But it has been nice to see you, Barbara, and to hear that you are not so badly placed as I thought."

" I am grateful that you found it possible to call, Mark."

Then there was the business of getting Mark's heavy body out of the low armchair and of exchanging hollow courtesies while she saw him to the door. At length he rolled away down the path, and she gently closed the door behind him, making an end and accepting all the consequences of a final break.

Secure again in the cabin of the four-wheeler, his own master once more, Sir Mark Oliphant considered the curious nature of the interview. Well, he concluded, as the vehicle splashed roughly through the puddles at the bend of the bay, she had always been a haughty, pugnacious bitch ; and if she thought now that a bankrupt business was a sign of success, good luck to her ! There was that American money, of course. . . . Anyhow—and now Mark indulged in a hoarse chuckle to himself—that women did not know that in his wallet was a letter from the Prime Minister himself, suggesting that he, Mark Oliphant, might, by the Queen's pleasure, become a Baron of the United Kingdom. Lord Oliphant . . . or it might be Lord Kempsfield, from that place he had bought in Hampshire. His son John would be the Honourable John Oliphant. The next rank above a baron was—what was it now ? . . . There were the Bishops, of course, but yes—Viscounts, and then Earls. You never knew. The Party could do a lot if you had the money and the power and the ability.

Barbara, on her part, returned to the sitting-room and shook out the cushions, ran a finger along the mantelpiece to see if that girl had done her dusting thoroughly, and then stood at the window, contemplating the sea, on which and by which so many of her personal fortunes had been decided. Baby would now be at Kitty's breasts and would thereafter sleep until the warm hour of the evening bath when the domestic discipline would relax and melt in a confusion of frankly female simplicities.   Meanwhile, Kitty would require a stimulating cup of tea after her sacrifice to the gluttonous child, Julius Walter Ivie Oliphant, and a salad remained to be prepared for supper. There was always something to be done.

THE END

10/60.